THE

FINAL

RESISTANCE

DARK UNIVERSE SERIES #3

ALEX SHEPPARD

My girls—sass and smarts, with mighty hearts.

THE
FINAL
RESISTANCE

Introduction to Dark Universe

Picking up the second or third book in a series always gets me debating — should I re-read the previous book(s) or should I jump into the new one and try to recall things as I go? While writing this book, I've wondered how to best relieve my readers of a similar dilemma.

After much thought, I settled on a super short recap. There's also a glossary at the end — a detailed compilation of people, places, and other terms present in the Dark Universe Series — to refer to as needed.

If you remember most events in *The Last Stryker* and *The First Covenant*, simply skip to the first chapter: Starbase Zeta.

The Story So Far

Ten years have passed since the Locusta-Vanga War. The invasion by the deadly Locustans had pushed the galaxy to the brink of extinction. It took a lot of valor and sacrifice to drive the Locustans away and finally the galaxy has settled back into a peaceful cadence.

The *Endeavor*, a battleship-turned-freighter commanded by Terenze Milos, the hero of the Locusta-Vanga War and former member of the Confederate Space Command, stumbles on a debris field in a remote star system. They find a lone surviving space-fighter and the crew hauls it in.

A few days later, Ramya Kiroff, the seventeen-year-old heir of House Kiroff, runs away from her educational institute, the CAWStrat, to avoid being forced into a marriage of convenience by her influential father, Trysten Kiroff.

While running away from CAWStrat and the clutches of her iron-fisted father, Ramya comes across a mugging in a deserted alleyway of the nearest spaceport. She chases off the thugs beating a man who turns out to be someone from the freight ship *Endeavor*. Hiding her identity, she offers to work in exchange for passage and becomes an apprentice to the ship's medic, Sosa.

Ramya discovers that the *Endeavor's* crew is on its way to meet the leader of the Confederate Space Command to hand over a craft — a space fighter they call a Stryker — salvaged from a debris field. The man Ramya saved is actually the Stryker's pilot, Habardein.

Habardein recognizes Ramya as Trysten Kiroff's daughter. He tells her that the Kiroffs had a factory in Sector 22 where they were secretly building the Strykers. However, something went wrong during the trials and of the five Strykers, four attacked the GSO space fleet protecting the area, destroyed them, and vanished. He chalks this up to a call from the Locustans to raise their fallen comrades from the last invasion. He warns of an impending Locustan invasion before falling back into a coma.

Captain Milos suspects Trysten Kiroff was experimenting with the Locustans' alien technology. He is worried because Locustans had deadly ways of proliferating their genetics, which the Confederacy didn't quite understand yet tinkered with. He wants to hand the Stryker to Confederate Space Command as soon as possible.

On their way to meet with Admiral Kanaa of Space Command at Alameda, a GSO ship intercepts the *Endeavor*. Lieutenant Gael Arlington of the GSO, who is evidently in the employ of Trysten Kiroff, commands it. Ramya also recognizes Gael as the man she danced with at the last gala at CAWStrat.

Trysten Kiroff demands that Captain Milos hand the Stryker over to him and not to Admiral Kanaa. When the captain refuses, Lieutenant Arlington tries to board the *Endeavor* and take the Stryker by force. However, the *Endeavor* escapes.

Captain Milos rushes to meet the Admiral, but takes a roundabout route to give Trysten Kiroff the slip. In the meantime, the Stryker that had not allowed anyone inside it so far allows Ramya access after detecting her Kiroff genetics. Inside the craft, Ramya meets Dakrhaeth, the AI of the Stryker, a Locustan entity known as a Viriskshi. Dakrhaeth warns her that the four missing Strykers are intent on weakening the galaxy from within while the Locustan forces prepare for the second invasion. He begs her not to give the Stryker away to Admiral Kanaa, and warns that the admiral will not spare the *Endeavor* or its crew when they try to hand the Stryker to her.

Captain Milos changes his plan to meet the admiral at Alameda. Instead, he decides to drop the Stryker off at the adjoining star system of Totori and then inform the admiral of its location. However, Admiral Kanaa is already waiting with a powerful fleet when the *Endeavor* reaches Totori. Captain Milos tries to convince the admiral of the real threat — the impending second invasion by the Locustans.

Admiral Kanaa ignores the captain's warning and orders her fleet to attack the *Endeavor*. The captain orders Ramya to take off in the Stryker and save the *Endeavor* from the fleet's attack. Piloting the Stryker, Ramya, with the help of Dakrhaeth and Commander Ross, fights the massive Drednots of the admiral's fleet and wins.

However, during the battle, the Stryker is separated from the *Endeavor*. Ross believes the captain will land the battered *Endeavor* on a nearby habitable planet; the most viable possibility is a Mwandan sanctuary on Morris II. Ramya steers the Stryker toward Morris II, a planet in the Kashiyap system.

On Morris II, Mwandan projectiles bring the Stryker down before they can pinpoint the location of the *Endeavor*. However, as the Stryker repairs itself, Ramya and Ross detect the presence of the *Endeavor* nearby. They start hiking toward the ship.

On the way, they run into a young Mwandan boy being beaten up by local law enforcement. Fearing they will murder the boy, the duo intervene. The boy — Ahool Petta, a part of the Berkari rebel group — teams up with them and leads them toward the sacred grove where the *Endeavor* is supposedly trapped. During the journey, Chief Dal, the leader of the Berkari, also joins them.

Entering the sacred grove proves tricky when Temihula, the resident spirit of the forest, is offended by the intrusion and refuses to let them in. Ramya gets into a debate and is challenged to a duel with the spirit. After a bloody battle, she finally wins and Temihula allows the party in. Temihula also gifts Ramya with a special jewel, a Drigganstone, which is valued for its use in weaponry.

On reaching the *Endeavor*, Chief Dal decides to join the cause of protecting the galaxy from the Locustans. He and some of his people come aboard the *Endeavor*. Captain Milos decides to head to Bucifer P9, a Mwandan sanctuary in the Fringe, to meet Chief Mifek.

Some urgent repairs need to be completed, so the *Endeavor* stops at a space station, Nebeca 21. Here, Ramya and Fenny are almost captured by troops from the Space Fleet but escape with the help of Lieutenant Gael Arlington.

The captain decides to meet with Trysten Kiroff on the way to Bucifer P9 to discuss a possible alliance. Halfway through, they are ambushed by space pirates sent by Octus Laurden, the owner of Nebeca 21, to steal the Stryker. *Endeavor's* crew manages to win a firefight and kill all the pirates.

Captain Milos meets with Trysten Kiroff. However, Trysten isn't interested in alliances. He only wants his Stryker back and demands that Ramya return also. During the stalemate, an urgent message from Chief Mifek reaches the Endeavor. Mifek announces that Locustans have reached his planet and are assimilating his people to form a Locustan army. He and a few members of his patrol team are hiding out.

The *Endeavor* rushes to Bucifer P9. Ramya takes the Stryker down planet to extract Chief Mifek and any other survivors, but she is not able to help. Ramya loses control of the Stryker when its AI is entranced by a call from a Locustan megaship. It turns out that the four other Strykers missing from the Kiroff factory in Sector 22 have morphed into a SuperStryker—a megaship that has been harvesting populations in the Fringe.

The Stryker, with Ramya, Ross, and Lefrasi in it, is about to be swallowed by the SuperStryker. With last-minute advice from Trysten Kiroff, Ramya is able to sever the connection between the megaship and her Stryker. She fights the SuperStryker, damaging it severely in the process. Ramya returns to the *Endeavor* with a heavy heart, having lost Chief Mifek and the rest of the Mwandans on Bucifer P9. However, as they leave Bucifer P9, Trysten Kiroff decides to join Captain Milos in his attempt to convince the Confederacy that the Locustan threat is real and immediate.

STARBASE ZETA

Admiral Zoho of the Confederate Space Fleet stared out of his observation station on Zeta and watched the carnage unfold. Waves of cold washed down his spine as he observed the systematic massacre of his people. His shoulders sagged with the weight of mountains. Every few minutes, he took a sip of water, but the dryness of a desert prickled his mouth the moment the cool liquid coursed down his throat.

A deep frown bunched Zoho's face like a prune. His mouth crinkled, not just from the fear of impending doom but also from anger and frustration. They should've known the Locustans would return. He had expressed his concerns, but when did Space Command ever listen to eccentrics like him? As the protector of the gateway to the galaxy, he had been caught off-guard by the foulest of enemies.

A space fighter blew into smithereens in the distance, and pieces flew out in all directions. Countless Locustan ships darted this way and that, obliterating his fleet. Zoho couldn't believe what he was seeing. So much for those expensive, state-of-the-art drones that monitored Anomaly Point—with the fight so close, the simple scopes built into the observation windows were enough. The battle he hadn't expected in his lifetime was right here at his doorstep.

With a sigh, Zoho slumped into the nearest couch and rubbed his temples. How in the name of the stars did he get here?

An assignment to Starbase Zeta was considered banishment in the Space Fleet, and when Admiral Zoho had been put in charge of the behemoth five years ago, his heart had sunk a little. True to his Norgoran heritage, he hid his despair well. Besides, he didn't have any family to speak of, so the task would suit him well, or so he had thought.

The starbase sat in the Alpha quadrant of the galaxy in the middle of dead space. It was dead far before the infamous Anomaly Point opened up and let the Locustan invaders in. With no habitable worlds in the area — the nearest settled system was two light-years away — interplanetary traffic in the direction of the starbase was scarce.

He always thought it was odd that the Super Luminal Highway (SLH) — the giant network of wormholes that connected the various systems in the galaxy — had three access points, or APs, right next to Zeta, which was in the middle of nowhere. Although most in Space Command chalked it up to a design idiosyncrasy, Zoho believed it was intentional. The long-extinct ancients had always known of Anomaly Point and the Locustan threat. That was why they had made room for three termination points in the area, so the galaxy could send reinforcements three times as quickly. He had no evidence to back it up; it was just an idea or another "Zoho brainwave," as the Space Command liked to call his theories in jest.

"Admiral," Alys, the human who sat at the communication station, said. "Space Command requests a word with you."

"On screen," Zoho said, tearing his eyes from the fierce battle that raged at the tips of the giant horseshoe that was Starbase Zeta.

The screen flickered and filled with the view of a spacious meeting room where Space Command — a group of twelve people in murky-brown uniforms who hadn't seen first-hand combat in a long while — sat around a dark-veneered table. They shuffled papers and communicators, trying their best to hide the fear that made their eyes jittery.

Marson Hale, the Chief of Fleets and the head of the Confederate Space Fleet, stood at the table and frowned. "Admiral, what's the latest?" he asked without the usual formalities. His sandy-blond hair seemed to have been generously sprinkled with gray overnight.

"We've lost two hundred and I fear we'll lose as many more before we can overcome this wave."

"So, we *can* overcome?"

Zoho stole a look outside. The two prongs of the horseshoe

stretched far into the darkness, away from the saucer-shaped midsection. At the ends, pale silvery shapes of confederate fighters streamed out of the starbase in a continuous line. There were at least two hundred fighters out there and Zoho's chest would've expanded with pride at the display of their might at any other time. But now their numbers seemed pitiable.

An unbelievable and endless stream of pitch-black Locustan craft swirled around the beautiful Wentworth-Busas of the Space Fleet like a curse out of the netherworld. There had to be at least a thousand of them and they were ripping into the Wentworth-Busas with the ease of a hot knife passing through butter. Zoho winced as a sizeable flicker erupted on the battlefield. His people were dying, one valiant soldier at a time.

"Admiral Zoho?" Marson called. "Can we beat them?"

"Possibly," Zoho said. "We've released less than half of our squadrons. If Anomaly Point doesn't reopen, I'd say we have a chance . . . *if* it doesn't reopen."

"The wormhole is closed now?"

Zoho nodded. Two hours ago, the heavens had opened up on them. The darkness was torn apart and for a moment Zoho had marveled at the glorious view, his first time sighting the gigantic wormhole. His wonderment had quickly turned into dread and there was barely time for him to send the first squadrons out. Not a moment too soon. A rush of spacecraft — precise, ruthless, and numerous — the likes of which he had never believed was possible, had streamed out of the almost-divine structure.

"Any signs of it opening again?"

Zoho couldn't tell. The wormhole had opened up without warning. The measurements they had been taking over years didn't show any telltale fluctuations. And just as suddenly, it had closed. Exactly the way it did during the Locustan invasion ten years ago.

"I don't know. You should send more scientists along with reinforcements. We need to study Anomaly Point better. What we have now isn't enough."

His words didn't have a happy effect on the people around the dark table. Vice Chief Romolo, a tall and gaunt Norgoran at the far end, shook his head. "Isn't enough? You have the best scientists there already," he said.

Zoho scoffed. No brilliant scientist—none sane enough anyway— came to Zeta. Coming here was as good as throwing their career away. Yes, there were scientists here, a scrappy and tenacious bunch, but there weren't enough of them.

"We can debate if you want, Vice Chief Romolo," Zoho said in an icy voice he hadn't thought he had in him. "But it has to be short. The front lines need my attention. Let me make sure I've made the situation clear to you: The second Locustan invasion has already begun. Our galaxy is under siege."

Anyone will ask for justice, not everyone will fight for it.

-Mwandan proverb

1

Ramya Kiroff guided the Stryker back into the *Endeavor's* belly with ease. It had been a smooth and trouble-free flight after the encounter with the Locustan megaship that had almost swallowed them alive on Bucifer P9. Ramya's attack on the megaship left it damaged badly enough, and no one pursued the Stryker as they'd fled the scene.

As soon as Ramya docked the Stryker inside the *Endeavor*, Lefrasi jumped to his feet. He didn't wait until the craft was secured or even offer to help Ramya and Ross.

"I have to arrange for a mourning," he said before rushing away.

Ramya climbed out of the Stryker after Lefrasi. As she set the locks that held the craft, her eyes swept over the sleek, dark body of the space fighter. The fight with the Locustan megaship had been close and the Stryker had taken quite a beating, its surface bent and torn in places. Ramya ran a hand over the Stryker's underbelly as she watched Lefrasi cross the shuttle bay with long strides and disappear into the hold.

Her heart grew heavier thinking of the Mwandans on Bucifer P9. They were all lost to the Locustans. Bucifer P9 didn't have as large a population of Mwandans as Morris II where Lefrasi was from, but at least five thousand souls had fallen prey to the Locustan ambush. Had the *Endeavor* arrived a little earlier, Bucifer P9 would've had a better chance. Now all they could do was mourn their loss.

Ross walked over to Ramya's side of the Stryker and frowned at her. "You look upset," he said.

Of course she was upset. They had just witnessed gigantic Locustans preying upon defenseless Mwandans. A Locustan megaship—a conglomeration of four Strykers—was out there and it was quietly harvesting populations in the Fringe. Yet there was not much they could do to stop it . . . at least not right away. However, there was hope—her father, Trysten Kiroff, had agreed to join the *Endeavor's* Captain Milos in the fight against the Locustans, but the fact remained that the Galactic Confederacy was still unconvinced of the threat of invasion. Wasn't that enough to be upset about?

Her father . . . . Ramya sighed. Her father was unquestionably the most powerful man in the galaxy. To say that they never got along was an understatement, but she was relieved by this new turn of events. Even if she didn't harbor much hope that their relationship would improve any, the galaxy could benefit much from Trysten Kiroff's backing.

Ramya flipped the final lock into place. "I'm worried," she huffed. A few days ago, her retorts to Ross would have had more of a bite. Since their encounter with the Confederacy at Totori and during their adventure on Morris II, the Mwandan sanctuary, Ramya had come to know Ross better. He seemed to trust her more and more. They had become . . . almost friends.

Ross shrugged and let out a long sigh. "Well, who isn't? But there's a long fight ahead of us and we can't lose focus."

Ramya smiled weakly. He was right, of course, but seeing people chased down by giant and deadly insects wasn't something you forgot in a hurry.

"You know, I always wanted to serve in the Fleet during the first invasion, but I couldn't get accepted," Ross continued. "My IQ was great, they said, but my physical condition wasn't at par. So I took up whatever vocation I could to help the fight."

Ross gave a sad shake of his head. "I helped the Fleet locate missing squadrons. I used to search for fleet debris." He paused, his flitting gaze settling in a distant corner of the hold. "I was just a kid back then. It hurt to see so much destruction . . . so little hope. I'd see pictures of these young pilots . . . lost, dead. There was no end in sight. The list of the missing kept on coming. For a long time, I couldn't get their faces out of my mind. But I had to, or I could get nothing done. So I forced myself to hope, to believe that we could . . .

win this."

He spoke in a strange, soulless voice and Ramya couldn't help but notice the pained, distracted look on his face. It was as if Ross had drifted far away, into a place devoid of light and life.

The Locusta-Vanga War was a dark time Ramya remembered well. It was hard for almost everyone. She imagined Ross, possibly a young teen back then, hard at work scouring the galaxy for debris. Her own memories still haunted her. Countless people she had known died, but nothing hurt as much as losing her grandfather Abelei. He didn't have to go to war—he was too old—yet he had rushed to the front lines. He had perished in the first wave and the Kiroff family home, Somenvaar, turned even colder than it had been before.

Even so, she couldn't imagine what Ross went through. During the war, her father, Trysten Kiroff, took over the planet Halperion, driving homesteaders like Ross off their land. Admittedly, without the Solandium from Halperion, Kiroff Industries wouldn't be able to churn out space fighters as quickly as it did, and without the space fighters there would be no stopping the Locustan swarms. The galaxy would've been lost. Still, there was no ignoring the fact that House Kiroff had robbed Ross and his family as well as many others of their rights.

Ross must've dealt with that at the same time as he was trying to come to terms with the senseless destruction of the war. It had to be a terrible time for him. And it showed. Anger, hurt, and fear spilled from Ross's eyes, the taut lines of his face making him look far older than his twenty-something years. Ramya wanted to console him, to tell him that she understood his pain or place a hand on his arm. She hesitated. Ross had just started acting normal around her after having called her a Kiroff spy, among other things, and she didn't want to bring awkwardness into the already complicated and fragile situation.

Ross broke the oddly comforting silence that had fallen between them. "I hope such times never come back."

Ramya wished she could reply with an assured, "They won't,"

but she couldn't. It would be a lie. Such times, if not worse, were looming already. The Locustans were coming again and the galaxy was terribly unprepared to face them.

"We'll fight them," she said in a voice that tried to sound poised but failed miserably.

"So we will," Ross replied promptly. The distant look in his eyes cleared in a heartbeat and his gaze turned razor-sharp again. He slapped the Stryker's nose. "All secure? We need to report to the captain."

Ramya nodded. "I'll ask Dakrhaeth to shut down. Then we can go."

She walked over to the open door and peeked inside the Stryker. In the middle of the entryway stood a pedestal that housed a dark ball. It was the only physical manifestation of Dakrhaeth, the Stryker's AI. It was dark, and the air was tight with an eerie silence. That felt . . . not good.

Anxiety made Ramya's insides twitch. A shudder at the base of her spine wanted to swamp her, but Ramya pushed it down with all her might. She was worrying over nothing.

There's nothing wrong with Dakrhaeth.

He was simply shaken like they all were. The Locustan megaship that was harvesting populations in the Fringe planets to build a Locustan army had asked Dakrhaeth to join them. For a long while, Dakrhaeth had been in a hypnotic trance, held captive by the other Strykers' call. He would've succumbed to it had it not been for a last-minute intervention by her father. Then he had veered away, and they had fought off the megaship.

Yet . . . Ramya just couldn't shake off the unease. Something about Dakrhaeth had changed since the encounter.

"Dakrhaeth," she called in a shaky voice. On getting no immediate reply, Ramya called again. "Dakrhaeth! You there?"

"I am here." His reply was steady but it lacked the chirpiness that was so characteristic of the AI. Once again, Ramya held her breath.

This lack of enthusiasm was different and unnerving. He didn't even address her as "Mihaal" the way he always did.

She must've stood silently for too long because Dakrhaeth said in an impatient tone, "Do you have a task for me?"

"Um . . . no," Ramya blurted. "No, I don't. Shut down, please."

"As you wish," he replied.

The Stryker's door slid closed and Ramya walked away, distracted by the dark thoughts that swirled endlessly inside her head.

What if the megaship's call had somehow changed Dakrhaeth? Ramya sucked in a lungful of air . . .

What if Dakrhaeth too had turned?

"All set?" Ross said, and Ramya almost jumped at the intrusion. His brows twitched just a little at her reaction but as soon as Ramya nodded, he started across the hold without further questions.

Ramya followed, her steps heavy and heart leaden with worry. The dark expanse of the hold passed like a blur, frenzied thoughts bombarding her tired brain incessantly. She kept telling herself that she was overthinking it, and Dakrhaeth was simply upset and tired just like the rest of them. After all, he was more than a machine. He had a personality that was just as alive and real as any live person's. So didn't it follow that he would be just as affected?

Still, as much as Ramya deliberated and as much as she wanted to get rid of her suspicions, she couldn't shake off that lingering doubt.

2

Ramya and Ross walked along the *Endeavor's* desolate corridors up to the main level in silence. Ross had cast a curious glance or two in her direction but didn't probe further. He would've continued his silence but for Ramya's distracted ambling out of the elevator.

After stopping Ramya from tripping over a box of fuses Flux had stacked along the side of the corridor, he frowned ferociously. "What's going on?" he asked. "You're somewhere else." Ross crossed his arms as he scanned her face.

"It's nothing . . . probably," Ramya said, debating if sharing her worries about Dakrhaeth with Ross was a good idea.

Ross was prone to suspicions—he'd jumped to a few unfounded ones about her not too long ago—and he never had much faith in Dakrhaeth to begin with. Ramya didn't plan to keep Dakrhaeth's change a secret; she'd have to confide in someone, but the only one suitable to hear her concerns was the captain, not Ross.

She wished she could simply shrug Ross off, but he stared grim-faced as she dithered, and Ramya realized it was too late to back out of the conversation. Her own relationship with Ross was fragile at best, and she didn't want to jeopardize what little trust had grown between them. With a cataclysmic invasion looming, now was not the time to create rifts. Regardless, she had to temper her comments carefully.

"Dakrhaeth seems distracted," she started slowly, mulling over every word she let out of her mouth. "Not quite his spirited self."

Ramya paused, hoping that would be enough for Ross. And it was.

"Don't see why he wouldn't be. We're all distracted," he replied. "I don't like that stupid AI one bit, but I'll admit he's . . . almost human. So it's normal, I guess, for him to be affected."

Ramya let go of the breath she'd been holding. "You're right," she said. If Ross was so casual about it, then perhaps she was overthinking it after all.

She would've happily abandoned her train of thought anyway but the sound of heavy boots coming their way made it easier. A glum, irritated look descended on Ross as Ramya's father, Trysten Kiroff, surrounded by his coterie of armored guards, strode up *Endeavor's* dreary corridors.

The moment he saw them, her father's gait stiffened—it was the slightest change in the arch of his neck, almost imperceptible, but Ramya had seen it far too many times to miss it. His face remained as impassive as ever as the group marched closer.

Ross frowned and fidgeted. "I should carry on," he said in a low voice. "The captain will be waiting to hear from us."

"I'm coming too," Ramya replied, somewhat crossly, before falling into step behind him.

She understood Ross was giving her privacy to speak to her father, but Ramya wasn't sure she wanted the chance. The only thing predictable about her father was his endless disappointment in her, and at the moment, she didn't care much for another bout of the same. If she was honest, it'd be good to get a nod of approval from him. However, Ramya didn't hope for it. She doubted her father was going to acknowledge her presence, let alone praise her fighting abilities, so she wasn't going to give him an opportunity to snub her. She had shown him enough of her needs and now finally, enough was enough.

Her father clearly had other plans. He slowed while his guards, at some invisible command, marched past and lined up along the walls a distance away.

"A moment, Lady Ramya." Trysten Kiroff gave her a slow nod, adhering to the decorum expected at the most formal of events.

Bound by years of habit, Ramya stopped right away and bowed. Ross cast a sidelong glance at her. "See you later at the COM," he whispered to Ramya, then with a curt nod at her father, Ross walked away.

Her father waited until Ross had turned the corner and disappeared from view. Ramya stiffened. She recognized that familiar glint deep in his always-glacial eyes.

"You seem to be quite friendly with him," her father said, the corners of his mouth curling in disdain.

Ramya furrowed her brows in confusion. "He's my crew mate. Why wouldn't I be friendly with him?"

He took a long time drawing a breath. "May I remind you, Lady Ramya, he doesn't belong with us." His words, cold and sharp, barely slipped past his gritted teeth. "You are practically royalty, he is . . . a nobody. He can serve you, but he can't be your equal. Do you understand?"

Ramya's fists curled. What in the stars was wrong with her father? Did he think the universe existed only to serve the Kiroffs? Perhaps he did, but she was not going to let him dictate whom she made friends with. Ross was no chum of hers, but he deserved more respect than Trysten Kiroff deemed.

"I'm sorry, Father," she retorted, rushing to get the angry words out, "but I disagree. Ross can belong anywhere he chooses to be."

His eyes turned to slits as they scoured her face. He grimaced and gave a disbelieving shake of his head. "Can't say that's unexpected of you. You always had a peasant's taste in everything."

What the . . . ?

As a fireball of curses threatened to spew out of her, Ramya suddenly realized that her father thought she was interested in Ross in a romantic sort of way. That explained his anger, his frustration, and his bizarre comments.

Ramya was about to break into a chuckle, but she resisted the urge and bottled the mirth up forcefully. While the idea of hooking up with Ross was interesting, it had never been on her mind. But her father didn't need to know that, did he? He could stew for eternity in his helpless anger for all she cared.

Ramya crossed her arms. "Well, then you should be happy that Somenvaar's rid of my lousy taste once and for all."

Her father glared at her. "This insolence doesn't befit your standing, Lady Ramya." His voice rose suddenly, its momentary loudness amplified by the corridors. The group of bodyguards shifted uneasily. Ramya winced but her father didn't stop. "No matter where you go or what you do, you need to remember where you come from."

I come from a family of cutthroats, Ramya wanted to scream, but she didn't. She held her breath and bit the inside of her cheek to stop from retorting. There would come a time for that, she reminded herself.

Her father looked up and down the corridor as if to make sure no one else had noticed his outburst. His shoulders seemed to have slumped a little. Perhaps he was ashamed of his temporary lapse of restraint. "I'm heading back to the *Kinvari* now." His voice had dropped to icy depths once more. "You could join me on the journey to El-Iss. It's much nicer."

Ramya bristled inside. He still didn't understand that she wasn't interested in "nice." But then again, at least he'd asked politely. That was a first and she couldn't totally ignore the gesture.

"This is where I belong now, Father," she said, keeping her tone calm but assured. "Nice or not, the *Endeavor's* my home."

"All right, all right," he said, impatience rushing his words along. "We'll meet at El-Iss then." Ramya expected him to march away to wherever he was going, but he remained still, his gaze scooting back and forth along the walls. There was something on his mind, Ramya deduced. And whatever it was, it couldn't be a pleasant thought for her father. He was uncomfortable, hesitant about something.

It dawned on her like a stroke of lightning. He wanted something. He wanted something from *her*. She recalled words Captain Milos had said once: *Everyone in the universe has needs, wants, hopes, and dreams, but powerful people hardly ever show their need to anyone. That's how they hang on to their power.*

At the moment, Trysten Kiroff was debating whether or not to give up his power, and his face was not a pretty sight. Ramya smirked. This was her moment, her opportunity, a mighty one if she chose to snatch it.

"What do you need, Father?" Ramya asked, forcing the glee in her voice to a minimum.

Her father's uncomfortable gaze stilled. His eyes narrowed and his lips thinned. He looked like a man teetering at the edge of a precipice.

"I don't see you having any use for the Drigganstone," he finally said.

You just couldn't ask for it directly, Ramya mused. Trysten Kiroff, the most powerful man in the galaxy, couldn't reveal his vulnerability to his own child.

The Drigganstone was tucked safely away in her room. Temihula, a Mwandan forest spirit, had gifted her the Drigganstone, a special jewel that was valued for its use in weaponry.

For a second Ramya considered refusing him. It'd be the easiest way to show him she was in charge, but it would be a petty move, and Ramya wasn't petty.

Ramya shrugged. "Sure, you can have it if you want," she replied, almost carelessly. "But . . ." She made a calculated pause and watched the spark of momentary relief in her father's eyes die out. "You have to promise that you'll tell me what you're doing with it. Every step of the way."

His answer came quicker than she expected. "Agreed."

"All right then," Ramya said with a loud chuckle. "It's a deal."

Her father squared his shoulders. "It is. I'll take the stone from you when we get to El-Iss. Have a safe journey."

With a nod, he turned and strode away, surrounded by his bodyguards. As they disappeared down the corridor, a satisfied smile curled the corners of Ramya's lips. For once in a very long time, she felt happy after an encounter with her father.

3

As soon as Ramya resumed her walk to the COM, she realized how tired she was. She also realized that in the anxiety of speaking to her father, she had forgotten to wonder about El-Iss and why they were headed there. El-Iss wasn't a new name for her—Kiroff Industries had built some factories there, although Ramya didn't know what those factories produced.

El-Iss was a moon of El-Soto, the fourth planet of the El system. The dry and rocky moon had a thin atmosphere and was inhospitable. While not a prime candidate for habitation, the moon was a lucrative piece of rock because of its extensive deposits of combustible carbon. Besides, it was almost in the Fringe, so the regulatory agencies of the Confederacy seldom ventured near. It was perfect for factories that needed to be run less than scrupulously to maintain a profit. Being near the Fringe had its disadvantages though, and they mostly appeared in the form of space pirates. However, Trysten Kiroff had pockets deep enough to keep the unsavory characters at bay.

Ramya's mind raced. Why was Captain Milos taking the *Endeavor* to El-Iss of all places? What happened to talking to Space Command and quarantining Bucifer P9?

As soon as she stepped inside the cramped Core Operations Module of the *Endeavor*, everyone turned to look curiously. Captain Milos and Ross were crowded behind Fenny's station, and Fenny peeked from in between the two men. Even Azzi, the Mwandan at the pilot's station, looked questioningly at her.

"What?" Ramya asked innocently, knowing fully well that they wanted to know how her encounter with Trysten Kiroff went.

Fenny's face scrunched as if she were trying to rein in a chuckle. She nudged Ross gently. "She looks all right to me."

"I'm fine," Ramya said, rolling her eyes. Did they think she'd burst into flames after talking to her father? Or collapse into a pile of mush?

Fenny's brows waggled. "You sure? Need a shoulder or something?"

"Oh, come on, Fenny," Ramya said, not trying to hide her annoyance.

"What?" Fenny feigned innocence. The ship's navigator had a tendency to be nosy. "I'm just asking. Hey, I could use a shoulder myself. Guess where his lordship's been spreading sunshine for the last two hours?"

Ross scoffed. "Well, get used to the sunshine, Fenny. We're gonna have that around us for a while."

While Fenny snickered, Captain Milos raised a hand to quiet everyone. Shaking his head, he walked over to his seat and slowly lowered himself into the chair.

"Respect, people," he said. "We have to respect each other, especially our allies. Sunshine or rain, these are folks we'll trust. Sometimes we'll need to put our lives in their hands. So . . ." He paused and rubbed his bandaged head gingerly.

"Captain, we're approaching the AP," Azzi announced.

"Take us in, Azzi," the captain said.

A shudder and a low hum later, the *Endeavor* entered the SLH to El-Iss.

"You have other matters to attend to, Azzi," the captain said right after. "Please go, see to them."

Ramya presumed Azzi was going to the mourning ritual Lefrasi said he'd arrange for the lost Mwandans on Bucifer P9. As soon as Azzi left, Ross slipped into the empty pilot seat and twiddled some buttons. "Two hours to El-Iss, Captain," he announced.

"Good, we have some time on our hands," Captain Milos replied. He sounded exhausted, and not without reason. Ever since Ramya joined the *Endeavor*, there had rarely been a full day of peace and quiet. On top of that, Captain Milos had been injured during the battle at Totori, and according to the ship's medic, Sosa, he had hardly gotten the rest his injury demanded.

Ross swiveled around and nodded. "We're good here, Captain. I'm perfectly capable—"

"You want the old man to get some rest?" the captain cut him off, smirking. "I will. In good time. Right now, I need a read of El-Iss. Fenny, please show us."

"Sure, Captain," Fenny said.

A few clicks and a splash of orange swamped the main viewer. Sharp peaks and ridges dominated the surface of El-Iss, with little or no vegetation. The moon rotated on the screen and soon a massive crack that stretched halfway across the orb from north to south came into view.

The captain sank back in his chair and scratched his chin. "They call that fissure the Deep," he said. "Trysten Kiroff has his base there . . . somewhere."

Even though no one asked her, Ramya felt somehow responsible because of her relation to the man. Her cheeks burned at the open display of her lack of knowledge.

Fenny's fingers danced over the buttons. The display zoomed to a location near the north end of the Deep. A ring of ten mountains formed a natural wall of sorts around a semicircular patch of land. Fenny tilted her head toward the series of geometric lumps dotting the area. "I think those are the entryways," she said. "I'm guessing whatever installation Kiroff has down there is underground."

The captain flashed a questioning look at Ramya.

"I don't know, Captain," Ramya said. "This was built recently and . . ." She let the words trail off, unable to say the truth—that her father had kicked her out of the Kiroff Industries main information network when she was a young girl. There were many days where she would dig and poke around the factory, as she'd loved the mechanics of things. "I didn't have access," she said.

"That's fine," the captain replied. "We'll find out soon."

"Why are we going there?" Ramya asked.

"Trysten offered to repair and retrofit the *Endeavor*. This ship does need a good mending. He also said the Stryker needs time to replenish its supplies."

Ramya nodded. Her father hadn't lied about the Stryker. The craft had regenerated itself once at Morris II, but the encounter with the Locustan megaship had cost them two new torpedoes.

"Besides, we need time to regroup and get our heads together," the captain said. "There's a lot of information Dakrhaeth transmitted to us, and we need to sort it all out. We need a place to camp and El-Iss is a good hideout."

"What do we do about Bucifer P9, Captain?" Ross asked. "We have to quarantine it, destroy that . . ."

"SuperStryker?" Fenny offered.

Ross gave her a listless shrug. "SuperStryker, yes. If we don't eradicate it, they're going to move on to the next planet and assimilate the population there. And keep on going."

Captain Milos sighed. "As much as I'd like to go after that abomination, we're not in a position to fight them, Ross. The Stryker's depleted, the *Endeavor's* practically stuck together with tape and glue, and Trysten's ship . . . well, he's not willing to use it. He says we're not an even match."

"Even match?" Fenny scoffed. "If we want to wait for an even match, we might as well hand over the galaxy to the Locustans."

"Patience, Fenny," the captain said. He looked over at Ramya and smiled. "Rami has damaged the Locustan ship enough. I believe she has bought us a day or two. We have to use the time wisely. Trysten will try to sway Space Command, as will the Mwandans."

"What if Space Command still doesn't budge?" Ross asked. "They don't seem particularly bright to me. Or interested in the well-being of the galaxy."

"Then we fight back on our own," the captain said in a steely voice. "Trysten is getting us space fighters. They're on the way to El-

Iss now."

"Yes!" Ross thumped the handle of his seat.

Captain Milos chuckled. "We'll still need to find pilots. We don't have enough of those."

"We'll find pilots," Ross said vehemently.

Even though Ramya didn't say anything, she doubted finding pilots would be so easy. Pilots didn't simply grow on trees. Good ones were even harder to find. She suddenly remembered Isbet, her best friend at CAWStrat and the finest pilot she'd ever known. A sigh immediately twisted its way out of her. She hadn't had time to miss her friend, but at the first thought of her now, memories came rushing back and her heart twitched.

"Rami, I need you to go over the information Dakrhaeth sent over," the captain said, rising to his feet. He picked up a small cube from the table next to him and offered it to her. "All of it is in there. Scan it."

"Yes, Captain."

Captain Milos rubbed his head and turned his bleary eyes toward Ross. "Commander, I will take that break you suggested. Buzz me when we're close to El."

"Yes, Captain."

Ramya tucked the memory cube in her pocket and followed the captain out of the COM. His bleary green eyes narrowed a tad when she voiced her concerns about Dakrhaeth.

"I hope it's nothing," he said after he had scratched the stubble on his chin for a bit. "Anyway, I'm sure Trysten's going to run a complete scan of the Stryker's systems once we reach El-Iss. So, either way, we'll find out."

He seemed eager to leave and although Ramya's anxieties hadn't abated much, she decided to drop it. Her steps were slow as she walked back to her room, but there was no time to rest. She *had* to find out about the directives Dakrhaeth received during the first invasion. And quickly.

4

Ramya hopped into the shower as soon as she reached her room. It couldn't be as long as she wished it to be since water was rationed, but even the short indulgence felt good and calming. Her eyes flitted over the mirror as she left the washroom, and she didn't miss how haggard her face looked. Sharp eyes—more a forlorn gray than a cheery blue at the moment—seemed to sneer at her.

"Tired already?" they mocked. "This is just the beginning."

Suppressing a sigh, Ramya hurried over to her desk and sank into the chair. She pulled out her notebook and hooked up the memory cube to the portal built into the nook near her bed.

Letters and numbers flashed across the screen in an endless stream. Ramya fell back into the chair and stared, more in sheer exhaustion at the volume of it than from disbelief. There was a *lot* of information, and it would take a long time to decipher. Time they didn't have.

Perhaps it would be faster to ask Dakrhaeth. These were his memories after all. Ramya mulled it over for a second and then sat up with a shake of her head.

Can't ask Dakrhaeth.

She was still not sure the Stryker's AI was in the clear after the encounter at Bucifer P9. She had to comb this data herself, no matter how long it took.

Ramya decided to look for any reference to "fading stars," the term Dakrhaeth mentioned quite a few times. It was a marker he had followed during their invasion of the galaxy, but that was all he remembered. Ramya was sure it was important, so she searched, not once or twice, but five times over, yet found nothing.

She was trying to focus every bit of energy left in her to think up another tactic to scan Dakrhaeth's memories when there was a knock on the door. An irritated grunt escaped her mouth and she walked over, muttering in frustration. The door opened with an annoying screech, revealing Ahool Petta's bobbing form outside.

"Rami!" he exclaimed. "I'm glad you all right."

Ramya chuckled, relishing the young Mwandan's glee at seeing her and his usual way of speaking in broken Galactic.

"Thank you, Ahool," Ramya said. "I'm glad too. I couldn't help Chief Mifek though," she added, heaviness sweeping over her at the thought. She had done nothing to help the Mwandans on Bucifer P9. She couldn't, rather. Dakrhaeth had been under the spell of what Fenny had aptly named the SuperStryker and she had no control.

"You look . . . not well," Ahool said, his bright red jewel-like eyes dimming.

Ramya waved casually. "Just tired." She wished Ahool would leave so she could get back to her task. But the Mwandan boy showed no sign of letting her go.

"Should sleep then. Maybe Pax can help," Ahool suggested eagerly. "I get you Pax from Sosa."

"No, no," Ramya protested. This love of Pax—a bright blue liquid that inhibited your senses—had gone far already, and it niggled her a bit. Besides, she had work to do. This was no time to get into a drunken stupor. "I'm working on something, Ahool. It's not Pax time now."

"Can I help? With work?" Ahool said. One look at those glittery eyes and Ramya didn't have the heart to refuse his earnest offer. Flashing a resigned smile, she beckoned him inside.

"Come on in," Ramya said. "Pull up that stool."

For as long as Ramya had known Ahool, she had never seen a dearth of enthusiasm in the boy. After Ramya explained what she was doing, he jumped into the task of going through the contents of the memory cube with zeal. It was a good decision to invite him in, Ramya realized. Not only was Ahool sharp as a whip, but it was good to have someone to brainstorm with, particularly when her own brain was as severely clogged as it was now.

"There no fading star anywhere," Ahool announced after they had searched through the data a zillion times over. "Am sure."

"I see that," Ramya said. "But Dakrhaeth mentioned it so many times. It has to be here somewhere."

Before he'd sent all the data over to the *Endeavor*, Dakrhaeth claimed that he remembered all about the fading star. It had seemed important at the time. He couldn't have lied . . . or could he?

"Here is something," Ahool said suddenly. "Not fading. But dying star."

Ramya leaned over to look. "That could be the same thing. Maybe Dakrhaeth remembered wrong. What else does it say?"

"The Hinterland is halfway to the dying star," Ahool said.

Ramya's eyes were stuck on a series of numbers that looked familiar. Even though she had no idea what the dying star meant, she had a hunch about the numbers.

"Could these numbers be galactic coordinates?" Ramya asked.

Ahool stared at the series of numbers for a while before shaking his head. "They look similar. But also wrong. Too big."

Ramya had thought the same thing. She knew the coordinates for the edges of the galaxy well, and they were small numbers compared to what they were looking at now.

"Maybe we should ask Fenny," Ramya said after they had checked and rechecked the coordinates. Fenny was the expert on star charts and she would likely have a solution to the puzzle.

"What is Hinterland?" Ahool asked, his spindly gray fingers dancing over the controls to highlight every reference to the word. There were many, and the highlights made the display light up like a screen full of fireflies.

Ramya pulled a blanket around her and settled back cozily into her chair. She didn't know, but the Hinterland—whatever it was—had to be important.

"Wait!" Ramya shouted. "The dying star is just a marker, right?

It's part of the directions to get to this Hinterland." Ahool nodded as Ramya continued to think aloud. "So . . . Dakrhaeth and his squadron were sent to the Hinterland and somehow they crashed into KS-5 in Sector 22?"

"But . . ." Ahool closed his eyes and shook his head with vigor. "But Sector 22 is far from battlefront, from the Fringe. Why go there?"

"That's what I've been asking. What was a squadron of Locustan fighters doing out there? They were looking for the Hinterland, whatever that is."

Ahool tapped his cheek thoughtfully. "Something very important is at Hinterland."

"Yes, has to be. But what?"

"Answer in here somewhere," Ahool said. He leaned closer to the display and started clicking away.

Together they skimmed over the endless stream of data. There was little of value; most of it was reiterations of the directions to the Hinterland. It almost felt like the same information being repeated. Could Dakrhaeth have bluffed and given them misinformation?

Dakrhaeth didn't lie, Ramya forced the suspicion away. He couldn't lie to her like that, not after having helped save their lives time and again. She was getting too paranoid, just like Ross.

A telltale shudder and a faint screech caused Ramya to look up. The scenery screen on the window changed to a real view outside.

"We're here already?" Ramya asked. Two hours had passed too quickly.

Ahool bounded off his seat and peeked out of the grimy window. "Where is this?" he asked.

"The El system," Ramya said, walking over to his side. "It's a triple star system. El-Enas and El-Dio are twins. See those lights over there?" She pointed at a double spot of light far to the right and Ahool nodded. "Those are the twin stars. The main star, El-Tyra, is closer, probably behind us."

"What planet we going to?"

"Not to a planet, we're going to a moon. It's called El-Iss."

"That where your father has factory?" Ahool asked.

"Yes, that's it," Ramya replied pithily and stepped away from the window. She sank back into her chair.

"You and your father fight a lot?" Ahool asked, and Ramya smiled. She had been expecting that question ever since Ahool walked into her room. The Mwandan boy wasn't exactly nosy but he was the curious sort. After all, he was a kid, and it was natural that his curiosity almost always overtook his restraint.

"Who told you about me and my father?" she asked, arching a brow.

"Wiz," Ahool replied without hesitation. "He tells me lot about everyone."

"I thought Sosa told him not to talk too much," Ramya said. The *Endeavor's* pilot, Wiz, was recovering from a foul head injury.

Ahool promptly looked up at the ceiling.

"You have to make him rest, Ahool," Ramya said. "That wound is . . . serious."

Ahool's face took on a purplish hue and his eyes dimmed. "I tried to stop. He won't listen," he said plaintively.

"You need to get away from him or tell Sosa," Ramya said. Ahool's wilted face tugged at her heart so she changed the subject. "Anyway, yes, my father and I fight a bit. Well, more like he tells me how worthless I am and I listen."

Before Ahool could respond, the comm on Ramya's wrist blinked. "What now?" Ramya muttered, frowning as she punched the "accept" button.

"Rami," Fenny called in a bristly voice. "To the COM, please. Lord Paramount Kiroff has instructions for landing."

Ramya shot a look at the window. El-Iss wasn't visible, which meant it was too early to prepare for landing.

"But, Fenny—"

"Hey, don't ask me. I'm just the messenger." Fenny's voice cut off with a sharp click, the abruptness leaving Ramya utterly baffled.

"Fenny very mad," Ahool said.

That was obvious. What Ramya didn't understand was what made Fenny so snappish. She quickly put on her jacket and strapped the M-gun to her leg.

"You want to keep working on that?" she asked Ahool before leaving, jerking her thumb at the portal still flashing Dakrhaeth's data. "If you want, you could."

Ahool's face broke into a huge grin and with an eager nod, he rushed back to the nook. Smiling to herself, Ramya left her room.

5

Trysten Kiroff was in a foul mood. Ramya didn't know what had set it off, but her father was soaking everyone with his ice-cold stare from the main monitor. Captain Milos was absent, so Ross and Fenny were getting the brunt of it. *No wonder Fenny snapped at me,* she thought.

Ramya slunk along the wall and found a spot behind the empty captain's seat. Her father's unfriendly gaze followed her.

"You," he called her with as much disdain as he could find. "You need to bring the Stryker in another way. I'm sending you the coordinates. My people will pick you up from there and bring you underground."

Confused, Ramya looked at Ross and Fenny. Neither moved or said a word. She gritted her teeth. Where in the stars was the captain?

"I don't understand. I thought we were getting the *Endeavor* repaired," she said slowly. "Why would I take the Stryker somewhere else?"

"Because the Stryker isn't like any other spacecraft. It needs special pods to replenish itself, which we don't have out here on El-Iss. Follow now?" he sneered.

His mockery of her was never subtle. His words burned through Ramya like hot lead from an assault rifle. Fists clenched, she held her breath and hung on to every bit of serenity she had within her.

"Not quite," she replied, her fingers curling around the cold edges of the captain's seat. "You want me to take the Stryker someplace away from where you're taking the *Endeavor* and everyone else? Why?"

His eyes flashed and his jaw tightened. Come to think of it, just this once, he had reason to be offended. Her words didn't paint a favorable picture of Trysten Kiroff. She'd made it sound as if he were plotting to separate her and the Stryker from the *Endeavor* and its crew—overall mighty dubious. She understood why he would be offended, but she didn't really care.

"I need the Stryker at a particular location where it can quickly soak up the most starlight," he said steadily. "Do you know what fuel the Stryker runs on?" The corners of his lips curled with derision at her silence. "The Stryker is fueled by Xebium packs, and they replicate well in starlight."

Ramya gulped. *Xebium? Really?* Her thoughts bounded away at the mention. Xebium was a synthetic element rumored to be under study and touted to be far more stable than those currently used in starship engines. Xebium would allow ships to travel ten times farther without refueling stops. Scientists said that it would revolutionize the space fleet. It was a miracle element, unbelievable almost, like horses with wings. Who could've guessed Xebium was already real, courtesy of Trysten Kiroff?

What other cutting-edge tech was her father playing with in Sector 22? He was experimenting with Locustan technology, teleportation, communication within the SLH, and . . . Xebium. Her father was indeed a force to reckon with, smart, cunning, and always ten steps ahead of the pack. She could almost be proud of him. If only he had a heart. If only he cared a little about her.

The sound of footfalls outside the COM was timely. It stopped Ramya from getting sucked into painful rumination. Captain Milos stumbled in, his face more haggard than it had been two hours ago. His eyes were reddish and bleary, and he almost seemed to drag himself into his seat.

Her father turned his attention to the captain. "Captain Milos, I spoke to the halfwits at Space Command. They laughed when I mentioned Bucifer P9. The imbeciles refuse to speak on the matter until you and your crew surrender and stand trial for the destruction at Totori."

Ramya scoffed. Stand trial? For what? For defending themselves? Did Space Command think the *Endeavor* was going to sacrifice itself to their whims?

The captain let out a thick chuckle. "Stand trial? Is that what they want? Well, I don't mind appearing before the senate, but I couldn't subject my crew to that farce."

"I told them they could go drown themselves in Pterostrich droppings," her father said. "No one's surrendering."

Someone snorted, and Ramya was pretty sure it was Fenny. Ramya wanted to laugh, but she didn't know how. She didn't remember when she had stopped laughing in the presence of her father.

"Ah well, since you've spoken so succinctly for all of us already, that's settled. Now what's the plan on El-Iss?" the captain said.

"I've sent your navigator coordinates for landing the ship. I need the Stryker to land at a different location."

Captain Milos nodded. "All right."

Ramya worried her lower lip. No matter what the reason, she didn't like the idea of being separated from the rest of the crew. At all. But she had no choice but to follow orders.

"Well, that's it for now. One of my people will guide you once you're near the landing site. I'll meet you on the ground." Her father nodded curtly and the screen faded to black.

The captain tapped the arm of his seat and looked thoughtfully at the dusty orange ball of El-Iss drawing steadily closer. "How far to the surface, Commander?" he asked.

"Entering atmosphere in ten minutes, Captain," Ross replied.

"Rami, prepare the Stryker," the captain said. "You'll take off once we are halfway to the landing site."

"Who's going with her, Captain?" Ross asked just as Ramya was about to leave the COM.

"Does she need anyone?" the captain said. "She's quite capable, isn't she?"

Fenny stared incredulously at the captain. "You're joking, right?" she said. "She's just a kid. Sure, she's good at flying around, but what if she needs a hand? Besides, this is Mad Kiroff's base. You can't let her go alone."

The captain stayed quiet for a while, his face impassive. "Take Ahool with you," he said finally.

"Ahool?" Fenny exclaimed. "That toddler?"

"Yes, Fenny, that Ahool," the captain replied. He turned toward Ramya and arched an eyebrow. "Go on, run. You don't have too long to prepare."

Ramya walked out of the COM a touch confused. She had been tasked with seemingly impossible jobs before, and this was a walk in the park in comparison. But still, she'd never been on El-Iss and hardly knew where her father was sending her.

Every time Ramya had been assigned a job by the captain, someone older, more experienced, was by her side. But this time, the captain didn't think of sending Ross or Fenny with her, not even Merin or Azzi. Instead, he picked the young and inexperienced Ahool. Ramya's steps slowed as the realization of her responsibility sank in.

Ahool was plucky, but what did he know of the world out there? He knew even less than she did. Hell, he'd never even flown in a spacecraft in his life. What if something went wrong and they were stranded on El-Iss? Who would help her? She'd have nothing to fall back on but her own and Ahool's minuscule knowledge of the universe.

Maybe that's precisely the idea. The captain always did things for a reason. And this job, Ramya was sure, was no different. For the first time, Captain Milos had put her truly in charge. Her feet picked up the pace. She had to do this right. She had to do this well.

***

The flight across El-Iss to the coordinates sent by her father was uneventful and quiet. Burnt-orange land stretched from one end of the moon to the other, like a fiery sea under the Stryker. Much of the land wrinkled into low mountains, their heights growing as they drew nearer to the gash across the moon, the chasm they called the Deep.

Ahool sat in the co-pilot's seat, rocking gently, his lips moving frenziedly as he scanned the busy control panel in front of him. He wasn't praying, Ramya knew. He was trying to memorize the controls. It was funny how Ahool had reacted to the news of their assignment. First, he had jumped to his feet; then, face paling, he'd slumped into his chair.

"Just you and me?" he'd asked, dimmed eyes scouring Ramya's face. "B-but I . . . I never fly before."

Ramya had reached out and patted the young Mwandan's shoulder. "It'll be all right, Ahool. Everyone learns one time or another. We'll be fine."

Her words had not brought much cheer but Ahool wasted no time in starting to learn. First, he had wrung out as much information as he could from Ramya, and as soon as they boarded the Stryker, he started memorizing the functions of every button and lever on the control panel. It continued even after they had launched from the *Endeavor*.

The *Endeavor* . . . Ramya scanned the rear viewer to look at the ship they had left behind. They were low, sinking nearer to the entrance of the factory. How her father was planning to get the ship to the repair crew, she didn't know. But they were getting farther apart—the *Endeavor* was heading east while the Stryker's nose was pointed due north—with every second that passed.

Ramya glanced longingly at the communicator. She thought of speaking to whoever was at the COM but resisted. Captain Milos wanted her to do this alone, so she would.

"Dakrhaeth," she called the Stryker's AI instead.

"Yes," he replied. The curtness made Ramya frown. Gone was the chirpiness. He didn't even call her Mihaal anymore. What was going on with Dakrhaeth?

"How long to the destination?"

"Six minutes and fifteen seconds."

Silence. Again. Ramya stifled a sigh. How did one diagnose an AI? She couldn't just take Dakrhaeth to Sosa. The captain was right. Only one person, her father, the one who had truly brought Dakrhaeth back to life, would know.

"That where we go?" Ahool asked as he pointed at the ground further up north. Ramya saw the spot of red right away, and the scopes on the Stryker clearly showed a blood-red flag with the Kiroff sigil drawn in gold on it. Two men in the standard Kiroff Industries gray overalls emblazoned with the same sigil stood next to it, watching them.

"Yes, that's it." She twisted the flight stick to descend slowly. "Try the stick, Ahool," she said. "Come on, try it. It won't bite."

He tried. The Stryker nosedived. Ahool shrank away, yelping. Ramya chuckled and eased the craft back to a stable position. Then she urged him to try again.

Any other time Dakrhaeth would've chimed in without fail and showered snippets of wisdom on them. Not now. For the first time in her life, she couldn't wait to see her father. Something was definitely wrong with Dakrhaeth and she was worried.

"You're getting better, Ahool," Ramya said, eyeing their destination, a large circular patch built on a mountaintop. It grew closer and bigger as they approached. "Have to be smoother, softer on the stick. We have to practice more."

"It is not advisable to let the co-pilot try to land us," Dakrhaeth said suddenly, the familiarity of the censure bringing a smile to Ramya's lips.

"Of course not," Ramya replied. She wrapped her fingers around the flight stick and straightened the craft for landing, lowering it steadily to the center of the landing patch. On touching ground, she cut off the engine and turned off the controls. "You're here to replenish your supplies, Dakrhaeth. Shut down, get your cloaking on, and start recharging. Any estimates on how long you'll need?"

"About ten hours to fully regenerate all supplies," Dakrhaeth replied. "Is this a secure place?"

"My father thinks so," Ramya said as she unstrapped herself from the seat. "He's usually right."

Ramya walked to the door, and Ahool followed.

"Will you be around?" Dakrhaeth asked as she was stepping out.

"I'm not sure. I may be taken somewhere else."

"See you later then," Dakrhaeth said crisply.

Ramya couldn't help another sigh. Dakrhaeth, his impertinence notwithstanding, had become a friend. His current aloofness pained her. She had no time to wallow in her sorrow. The door slid open and a burly man with big, crooked teeth greeted her with a large smile.

"Lady Ramya," he said and bowed low. A small man stood behind him, his face pensive. He bowed a few times in quick succession, in a nervous sort of way, as if not sure what would impress her.

"I'm Mola and this is Nine," the burly man said, tapping his chest and then gesturing at his smaller mustached partner. "We will take you . . ." He paused when he saw Ahool, his eyes bulging. Although funny, his reaction wasn't unexpected — Mwandans were a reclusive race and one didn't come across one of them face-to-face very often, if at all. Mola recovered quickly enough. "We will take you both to the base."

"The base?" Ramya blurted. These were supposed to be factories, but "base" sounded like fortification.

"Yes, underground. That's where the Lord Paramount took his ships."

Ramya held up her hands in disbelief. "Wait, he took both the *Kinvari* and the *Endeavor* underground? Two entire ships?"

Mola shrugged. "Yeah, of course. Why wouldn't he?"

Taking two hulking battleships underground to some bunker seemed nothing out of the ordinary to the big guy. Only Ramya couldn't fathom what sort of operations her father had going here on

El-Iss.

"You'll see. That's where we're going," Nine chimed in. He was a nervous sort, and even his speech rushed as if fleeing his mouth. "We'll ride to the entrance in our komodo."

"What is komodo?" Ahool asked.

"That," Mola said, pointing at a grayish contraption on an endless set of tracked wheels that looked like a squished caterpillar. "It's fast."

"All right. Who stays with the Stryker?" Ramya asked.

"Watchers are watching," Nine said, gesturing at the edge of the landing site. Turrets, quad-barreled and camouflaged to match the orange landscape, ringed the circular patch. Ramya sighed in relief. Even though Dakrhaeth was going to get his shields up and stay invisible, it felt good to know that someone was watching over him.

Mola and Nine led them to the komodo and ushered them in. As soon as they had settled in—Mola in the driver's seat, Nine in the passenger side, and Ramya and Ahool in the rear—the komodo growled to life. It crawled away from the landing site, slowly at first, then at a breakneck speed along the side of the mountain.

Ramya grabbed the arm of her seat and held her breath. Flashes of scenery sped past and orange walls rushed up to them and fell away. The komodo thundered on, relentless and determined. Gritting her teeth and clutching her stomach, Ramya fought the nausea churning her guts. She had been scared plenty of times in the last few days, but this rollercoaster ride was a punishment like no other. She only hoped she wouldn't throw up on Nine's back.

The komodo had clambered down to the bottom of the hill and shuffled across the arid flatland before Ramya breathed easy. Ahool sat with his eyes glued to the front windows, his face ashen. As the komodo dipped and dropped, Ahool yelped.

"It's all right, Ahool," Ramya whispered. "These guys know what they're doing."

Ahool didn't seem to hear. He raised a shaking hand toward the southern sky. "What are those?" he whispered.

The pit of Ramya's stomach dropped. A cluster of dark specks had appeared in the sky and was streaking toward the Deep.

For a second she forgot to breathe. The world turned a shade of gray and closed in on her. She did not even know when words slipped out of her mouth. "Iffin hell! Where did those come from?"

6

Locustan invaders, Ramya thought, as she clutched the back of the seat. She was sure it was a swarm, albeit a small one, but a Locustan swarm nonetheless.

"Stop!" she shouted. "Stop right now."

The komodo lurched violently forward as Mola brought it to a halt. Ramya's shoulder crashed against the side but she hardly felt any pain. Her heart was laden with fear, thumping wildly against her chest.

Mola turned around and gave Ramya a bewildered look. "What's wrong?" he asked.

Ramya pointed at the cluster of at least twenty space fighters to the south. "That. Do you see that often around here?"

Mola looked at the sky, then toward Nine, and finally back at Ramya. When he shook his head, his face was ashen. "No. Never. Are those . . . do you think they're . . . L-Locustans?"

"Shut up, Mola," Nine growled. "There's no invasion. Locustans are gone. Those are . . . just . . ."

"Just what, eh?" Mola snapped back. "No one just drops by El-Iss. We'd have heard if Lord Paramount had allowed anyone in. Just like we knew he was visiting. Him and his guests in that rust bucket."

"You two, quiet!" Ramya said impatiently. The two stooges her father had sent were undoubtedly clueless duds. There was no time to listen to their bickering. She needed to find out who the fighters were.

"Do you have scopes on board?" she asked.

Nine fumbled around and pulled out a pair of binoculars. Ramya snatched them and wriggled out of the komodo. The fighters were still a few minutes away from the Deep but with the scopes she could see them clearly. They were all Wentworth-Busas, brown and splotchy all over with a red-and-black star on their tails.

Confederate fighters!

"These aren't Locustan," she yelled. "Confederate fighters . . . all of them."

"And that's not good, I assume," Mola said.

"No, it's not."

Space Command had found them somehow. She had to warn her father and Captain Milos. Ramya punched her wrist-comm on. Just as she feared, the proximity sensor at the center of the device stayed red, indicating they were out of range of the *Endeavor's* radio.

She peeked inside the komodo. "Can you call the base from here?" she asked.

"We could try calling Gate. Should we?" Nine said.

"Yes, you should," Ramya snapped. "Call them. Tell them a confederate squadron is" — she looked up at the sky to assess their distance — "two minutes away."

Mola and Nine exchanged a look before Nine started fiddling with the instrument cluster. A series of bleeps and bloops later, Nine nodded. "Sent them a message, Lady."

"What did they say?"

Nine shrugged. "I don't know. Komodos aren't set up for two-way communication." Seeing Ramya's eyes widen, he added, "We don't have combat situations every day."

Mola flashed a crooked yellow grin. "Heck, we don't even get out to the surface that often."

"If ever." Nine chuckled throatily.

Ramya groaned. *What a pair idiots!* And what was her father thinking sending her this useless vehicle that didn't even have a two-way communication channel? He always made fun of the old and beat-up *Endeavor*. Didn't the almighty Trysten Kiroff have the money and the tech to get decent vehicles at his top-secret base?

Ramya sucked in a lungful of air and calmed her rising temper. She had to think this through . . .

Maybe, just maybe, this wasn't much of a threat at all. What could happen really? The pilots could bombard the entryways, but the base was underground, and unless they fired a fission warhead into the ground, they could do nothing. And fission warheads didn't get chucked around at the drop of a hat. Besides, what good would bombarding the base achieve? All Space Command wanted was to make Captain Milos stand trial for the confrontation at Totori, not kill him. She had to be overthinking this. This was simply a recon mission, nothing else.

"Lady Ramya," Mola yelled. "What do we do now?"

Ramya crawled back into the komodo, thinking furiously. What could they do? Follow the original plan, whatever it was?

"What were your instructions? Where were you taking us?"

"To the main entrance, of course," Nine said.

Ramya mulled it for a second. "Is there another entrance to the base?" she asked.

Mola and Nine looked at each other again. Then Nine shrugged.

"There's one side door we know of," Mola informed. "But it's not much used. It's a bit . . . mucky."

"Mucky is fine," Ramya said and strapped herself in. "Take us there. Quick."

The komodo growled and rolled forward in a heartbeat. The sharpest tack he was not, but Mola was a skilled driver. He steered the komodo across the rocks and dust, up, down, and along the sides of the mountains. Ramya's gut churned and her body ached from being hurled from side to side, but she couldn't complain — they were covering the distance fast, just like she wanted.

"We're close," Nine announced after they had circled around a fat hillock and headed to the next. For the next five minutes, the komodo crept upslope until it reached the crook of the mount. There it crawled underneath an outcropping and stopped.

Mola and Nine jumped out of the komodo, and Ramya and Ahool followed. While Mola and Nine started digging near the wall of the mount, Ramya looked around. They didn't have a clear view of the basin where the *Endeavor* was supposed to land. However, it wouldn't be too difficult to steal a look if she could circle the mount fast enough. Ramya cast a look back at their escorts. They were still digging. Perhaps she had enough time to get to the other side and back again.

"Hey, Mola, Nine!" Ramya called. "I'll take a quick look at the other side, all right? Be back soon."

She ran a hand over her weapons; the M-gun was tucked inside her jacket and the blaster on her leg. She looked for Ahool and found him standing behind her, silently observing.

"You've been too quiet," Ramya observed, suddenly realizing that Ahool hadn't spoken since boarding the komodo.

Not waiting for a response, Ramya walked in the direction of the basin with long strides.

"What you planning?" Ahool asked, following her.

"I want to check what the fighters are doing," she said. "I didn't see them return so they must've landed."

"They want to catch Captain Milos?"

"I think so."

They walked in silence for a bit.

"How we going to stop them?" Ahool asked in a worried voice.

"We'll see," she said. Truth was, Ramya didn't know. She didn't know if they could stop anyone from capturing the captain, but she would do everything in her power to make sure that didn't happen.

Ramya clambered up a dirt hill, grasping at roots, and made her way to the top of a boulder where a sliver of the basin was visible just beyond.

"They *have* landed," Ahool said. He had climbed next to her and stared at the two neat rows of Wentworth-Busas. There were at least twenty of them. A few people—five or six soldiers dressed in the confederate green—were patrolling the area, cradling Meson cannons.

"They sure don't look friendly," Ramya said. "Come on, Ahool. Let's get back. We got to get inside."

Ramya scampered off the boulder and rushed back to the komodo with Ahool in tow. When they reached the outcrop, Mola and Nine weren't digging anymore. Instead, they were peeking at a cavernous hole in the ground.

Mola pointed down. "That's how we go in," he said.

It was more like a well, a deep one with rungs built into the sides. It was dark within, strung with cobwebs. A musty odor of stale, dead air hit her nose.

"How deep does it go?" Ramya asked.

"Not too deep. Two standard levels maybe," Mola said.

"And how far is this from where my father would've entered?"

Mola looked at Nine who nodded diffidently. "Not too close," he said, then paused. "Not too far either."

His answer didn't inspire much confidence. *Do they even know where the well leads to?* Ramya wondered. *What if we get trapped inside?* She shivered at the thought.

"You know the way, right?" Ramya said, eyeing the well.

"Of course," Mola replied. He cast a wary look at Nine. "You do, don't you?"

"Yes, yes, I do," Nine said impatiently. He slung his legs over the edge and grabbed a rung. "Come on, I'll show you."

You're in charge, Rami! This is all on you, Ramya reminded herself. She was about to lead the two men and Ahool down a hole that no one had been in recently. Their safety was her responsibility, their lives in her hands.

"Coming, Lady?" Nine asked.

Ramya hesitated and immediately steeled herself. The captain's life and honor were at risk. Perhaps the honor of House Kiroff as well. Most importantly though, the entire galaxy was in danger. This was no time for wild-goose chases and petty politics. Yet Space Command was doing just that.

Ramya gritted her teeth. She had to do everything to keep the Locustans away. And right now that meant helping the captain escape the Confederate troopers.

Fists clenched, Ramya walked over to Nine. She looked at her ragtag team once and nodded resolutely. "Let's go. Let's find out what the troopers are up to."

7

To call the well mucky was an understatement. The entire length was dark, smelly, and covered with cobwebs. It was only by sheer force of will that Ramya and her companions continued. Ramya's palms burned from holding the rungs and her guts roiled every time she breathed in the musty air. She heaved a sigh of relief when Nine slowed below her.

"Are we there?" she asked.

Even in the dim light, Ramya didn't miss his tentative nod. Nine let go of the rungs and turned around to shine a light on the gaping hole on the opposite side.

"There's the tunnel," he said between long breaths. "We go in there. Follow me, Lady."

The tunnel was even worse than the descent into the well. Strewn with what could only be rodent droppings, the stench of rotting carcasses filled the air. Ramya even heard scurrying paws and saw a pair of shiny eyes or two. She only hoped there wasn't an animal that would decide to feast on them. Nine carried a tiny penlight and led the way, while Mola lit the way from the rear.

"How long is it, Nine?" Ramya whispered after they had walked for at least five minutes.

"I dunno, Lady," Nine said. "I don't come here every day. All I know is that this opens into the ventilation shaft near the main entrance."

Fair enough. Ramya decided not to ask any more questions after that. As long as Nine led them to the main entrance safely, she was fine with it.

After five more minutes of tramping in the dark, Nine slowed. He flashed his light around, looking for something. Ramya was about to ask him what was going on when he rushed to one side and felt the wall of the tunnel. Then he grinned triumphantly at Ramya.

"There it is, Lady," he said before beckoning Mola. "Hey, come on. Give me a hand here."

Together they pushed against the wall until a square-shaped piece slid to the side.

"That's the ventilation shaft, Lady Ramya," Mola said, pointing at the opening. "We're almost there."

Almost there! Almost? This was turning into a never-ending quest. Time was slipping past like water through a sieve and Ramya doubted if they would reach the entrance in time to make a difference. Or if they would reach the entrance at all.

"Coming in, Lady?" Nine had already hoisted himself into the ventilation shaft. He peered curiously at Ramya.

"Yes, sure," Ramya replied. What choice did she have but to keep going? She crawled in after Nine, wincing when her knuckles scraped against the sharp edge of the opening.

"You all right, Lady?" Nine asked, noting her pained expression.

Skin had peeled right off and it burned like hell but this wasn't the time to discuss trivial injuries. Ramya simply nodded and looked around. This tunnel — the ventilation shaft — was dark just like the previous tunnel, but it was surprisingly clean. There was no smell, no animal droppings, only a bit of dust. But it was far smaller in girth, so the only way to move through it was to crawl. That, in turn, made their journey even slower than before. Not to mention that it almost triggered Ramya's claustrophobia. She fought off the fears with everything she had and pushed herself on.

It seemed like an endless while had passed before the shaft suddenly turned sideways and grew wider. This section also seemed less dark and the reason soon became apparent. Large, square air-vents were built into the bottom of the shaft at regular intervals, through which light streamed in. Ramya kneeled near one of the openings and looked through the slats. A corridor stretched below — gray, clean, and sterile like a laboratory. It was empty.

Where are all the people?

"Keep moving, Lady," Nine's sharp reminder made Ramya hasten. They moved along stealthily until Ramya heard *the* voice. Her father's voice. She couldn't understand what he was saying, but there was no doubt he was angry.

"Do you hear that?" Ramya whispered. "That's my father. But where is he?"

Nine gulped noisily. "He doesn't sound too happy, does he?"

He's never happy, Ramya mused. "We need to reach him fast," she said. "Where do you think he is?"

Trysten Kiroff's voice thundered again and Nine's mustache suddenly drooped. He licked his lips and shuddered a little. "C-come this way," he said finally.

It didn't take long to locate him. A bit further down, where the shaft crossed a large hallway, Meson cannon-wielding Confederate troopers had corralled the *Endeavor's* crew and about twenty other people sporting the Kiroff sigil. There were a few battered and bloody bodies on the ground as well. All dead, Ramya presumed. There had been a firefight when the troopers came in, but not a long one.

Trysten Kiroff and a tired-looking Captain Milos stood in front of a tall, strapping, red-haired woman in fleet officer's uniform. She was a high-ranking official given the number of stars on her lapel. Ramya counted them . . . an admiral. *Is that Admiral Kanaa?*

"We need to talk, Admiral," Trysten Kiroff said to the woman.

"We don't have the time," the woman snapped in a wheezy voice that Ramya recognized right away. It was the same voice that had asked them to surrender at Totori. This was indeed Kanaa.

"I let you walk into my factory because I trusted you'd do the right thing. Instead, you turned around and killed my people. Now you're hauling more of my own away. You can't do that," her father said.

"By the power bestowed on me by Space Command, I can. And I will."

"You at least owe me a conversation."

"Then converse, Lord Paramount Kiroff."

"Not like this," her father replied. He cast an annoyed look around at the people around them. "One to one. In privacy."

"There is no time for that at the moment, I'm afraid," Admiral Kanaa said. "We can talk and we will talk, but right now I need to take this man away." She jabbed a finger in the direction of Captain Milos. "He needs to stand trial for his crimes at Totori. The deaths of nearly a hundred fleet personnel are on him."

Ramya's nose scrunched indignantly. Kanaa had started firing at the *Endeavor* first. What did she expect? That the *Endeavor* wouldn't fight back?

She calmed her thoughts. Right now, she had to find a way to turn the tables. She had to focus.

"Perhaps you're right," her father said. "But perhaps not. I have a proposal for you. Please hear me out."

He was stalling, Ramya realized. She understood that this was her chance to come up with a plan of her own.

An ambush, perhaps?

Ramya started to count the troopers but stopped. There were too many of them and they were too heavily armed. Ramya and her team didn't stand a chance in a face-to-face combat. The troopers would mow down her ragtag band before they could blink. No, there had to be some other way.

"How far does this vent go?" she whispered to Nine. A plan — insane at worst and suicidal at best — was taking shape in her mind.

"All the way to the entry gate," Nine replied, pointing ahead.

"Good. Can you pry open one of these vents?"

Nine's eyes widened and he exchanged a quick look with Mola before shaking his head vigorously. "That's crazy," he said, his words rushing out at breakneck speed. "Do you see how many people they've killed? These are professionals. They'd cut us down before you even fired a shot."

Ramya held his gaze steadily for a bit, then she asked again, "Can you pry open one of these vents, Nine?"

Nine gave out a resigned sigh. "Yes, probably."

"Then I need you to open the one nearest to the exit," Ramya said. In the hall below, Trysten Kiroff was talking up a storm. "We don't have too long."

Nine and Mola crept forward with Ramya and Ahool at their heels. On reaching the vent nearest to the exit, the two men hunched over the grill and started tinkering.

Ramya hung near the next vent, studying the layout of the hallway underneath. She panicked for a moment. The hallway where her father was still debating with Admiral Kanaa ended before the last two vents. From there, a long bridge connected the main level to the exit.

Kanaa and her troopers would have to pass under the vents, but if she swung down onto them, it would only take a small mistake to miss the catwalk altogether and fall to some floor below. Even if she survived, she'd be in no shape to fight Kanaa.

"He's sick, don't you get it?" her father bellowed.

"Round up all of the crew," Admiral Kanaa ordered. "Lord Paramount, you're coming outside with us."

Ramya couldn't see them from where she was, but she knew the troopers were about to leave.

Heart pounding, Ramya scooted over to Nine and Mola. "Almost there, Lady," Nine informed.

"Hurry up," Ramya said, "they won't stay here forever."

"There might be some noise when I tug," Mola said. He didn't wait for an order but simply grabbed the bars of the vent and yanked. Ramya hadn't hoped for an effortless removal, but the vent snapped out of place right away, leaving a perfectly square hole that looked straight down on the catwalk.

"Put it back on," Ramya instructed. "Can't have it open until they're passing underneath. Someone might notice."

Commotion drifted in. Yells, orders, the sound of boots striking the floor.

Ramya pulled out her blaster and checked it a few times. She looked up and saw three pairs of eyes staring at her.

"What?" she asked, looking from one face to another.

"What the plan, Rami?" Ahool asked. "How do we attack?"

Ramya looked at their faces once again. They were fearful, but they were also ready to help.

"*We* don't." She pulled out her M-gun and checked that as well. "I attack. You come out only if I win."

"B-but, Lady Ramya, you can't do this alone," Mola protested. "They're so many."

"I have to do it alone. That's our best chance," Ramya said. "I'll aim for Kanaa. If I can land on her or at least near her, I can hold her hostage. Then they'll have to listen."

"But if you miss—"

"If I miss, there'll be a whole lot of trouble coming our way, Nine," Ramya said. "So I can't miss."

A thunderous stomping of boots grew in the distance. It could only mean one thing: the admiral and her troopers were leaving with their prisoners.

"Ahool, if something happens to me, you talk to Dakrhaeth and bring the Stryker to my father. No one *but* my father, all right?"

Ahool nodded. His face was gray like clouds on a rainy day, and his eyes a dull red. "I want to come with you," he said, his gaze pleading.

The sound of boots drew near.

"Get your weapon out, Ahool," she said to him. "I'll do fine."

That was a lie. Just the fall down to the bridge—at least a story and a half below—would be painful. The chances of landing anywhere near Kanaa were not great, but she couldn't say all that to the kid.

Ramya turned to Nine and Mola. "Be prepared to retreat. If I fail, they'll shoot the roof down."

Admiral Kanaa's party marched into view. They led the *Endeavor's* crew out first. Ramya crouched near the vent, M-gun in hand. She signaled Nine and Mola to slide the vent cover when the first row of troopers came below them.

Fenny was cursing non-stop as they led her out. Along with her was Ross, Wiz with his bandaged head, Flux, Sosa, and the whole Mwandan gang. The captain was propped up by two soldiers. Her father marched next, back stiff and jaw tight. At the end of the line was Admiral Kanaa with four troopers on her side and back.

"Help me, God of stars," Ramya muttered.

Admiral Kanaa marched into sight.

Ramya sucked in a mouthful of air. Her fingers tightened around the M-gun's grip. Then she hurled herself out of the vent hole.

8

Ramya swung toward the admiral and her guards, her eyes fixed on Kanaa's red hair. She was right on target . . . almost. She landed on her feet between the admiral and the two guards in the rear. Searing, scorching pain shot up her legs, numbing her for a bit. She saw a blur of weapons around her, nozzles swinging in her direction. She knew she had less than a second before they'd riddle her body with hot metal. Ramya lunged, desperate to reach the admiral. She grabbed Kanaa around the waist and together they toppled and fell to the ground.

Ramya rolled to one side, dragging Kanaa with her. More screams, gasps, shouts, and orders . . . an elbow crashing painfully into her ribs, her lungs screaming for air. Ramya didn't know for sure what was happening around her except for two things: she was still alive, and she had Kanaa in a chokehold, her M-gun steady against the admiral's skull.

By the time Ramya's breathing had slowed to normal, her vision also cleared. Almost every trooper had their cannon aimed at her. Their faces were grim, their eyes stony. The only thing that stopped them from shooting her was Kanaa—her body covered Ramya and protected her like a shield. But Ramya knew it was a fragile and unreliable barrier. One mistake and they'd blast her off the face of the universe. Icy fingers tapped at the base of her spine and a shudder threatened to swamp her. Ramya fought it down and tightened her grip on the gun.

"No one move. Let the captain and the crew go," she said in the steadiest voice she could muster. "I have your admiral. You don't want her dead," Ramya added.

The soldiers didn't move. They didn't even seem to bat an eyelid.

"Didn't you hear?" she shouted. "Let them go." She shook the admiral a little. "Tell them to drop their guns."

"Don't listen to her," the admiral said through gritted teeth. "Take the prisoners. Just take them and leave."

Ramya couldn't believe her ears. Kanaa was willing to die rather than let the prisoners go? She hadn't thought of that. What now?

Anger at herself rose like a squall in the pit of her stomach. This was a stupid, brainless, and irresponsible plan. What was she thinking? Now she had not only blown up a Drednot at Totori and killed hundreds of people, she had also pulled a gun on an admiral of the Space Fleet. That too in the presence of a zillion witnesses. What a record she'd have!

No, Rami, you can't just give up.

She had to make this work, turn this around. One last try.

"Last chance, Admiral," she hissed at Kanaa, trying to sound like a homicidal maniac. "Tell them to drop their guns or I'll blow your head off."

"Go ahead then," the admiral wheezed back. "Pull the trigger. I've lived long enough. The success of my mission is far more important than my life."

Damn the old, stubborn witch!

"You heard me, soldiers," Kanaa yelled. "Take the prisoners and leave. Take Trysten Kiroff also."

Ramya looked at her father and shriveled inwardly. The look he gave her almost made her want to curl into a ball and cry.

Brilliant, Rami! You've managed to make things worse. At least her father was free before, but now, thanks to her stupid plan, even he would be arrested.

"But, Admiral, we just can't leave you here," one of Kanaa's guards said.

"That's an order, Trooper Rian," the admiral shouted. "I'll deal with this assailant myself."

The soldiers started moving around them and Ramya thought of surrendering. What if she begged the admiral to let her father go? No,

Kanaa would never relent.

There was no way to fix this. She had messed this up too much. It was no wonder that even the crew of the *Endeavor* had stayed quiet. The best thing now, Ramya concluded, was to keep her mouth shut.

Just then, the trill of a communicator shook the living daylights out of Ramya. The furious ring came from the admiral. It rang and rang, setting Ramya's nerves on end.

The admiral looked askance at Ramya. "I need to get that, please. It's an urgent message."

The soldiers who had started filing out stopped. Ramya hesitated. Maybe Kanaa was telling the truth about its urgency, but what if Kanaa also had a gun in her pocket?

"Please," the admiral said. "You can take it out yourself if you want. It's in my right pocket."

Ramya bit her lip. *Her right pocket?* That meant she had to switch hands with the gun. It also meant she had to release Kanaa from the chokehold. That was risky. Probably riskier than letting Kanaa take it out herself.

"You take it out," Ramya ordered. "But no tricks."

"I promise." Kanaa slipped a hand into her pocket and dug out a sleek, silver communicator. She turned off the sound and raised the device to eye level. Flashing red letters spelled out a message and Ramya couldn't help reading it along with Kanaa.

It was indeed urgent, made evident by the bolded "Urgent" that flashed at both ends. Within the urgent tags was a message: "GSO personnel requests permission to meet. Has critical news from Space Command to deliver." Ramya figured it had been sent from the troopers who were outside.

"What is this?" Kanaa muttered.

The gears in Ramya's head had already started spinning furiously. GSO? Could it be Gael? Could this be something her father had orchestrated to escape Kanaa? If so, this could be her chance to fix the situation. Sure, it meant seeing Gael again, but . . .

"Ask them to come in," Ramya said quickly.

The admiral gave half a nod. Her fingers clicked and clacked over the tiny keyboard until she sent an order out.

"What's the command, Admiral?" Trooper Rian asked.

"Open the main door. The GSO is here with some critical news. Let's hear what they have to say." Kanaa turned her head a little toward Ramya. "Listen, girl, how about you let me sit up? This is a rather undignified position to see people, don't you think?"

She had a point. They were still sprawled on the floor and it was awkward. Not to mention Ramya could barely feel her right leg, as it had fallen asleep. But sitting up could mean losing her cover and that was a chance Ramya didn't want to take.

"Ask your people to lower their guns and then we'll talk," she said.

"Troopers, lower your weapons," Kanaa ordered immediately. It was interesting how dignity carried more weight than life.

As soon as the guns pointed at the floor, Ramya let the admiral sit up. Holding her neck just as tightly, she backed up to one side, making sure Kanaa still provided her the cover she needed.

The main door leading outside had opened and Ramya saw a row of dark figures march up to it. The light outside blinded Ramya too much to see their faces clearly, but as soon as they stepped inside, she realized her hunch was right. Gael Arlington led three other officers of the GSO, his face impassive as he took the scene in.

"Admiral Kanaa," Gael called, his sharp eyes scanning the room until it settled on them. Ramya could have been mistaken, but she thought his eyes widened just a tad when they fell on her. There was no trace of recognition on his face when he marched up to the admiral. He snapped a salute before addressing Kanaa. "Admiral, Starbase Zeta has been attacked. Space Command asks you to abandon your current mission and report immediately." He held out a small ordnance device that was used to deliver secure and sensitive information.

"You can take it," Ramya said, her heart thumping wildly at the news Gael had just delivered. Starbase Zeta sat guard over Anomaly Point, and if Zeta had been attacked, it could only mean one thing: The Locustans were here, the invasion had begun.

"Is this true, Lieutenant?" Kanaa, who had moments ago showed no fear of death, shuddered after reading the message.

"That is a signed and sealed directive, Admiral."

Kanaa let out a long, ragged breath. "Locustans are really here then?"

A rumble rose in the crowd. The troopers looked at each other, as did their prisoners. Some whispered and some exchanged fearful glances.

"I do not know the details, Admiral," Gael replied. "But that is my understanding, yes."

If the tiniest mouse had scurried across the hallway at that instant, Ramya could've heard it clearly — such was the silence. It seemed as if the entire room, even the building itself, had forgotten to breathe.

Then her father spoke, his voice rolling across the hall like thunder. "Admiral Kanaa, I've been pleading for a chance to speak. Please, let us set our misunderstandings aside and speak. It is time to come together and act."

Kanaa nodded. "Yes, let's. Stand down, Troopers."

Trysten Kiroff strode up to them, only quickly glancing at Ramya. "Captain Milos needs urgent medical attention," he said. "If you'll allow —"

"Yes, yes," Kanaa said impatiently. "Can someone get this girl off me now?"

"Apologies, Admiral." Her father bowed slightly then glowered at Ramya. "Let the admiral go. Now."

Ramya knew well how her plan had backfired and how close she'd come to ruining everything they'd fought for over the last few weeks, but her father's public dismissal still stung. She fought back a retort and the barrage of tears with all her might. As if by instinct, her grip on Kanaa tightened even more.

Kanaa choked and coughed. Her father growled. "Did you hear me? Let her go."

Ramya winced and tore her gaze from her father's stony face. It came to rest on Gael who had been observing quietly. As soon as their eyes locked, he nodded. It was a subtle, rather surreptitious nod, but somehow it promised understanding. And it calmed Ramya.

She released Kanaa and scooted backward, the gun in her hand rattling in an annoying way. Kanaa breathed deeply and massaged her neck while frowning at Ramya.

"You're a dangerous girl, and strong," the admiral said, then turned to Trysten. "Do you know her?"

"She's not important," her father said carelessly. "There are other critical matters at hand. We have to speak to Space Command."

Kanaa nodded. "Yes, we will. But until this is all sorted out, I want this girl held. As well as the *Endeavor's* crew."

"I'll secure her, Admiral," Gael said. Ramya thought he was a little too eager to offer his services to the cause.

"Thank you, Lieutenant."

Kanaa walked away with her father. A bunch of the troopers followed her while a bigger bunch marched the *Endeavor's* crew another way.

Gael cast a quick look around and kneeled next to Ramya, his eyes scouring her downcast face. "You decided to hold an admiral hostage?" he said in a low voice that brimmed with incredulity. Or maybe it was mockery, plain and simple. Ramya gritted her teeth. It was a stupid plan, she knew that, but did he have to rub it in? "I have to admit, Kiroff, you're the most daring girl I've ever known. And just as reckless."

"Aren't you going to secure me?"

"Of course," he said, rising to his feet again. "To your feet, prisoner."

Ramya looked up at the vent on the roof through which she had jumped. She knew Ahool was still there, as well as Nine and Mola.

"Do me a favor, Arlington?" she said.

Gael gave her a curious look. "A favor for you? Absolutely. But what's this? You . . . asking me for a favor . . . are you all right?"

She ignored his dig and collected her thoughts. "See that vent up there? I have friends hiding in the ventilation tunnel. Can you get someone friendly to escort them out? Please?"

"You've got an army, huh?" Gael flashed a wicked grin. "Of course, my lady. Your wish . . . my command, right?" He slipped a pair of cuffs around Ramya's wrists and tugged her arm. "But first, let's get you to a holding cell."

9

Gael put her in a room and left. It was almost like a real prison cell—Ramya briefly pondered the need for one anywhere in a factory—bare and cold, and it felt every bit as punishing.

Gael had taken off the cuffs before leaving. He'd also given her a pleading look. "Please don't try anything funny." Then he was gone.

Ramya looked around at the empty gray room and sighed. There was nothing left to try. Perhaps there was no need to, either. Since Space Command had now realized that a second Locustan invasion was real, they'd come together and fight. But would there be anything left to fight for? Ramya sank to the floor and rested her back against the wall. The cold hard surface was unexpectedly comforting, calming.

While Ramya's body relaxed a bit, her mind whirred endlessly. Starbase Zeta had been attacked. Were they able to hold off the Locustans? Or was it completely destroyed?

It couldn't be entirely destroyed, couldn't be. She remembered what Captain Milos had once told her: a third of the Space Fleet was stationed at Zeta. Zeta being destroyed meant a third of the galaxy's fighters had already fallen.

The air turned heavy and stale . . . and not enough to fill her lungs, no matter how deeply she breathed.

They could've prevented this. How long ago had Dakrhaeth told them about this? Was it a week or more? Hours and days jumbled in her head in a wretched mess. Every muscle in her body ached, relentlessly. Ramya pulled up her legs to her chest and rested her throbbing head on her knees. She craved a warm, soft bed and a good night's sleep.

Closing her eyes, Ramya tried to think of something else altogether. Something . . . anything that'd make her stop worrying.

There was nothing she could do by fretting and fuming in this room anyway, so what was the point? Her thoughts flew back across years and light-years, to Somenvaar. And to Grappa Abelei.

It was a warm afternoon and she sat on the floor, in tears and surrounded by pearls . . . pearls that had scattered all across the room when she accidentally broke her mother's favorite necklace.

How old had she been then? Five? Six maybe?

Her grandfather had scooped her up in his arms and wiped her tears away.

"We will fix this together, Bella," he had said. He always called her Bella. It meant *beautiful*, he had told her. "I promise you, we shall hunt down every naughty pearl that's run away from you. Each one of them."

They had. It had taken the whole afternoon. They had crawled all over the room and wriggled under furniture and shaken every rug. Together, they had found them all.

"You see, my Bella," Grappa said later that evening as they both sucked on ice-cones Gramaman Otis had made for them, "there's no use crying when things fall apart. What you really need is a good plan and a stout heart to put it all back together."

The ice cone was good—cold, tangy, and perfect for that day. Ramya could still almost taste it. Up until now, she'd clung to the taste of the cone and the happiness of finding all of her mother's pearls. This time, Grappa's words came back with clarity and force like never before and made Ramya sit up again. Her fists curled slowly into tight balls—the situation was bad, but she wasn't going to stop fighting.

The door flew open at that precise moment, startling Ramya. Gael careened in, a piece of paper in hand. He slowed for a moment at seeing her on the floor and his eyes narrowed on her face. Then he walked over and sat down unceremoniously next to her.

"All good?" he asked, throwing her a sideways glance.

"I'm fine. Did you find my friends in the ventilation shaft?"

Gael gave her a telling look. "The Mwandan kid is worried sick

about you. He tackled me to the ground and almost bit my ear off."
Gael rubbed his left ear tenderly. "So much for trying to help."

"Sorry," Ramya said. Ahool must've been really scared and
anxious. "Where are they now?"

"The kid is with the rest of the crew. The other two went to report
to their supervisor."

"Thank you," Ramya said sincerely. The miserable failure of her
ambush plan didn't bother her as much as risking the lives of Ahool
and the other two men did. Now that they were safe, the biggest
burden was off her shoulders. "I should've never dragged them into
this . . . stupid mess. What was I thinking?"

Gael scoffed. "Oh come on, Kiroff. You had an idea and you took
a chance on it. Maybe you failed. So what?"

"So . . . I made a fool of myself. And the admiral will probably
throw me in prison."

"She'll do nothing of the sort. First off, she can't afford to lose a
skilled pilot. Second, your father will never let her lay a finger on
you."

Ramya held her breath. Her father would do what? She turned
toward Gael looking for signs on his face that would tell her he was
putting her on. He looked quite serious, she discovered.

"My father?" Ramya started slowly. "The same one you saw
sneering at me in front of the whole wide world?"

Gael chuckled. "Hey! It wasn't the whole wide world. Just fifty
people, give or take." His face turned grave in the next moment and
he held her gaze steadily. "But yes. The same one. Lord Paramount
Trysten Kiroff. Or as you prefer to call him, the all-powerful puppet
master."

Well, sure. That made sense. Just like always, he couldn't let
House Kiroff's name be dragged through the mud. Of course.

"Never mind all that." Ramya waved at Gael to divert him from
the topic. "What happened at Zeta?"

Gael exhaled noisily. "Apparently, Anomaly Point opened up. It didn't stay open for too long, thank heavens for that. But just long enough to let a squadron of Locustans in. Zeta is badly damaged. At least a thousand dead, half of our units stationed at Zeta gone."

Ramya could hardly believe what he was saying even though she had long known this was about to happen. Or maybe she didn't want to believe it was happening. She couldn't find her voice for a while.

"The wormhole closed, right?" she asked. As soon as Gael nodded, Ramya jumped to her feet. "So, it isn't too late. We still have time to prepare."

Gael forced a small smile to his lips. "Yes, we do."

"Then why are we sitting here talking? Let's go do something useful."

Gael arched his brow. "You don't think this beautiful conversation is of use? Really?"

Ramya couldn't decide if she ought to be mad at him. Gael broke into chuckles before she could come to a conclusion.

"You're too much fun to mess with," he said. Once again, before Ramya could decide whether to take that as an affront, Gael turned serious. He hopped to his feet and held up the paper in his hand. "Here's something useful that we need done right away. Go to Bucifer P9 and eliminate the Locustan scourge there."

Now they were talking!

"You're going to Bucifer P9?"

"Of course. After seeing the recordings Captain Milos and your father showed us, Space Command deems a cleanup of Bucifer P9 Mission Priority 1," he said. "My unit and all of the admiral's troopers that are here are coming as well."

Ramya's heart pounded. Finally! Things were coming together after all. All they had fought for was coming true. Ramya let a silly grin spread over her face.

She was still smiling when Gael opened the door and beckoned her. "Come on, let's go."

"Where am I going?" Ramya asked, genuinely surprised.

Gael shot her a curious look. "You think you can sit out a top priority mission after the stunts you've been pulling?" he said. "Come on, Kiroff. You're going to Bucifer P9 to kick some Locustan behind."

10

It seemed to take forever to get to Bucifer P9. And even after they reached the planet, things didn't go as planned. The trouble was that the Locustan megaship, a.k.a the SuperStryker, was nowhere to be found.

They first scanned the location where Ramya had last seen the megaship, Ramya directing the search from the Cutlass Gael commanded. A Drednot from Admiral Kanaa's fleet accompanied the Cutlass. Together they scoured the area but found nothing. Then they circled Bucifer P9 a couple of times, scanning every bit of the planet. Once again, they found no sign of the Locustan megaship.

It had been a few hours already and frustration crept in. Ramya sat at the Cutlass's COM watching Gael converse worriedly with his team and on screen with Rida, the Space Fleet lieutenant in charge of the Drednot. Ramya's heart steadily filled with dread and the weight grew with every passing second. Where did the SuperStryker go? She had damaged it quite a lot. It hadn't seemed like the megaship could leave Bucifer after she'd torn one of the main spans between the Strykers. But if it wasn't here, then—

"These are the correct coordinates, right?" Rida asked snappishly from the screen.

"Yes. Of course they are."

"Sorry if the question offended you, Lady Ramya," Rida said. "I just don't understand why we can't see such a big ship."

"It's obviously cloaked," Gael's second-in-command Amireh commented.

"Obviously," Rida replied in an irritated tone. "But we have the best scanners. And we've already scanned the whole planet twice."

"Maybe its stealth tech is far beyond our detection equipment," Gael said.

"It has to be that. I know I damaged it enough. It couldn't have left the planet altogether," Ramya said.

It better be that, Ramya prayed. It better not have moved on to the next system.

"There's nothing, Lieutenant," the woman in charge of scanning the planet surface announced in a tired voice.

"It's hiding," Ramya said. She had been standing to one side, observing mostly. Now she strode over to Gael and Amireh, her eyes focused on the view of the dim planet below them. A plan grew in her head, one that could work to break the stalemate. "I know just what to do. I'll take the Stryker out."

Gael's eyes narrowed, Rida's also. Ramya hurried to add, "I'm going to lure the megaship out by using the Stryker as bait. I know it's hiding. But it'll come out when it sees the Stryker. It won't be able to resist trying to get my Stryker on its side."

Gael didn't seem convinced. "Your Stryker attacked the megaship the last time. Damaged it. Tried to destroy it. And you think it'll still try to win the Stryker over?"

Ramya nodded. "I hope so. If not, it'll try to destroy the Stryker. Either way, it has to come out of stealth mode. The Strykers' cloaking system is an energy drain. It can't simultaneously cloak *and* fight us."

"It's a good plan," Rida said from the screen.

"It's a dangerous, half-baked plan," Gael snapped.

"Well, it's the only plan," Ramya said. "And I'm going with it." She took off, hurrying toward the exit, heading to the hold where the Stryker was docked.

"Wait." Gael's voice was sharp and it slowed her a bit. He spoke hurriedly to Amireh before following Ramya out. His face was grim when they got into the elevator but Ramya was not prepared for the scathing words that followed. "What the hell do you think you're doing?"

For an instant, she shriveled. Then a fiery ball of anger erupted in her gut. Who the hell did he think he was, talking to her that way? But she didn't shout back, simply raised a curious brow at him.

"What do you mean?" she said through gritted teeth.

"You can't just take off like this when you're working in my team. You have to think through a plan, vet it, and get approval before you jump to your death."

"I've thought enough," Ramya said coldly. "It's a fine plan."

The elevator came to a stop and Ramya was about to walk out when Gael blocked her way. "We're not done talking."

"I am," Ramya retorted. Noting Gael's face rigid with anger, she eased her own fury a bit. "I don't need you to protect me, all right? I can take care of myself quite well."

His eyes widened a little before he voiced his protest. "I'm not trying to protect you, Kiroff. And you don't need to prove to me you're capable. I already know."

Ramya's thoughts stumbled a little. "What is it then? My father asked you to—"

"Oh come on. Not everything's about your father."

"I don't understand," Ramya blurted. She really didn't. "Getting the Stryker out there is a good plan. And the only way to get that monster out of hiding."

He stayed silent for a bit as if he were carefully weighing his words. "A good plan it may be, it's still risky as hell. But that's not the point."

"Then what is?"

"That you decided you're going to take the Stryker out no matter what. That you forgot we're a team. This mission is not yours alone, it's ours. We work together."

He had a point. In her desperate need to get the monster destroyed, she had forgotten about the team. Gael, his unit, and Rida's fighters would follow her into battle, and they deserved to know and think through the plan.

"I'm sorry," she said earnestly. "I've gotten used to taking the Stryker out alone. Never went out with a squadron before this."

Gael's face softened. "I understand."

"Should we go back up and walk this through? I don't really have a detailed plan. I'm hoping once I get the Stryker out, Dakrhaeth will feel its presence."

"That's all right. What's done is done," he said. "I'll fill in the team. But please, when you're out there, don't just fly off. We coordinate the attack, all right?"

"Got it," Ramya said. This was new. She had no experience of flying with others on a real mission outside of CAWStrat, but she had to learn.

As they geared up, Gael talked to Amireh over his comm. The final plan was simple: Ramya would drop out first, Gael would follow. The rest of the squadron would wait until the megaship revealed itself. Then they'd all engage and bring it down.

"Prep for launch," Gael said to Amireh as they strode into the launch bay. "The Stryker goes out first, then me."

The Cutlass's launch bay was a far cry from the *Endeavor's* old, battered one. This was shiny and bright, almost as good as their living quarters on the *Endeavor*. When Ramya had docked the Stryker before leaving El-Iss, most of the bays were dark. Now all the lights were on and she could see everything inside.

Five gleaming Astro Scouts, the GSO's favored fighter craft, were closest to the entrance and Ramya couldn't help smiling at them. The Astros were petite but their looks were absolutely deceiving. Fast and packed with firepower, Astros were far more lethal in combat than the larger Wentworth-Busas or WBs used commonly in the Space Fleet.

"Must be fun flying an Astro?" Ramya asked, looking longingly at the nearest fighter with a bright red stripe from tail to nose. She had always wanted to fly one, but Astros were hard to come by. CAWStrat mostly used WBs for training.

"It is," Gael replied. His brows bunched a little. "Haven't you ever flown one?"

"No," Ramya said quietly, a hard lump growing bigger in her

throat. Kiroff Industries built the Astros on Nesbo V, and she had only visited the factory once. Flying an Astro? That stayed a dream. "Show me your flight honor badge and I'll let you fly one," Trysten Kiroff had said when she'd asked. She had never asked again.

Gael probably gauged the grimness on her face since he didn't probe any further. Ramya forced her memories away. Those days were over. There was no point brooding over it. "Which one's yours?" she asked cheerfully as they came to the second row of Astros.

It was odd how his face tightened, as if she had asked him the wrong question. Ramya didn't understand why he didn't reply, not until she had taken a few more steps toward the end of the launch bay.

The shimmering shape of the fighter craft of her dreams stood right across from the Stryker, looking no less impressive than the Locustan hybrid. Its silver was a sharp contrast to the Stryker's dark coloring, its nose tipped with dark red. Ramya blinked a few times before she could really believe what she was looking at.

"You have a Mossin?" she asked, looking wide-eyed at Gael. It was odd that he looked so guilty when he should've been bursting with pride. Anyone who flew a Mossin would show it off. She would.

Mossins were not mass-produced. Heck, they were barely produced at all. Every bit of a Mossin was handcrafted and it took years to build one. Her father had a Mossin, of course. He had to--he owned the factory. Ramya hadn't known of anyone else that did, until now.

A thought, strong and searing, that made her look away from the Mossin's sleek contour to Gael, hit her. "My father gave you this, didn't he?"

She didn't need him to answer. It was already written on his face. And Ramya couldn't help shaking her head at the gut-wrenching unfairness of it all. There she was, the heir to it all, begging for a simple ride on an Astro and being refused, while Gael was being gifted the most coveted craft in the universe.

Ramya hadn't noticed when her nails started digging into her palms but the pain surely felt good. It helped immensely, yanking her out of her misery and planting her firmly in the middle of the mission ahead. She couldn't lose focus, she just couldn't.

"Well, let's go," she said. Turning around she strode toward the Stryker.

"Listen, Kiroff," Gael called. "I'm —"

Ramya held up a hand. She had to put a stop to this or it'd tear her apart. "Forget it, all right? You don't owe me an explanation. You don't owe me anything."

"Maybe I don't. But I don't enjoy seeing you hurt either. I —"

"Thanks, Arlington," Ramya cut him off. "Appreciate your thought but all I care about is this mission. Let's just get it done and go our own ways."

She didn't wait for him to answer. Resolute steps brought her to the Stryker and before she had touched the craft, the door fell open. Ramya plunged into its cool, dark interior, eager for some quiet.

***

Dropping out of the Cutlass was liberating. Everything felt strange — Dakrhaeth was quiet, her own thoughts were drifting, and it felt weird being the only one inside the Stryker. However, Ramya also cherished the quiet. She stared at the dark surface of Bucifer P9 beneath them, her eyes scanning it repeatedly.

"All good, Kiroff?" Gael's voice came over the comm and Ramya stirred.

"Yes, all good." It had taken a few minutes to get the Stryker's radio synched up with the others, but it worked quite well in the end. "I'm going to get near the surface," she said.

"All right. I have my eyes on you," Gael replied.

Ramya slapped the comm to mute. She needed to speak to Dakrhaeth before the battle began. The engineers at El-Iss had scanned the Stryker's systems and cleared it for flying. But doubts still prickled Ramya's mind. Dakrhaeth's silence was unnerving. What if he had planned to join the others? She had to find out.

"Dakrhaeth," she called.

"Yes, Mihaal," the reply came swiftly enough. But the voice shook Ramya; it sounded as if Dakrhaeth had aged years.

"Are you well?"

Dakrhaeth gave out a dry chuckle. "I'm trying to stay well, Mihaal. Although you don't seem very happy to me."

"All right, Dakrhaeth, let's just be honest," Ramya said with a resigned sigh. "We're both in a bad spot. But nothing too worrisome, is there?"

The sliver of silence felt like forever. "No. None."

Ramya took in a long breath. No matter what Dakrhaeth said, there had to be something bothering him. Ramya only hoped he wasn't making plans to desert her.

"I'm guessing you've heard about the mission?" she asked.

"Yes, Mihaal," he replied. Dakrhaeth always enjoyed eavesdropping and Ramya had no doubt he'd been listening to every conversation on the Cutlass since he had docked. "We're here to destroy the others."

Ramya wanted to ask if he was all right with that task but decided not to in the end. Who in the universe liked destroying their own?

She turned the comm back on and hovered near the coordinates of the last sighting. "Do you feel them? Are they near?"

Dakrhaeth stayed quiet for a bit. "I don't," he said finally.

"All right then, let's circle around." Ramya tugged at the flight stick and veered away from the spot. An ear-splitting yell made Ramya jump barely a second later.

"Mihaal," Dakrhaeth shouted. "Incoming!"

A ball of fire erupted in the sky and streaked toward her. Before Ramya could blink, a hot wave of turbulence swept the Stryker, flinging it backward. Ramya crashed against the window. A sharp pain exploded in her shoulder and punched the air out of her lungs. Ramya screamed but heard no sound.

The last thing she remembered was falling. She sank like a stone, along with the Stryker. The dark surface of the planet rushed up toward them at a breakneck speed. Ramya gasped for breath and the world faded.

11

A shrill beep cleared the fog from Ramya's senses. Clutching the edge of her seat, she tried to sit up. Alarms blared around her. Every light on the instrument panel kept flashing. They were still falling. Ramya threw herself against the flight stick and pressed on the throttle, frantic to straighten the Stryker.

"Kiroff!" Gael's frenzied voice streaked out of the comm and filled the Stryker's inside. "Kiroff, answer me. Kiroff!"

"I'm alive," Ramya shouted back.

She tried to focus. They were still plummeting but it seemed to be slowing. The shield panel was blinking a large orange 60% at her.

"Dakrhaeth," she called.

No one answered. How she wished Ross were here to help. Anyone for that matter. But he wasn't. No one was. She had to figure this out by herself. Or die.

"I can't die. Not this way."

She adjusted the thrusters some more and pulled on the flight stick. The Stryker slowed a little and straightened a bit.

"Some more, some more," she muttered to herself, fingers dancing over the thruster controls. They seemed slow, unwilling to respond to her touch. They sank lower and lower still.

She had to get Dakrhaeth to help. Why wasn't he responding? They had to have got to him somehow.

The muffler!

Ramya hit the green, mushroom-shaped button hard, the stinging impact making her yelp.

"Dakrhaeth," she yelled again and this time there was a response. Not a verbal one, but the controls started responding better immediately.

"I've engaged emergency stabilizers, Mihaal," Dakrhaeth said in a raspy voice. Sure enough, the Stryker's rapid descent slowed and a moment or two later, Ramya was able to tip its nose upward.

Before Ramya could let out a breath of relief, Gael's anxious voice floated in once again. "Kiroff!"

"I'm fine. I'm fine," Ramya said. She looked up ahead and saw a stream of fighters circling an area in the sky. That was the area the fireball had come from. It had to be where the megaship was hiding. She pressed on the throttle and headed in that direction. "Dakrhaeth, how much damage did we take?"

"The shield took most of the hit, Mihaal. It's at 62% now," Dakrhaeth said. "Everything else seems all right."

"Good."

"Thank you for getting me out, Mihaal," Dakrhaeth said. He was referring to her using the muffler, Ramya guessed.

"Once we get back, we have to do something about that. Maybe put a permanent muffler on you or something," Ramya said, forcing a chuckle. A gasp came out of her instead at the sight ahead. Another ball of fire shot out of the skies and ripped through the row of WBs. A wave of panic erupted on the comm.

Rida's sobering voice came moments later. "We've lost Karron and Lief. Keep moving, people. Slow down and you'll make yourself a target."

Ramya pushed on the throttle some more. "Dakrhaeth, how could they fire with cloaking on? You said cloaking sucks too much energy."

"It does," Dakrhaeth replied. "They can't hold it for too long."

"We'll engage," Gael said. "We'll force it into revealing itself. All units, open fire," he ordered.

The WBs kept circling above the spot where the blast had originated, their guns focused on the space below. Ramya didn't join them but kept zigzagging above. After a few more blasts, it didn't take long for the first shimmering outline to show up. Then, slowly, the immense shape came into view. The WBs scattered like flies, the comm filled with awed chatter.

Ramya had hardly expected to be daunted by the megaship, yet she was. Not by its size but because it had morphed again. The star-shape was gone, as were the connectors Ramya had broken during the last encounter. She could still discern the original shapes of the Strykers, but it was harder now. They had come together, back to back, and formed a cone. It was one large, menacing cone.

"They must be firing in unison," Ramya said, studying how the front ends of the Strykers had fused together to form the tip of the cone. "No wonder the blasts are so powerful."

"It's regenerating its shield, Mihaal," Dakrhaeth said. "You need to attack now if you want to bring it down. There are no weapons around the middle, so—"

"I'm going in," Ramya announced. "Arm the torpedoes, Dakrhaeth."

"Kiroff, wait," Gael said. But she couldn't. The megaship was rebuilding its shield fast and she had to strike while it was still vulnerable.

"We can't wait," she yelled. "Get everyone to strike now."

"Remember the midsection, Mihaal," Dakrhaeth reminded.

"Aim for the middle."

Ramya pressed on the throttle until her fingers hurt. She zoomed on the dark, rippling surface of the megaship, her hand tight on the flight stick.

"Ready, Dakrhaeth?" she whispered. "Fire now!"

The torpedoes streaked out from under the Stryker's belly, leaving a ripple of warmth under Ramya's feet. The dark surface of the ship melted into an ocean of fire. Ramya pulled on the stick and fell backward. She felt the blast reverberate against the Stryker's belly. Ramya careened away, gritting her teeth as a wave of heat and light swept across her.

By the time she circled around and faced the megaship again, the WBs and Gael's Mossin had jumped into the attack. The fighters moved in perfectly synchrony, their relentless waves of fire hitting the

Locustan ship in unison. Ramya could see the blasts eating away the midsection of the cone. The SuperStryker was falling apart, but far too slowly. They needed something stronger to end this before the megaship could regenerate its shields.

Ramya slapped the comm off and called Dakrhaeth.

"Dakrhaeth, prep the plasma guns," she ordered.

"Are you sure, Mihaal?"

"Yes, Dakrhaeth."

"I hope you remember that discharging the plasma weapon severely drains our power. We won't be able to move out of the enemy's firing range as quickly, if at all."

"I remember quite well, Dakrhaeth. Do it now." She had to eviscerate this monstrosity fast, make sure nothing of it remained. The plasma gun was the only way. Ramya turned the comm back on. "Lieutenant Arlington, I think it's time to take this thing out once and for all."

"That's what we're doing, Kiroff."

Ramya took a moment to collect her thoughts. What she was about to say wasn't going to be pretty. But it had to be said.

"Your weapons aren't strong enough. It's taking too long."

A prickly silence hovered on the comm. Then Gael's voice crackled. "Do you have a miracle up your sleeve, Kiroff?"

"If you'll step back, I'll use what I have," she said.

"All right. All units, disengage," he ordered. "Pull away."

Ramya didn't expect him to come around so quickly. She'd thought he'd question her claim, or at least ask what the weapon was. The unexpected freedom he handed her so fast brought a smile to Ramya's lips. She was still smiling when she positioned the Stryker to face the worst-hit part of the megaship.

"All set?" she asked Dakrhaeth.

"Plasma vents aimed and ready, Mihaal."

Ramya's finger stabbed at the control and with a shudder, the Stryker unleashed waves of energy at the megaship. They rammed its burnt body, making it shatter and peel. Debris flew up, down and sideways. The shield monitor erupted with complaints.

"Fall back, Kiroff. Fall back." Gael's voice, distant to begin with, faded as a wall of fire swept over the Stryker. An intense blast of heat sucked the air out of Ramya's lungs. She gasped for air, her eyes blinded by the immense, dazzling fireball that had engulfed the Locustan megaship.

Ramya lifted her finger off the gun controls and wrapped her hand around the flight stick. The Stryker veered away, so slowly that it hardly seemed to move at all. For moments that felt like an eternity, Ramya was sure she'd be consumed by the fire. The broken pieces of the megaship seemed to freeze in the air, hanging around the Stryker in a cloud of molten metal and fire. Then, in a sudden burst of power, the Stryker zoomed forward and out of the sea of fiery debris.

"In the name of the stars! I thought we'd lost you, Lady Ramya," Rida's relieved voice filled the Stryker.

"Yes!" someone else shouted on the comm. "The bastard's down."

Laughter and cheering broke out.

"Good work, Dakrhaeth," Ramya said. Sweat trickled down her face as she eased back into her seat and let out a long, satisfied breath. They had done well indeed. She hadn't been able to save Chief Mifek or his people, but at least she had avenged their deaths.

By the time the Stryker was back inside the Cutlass, the fleeting joy had subsided and Ramya once again worried about the impossible battles ahead of them. Distractedly, she rolled the Stryker into position and engaged the clamps.

"Have you found out any more about the fading star, Mihaal?" Dakrhaeth asked as she unstrapped herself.

"We found no fading star, Dakrhaeth," she said, recalling what she and Ahool had dug up from Dakrhaeth's memories. "There's a dying one, though."

"Perhaps they're the same," Dakrhaeth said.

"There's mention of a Hinterland."

"Aah, yes, Hinterland, I remember. People lived there many stars ago . . . wise people, people with much power. We despised them," Dakrhaeth said in a distant voice. "There is something in the Hinterland, Mihaal. They said it holds the keys to our triumph and theirs. Victory will come to whoever reaches there first."

"Your memories don't clearly state what the keys might be," Ramya said.

"Perhaps we could go there and check?"

"Yes, we need to decode the marker, the dying sun, and the coordinates. I'll have to ask Ahool to get on it."

"I'd suggest you hurry."

That went without saying. But with nothing but cryptic clues, how could they get anywhere quickly? Ramya walked out of the Stryker absentmindedly, barely noticing the other pilots securing their own crafts, unless they waved at her.

As soon as she stepped outside the launch bay, Gael, who had been talking to a group of people, strode up to her.

"Great flying today," he started in a hesitant sort of way. Ramya could tell that wasn't the only thing on his mind.

"You too," she replied regardless.

He stared at her for a second, as if trying to make up his mind. Then he almost threw the words out. "Listen . . . I know you don't want to hear this but . . . I have to tell you. I'm sorry about how things are between you and your father. I really am. When I got dragged into this marriage agreement, I . . . didn't know . . . I'd no idea you were against it. It's too late now to change our pasts but . . . let's at least try for a better future?"

A better future? They had no future. Not together anyway.

"Sure," Ramya said, hoping he'd drop the topic fast.

"I hope you understand."

She understood quite well. He wanted to normalize their relationship, but that wasn't going to happen. There was no normalizing something that was utterly broken. Besides, even though it wasn't the right thing to do, she couldn't help thinking of him as the symbol of everything that had been wrong with her life. He was the past she was desperately trying to escape from and he always brought a stream of hurtful memories. She couldn't let him. She couldn't let her past drag her down. Not anymore.

"Of course, Arlington," she said with as much pleasantness as she could afford. Chances were he'd realize she was pretending. She didn't care. She just wanted to get away from him. "Is there a private room where I can rest for a bit?"

"Yes, of course," he said.

They walked all the way in silence, and Ramya breathed a sigh of relief once she had reached the quiet seclusion of the room.

12

One of Trysten Kiroff's aides—a tall, mustached and uniformed man—was waiting near the entrance of the factory and as soon as Ramya walked in along with Gael and the rest of the pilots, he rushed up to Ramya and gave her an extravagant bow.

"Lady Ramya," he said. "Lord Paramount requests your presence, my lady." His address felt strangely out-of-place and rather embarrassing in the presence of a group of people who had just returned from a hard-won battle. Ramya nodded hastily in response.

"Good luck," Gael said. Just like most times with Gael, Ramya couldn't be sure if he was teasing or if he was seriously offering his wishes. She didn't have time to look back at his face because the aide had already whisked her away into an elevator.

"I'm honored to serve you, my lady." The aide gave another bow as soon as the elevator doors had closed. "Tales of your valor are—"

"What's your name?" Ramya cut him off, desperate to stop the grating adulation. Her father reveled in such words, but she had trouble swallowing them, even when they were true.

"Casten, my lady," he said, bowing once again.

"Where are you taking me, Casten?"

"To Lord Paramount Kiroff, of course," Casten replied. He bowed again but thankfully, it wasn't the full floor-scraping spectacle. It still made Ramya frown.

"No, I meant where is this place we're going?" she said.

Casten's face reddened. "My apologies. He is in the regent's office and that is at the base's . . . lowermost level."

No wonder the elevator kept on descending.

"Who else is there with him? Do you know?"

"At present, no, I do not, my lady" he replied. "But when I left the room, Admiral Kanaa and Captain Milos were with him. Although the captain was being taken to the infirmary soon and the admiral was planning a trip to Xandria."

"How is Captain Milos?" Ramya asked. Although Gael had said the captain felt better for the moment with medication, she worried it was only a temporary fix until they found out what exactly was troubling him and treated it.

"The Lord Paramount's personal medical team is examining him. The captain should be fine soon."

Ramya sure hoped so. She didn't have much faith in Kanaa and the Space Command. Had they not taken so long to heed the warnings, Zeta would've been in better shape. They needed Captain Milos, now more than ever.

The elevator came to a stop while Ramya was still stuck in worrisome thoughts. The door slid open and Ramya held her breath for a second at the sight outside. This floor could have fitted right in to a top-class luxury resort. It had no business being in a factory and it was an impossible sight so deep underground.

Impeccably furnished hallways complete with human-length chandeliers, water fountains, and tastefully manicured foliage caught Ramya's color-starved eyes. She followed Casten, almost in a trance, along a long corridor that ended at a door as dark as the night sky that shone like a mirror. Two liveried guards flanked it, and as soon as Casten approached with Ramya, they bowed. Suppressing an irritated frown, Ramya forced a nod.

Casten opened the door and showed Ramya in with a sweeping gesture. Ramya's heart pounded a little faster at the thought of facing her father, her fingers turning a tad cold at the tips. It wasn't so much fear, but more of a cold fury that remained. With a bracing breath, Ramya walked in and looked around.

A large, rectangular table extended down the center of the room and at its farthest end, Trysten Kiroff sat alone. There was no sign of Admiral Kanaa anywhere.

"Lady Ramya," Casten announced.

"You may leave, Casten," her father said. It was amazing to see how fast Casten could move. Before Ramya could blink, Casten bowed and darted out.

Trysten Kiroff had perfected the art of making his power felt with the simplest gestures. Or the lack of them. As he did now. For a while, he didn't even look at Ramya but simply continued to study the contents of a folder in front of him. Ramya had been taught to wait until she was spoken to all her life, particularly when it came to her father. So by force of habit, she waited at the door, expecting him to beckon her near. He didn't.

Ramya shifted her feet, anger and frustration stirring restlessly to life inside her. She wasn't going to wait forever. Not anymore. Another breath and she marched forward until she stood at the chair next to him.

"You need something, Father?" she asked, as calmly as she could.

He looked up, brow raised appraisingly. Then he nodded at the nearest chair. "Sit."

Ramya had barely sunk into the chair when her father hissed at her. "What were you thinking holding the admiral hostage?"

Not that again! That was the one time she had failed. Didn't he remember the numerous times she'd burned the Locustans to the ground, as in her last mission to Bucifer P9? Where was the praise for that?

Her father drummed the table, his stony eyes scouring her face. "Don't forget, Lady Ramya, you're not just one of *them*." He waved at invisible scum somewhere. "You have a reputation to uphold and protect."

Ramya's first instinct was to tell him that the random scum was better than most liere-wielding highborn. But she stopped herself. There was no changing Trysten Kiroff's view of ordinary people. Instead, she took a different tack. "So I should have just sat and watched them haul away the one person who knows the most about the doom that's coming?"

His brows wrinkled a bit. "That wasn't going to happen. I wouldn't let it," he said gruffly. "Once I make a promise to someone, I keep it. And I promised Milos I'd support him."

Her hunch had been correct. Her father had a plan, likely with the GSO.

"So you had already summoned Gael. But how was I supposed to know?"

Trysten Kiroff leaned back into his chair and his eyes narrowed. "I see you're on a first-name basis with Lieutenant Arlington. What do you think of him?"

Ramya balked. That was all he could think about? How she liked Gael? What about matters like the galaxy being ripped apart by the Locustans?

"That's not important," she snapped, her fears flying out the door in an instant. "We should be talking about how we're going to stop the Locustans."

"You don't have the capacity to understand what's important," her father snapped back and swiveled out of his chair. "You only focus on a tiny bit of the future, and you miss the whole view." He paused and grabbing the back of his chair, he pursed his lips, as if he were holding in a barrage of slights with a lot of effort. "Anyway, I called you here to let you know that you're coming with me to the senate in a few hours. So you need to prepare."

"Senate?" Ramya blurted. "Why?"

"We've been summoned to provide a first-hand account of the Locustan threat," he said. "It might not come to your testimony but in case they want to speak with you—"

"But I'm not . . ." Ramya's thoughts wouldn't behave. They kept on flying all over the place. "Captain Milos should be the one—"

"He's unwell."

"Then Ross should—"

Her father's jaw tightened before he swiftly cut her off. "The Galactic Senate isn't a playground, Lady Ramya. We can't let just anyone go romping in there." He paused for a second, his glacial gaze lingering on Ramya's face. "I will have Lefrasi join you. Having a Mwandan with us will be good optics."

So Lefrasi was fine and Ross wasn't? Why did her father have to keep snubbing him like that? Just because he assumed she was interested in Ross?

Ramya forced her thoughts away from Ross. He could wait. Now she had her own battle to fight. "I'm not even an adult. What makes me so worthy? That I'm your daughter?"

"Obviously, lineage matters a lot. Besides, you're the one who found out about the Locustans. You've flown the Stryker. You know a lot more than any of us."

"B-but . . ." Ramya would've happily chosen a field of quicksand to walk over rather than take a stand on the senate floor. *If* she were given a choice.

"You're afraid?" he asked as if she had committed a sin.

Ramya resisted the terrible urge to roll her eyes but instead only stuck a defiant chin out. "Yes, I am. Is that so disgusting?"

"Coming from a girl who has been fighting the godawful Locustans without any serious military training and still winning, I'd say yes," her father retorted. "The senate won't bite or fire their cannons at you. What's there to be afraid of in a few useless talkers?"

Ramya doubted the senate was as useless as her father was making it sound. Besides, that was the problem. She could return cannon fire or blast a ship out of the universe, but standing at the center of the senate floor and answering devious questions from a hundred pompous windbags? That was something else altogether. Even thinking of it made her spine tingle with dread.

Her father drew a sharp breath, perhaps on seeing her face wilt. Arms folded across his chest, he strode to her side. "All you have to do is tell them what you know." He paused a second and exhaled. Ramya knew that sound well; it always came when he was particularly disappointed in something. At the moment, it was her behavior. She braced herself for another round of scathing remarks. "You're a Kiroff. This is in your blood," he said through gritted teeth. "Don't cower like a kicked dog."

Ramya's fingers clawed into the edge of her chair. She gritted her teeth and fixed her gaze on the far end of the table, wishing this would end quickly. She couldn't take this onslaught of words much longer.

Her father was not good at giving up. He shook his head while towering over her. "The first time I faced the senate, I was fifteen. Father was sick and I had to take his place and fight for our rights on Nesbo V. We *had* to win the case, convince those talkers that House Kiroff was the best path forward. I did. Fear didn't dare cross my path. I didn't let it."

"I'm not you," Ramya spat out, her chest heaving under the burden of his words. Her eyes stung and her throat ached but she managed to throw more words out at him regardless. "I don't want to be you." The truth was that she couldn't be him if she tried for a million years. But she wasn't going to tell him that.

Her father's eyes stilled. His mouth opened slowly, far too slowly considering how fast he usually responded. But before he could frame words, a rap sounded on the door and in the next moment the panel swung open.

Casten shuffled in and bowed. "The lady's maid is ready, Lord Paramount."

For a second, only a stifling silence hung in the air. Then her father nodded. "The maid will help you dress appropriately," he said, his voice missing the usual bite. "I'll meet you on the *Kinvari*."

Ramya lurched to her feet, avoiding looking at her father. She turned around when she was almost out the door. There was one thing she needed to do before she left.

"I can't leave without seeing Captain Milos," she said.

Her father had been absentmindedly flipping the files on the table. At her declaration, he looked up and stared for a moment.

Ramya thought she saw a dark flash in his eyes. It wasn't anger, but something else. He nodded before she could fathom what it was. "Go see whomever you need to," he said before turning back to his papers.

Ramya followed Casten out into the sumptuous corridor, happy to get away from Trysten Kiroff and eager to see Captain Milos and her crewmates.

13

The *Kinvari* took off soon after. The preparation for the journey, particularly the fitting session with the maid, had stretched longer than Ramya would've liked. But presentation mattered immensely at the senate, so she had to endure. After the maid finished fitting her formal attire, Casten had led her to the room where Captain Milos was being treated. After a brief word or two, she had gone on to meet the rest of the crew before Casten brought her to the *Kinvari* and showed her to her personal section of the ship.

Ramya had expected her father to join her and braced for a long, uncomfortable journey to the fabulous Xandria, the Confederacy's magnificent capital, but it didn't happen. Trysten Kiroff didn't show. Lefrasi didn't either. Other than the frequent—too frequent for Ramya's taste—visits from the ship's charming host, she was left to herself.

For a while, she struggled to find a comfortable position. The couch was sumptuous, as was everything else on the *Kinvari*, but the meluscoat—the formal attire of the senate—was annoying. A meluscoat was usually a black, knee-length coat worn over an under-suit in house colors. In Ramya's case, the suit was blinding in red and gold, which was smothered by the drabbest, darkest and tightest long coat she'd ever worn. The worst part of the meluscoat was its high stiff collar that made Ramya's neck itch constantly. The fasteners were complicated and it had taken the maid agonizingly long to put together, so Ramya didn't dare adjust them. But she fidgeted endlessly.

The main floor of the ship was not visible from where she sat, but the windows provided a clear view of El-Iss and its dusty terrain as the *Kinvari* glided out of the underground cavern and shot out into the skies. Ramya scanned the surface, trying to detect the mound where she had landed the Stryker. She couldn't spot it.

It was odd how empty she felt at that moment, as if she had suddenly been robbed of all her possessions, as if she was leaving behind everything she knew. Somehow, this dread was stronger than the fear she had felt when leaving CAWStrat. She had left behind a life of seventeen years then, yet it had been far easier.

Ramya was pulled out of her thoughts when the ship's host sashayed into view for the umpteenth time. He deposited a silver tray with an array of delicacies on the table. Then with the customary bow, he left. Ramya reached for a piece of meat, relishing its butter-like softness. It had been a while since she'd had good food. A sigh coiled out of her immediately as she wondered what her crewmates had been served.

Surely not this! Meat so succulent couldn't be served to *just* anyone, Ramya mused, thinking of her father's words. *Ah well*, she reassured herself, *at least they are all safe*.

By the time Ramya had finished every morsel, the *Kinvari* had entered the SLH. The ship's host appeared again to clear the table, and he didn't leave after his task was complete.

"My lady, we're on our way to Xandria. The captain expects to reach it in five hours," he stated solemnly. "Is there anything I can serve you with?"

"No, thank you," Ramya replied. She wanted to find out what was happening on the main deck, but she didn't ask the host. He wouldn't know, and even if he did, it would be against decorum to talk about the ship's operational activities with him.

Ramya's thoughts lingered on his words long after he left. Five hours? That was too quick given how far Xandria was from El-Iss, but then the *Kinvari* was beyond state-of-the-art.

Five hours! She could use some sleep. She needed the rest, particularly before facing the hawks in the senate. Ramya leaned back and closed her eyes. Her thoughts lingered for a bit on the joyful reunion she'd had with the crew of the *Endeavor*. A smile tugged her mouth when she recalled how Ahool had pranced around her.

"Give 'em hell!" Fenny had told her on hearing about her dread of facing the senate. "Someone needs to get those oafs off their behinds."

More than Fenny's fiery words, the captain's calm directive stood out in Ramya's mind. They had sedated him and his words came out slightly slurred, but that didn't stop him from telling her what was needed.

"You can do this, Rami," he had said. "I don't have a smidgen of doubt and you shouldn't either. Tell them what they need to hear. We need a declaration of emergency so we can mobilize every person on every planet to counter this invasion. There can be no more delays."

"But Captain, Zeta has been attacked already," she had said, not understanding the need for her testimony. "They already have proof. What more do they need?"

Captain Milos had taken a long pause to breathe and Sosa's lips had thinned. His cure was rest, the Norgoran medic had told her once already. He needed time to recover from the loss of blood. Ramya knew this conversation was not helping that happen.

"Space Command is a lazy bunch of cowards. Now that Anomaly Point has closed again, they'd rather go back to sleep and hope it'll never open again. But it will. Zoho thinks it will. I know it will."

"Who's Zoho?"

"I think you should let Terenze rest now," Sosa had interrupted sharply at that point. "Just go give them your account."

Captain Milos nodded slowly, his eyelids heavy with sleep.

"The senate has to approve a galaxy-wide call-to-arms, so Space Command can recruit people. Every citizen who can fight has to be at the front lines," he whispered. "The senate needs to understand the urgency. Space Command isn't very interested in making that happen, so we have to push them. Show them what's at stake. Show them. You can."

Why in the stars would anyone believe her? She was not even an adult and after all, she was Trysten Kiroff's daughter. He was no darling of the Galactic Senate. Their claws were always out when it came to House Kiroff and its arguably shady business practices.

She hadn't had the chance to ask. The captain had drifted into sleep. Now she wondered if her testimony would help the cause or if her inexperience would simply burn down what little progress they had made thus far.

***

Ramya woke up with a strange feeling. It was cold and someone was watching her. She sat up with a start, and for a second, she couldn't recall where she was. Then she noticed her father.

He was seated across from her, his blue-gray eyes fixed on her face. There was no anger in them, and no disgust either. He simply looked. And that was weird.

Isbet, her best friend at CAWStrat, sometimes told stories of her own father, of how he often sat at her bedside, reading her stories until she fell asleep. Ramya had never had such luck. Heck, she would consider herself lucky if Trysten Kiroff flashed a half-smile at her.

"I'm sorry," Ramya blurted, smoothing the folds of her meluscoat as she sat up. "I dozed off."

"Good," he said. "You needed the rest. We're close."

Ramya balked at his words. "I slept for five hours?"

"Four, I think. We're still half an hour out," he said. He sat up and pointed at a bright red digital folder at the center of the table. "So, time to get to work."

Ramya blinked. She looked from her father's face to the folder and back again.

"Work? What kind of work?"

"We don't just walk into the Galactic Senate. We prepare. We strategize. That way, when we get there, we're ready to attack. Or defend as needed." He paused and nodded meaningfully at the folder. "That's our strategy."

"Our?" Ramya blurted.

Her father's brows crinkled just a bit. "I'm an ally of your captain. So yes, we work together."

Ramya could barely keep the chuckle in. Work with Trysten Kiroff? That sounded like they were equals . . . almost.

"Work with *you*?" The disbelieving words slipped past her lips before Ramya could rein them in.

"You don't want to?" he asked, his voice tightening.

Of course she did. Wasn't that what she'd always wished for? That he'd consider her worthy enough to trust her with his ventures? To be entirely honest, she wanted to squeal. But that would make her look like a mongrel giddy over a scrap of leftovers. And she couldn't let that happen. She couldn't let him see her joy.

Ramya simply shrugged, a little too carelessly. "I don't mind working with you."

"Good. Until Milos is back on his feet I'm all you'll have," he said.

"Where's Lefrasi?" she asked. "Shouldn't he know this too?"

Her father shook his head. "*You* will lead the conversation, so this is *your* weapon. Troops don't need to know strategy; all they need is guidance from their leader."

Ramya couldn't help but notice how different her father was from Captain Milos. The captain worked another way, letting everyone on the *Endeavor* figure out a way to deal with challenges, hardly ever imposing himself on them or their decisions. Trysten Kiroff, on the other hand, was all about keeping his control from slipping away. It had served him well but—

"Now get started. We don't have all the time in the universe."

Ramya hurriedly flipped the file open. Rows of faces greeted her, all of them dressed in senators' white meluscoats or Space Command's turd-brown uniforms. Brief biographies of each person followed their pictures, but it was the letters across their faces that caught Ramya's attention the most.

Words were stamped in big, bold red letters that screamed either

"Ally" or "Opponent." Ramya flipped through the entries, heart sinking fast as she noted how overwhelmingly their opponents outnumbered their allies.

14

Xandria was the heart of the galaxy. Obviously, it wasn't the physical center of the galaxy since a super-massive black hole took up that spot, but Xandria was the center for all practical purposes. It was the spatial midpoint of the galactic confederacy and the coordinates of every other system were measured relative to Xandria. The standard 30-hour Confederacy clock was based on the duration of a day on Xandria, and the time Xandria took to revolve around its star was a standard for measuring years across the galaxy as well. The third planet of a yellow star, Xandria, the capital planet-city of the galaxy, was an important and magnificent place.

It had been that way since before the Confederacy came to be. It was said that the first settlers of the galaxy found a grand city on Xandria—a megacity rather, one that extended over most of Xandria's largest continent. Curiously enough, it was entirely uninhabited.

The mystery behind the abandoned city didn't deter the newcomers from staking a claim on it. What famished settler gives up on a pre-built settlement in perfect working condition? Even if it had seemed strange, eerie even, that not one of the people who had built that sprawling structure remained, the first settlers didn't care. Numerous studies and hundreds of years later, questions about the ancients who had built Xandria remained unanswered to this day.

Ramya stared at the green and gray planet in the distance and wondered, the way she always did on seeing it. Where had the builders of the magnificent civilization gone? Why did they leave? No one knew. Those questions became one of those timeless mysteries that were still waiting to be solved. Just like the mystery of the SLH, how no one knew who built it.

During the time of the Confederacy, Xandria had been built up some more. The megacity that had once stretched across half the globe now almost covered it altogether. From an approaching spacecraft, it was a sight to see. Particularly on the night side when the lights came alive.

Xandrians were a proud people, prouder than the inhabitants of any other prime planet. They considered themselves the oldest of the old blood in the galaxy. They had the best intellect, and they were ahead of the galaxy in every way. Ramya had been to Xandria a few times, and even though she was the heir of the venerated House Kiroff, she had always felt like a peasant in the presence of the Xandrian highborn. In a way, Xandria and its people had always awed her.

This time, all she felt was annoyance. Where was all that intellect when it was needed? What was the point of pomp and grandeur when they lacked the intelligence and drive to counter an invasion?

Her thoughts scattered seeing the ship's host walk in with a plate of refreshments. Placing the plate in front of Ramya, he bowed. "We will dock in five minutes, my lady," he said.

Ramya grabbed the smallest snack from the plate and jumped to her feet. She wanted to be on the main deck when they docked, not sequestered away like this.

"Show me to the main deck, please," she ordered. His face tightened a bit but he nodded nonetheless.

By the time she reached the main deck, the *Kinvari* had already lurched to a stop. The host led her to one of the central rooms where Trysten Kiroff sat with Wultoph Aristide and a few other people Ramya didn't know by name. On seeing her, her father's brow arched. Ramya knew that withering 'what the hell are you doing here' look. But that was not why Ramya immediately regretted coming here. It was because all of his aides started bowing frenziedly. She should've and could've easily saved herself from this. Thankfully, halfway through the demonstration, her father intervened.

"Let's get started," he said, leading Ramya out of the room. As soon as Lefrasi—flushed and grumbling about how uncomfortable the meluscoat was—joined them, a pair of aides led them out of the *Kinvari*. Another group of people with sweeping bows and unending smiles accosted them as soon as they set foot outside the security screening area. Ramya grimaced at the spectacle. It was no wonder she had little trouble leaving home. She hated this endless show that was her life as a Kiroff heir.

"Ramya," a dulcet voice rang above the dizzying din of the aides surrounding her. She knew that voice. It belonged to Lynden, the sweetest and the most charming of the three older Kiroffs. Although Lynden was not as favorite an uncle as Bryn had been, he had always been kind. Ramya's heart lifted a little seeing his bright and smiling face.

Uncle Lynden didn't altogether dispense with the obligatory bow and the light kiss on her hand but he didn't hesitate to pull her into a warm embrace either. "Look at you, you're all grown up. I didn't know you'd be here," he said and shot a curious look at his brother as soon as he noted her attire. "Is she—"

"Let's speak on the way," her father said.

Lynden nodded and whisked them away, the two brothers speaking in hushed whispers as they walked. Ramya fell back to talk with Lefrasi who groaned at the first chance he got.

"This is terrible, Rami," he said with a sigh. "I didn't sign up for this."

Ramya chuckled. "Well, I didn't either, but . . ."

She couldn't finish the sentence. They had reached a waiting retinue of transporters. There was a hum of aides around them once more and Ramya found herself taken away from Lefrasi to a vehicle in the middle of the procession.

"Hold on," she said as they herded a distraught Lefrasi away to another, likely a less premier transporter in the group. No one heard her. No one even looked.

This was a mistake. Lefrasi had to be with her for as long as they were on Xandria. Ramya rushed up to her father and uncle. They were still talking, Ramya guessed about the upcoming testimony at the senate. Ignoring decorum, she interrupted.

"Father, they're taking Lefrasi to a different transporter. We shouldn't do that."

Her father's lips thinned. Uncle Lynden stood with a stunned, rather horrified look on his face. He had reason to be surprised. No one in their right mind interrupted Trysten Kiroff, and certainly not as publicly as she had just done.

"Why not?" That her father even asked for an explanation was leeway enough for Ramya.

She had a reason for this, and not just because she didn't want to abandon a completely bewildered Lefrasi. She collected her thoughts quickly and made her case as calmly as she could. "Lefrasi needs to look like one of us. Like we're on the same team. If he's separated from me, anyone would think he's a stooge. People would think this was *our* show and *our* agenda, not the galaxy's cause." Ramya paused a moment to take a breath and study her father's face. He wasn't livid yet, and that meant he was buying into her explanation. She soldiered on. "First of all, that's not the truth. And even if that were true, we wouldn't want anyone to know."

Her father's eyes crinkled, and it almost seemed to Ramya that he found her suggestion humorous. But a second later he waved at the nearest aide. "The Mwandan rides with us."

Ramya was as happy as a clam when they settled down inside the transporter. Lefrasi seemed relieved to be back with her and the eased expression on his face drove away more of Ramya's worries about facing the senate.

Her father and uncle continued to talk, Lynden's face changing from worried to fearful as time passed. Once he cast an anxious look at her and Ramya caught his whisper. "Are you sure she's ready? She's too young to face the senate, Trysten."

"She might not be called upon at all."

"And what if she is? Can she stand up to those hawks? They're a vicious bunch, Molen in particular."

Lynden's concerns were not entirely misplaced. This was not an easy job for anyone, let alone a greenhorn like her. The task was to convince the senate to declare a galaxy-wide emergency, something Space Command didn't seem convinced about. And not just Space Command--the senate was not a very proactive bunch either, not when Molen Danukis was leading the charge as chief inquisitor.

House Danukis had always been a fierce opponent of House Kiroff and Molen was no exception to the rule. On top of that, Molen, according to her father's dossier, was a staller; his reputation built on opposing every demand that came to the senate floor for a hearing. This wasn't going to be any different.

Ramya didn't expect her father to look at her. She had been observing him, his face, the changing expressions, so when he glanced her way she was caught in an unguarded moment, gawking like a fool. Even though her first instinct was to look away, she didn't. She wanted to hear what he had to say, she had to know his opinion.

Her father didn't look away either. He scanned her face the way a jeweler would examine a stone to evaluate its worth. Even holding his gaze felt tiresome, but she hung on to it.

"She'll do fine," he said finally, and with a subtle nod at Ramya, he turned once again to Lynden.

Ramya sank back into the plush seat and closed her eyes. It was funny how the heart worked. Her father had yelled at her and snapped at her, but all it took to drive her fears away was a show of faith. She couldn't find a shred of dread within her. She could take on a hundred Molen Danukises and more. One kind word had done much more than a thousand rebukes.

15

The Galactic Senate was almost as massive as three Drednots put together. It was a building of gleaming white stone at the center of a gigantic plot of manicured gardens and divinely landscaped patios. It was a famous building, so the façade was familiar. However, Ramya had never been near it, so she held her breath all along the drive up to the front of the building. Guards in uniforms — white, with the confederate sigil of a black and white four-pointed star emblazoned on their chests — screened them one by one. It took a while to get everyone in the party cleared.

Their destination was the Hall of Narratives at the center of the building. Everyone, according to Wultoph Aristide, had already gathered in the hall to hear testimony on the Locustan situation. That left the cavernous hallways leading up the Hall of Narratives mostly empty. Ramya noted that they did not walk to the main entrance of the hall, but instead took a path that led them to the side and to a door that was puny compared to every other door she had seen thus far. Liveried guards checked their credentials before letting them inside.

As soon as Ramya entered the Hall of Narratives, she blinked. She had seen pictures of the place and she had heard about it plenty of times, but nothing prepared her for what she saw. The Hall of Narratives at the Galactic Senate was just as immense as everything else there. From where Ramya stood, she could not even see its roof, not just because the place was dimly lit, but because it was so high up.

Simply described, the hall was a gigantic domed room, designed like an amphitheater. The viewing galleries were spread out in the shape of a cone facing a platform where a lone lectern stood. Behind the podium where unfortunates such as herself were summoned to address the senate, a giant viewing screen rose to the roof.

The already dimmed lights dimmed some more as soon as they

reached their seating area. It was a small, cordoned-off section, close to the podium, and Ramya assumed it was assigned to House Kiroff. Ramya sat between her father and Lefrasi, her heart pounding like a drum as the reality of the situation sank deeper into her head.

She was going to have to stand up there, alone perhaps, and answer blistering questions in front of a thousand or more people. They would watch her and enjoy seeing her fall apart.

"The Honorable Chief of Chairs, Molen Danukis, will address the assembly," a booming mechanical voice announced and promptly pulled Ramya out of her thoughts.

A stout man walked across the platform. As soon as he reached the lectern, the screen behind him lit up with a close-up of his face. Molen was the elder brother of Ramya's ex-classmate and nemesis at CAWStrat, Armand, and the family resemblance was strong. Even the way he walked reminded Ramya of Armand and her nose crinkled with disgust.

"Welcome, one and all, to this exigent session," he said, pausing and raising his arms above his head as a low murmur grew. "I know, I know. I didn't like being summoned away from my private time, but . . ." he paused again and shook his head for effect. "But . . . it seems there has been an incident involving our dear old friends, the Locustans."

Even with gritted teeth, Ramya found it impossible to stop an angry grunt. Her father shot her an admonishing glance but Ramya's anger did not abate one bit. Did Molen have to make light of the situation? Thousands of people had already died, and here he was joking about Locustans and complaining about being yanked out of his private time?

At the podium, Molen grated on. "I promise, this will be short and we will get back to our lives as fast as we can." Ramya inhaled sharply at his flippant words. Was he that daft? Didn't he get it? There would be no life in the galaxy if Anomaly Point opened up for good.

Her father turned a bit toward her. "This is only the beginning," he whispered. "My lesson from the first time I visited here—learn to shut out your emotions. You should be thinking of nothing except your goal."

It was good advice delivered pleasantly. Ramya decided to try her best to follow it.

"We shall begin with an address from the Chief of Fleets, Marson Hale," Molen Danukis declared before stepping away.

A sandy-haired man in Space Command's uniform slunk up to the vacant lectern. As soon as his face filled up half of the viewing screen, Ramya saw fear in his eyes. He was trying hard to hide it, but she didn't miss the telltale ripple. This man knew how real the threat was, yet according to her father's dossier, he wasn't keen on a call-to-arms. Why?

"Please state your name for the assembly," Molen's voice boomed. The other half of the viewing screen had filled with a view of the inquisition committee. Molen sat in the middle of the row, flanked by two others. To his left was a man, Babbus of House Konnem, classified as an opponent in her father's dossier. A Norgoran female—Eliah, an ally, Ramya recalled the name from the file—sat to Molen's right. Ramya tried to pinpoint their physical location in the hall but couldn't. Molen's voice, however, seemed to come from a section located similar to theirs, but on the other side of the podium.

"Marson Davidus Hale, Chief of Fleets, Space Command of the Galactic Confederacy."

"Please proceed with your testimony."

"Salutations, everyone. Last night we received word that Anomaly Point had reopened. Anomaly Point, if you recall, is the wormhole in the Alpha Quadrant through which the Locustans entered our galaxy during the invasion ten years ago."

"We are aware of what Anomaly Point is, Chief," Molen's sharp voice cut in. "Let's please adhere to the critical bits. Who told you about the breach at Anomaly Point?"

"Admiral Zoho."

"And what is his function?"

"He is in charge of Starbase Zeta. Zeta is the closest presence Space Command has to Anomaly Point."

"We know what Zeta is, Chief," Molen said. Ramya pushed down the simmering annoyance inside her. Her father was right; she could lose her mind over every snub Molen unleashed. "Please tell us what Admiral Zoho told you."

"Locustan fighters had streamed out of Anomaly Point and attacked Zeta. Admiral Zoho sent out our squadrons stationed at the starbase. There was a long encounter with the invaders."

"What happened at the end?"

"Our squadrons were able to subdue and wipe out the enemy."

"All of them?"

The chief nodded. "Yes."

"So we won?"

"Yes."

"Do you anticipate any more attacks?" Molen asked.

The chief seemed to hesitate before answering. "We do not have the ability to predict when Anomaly Point will open again."

"So you don't know if it will open at all?"

"That's correct," Marson Hale replied, but clearly, he didn't seem happy.

On the screen, Molen Danukis smirked. "There is a request to authorize galaxy-wide call-to-arms to resist this so-called invasion. But I do not see an invasion. Do you?"

The chief shifted uncomfortably on his feet. "As I said, we can't predict how Anomaly Point will behave and —"

"Sorry to interrupt, Chief Hale, but do you see a necessity for a galaxy-wide call-to-arms at the moment?"

He took forever to answer. In the end, he shook his head decisively. "Not at this time, no."

What in the name of the stars? Ramya breathed in with all her might to keep another angry grunt from escaping her mouth.

"Thank you, Chief Hale," Molen said, almost too eagerly. "You may step down now."

Lefrasi leaned toward Ramya and sighed. "That went well, don't you think?"

Ramya chuckled at the Mwandan's sarcasm and nodded. "Yes, definitely." She was sure their testimony would be received just as warmly.

"The next on our list is Admiral Zoho," Molen announced. "Please bring him up."

Zoho's tired face filled half the screen instantaneously. Ramya understood why Molen had asked to "bring" Zoho up; the Norgoran admiral was not physically present at the senate. He was clearly at Zeta, probably at his command center.

Molen quickly completed the introductions and started questioning. "We just heard from the Chief of Fleets. Congratulations on your win."

"I wouldn't call it a win," Zoho snapped right back.

"No? Why not?"

"Because you don't win until you've won the war, and the war has only just begun." Ramya stirred happily in her seat. The dossier had marked Zoho an ally and she was starting to see why already.

Molen Danukis drummed the table, his brows furrowed. "All right, I'll give you that. War has only just begun and there's more coming. Still, we've won against them before, ten years ago. We were less prepared then, and our tech was far more primitive. Yet we won. Can you make me understand why we're already in a panic-and-run mode this time around?"

Zoho exhaled noisily. "Because . . . in these ten years, their tech has evolved far more than ours. Their fighters are stronger, more agile, their weapons more accurate and deadly. If they keep on coming at full force, our fleets will be wiped out in a matter of days. So, no, Chief of Chairs, we won't win so easily this time, if we win at all."

For a whole minute or so, the Hall of Narratives stayed quiet. Then a murmur grew, low but persistent.

Molen shuffled in his seat and cleared his throat. "*Only* if they keep on coming, yes? But the Chief of Fleets told us that Anomaly Point has closed. Do you disagree with that statement?"

"No, I don't. But it's not the entire truth," Zoho said. "It can open again. It *will* open again."

"How do you know that? Do you have scientific evidence?"

Zoho sighed. "No, but I have experience."

Molen flashed an annoying smile. "And in your opinion, the Chief of Fleets doesn't have any experience. Is that what you're trying to imply?"

Zoho's jaw tightened and Ramya could tell he was losing his patience. The admiral had lost a huge number of his people during the attack on Zeta and it was understandable that he didn't have the tolerance for Molen's ridiculous questions.

"I did not say that. I only stated *my* opinion based on *my* experience. Anomaly Point won't stay closed forever. It'll open. Soon."

"All right. Say it opens. You've won one encounter. You'll win another. What's there to fear?"

"Half of our squadrons perished in this encounter. That is a sixth of the entire space fleet." The admiral paused and took a long bracing breath. "Do you know how long Anomaly Point was open? Only . . . ten minutes. So, what happens when Anomaly Point stays open for an hour? What will we do then?"

"All right, so . . . you're in favor of a call-to-arms?"

"Of course," Admiral Zoho said vehemently. "But even that might fall short."

Molen raised an eyebrow. "Please explain, Admiral."

Admiral Zoho stayed silent for a while and then he spoke in a worried, exhausted voice. "I'm afraid they're trying to keep Anomaly Point open forever."

"Who's they?"

"The Locustans."

"Hmm . . . I see. How do you know that?"

"I believe this has happened before," the admiral said, haltingly. "Before us."

Molen sat up and a sarcastic smile curled the corners of his mouth. "Before us?"

"The ancients who built the SLH knew about Anomaly Point. That's why they built three termination points near it. The Locustans must've come before. Perhaps they were the ones who claimed all the ancients. Perhaps that's why Xandria . . . the entire galaxy was empty when our ancestors arrived."

"That's a whole lot of speculation, Admiral Zoho," Molen said. "Assumptions that no one else in the galaxy thinks worthy of — "

"The Hand of Darkness has written long treatises on it. Their works are built on scientific premises."

Next to Ramya, her father stirred uneasily. Ramya thought she understood his impatience. The admiral had started off nice and solid, but now his testimony was fraying. He was bringing up conspiracy theories that had no place in this forum. Or did they?

"The Hand of Darkness is an outlawed cult that practices the dark arts," Molen said caustically. "We cannot build our defenses based on a treatise they have written."

Zoho's eyes sparkled. "But they might know of a way to shut down Anomaly Point permanently. They say — "

"It's been a while since you took command of Zeta, isn't it?" Molen cut the admiral off. "When did you last have a detailed psychosomatic evaluation?"

Zoho frowned and his jaw turned rock hard. "You think I'm insane?"

Molen held up his hands and shook his head vehemently. "Absolutely not, Admiral. But sometimes, when we are away in a secluded place, sometimes we become more prone to a vivid imagination. That's all."

"This is not my imagina—"

"I've noted your stand in favor of a call-to-arms, Admiral," Molen interrupted Zoho again. "I'm sure you have a great many things to attend to. We will release you now."

Zoho barely had time to be surprised at his abrupt send-off, his image on the screen vanishing before his eyes could widen.

"We shall now take a small pause," Molen announced. "After that, we shall hear from Admiral Kanaa of the Second Fleet."

The way her father rubbed the bridge of his nose told Ramya her suspicions were correct. Zoho's statements, honest and vigorous as they were, had not helped the galaxy's cause much.

16

The lights in the Hall of Narratives brightened a little and people started walking about and talking amongst themselves. Ramya leaned over to check on Lefrasi. His face had lost color and Ramya knew he was tired and hopeless. Much like the way she felt herself.

"Don't give up just yet," she said to the Mwandan who didn't seem to find much cheer in her words. "Kanaa will tell them about the Locustans in the Fringe. That might make them understand the situation."

"So many are already dead, Rami," Lefrasi said with a sad shake of his head. "And these folks here are just . . . joking about it."

A long sigh tore through Ramya and she let it. It was sad, almost unbelievable that while the galaxy was on the brink of total annihilation, people like Molen were senselessly indulging in their fantasies of safety. She found no words to counter Lefrasi's thought. They were a doomed lot, with barely a month or two to live.

"Trysten Kiroff!" The brassy voice made Ramya jump. Her heart was still pounding when she saw the man — a massive specimen of a human with a shock of red hair and a flaming red beard — plodding toward her father who watched him approach with a stricken look on his face.

Ramya shrank back in her seat but it was already too late. The man's gleeful eyes moved quickly from Trysten to settle on her. "And Lady Ramya," he declared even more loudly.

"Who's that?" Lefrasi asked, but Ramya didn't have time to respond. Gael Arlington's father Tucker Arlington, or Tuck as he liked to go by, descended on them like a thunderstorm.

"What a beautiful surprise," he bellowed. "You didn't tell me you were bringing your lovely daughter along," he said, planting a sloppy kiss on Ramya's hand. In the next second, he shook his head at her father. "This is no way to meet such an enchanting young lady for the first time." Tuck's mighty arms flew through the air. "We ought to have a grand ball, an exquisite feast, and —"

"In good time, Tuck," her father interrupted hastily. "We will."

Tuck nodded. "We should. We have to." He turned toward Ramya and flashed rows of oversized teeth. "I say you deserve the best for the best event of your life. Right, my lovely?" he asked.

Ramya had no doubt it was her planned marriage he had negotiated with his son, Gael — one she was never going to let happen — that Tuck was alluding to. Well, it was hardly an allusion anymore. Nothing was with Tucker Arlington around. Five more minutes of this and the whole universe would know.

Tuck rubbed his chin with a meaty finger. "Hey!" he shouted suddenly, furiously beckoning someone from the far end of their seating area. "Hey, Gelly! Come here! Have you met the beautiful —"

"Tuck, they've met," Trysten Kiroff said, almost sounding frantic.

"They have?" Tuck said. He didn't stop waving at whoever he was calling. "Come on, Gelly. Hurry. Molen is gonna start strutting around soon."

Ramya couldn't decide which was better — seeing Molen strutting around or enduring Tuck's showboating.

"There you are," Tuck said and Ramya's mouth fell open a bit seeing who Gelly was. She had suspected as much already. It made sense that a lieutenant from the GSO who had fought the Locustan megaship on Bucifer P9 would be present for the testimony. Still, seeing him flinch every time Tuck called him Gelly or thumped his shoulder surprised Ramya a bit.

So this is how you survive, Gael Arlington, Ramya mused.

"Here's Lady Ramya Kiroff," Tucker announced to a rather red-faced Gael, who politely bowed and stood stiffly to one side. His father looked curious for a second before thumping his back. "Go on, speak to the lady."

"They've met already, Tuck," Trysten said again, this time

through gritted teeth. Tuck, however, didn't hear, or pretended not to hear, likely the latter. He almost pushed Gael next to Ramya and smiled triumphantly at Trysten Kiroff. "There, done."

This had to be the first time Trysten Kiroff had ever rolled his eyes at anyone in public. Looking at her father's annoyed expression and the burning flush on Gael's ears, Ramya could hardly keep a straight face. Watching them wriggle awkwardly was fun. However, the booming mechanical voiced announced the beginning of the next session and Gael hurriedly nodded at Ramya. "Good luck," he whispered.

Ramya couldn't help herself. "You too, Gelly," she said, giggling.

Gael shot her a withering look. "Drop it, Kiroff," he said before walking away.

Ramya was still smiling when she settled back into her chair, probably a little too much, because Lefrasi looked curiously at her. "What's going on?"

"Long story," Ramya said. "How about I tell you on our way back to El-Iss?"

The story would definitely have to wait since Kanaa had already taken the podium. The usual introductions later, Molen started with his questions.

"I gather you've had some illuminating experiences regarding the Locustans recently. Please enlighten us, Admiral."

Ramya held her breath. Molen's question was broad and it left Kanaa with plenty of room to bring her involvement with the Stryker to light. While that was something she couldn't avoid forever, now was not the right time. If Molen got wind of it, he would pounce on the chance to take a Kiroff to task and happily derail the current conversation. Ramya only hoped that her father had brokered some sort of understanding with the admiral.

"Locustans have invaded the Fringe," Kanaa said simply. She paused a bit after that statement and all Ramya could hear was the dull thump of her heart beating. It was as if that enormous chamber was collectively holding its breath. "They have harvested populations of multiple planets in the Fringe. We have thwarted them from spreading out more, but that is only a temporary fix."

"A moment, Admiral," Molen interjected loudly. "Locustans? In the Fringe? They've been harvesting populations?" He stopped and let out a chuckle, albeit a nervous one. "This is hard to believe."

"There's footage," Kanaa said calmly. She gestured at someone to the side of the podium. "With your permission, Chief of Chairs."

The screen filled with the recording the Stryker had made on Bucifer P9, of the Mwandans being chased down by the massive insectoids. Lefrasi let out a pained sigh but it was lost in the swell of gasps and murmurs that broke all over.

When Molen's face came back on the screen again, he looked a little pale. "How long has this been going on? Why are we hearing of this only now?"

"We only became aware of the situation recently."

"And what is being done about them?"

"We have eradicated their mothership."

"We? You mean the Second Fleet under your command carried out this mission?"

"Yes," Kanaa replied. "A GSO unit led by Lieutenant Gael Arlington was with us also. As well as some of Captain Terenze Milos's crew."

Ramya shrank a little as Molen's eyes narrowed at the mention of the captain's name. "Terenze Milos? As in *the* Terenze Milos of the Locusta-Vanga war fame? I'm a little confused about his role here. But we shall get to that later. We want to hear now about this mission against the mothership. Let's see . . . Lieutenant Gael Arlington of the GSO, please take the stand. And Admiral, please don't leave us just yet."

As soon as the opening statements were over, Molen started questioning Gael. "Tell us about this mothership, Lieutenant. How big is it? How many Locustans was it carrying?"

"It was half the size of a Drednot. We do not know how many Locustans were inside because we didn't investigate."

"You didn't? Why not?"

"Because we lacked the personnel. As you saw from the footage Admiral Kanaa shared, Bucifer P9 is overrun with Locustans. A squadron or two doesn't stand a chance against them. We'll need a lot more people on the ground, and that's just one planet we're talking about. We don't even know how many others have been harvested already. Each planet in the Fringe needs to be checked for the presence of Locustans and — "

"All right, all right." Molen raised his arms impatiently and Ramya understood why. Gael had effectively steered the questioning away from the direction Molen wanted to go and brought up other troublesome questions. Molen, being Molen, didn't appreciate that. "Please answer my questions in a simple sentence or two, Lieutenant. We do not need a discourse from you on what needs to be done. We, your superiors, will decide that. Now tell us, please, has this mothership been completely eradicated?"

"Yes, it has," Gael replied tersely.

No, no, no! Don't back off! That's what he wants you to do. But Gael had already given Molen an opening.

"You were witness to this, is that correct?"

"Yes, I was."

"Excellent," Molen said. "That's one less thing to worry about, then."

"I wouldn't — "

"Do we have footage of this mothership?"

Gael didn't reply and Ramya didn't understand why. They had good footage of the mothership he could show them. The answer hit her suddenly — showing the mothership would lead to questions about its origin, which in turn would turn all attention to Kiroff Industries and her father. That was a distraction they could do without.

"Please answer my question, Lieutenant," Molen asked sharply. Ramya worried that he had already smelled blood in the water. She wondered if Gael would lie about the footage.

"Yes, we do."

"Please show us."

The shimmering superstructure of the four Strykers meshed into a megaship flashed on the screen a moment later. There were more gasps, some yells as well.

"Where did this ship come from?" Molen's question was expected, but it drained hope out of Ramya. She heard her father draw a sharp breath and realized her fears were not misplaced. The drama Molen could've only dreamed of creating was now within his grasp. "There was no breach of Anomaly Point before this. So, where did a ship of this size materialize from? Can you think of an explanation, Lieutenant?"

Gael pursed his lips and mulled the question for a second. Then he glanced quickly at Admiral Kanaa before he let his answer shatter the quiet. "This didn't come through Anomaly Point. It came from Sector 22. This is the product of an experiment approved by Space Command."

It was smart of Gael to bring up the fact that the Strykers had been built with the blessing of Space Command, but Ramya doubted how much good it'd do.

"I shall call back the Chief of Fleets again, but since you're here, Admiral Kanaa, please tell me, as per your knowledge, is the lieutenant's statement true?"

Kanaa plodded to the center of the podium and nodded gravely. "Yes, it is. We had authorized experiments on debris we recovered after the first invasion."

Molen tapped his chin thoughtfully. "So . . . first of all, Space Command never came to us for approval on this project as is protocol. That's a grave offense and someone will stand trial for it. However, the bigger question is, how did we go from debris to this murderous monstrosity? Who created this?"

Molen had not only smelled blood, he now had his prey in sight. He knew only one person could be at the other end of his questioning and that was his nemesis, Trysten Kiroff.

"I don't think this question bears any value—"

"Please let us be the judge of that, Admiral," Molen cut her off deftly. "Who built this monstrosity?"

Kanaa drew a long breath and frowned at Molen. "No one person built this whole ship," she said with deliberation. "But parts of it were made by Kiroff Industries."

If Molen could've squealed with joy, he would have. Since he was skilled at masking emotions, the happiness at having cornered his family's greatest enemy only showed as a flicker in his eyes. Ramya saw it nonetheless. She knew that smirk that had curled Molen's thick lips almost imperceptibly. She had seen it on Armand's face each time she got into a fix at CAWStrat.

"Kiroff Industries," Molen said, shaking his head. "We should've expected this. This is all the work of one family that's set on profiting off anything, even our lives." He paused for a moment and looked toward where the Kiroffs were seated. "Lynden Kiroff will please take the stand." Babbus leaned toward him and Molen immediately nodded. "I've just been told that Lord Paramount Trysten Kiroff is here with us today. In that case, I ask him to take the stand instead."

17

Ramya stared at her father's impassive face on the giant screen and prayed. If anyone could turn this around, it was Trysten Kiroff. They couldn't let this entire proceeding derail into a personal fight between House Danukis and House Kiroff. Every minute they spent fighting here was a minute wasted. No one knew when Anomaly Point would open up again and for how long. It could very well be opening up now, and forever. They could actually be nothing but dead people talking.

"We shouldn't have come here at all, Rami," Lefrasi said in a low voice. "I'd rather clean the planets that have been touched by the scourge. Who knows what those things are up to while we're wasting time debating?"

This wasn't even a debate. Molen was getting ready to settle personal scores. However, Ramya didn't want to tell Lefrasi that. "My father is good at fixing things," she said, really hoping that he could.

"Lord Paramount Kiroff," Molen started in a caustic voice, a smirk pulling down the right side of his mouth in a grotesque way. "You seem to be a permanent resident of this hall. We meet almost every other day to resolve one dispute or another."

Her father didn't reply. A cold, inscrutable stare was all Molen received as a response to his non-question. It didn't sit well with the chief inquisitor, his eyes narrowing to slits as he locked stares with Trysten Kiroff.

"So, what are you getting out of this ruse, Lord Paramount?" Molen said finally.

"I do not follow your question, Chief of Chairs."

"I believe this is an elaborate farce you've created," Molen said. "This call-to-arms, this panic, this ruckus, it's all a front to cover up your mistake—that a monster you created went out of control and on a rampage. Isn't that true?"

Her father's eyes narrowed, then he chuckled. Ramya couldn't remember when she had last seen him laugh, but she was sure it had been a long time. "You saw footage of Anomaly Point opening, you saw the footage of Locustan fighters attacking Zeta, you heard testimony from admirals of the Space Fleet, and yet you think I made all of that up?"

Molen crossed his arms and crinkled his nose. "You've worked up convoluted schemes before."

"You must really think *very* highly of me." Trysten Kiroff laughed again. "I wish this were all a ruse, but it's not. I wish I could open up wormholes in space whenever I chose to, but I can't. The only truth is: the Locustans are coming and we need to mobilize. Right away."

"Mobilize? You know what a call-to-arms will do? It'll disrupt everything in the galaxy. Trade, business, every aspect of our lives. What's to say you won't profit from that disruption? It won't be the first time you've played dirty."

Her father took a long breath. His face had hardened and Ramya knew he was ready to throw a pitiless reply at Molen. She was not ready for what she heard. "My apologies for everything I might've done in the past. I'm open to any sanctions you deem fit. But not at this moment. Now is not the time to discuss me or how I do my business and earn my profits." He paused a second to look up and around the Hall of Narratives. Ramya could see the pain in every taut muscle on his face. She knew, as did anyone else who had known Trysten Kiroff, how hard it must've been to swallow his pride and beg. Yet he did. And Ramya had never felt prouder. Her father continued. "This is my plea to all of you, open your hearts and minds. This is beyond me, and beyond our differences. The Locustans are coming and they are vicious. And smart. And efficient. If we don't mobilize right now, it'll be too late."

The hall erupted into murmurs louder than before and Ramya knew something had changed. Babbus and Eliah clustered around

Molen who looked utterly frustrated with how things were going.

"Silence, please," Molen yelled when the murmurs grew to a low rumble. "Yes, we shall take a vote. But only after we have completed our questioning. Please bear with the inquisitors."

Ramya could've jumped for joy. If there was a call for voting already, it meant Molen's throttling wasn't working. Her father had done it, turned things around. However, Molen wasn't done yet. He tapped his chin and frowned at Trysten Kiroff. "What's your deal with Space Command?"

"I do not follow your question."

"They must be dangling some mighty carrot in front of you to make you grovel on your knees like this." Molen paused to smirk and Ramya braced herself. Those were stinging words and they could break her father's resolve to rein in his pride. Gritting her teeth, she prayed that wouldn't happen. "What are they paying you, Lord Paramount Kiroff? It has to be an enormous sum because you're begging even better than my dog."

Ramya held her breath, fists turning into balls as she glared at the image of Molen on the giant screen.

Her father's eyes flashed. He scoffed. "I wish they could pay me. Instead, I've pledged every craft that comes from every factory I own to Captain Milos. So he can defend the galaxy when you can't. Or won't."

For a second there was silence. Then Molen arched a brow. "Why is Captain Milos being mentioned so many times? Didn't he retire ages ago? I thought he was long dead and buried."

"He's doing fine," Trysten Kiroff retorted. "He's the one who's been trying to warn Space Command about the Locustans, or should I say . . . trying to knock some sense into their heads."

"Hmm . . ." Molen leaned back into his seat with a satisfied smile curling his fat lips. Ramya's heart sank. Molen Danukis looked very pleased and that wasn't a good sign. Molen scratched his nose thoughtfully. "How does Captain Milos know about such things as the next Locustan invasion? Do the Locustans send him notes?"

Molen ended with a sarcastic smile and Ramya found her fists tightening. House Danukis was made up of stellar specimens, but Molen had to be a shining star among them. She almost wished she could land a punch on his face, the way she had on his brother Armand's.

Molen tapped his forehead meaningfully. "Or perhaps Milos has gone a little rusty up here? The man was always a bit on the loony side."

"The man is a legend who deserves respect," Trysten Kiroff snapped. "Terenze Milos was always fine. He only lacked interest in reconciling with traitors."

Ramya sat up. What did her father mean by that? Something about the captain's past?

Molen raised his arms. "All right, all right. But can you explain how he knows about the Locustans?"

Her father hesitated for a second. "Because he was the one who came across one of the hybrid crafts we built in Sector 22. He found the one Stryker that hadn't gone rogue."

"Aha! And this craft, this baby monster you created, talks to Milos?"

Trysten Kiroff's face stayed expressionless but his eyes narrowed a tad. Ramya shifted uneasily in her seat. They were veering close to her now, too close for comfort. "The Stryker has an AI that can speak to people."

"Is the illustrious man, the legendary Terenze Milos, here with us? I'd like to hear about what this AI told him."

"He is unwell and couldn't be here."

Molen's mouth twisted. "That's pretty convenient, isn't it?"

Babbus whispered in Molen's ear and he waved dismissively at Trysten Kiroff right away. "You can leave, Lord Paramount, we're done with you for now." He spoke animatedly with Babbus some more before facing the podium again. "I'm told some of Milos's crew is present here. Could we have them step up, please?"

Ramya had never felt dread as heavy and crushing as this before. Even when she had faced the Locustan megaship or fought the Drednots, she had a sliver of hope inside her. This moment felt different . . . too hopeless. Or maybe things always looked better in hindsight. They had to. Maybe this too would not turn out to be a disaster after all. Fists curled, she got to her feet and along with Lefrasi, walked toward the stairs leading up to the podium. Her ears buzzed and her head was light when she came face to face with her father. All she remembered was the look on his face. There was no anger in his eyes, only a cloud of concern. He gave her a solemn nod and whispered, "Just be yourself."

The air felt cold around the podium and the spotlights that burned into her face were disorienting. But Ramya got some reprieve, thanks to Lefrasi. The Mwandan's presence had stunned Molen, and his attention stayed away from Ramya for a while as Molen probed how the Mwandan had come to join Captain Milos. It wasn't until Lefrasi voiced his opinion about the inefficiency of the ongoing inquisition that Molen swiftly turned his attention to Ramya.

"And you, dear. You are a crew member of this freight ship as well?" Molen flashed a gratifying smile.

Ramya nodded. *Just don't ask my name, please.*

"State your name and occupation for the record, please."

She had pondered this moment, yet when the instant of announcing her name arrived, Ramya hesitated. She could lie and there was a chance they'd never find out. However, if they found out later anyway, it'd look even worse.

To hell with it!

"Ramya Kiroff, medic's assistant."

Molen's face froze and Ramya would've enjoyed a hearty chuckle had the situation not been so dire.

"What did you say, dear?" he stuttered to life a moment later.

"Ramya Kiroff, medic's assistant."

"Kiroff, you say?" Molen's chest heaved as if to catch his breath. "Are you related to Lord Paramount Kiroff?"

Ramya nodded slowly. "He's my father."

For a while, they simply stared at each other. Then Molen blurted, "I don't even know what to say." He rose to his feet and then sat down, before rising again. "What does the Kiroff heiress do on a rundown freight ship?"

"I assist the medic. And I run errands."

"Run errands? You? On a rundown freight ship?" Molen scoffed. "Lady Ramya, are you making fun of this esteemed venue?"

"Absolutely not! It's the truth. Lefrasi is my crewmate. You can ask him."

"No, I won't ask him," Molen yelled. "I won't let you and your arrogant father turn the Galactic Senate into a joke. This inquisition is over. I don't know what it is that you and your infernal family have planned but I refuse to be your plaything. There can be no call-to-arms, not now."

"Then you will be responsible for the annihilation of this galaxy," Ramya shouted back. She felt no fear, no hesitation. She didn't care what they thought of her. She knew she had to say it and she did. She tore her eyes from Molen's livid face and looked up and around the hall. "Please, forget my name. Who I am is not half as important as what I've seen. I have seen the Locustans up close, I have seen them hunt down people. The footage you saw of Bucifer P9, I was there. They came at my Stryker with their enormous wings and crooked bodies. Believe me; no one stands a chance against them in hand-to-hand combat. Even before they strike you down, you'll be paralyzed and dead with fear. They are death, an army of death."

Ramya paused a moment and realized how quiet the assembly was. They were listening. A trickle of hope came back into her heart and she started again. "We cannot let them in through Anomaly Point. We have to get everyone . . . anyone who is old enough to fly . . . out there, guarding Anomaly Point. We have to do that before it's too late.

And I fear while we argue here, it might already be too late."

Eliah, the Norgoran woman on the committee of inquisitors, leaned forward suddenly. "You have engaged in combat with the Locustans? In person?"

"Yes, I have. Multiple times. I was part of the team that took down what you've named the mothership." The Norgoran seemed genuinely interested and it spurred Ramya on. "We do not even know how many planets in the Fringe have been taken over already and if they have discovered the means to spread further. Those planets need to be identified and quarantined. As soon as possible. That effort needs a whole lot of people too."

"And what else, Lady Ramya?" Molen almost elbowed the Norgoran aside. "Don't you need us to discover a miracle to shut down Anomaly Point as well?"

She did. They all did. And Ramya believed there was such a miracle out there. Dakrhaeth had hinted about it. Admiral Zoho had some ideas. There had to be something.

"I believe there's a way to shut down Anomaly Point, yes," she said. "I believe there's truth in what Admiral Zoho said. The ancients knew the answer and we have to find it. That's what will save us."

Molen burst into laughter. Anger coiled at the pit of Ramya's stomach and her fists balled.

"You, my dear, need to give your overactive imagination some rest," Molen said. "Go on, go with your father. Go home. I don't know what you were doing fighting in the Fringe. My guess is you were assisting your father in some sort of an elaborate scheme to rob the galaxy's coffers. But whatever it was, it's over now. Leave this to the grown-ups, dear. Go home and play with some dolls."

Anger that had been smoldering within burst into flames at Molen's words. Ramya clutched the edge of the lectern to stop her body from shaking. She glared at Molen, wishing she could burn him down.

"You're excused, dear," Molen said again in an infuriating tone that clawed at Ramya. "Now is when you leave."

"No, I shall not leave. Not until I'm done saying what I need to say. And you shall not interrupt me. Not until you've stared the Locustans in the face and taken their fire the way I have."

Ramya paused for a breath, relieved that she'd stunned Molen into silence. That was all she needed. She was going to crash and burn in the end, that Ramya knew, but her ruin had to amount to something.

"I get that you hate my father. I don't like Trysten Kiroff much either. He's brash, arrogant, a know-it-all. I avoided telling you, but the truth is I left home to get away from him and my house. That's why I work for Captain Milos in a rundown freight ship. Right now, I don't much care if House Kiroff burns to the ground. So your accusation that my testimony is fabricated to aid House Kiroff is nothing but a fable. It's remarkably stupid, really. But I'd expect nothing less of House Danukis."

"Lady Ramya," Molen growled as he rose to his feet. "You're in contempt and I'll have you removed."

"You won't have me removed. I'll leave on my own when I'm done. But first I'll tell you why I just called you stupid," Ramya said. She was on a roll and no Danukis was going to stop her now. "Those things you saw on the screen, they don't care about who you are and what family you come from. They just kill anything they come across. They won't stop when you flash your fancy badge that says Chief of Chairs and they won't stop when you tell them how noble and powerful your family is. You're going to die just like any other person out there on the streets."

Ramya noticed Molen summoning the guards at the door and she knew she had to finish quickly before they dragged her off the stage.

"Right now, you still have a choice--you can fight them before they get too far. But that window won't last long." She paused and looked around the Hall of Narratives, at the people she couldn't see from so far away, some of whom she knew cared. "I know I'm not even an adult, so I don't expect you to heed my advice. But I plead to you, all of you, for the sake of the people you lead, listen to what Admiral Zoho told you, what Captain Milos has been saying, and what my father Lord Paramount Kiroff just recounted. It's the truth, and you'll be sorry if you disregard it."

A commotion grew behind her and Molen Danukis stormed onto the platform, flanked by four armed guards. Lefrasi stepped forward and from the corner of her eye, Ramya saw her father and uncle jump to their feet.

"All members of the Galactic Senate, I appeal to your good sense," Ramya pleaded, ignoring the hubbub behind her. "You can investigate as much as you choose and punish people as much as you want to. But now is not the time. The only thing we need to do right now is fight the nightmare that's coming. Everything else, every other difference we have among us can wait until later. Until we survive the Locustans."

"Take her away," Molen yelled. "She's in contempt of the Galactic Senate. You Kiroffs think you own the senate? I'll show you your place right now."

Ramya turned away from the lectern. "Keep your senate, Molen," she said, calmly and collectedly. She walked past him, stopping briefly to stare into Molen's blazing eyes. "You should be more afraid of the Locustans than I am. Because you know what? We Kiroffs might not own the senate but we sure own a lot. And you know my father just might have the intellect to find a way out of this and save his family. That is not something you can say about yours, can you? So if I were you, I'd make sure there were people fighting to keep the Locustans away. Because once they come past the Fringe, you're as good as dead."

"You'll be penalized," Molen yelled as she walked down the stairs, Lefrasi following. She hardly heard what Molen kept hurling at her. She only saw her father's grim face.

"I'm sorry," she blurted. For the first time in her life, she was prepared for a scathing rebuke. She almost wanted it. "I didn't plan to insult you publicly. But I thought . . . I thought it'd help."

Her father nodded. "A means to an end--I understand."

"You're not offended?"

"I am," he replied without hesitation. "But it's an offense I can . . . I will choose to overlook." He tilted his head toward the giant screen. "They're taking votes now."

They were? Sure enough, numbers were scrolling, fast and furious, on the giant screen.

"And we'll lose," she whispered, stumbling back into her chair.

Her father sank into the chair next to her. "Perhaps not."

Ramya blinked at the screen, only seeing a blur of digits. Her parched throat ached, and her thoughts were a jumbled mess. Ramya cradled her head in her palm and tried to fight back the sting in her eyes. She wanted to cry, but she couldn't. Not in the presence of her father--he wouldn't approve.

Yet, she couldn't stop a tear from trickling out. She couldn't prevent herself from mourning the end of the galaxy. She let them slip, one drop at a time.

Someone yelled. Someone cheered, and one shout quickly grew into a deafening roar. "Yes!" Lefrasi shouted.

Ramya looked up, the world around her a haze. Ramya's heart pounded. Had they won approval? She blinked furiously to clear her sight.

A hand patted her shoulder. "Well done, Lady Ramya." Her father's voice cut through the fog. "You've won your first battle at the Galactic Senate."

18

Things kicked into high gear after the senate approved the call-to-arms. The Galactic Confederacy was a mighty powerful wheel when it moved. And now, finally, it started to move and more importantly, in the right direction.

Overnight, El-Iss turned into a base of sorts for the Confederacy. Trysten Kiroff's factory being located there as well as El-Iss being close to the Fringe made it an ideal choice. Space Command piled personnel and craft on El-Iss. Even more had gone to Zeta. In addition, the Kiroff factories churned out craft every day and a gigantic fleet quickly grew in El-Iss.

Anomaly Point had stayed closed and while much of the effort was focused on the getting forces deployed around Anomaly Point, major work had started cleaning up the planets in the Fringe where the SuperStryker had harvested populations.

As much as Ramya wanted to actively participate in the action, she was pretty much grounded on El-Iss. Her first shackle was the Stryker—it had to be repaired after the damage it had sustained on Bucifer P9. An unbelievably mellow Trysten Kiroff put her in charge of the repairs and upgrades for the craft.

"This is what you always wanted," her father said as he showed her around the factory floor deep underneath the surface of El-Iss a day after they had returned from Xandria. "Yet now that you have the chance, you don't seem happy."

Shifting her feet, Ramya took in a long, deep breath. He was right. On all counts. This was what she had wanted all her life—that her father would put her in charge of something important. Still, now that she was getting some of it, it felt . . . not enough.

She stared at the Stryker on the floor below them. It was unique, impressive, formidable. It was hers to keep and protect. She was, in

Fenny's words, the luckiest girl alive in the iffin universe. Yet . . .

"You want to fight the Locustans?" her father asked, fixing a tight gaze on her face. He didn't seem angry, just fretful. "You've already done that. And this is just the beginning. There's much more coming our way. This, however—" he nodded at the factory floor below them, "—might not happen for a while."

He was right again. The ugly truth stared Ramya in the face. She was being a brat—a selfish, ungrateful brat. This was the chance of a lifetime and did she even thank her father for that? No! She had instead moped, yearned for more. What more, she didn't even know.

Admit the truth, Rami, she told herself.

"I'm sorry, Father," she said, expecting a scornful reply at best. "I-I should've . . . I'm grateful for this chance. I should've said that before. Thank you."

"No need to thank me," he said. "You earned it."

The world suddenly felt too small. Ramya's heart soared, her father's words tinkling in her ears, and a smile stretched her mouth into a silly grin. Perhaps she wasn't as ungrateful as she'd thought.

Ramya diligently supervised the Stryker's repairs after that. It was fun working with the engineers, as well as hearing how pleased Dakrhaeth was with the new suppressor module or the upgrade to his cloaking unit.

On the third day after they'd returned from Xandria, Captain Milos summoned her to his chamber. His quarters were in the lowermost level, close to Ramya's own suite, while all the other members of the crew had been placed at various other levels. Ramya found him with Ross and Rida of the Second Fleet. A large square table in front of them was covered with maps, charts and holographic projections of various places.

"Where are we with all the information Dakrhaeth gave us?" he asked as soon as Ramya entered.

He handed her a cup of his typical blood-red and runny noja. It was good to see him being himself again. The bandage on his head had shrunk considerably and he looked almost normal. His noja was sharp, bitter, and better than ever.

"Not far," Ramya admitted. She told them about the faded star clue and about the Hinterland. Truth was, she was stuck.

"You can't take your eyes off this, Rami. There's more to this, I believe," the captain said. "Most of our resources are focused on fighting the Locustans, so I'm counting on you. You have to keep digging. Ask for help if you need it."

"I have Ahool," Ramya said. Over the past three days, the Mwandan boy had been hard at work alongside her, sifting through maps of the galaxy, plotting trajectories, and making calculations.

"You know who's good with clues and things like that?" Rida said suddenly, smiling at the captain who chuckled wryly right away.

"I know. Zoho."

"Yes, Captain. Zoho's the man." Rida nodded and gave Ramya a telling look. "I think you should run this by him. He has ideas."

"Ideas that got him placed in charge of Zeta?" Ross commented.

Captain Milos frowned. "Ideas get a lot of people in trouble, Ross. The ones who stand by their beliefs despite everything going against them are worth something."

Ramya couldn't decipher the true intent behind the captain's comment, mostly because she had started thinking about how to speak to Admiral Zoho. He had ideas indeed. Strange, almost blasphemous ideas involving the Hand of Darkness. Ideas that had left her curious.

"He must be very busy," Ramya said. "With all the prep going on at Zeta —"

"I'll look into that," the captain said. "I'll get you to talk to him."

Days had passed since then. Troop build-up on El-Iss grew, and dread of an imminent invasion rose to fever pitch across the galaxy. Ramya couldn't stop her growing desire to be out there, along with the soldiers that were combing the Fringe and wiping clean the harvested planets, or going farther out to Zeta. She realized she had gotten used to a breakneck pace, to running around from one crisis to another. This sudden slowdown left her antsy and exhausted her. Yet she had no choice but to wait until the Stryker was completely upgraded.

***

On the fifth day after her return from Xandria, the Stryker's upgrades were complete. As soon as the chief engineer gave her clearance, Ramya took the Stryker out for a spin. She, along with Ahool, spent a while flying the craft over El-Iss. Ramya relished the change in her routine and the freedom. Ahool seemed happy as well and Dakrhaeth was back to his chirpy self again.

Ramya had been practicing some loops, much to the delight of Ahool, when Fenny's sharp voice broke out of the comm. "Rami, are you done showing off? I've got news for you."

"Go on, say it," Ramya said.

"Get your behind back on the ground first," Fenny snapped. "Waiting for you at the gates."

Fenny had to have a reason to call her back, and Ramya didn't argue. She steered the Stryker to a nook near the main entrance that the engineers had fashioned, and within a few minutes she reached the gates.

Ahool gasped and slunk behind Ramya as soon as they spotted Fenny. Ramya couldn't blame Ahool for his reaction. Fenny, after all, was strutting around the entrance with her pet Pterostrich, Vi. Ramya wanted to hide somewhere as well, but it was already too late. Fenny spotted them and strode up, Vi in tow. Although Fenny had fashioned a nice muzzle, as well as a saddle and stirrups to ride the chick, Vi and her yellow gaze scared the heck out of Ramya every time. It didn't help that Vi towered above them and each of her legs was already half as thick as a standard human torso. Even now, Ramya held her breath as Fenny and Vi approached.

"Vi's fine, Rami," Fenny said, scrunching her nose at them. "She won't hurt a fly."

Right! As if Vi had pledged not to. But there was no arguing with Fenny. Ramya decided to dodge the topic altogether.

"What's the news?"

Fenny stopped glaring at Ahool and looked at her. "Well, the *Endeavor's* all fixed, thanks to your father. It's actually even better than it was before. Anyway, we'll be off soon."

"What do you mean by off?"

"Chief Dal and his Mwandan contingent have arrived on Bucifer P9 and the captain wants to meet him there. We'll go on to Zeta, I'm guessing."

"I'll pack up then."

Fenny held up a hand. "Oh no no. You're not coming with us. Neither is your sidekick. You stay and work on Dakrhaeth's memory dump."

A hole opened up inside Ramya. How could they just leave her? She belonged on the *Endeavor*.

"I could work on the puzzle anywhere. Even on the *Endeavor*."

"Well, the captain told me to tell you that you're not coming," Fenny said in a slow deliberate way. "You have to stay here."

"My father got to him, didn't he?"

Fenny shrugged. "I don't know about that. But this is captain's orders." She straightened the stirrups on Vi's saddle and was about to mount the Pterostrich when she stopped suddenly. "I forgot the most important thing. Here you go." She held out a piece of paper. "That's information on getting in touch with Admiral Zoho. The captain said you should do that right away. Also, he promised Zoho you'd investigate some of Zoho's theories. You got that, right? Rami?"

Ramya barely heard anything. She couldn't. Her mind was circling around one thought — the captain was abandoning her.

19

Ramya was in a very foul mood that night. Even as she busily set up the communication channel to Admiral Zoho with Ahool, she was distracted. And annoyed. The *Endeavor* was about to leave for Bucifer and she couldn't understand why the captain wouldn't take her along. She belonged in that ship, with its crew, not in a suite stacked with indulgences.

A sudden rap on her door made Ramya jump and drop the controller box of the makeshift communication pedestal they were setting up in her room.

"Iffin hell," she blurted.

"You go get door, Rami," Ahool offered helpfully. The boy had tiptoed around her since the morning and even though Ramya felt guilty about it, she found it difficult if not impossible to get back to being her usual self.

Muttering slightly under her breath, Ramya threw the door open. There was a flash of white and gold. A shout rang out and a girl threw herself onto Ramya.

"Rami!" she yelled.

"Isbet?"

Giggling like a gushing fountain, Isbet wrapped her arms around Ramya's neck. "I knew I'd see you soon," Isbet said.

Ramya laughed, suddenly realizing she hadn't laughed so loud in a while. It was good seeing her best friend. Better yet, in the joy of meeting with Isbet again, Ramya's grief over parting with the *Endeavor* ebbed considerably.

Isbet threw an accusing glare at Ramya, recalling how she had sneaked out of CAWStrat on Concert Night.

"You lied to me," Isbet said.

"I didn't exactly lie," Ramya tried to explain. "I just didn't tell you everything. I couldn't."

Isbet waved away her explanation. "That's all right. As long as you're safe and sound. I was sick with worry. And no one would tell me what happened. That bitch Leona said your father had you pulled out of CAWStrat. I didn't believe that for a second."

Ramya told Isbet about everything that had happened since leaving CAWStrat and soon Isbet was telling her how she came to El-Iss. "The GSO offered me an apprenticeship, Rami. Can you imagine that?"

Ramya was happy for her friend. She knew this was a dream come true for Isbet.

"And guess what? Rownack is in my unit too."

Seeing Isbet's beaming face, Ramya chuckled. Rownack was a senior at CAWStrat and Isbet had an immense crush on him.

"We have to speak to Admiral Zoho about something," Ramya said. "But you can stay. You might even enjoy the conversation."

Isbet flipped her hands. "Why not? I don't have much to do tonight."

"So you really made it into the GSO, huh?" Ramya said. "Can hardly believe it, but I'm so proud of you, Isbet."

Isbet laughed. "I couldn't believe it myself. The first ones the GSO asked for were Rownack and me. That idiot Armand was so mad."

Ramya chuckled some more. Both Rownack and Isbet were top fliers at CAWStrat, both winners of the coveted Flight Honor badge of their respective years. It was expected that the GSO would invite them first. How could Armand Danukis even hope to be pampered the same way? All he was good at was being obnoxious.

"Which unit are you in?" Ramya asked. She knew some of the GSO squadrons stationed at El-Iss quite well.

"Unit 31. Guess what? Our lieutenant knows you. His name's Gael, Gael Arlington," Isbet said casually. Her brows bunched when she saw Ramya's face tighten. "Something wrong with him?"

"Everything," Ramya muttered as she pulled a couple of chairs close to the communication pedestal. She was sure it was no coincidence that Isbet had been placed under Gael's command. But seeing Isbet's anxious stare, she cut back on her outburst. "He's fine."

"Rami, we ready," Ahool said, pointing at the flashing green light at the base of the pedestal that signified a cleared channel to Zoho.

"Good, let's go."

Admiral Zoho's grim face soon appeared above the pedestal, a projection from distant Zeta.

"Greetings, Admiral," Ramya started, quickly introducing Ahool and Isbet.

The admiral's face turned grimmer by the time she finished speaking. "You're very young," he pronounced a short pause later.

Ramya was sure he didn't mean that as a compliment. She pushed down the retort that bubbled up in her throat and instead flashed a smile and forced a cheery reply. "We're hard workers too, Admiral. And we're good at what we do."

"I was expecting only you and Ahool Petta," Zoho said, his sharp gaze landing on Isbet who was sitting behind them. "Why is a third person here?"

Ramya's breath hitched in her throat. She hadn't thought inviting Isbet would be such a big deal. They were working for the same cause. Now it seemed like a mistake.

"Isbet's my friend, a GSO apprentice," she said. "We just met again after a long time, so I invited her to join us."

"Does this look like a picnic to you?" the Admiral snapped. He shook his head and looked away, sighing.

Isbet jumped to her feet behind them. "I'll leave. Please excuse me," she said.

Zoho waved impatiently. "No, sit." A frown was etched deep on his forehead when he looked back at them again. "I hope you take this seriously because otherwise you're not just wasting my time, you're squandering the galaxy's chance of survival."

Ramya stiffened a little. His words came from years of being laughed at, she understood that, but to assume that they were joking about the matter was rude.

"Captain Milos is not someone who takes the galaxy's well-being lightly, Admiral," she shot back, even though she knew her voice lacked fire. "If he thinks we're capable enough to look into this, I'd say there's weight to it. And we may be young, but we've been through enough and proven ourselves enough."

Zoho's eyes narrowed. "Big words," he said. "I'm no fan of big words and fancy promises. They're always the tools of empty people." He pursed his lips and gave a firm shake of his head. "This is wasting my time. I'll tell Milos to find someone with more experience."

Ramya shot a quick glance at Ahool. The Mwandan's face had paled and his eyes had lost their glitter. Ramya's heart twitched. The boy had worked so hard on this and the admiral's dismissive stance wasn't fair.

"Admiral, I don't know if you've heard of me but—"

"I know who you are, Lady Ramya," Zoho interrupted. "Your parentage is half the reason I doubt your suitability in this venture. Big names like yours come with heads full of preconceived notions and arrogance, things that are bound to fail against the Hand of Darkness. On top of that, you're just . . . a child."

Ramya wrapped her arms around her torso, her eyes fixed on Zoho's face. "A child who has done plenty."

Zoho shook his head. "I've heard of your . . . accomplishments. I wonder, though . . . how much of it did you accomplish because Milos or your father or someone more knowledgeable was helping you? What do you think?"

Ramya didn't know what to tell him. His words stung, like a backhanded slap across the face. It was as if the floor that she had so painstakingly built was yanked out from under her feet. He wasn't entirely wrong: anytime she won a challenge, someone older and wiser had always been by her side. The one time she had led, the time she ambushed Kanaa, had been a massive failure.

Perhaps seeing her dimmed eyes, Zoho's face softened a bit. "I'm sure you're just as plucky as Milos says you are. But this is by no means an easy venture."

"If you'd let us try," Ramya said. Her voice came out more subdued than she wanted it to be, her faith in herself seeping out like water out of a closed fist. "There's not much to lose by trying, is there?"

"We'd lose valuable time. Besides, I don't want to be responsible for sending you to your deaths."

"Why would we die?"

Zoho closed his eyes and let out a small sigh. "I looked into the summary Milos sent me. It seems the things the Locustan AI told you are the same things the Hand of Darkness allude to in their treatise," Zoho continued in a gruff voice. "But the Hand of Darkness is not something you trifle with. They are a vicious clan of fanatics, and that's putting it mildly."

"You want us to speak with the Hand of Darkness, Admiral?"

"How else will you know what's in the Treatise of Ed? Those scrolls aren't in some library. I've only pieced together bits and pieces of hearsay."

"Then we go ask Hand of Darkness," Ahool said spiritedly.

"If you can find them. They aren't easy to find. Besides, you being Trysten Kiroff's daughter doesn't help. If you make a spectacle of this . . ."

"I won't. Give us a few days, Admiral," Ramya said. "Perhaps we can find a way to locate them. If we can't make any headway, I'll hand this mission over to Captain Milos myself."

Perhaps it was her pleading voice. Or perhaps Zoho thought a few days would wear them out anyway. His gaze softened a little.

"All right. So here's what I think. This Hinterland your AI speaks of is the same as the Core mentioned in the Hand's seventh treatise on the ancients, or the Unosi, as the Hand likes to call those who came before us," Zoho said. "They say the Unosi fought off the darkness with a jewel that now lies in the core."

"A jewel?" Ramya asked incredulously.

"I think it's a metaphor for a weapon," Zoho said. "Something the ancients used to drive the Locustans away."

"But if it's a weapon to drive the Locustans away, why are the Locustans so eager to find it?" Ramya wondered aloud. Dakrhaeth and his squadron had traveled far into Sector 22 looking for the Hinterland. It didn't make sense they'd hand the galaxy the tools to their own destruction.

"Perhaps they want to destroy it for good," Zoho said. "To ensure there's no known way to stop them anymore."

"We *have* to find it before they do," Ramya muttered distractedly. Remembering their recent progress, she turned toward Ahool. "Ahool, tell the admiral about your calculations."

"Yes. I deduce possible locations of Hinterland. Dying star Dakrhaeth says about might be a star that went supernova or going to be soon. There is one in line of sight from Sector 22."

"Why Sector 22?" Zoho asked.

"We have theory," Ahool chirped, excitement making his sentences far more disjointed than usual. "Because that's where Dakrhaeth and friends crashed during last invasion. They must be going to Hinterland that time. So Hinterland must be in Sector 22."

"Hmm. That's interesting," Zoho said. "But Sector 22 is a large place. We can't look through every planet."

"Well, the Hand might help narrow it down," Ramya replied.

"Yes, they might. If you manage to find them. And they aren't hospitable to intruders. So, the chance of talking to them is — "

"Do you know where we find the Hand?" Ahool asked.

"They've always stayed in the Fringe to avoid the Confederacy's crackdowns on cults," Zoho said. "Some say they don't stay on one planet for too long. But Novostra is a favorite of the clan."

Ahool turned expectantly at Ramya. "So we go to Novostra then."

"Whatever you do, please don't make a situation out of this. The stars know I have plenty on my hands already," Zoho said before his projection dissolved.

A situation was the last thing Ramya wanted. She had to get the captain's approval on this before he left for Bucifer P9. No one else would let her go there — it was one of the wildest places in the Fringe — and Ramya wasn't sure she wanted to go there either.

20

Captain Milos grunted when Ramya brought up Novostra. While he kept worriedly tapping his chin, Ross and Fenny, both of whom the captain had called to his room when Ramya came to update him, exchanged a quick, knowing glance.

"You can't go there alone," the captain said finally.

"Ahool's coming," Ramya informed him, and Fenny scoffed immediately.

The captain shook his head. "Ahool's just a kid. I'll get some of Rida's people to go along."

Ramya struggled to not let her frown show. Rida was surely capable, but she had never been too friendly. All of Admiral Kanaa's troops were icy to her for that matter, and it didn't take much to see why. She had not only destroyed an entire Drednot and killed their compatriots at Totori, she had even had the gall to hold their leader hostage.

"It's an iffin crap hole, Captain," Fenny declared. "And not a small place either. These crazy people could be anywhere on Novostra. How will Rami even know where to look?"

"Admiral Zoho said he has some clues," Ramya offered, but Fenny rewarded her with an eye roll.

"Captain, I can go with her," Ross said. While the captain raised a curious eyebrow, Ross continued. "Bucifer is just a simple recon mission. I don't think I'm critically needed there. Lefrasi and his people are fine. Novostra, on the other hand —"

"I'll come too," Fenny said.

The way Ross and Fenny rallied around her lightened Ramya's heart. The three of them had been through many iffy situations together and if they were with her, Ramya knew she had a chance to get through this safely. Still, a thought niggled. Once again, she was relying on friends to solve the problem, just like Zoho had pointed out. She'd only get so much credit for the success of this mission. Yet she couldn't bring herself to protest Ross and Fenny's offer.

The captain didn't seem to appreciate the situation much. His brows crinkled. He opened his mouth as if to say something, and then shut it abruptly. Ramya couldn't tell if he didn't like Ross and Fenny jumping in the way they did or if it was something else.

"Not Fenny. I'll need you," he said in a gruff voice. "But you can go, Ross. You get one shot to find the Hand. If not, we go back to what we have."

"Yes, Captain," Ramya said.

Ross walked over to the table with stacks of maps and flipped a few over. "Novostra was flagged for Locustan infiltration, wasn't it, Captain?" he asked, flipping through more of the stack.

"Yes, but I think it was just cleared. Check with Rida."

Ramya sat up a little. This she hadn't considered. Novostra was in the Fringe, relatively close to Bucifer P9. Obviously, it was flagged as one of the potential planets the SuperStryker had harvested.

She wondered if the Locustans had infested Novostra as badly as they did Bucifer P9, her hopes sinking like a stone to the bottom of her gut. What if, like the Mwandans on Bucifer P9, no one had survived on Novostra?

***

Novostra was a water world. A green cloak of ocean covered it; islands dotted it sparsely in the south and more densely toward the north. Rida's Wentworth-Busa was headed to a medium-sized island. Shaped like the blade of a scythe, this island called Motolo was at the tip of the long archipelago near Novostra's equator.

According to Zoho, the Hand of Darkness considered Motolo sacred and always maintained a presence on it. "You might even find one of their high priests there," Zoho had said.

Ramya stared worriedly at the island drawing rapidly closer. A green canopy of trees covered the land except for the western tip where a large clearing tapered into a road through the trees. It ended near a structure the shape of an upturned bowl at the center of the scythe, which Zoho said was the temple of the dark god, Bu'Dai, whom the cult worshipped. The plan was to get near that temple, hoping to come across members of the Hand of Darkness or preferably a priest who scribed and protected sacred treatises.

Ahool was seated across from them and as far as Ramya could tell, Rida was tutoring Ahool on combat techniques. Rida's core unit of four was clustered further to the front. Only Ross sat next to Ramya and had been quiet all along. At the sight of the islands below them, he sat up. "It looks too beautiful to be home of a cult," he commented.

"Yes," Ramya said.

She must've sounded worried because Ross frowned at her. "You've been to worse places," he said. "There's nothing to worry about here."

A wry chuckle escaped Ramya's throat. "Really? The cult is famous for roasting trespassers alive. And we're entering their territory without permission, which puts us in a very bad place."

Ross laughed a little. "We keep on intruding into people's sacred sites. No wonder they don't like us much." He paused a bit and looked at the sparkling ocean below. "But we're not in as bad a situation as we were on Morris II. At least now we're well armed with a lot of back-up."

Ramya looked askance at Rida's troops. They were indeed a bracing sight. Dressed from head to toe in battle gear, they looked formidable. Yet, even though looking at them made Ramya sigh with relief, it also saddened her a little. Even if she were to complete this mission to perfection, people like Zoho would once again wave her contribution off.

Her sober face didn't go unnoticed. "What's going on?" Ross asked.

The first thing Ramya wished was that Fenny could be asking that question. Ross, from the first day she had stepped into the *Endeavor*, had been cold to her, to the point of accusing her of spying. Since their adventures on Morris II, he had warmed considerably, but memories of his unkindness still lingered.

"You don't have to tell me," Ross said, probably noticing her hardening face. "But I'm here if you need to."

What the hell! She did want to talk about it with someone.

"Zoho doesn't think much of me," she blurted. "He thinks I got out of sticky situations because of people around me. If others didn't help, I didn't stand a chance."

Ross raised an eyebrow at her. "Really? Well, he hasn't seen you in action. Besides, we're not superheroes with miraculous powers who can blast our enemies away with a wave of our hands. We're just people. We need other people with us to fight a war. That doesn't make us weak. When we trust people who are better at something than us, it makes us smart."

She knew he had a point. But it was hard to keep seeing it through the blur of hurt. "The captain didn't like you and Fenny volunteering," Ramya said. That thought also niggled her constantly. "I think he wanted me to do this on my own."

"Perhaps. But he was fine with it in the end," Ross said. He leaned over to pat her hand. "Don't worry about it."

Not worrying was difficult. Trying to prove herself had seeped into Ramya's bones since childhood and it stung when anyone doubted her. If such doubts came from someone like Captain Milos who had trusted her completely so far, it hurt even more. To be honest, it rattled her to the core.

"Ten minutes to ground," a hollow mechanical voice sounded.

Ramya drew a sharp breath. She instinctively patted her armor and weapons and looked up at Ross. She hesitated for a second, but then her thoughts streamed out. "You know what's worse? That I was relieved when you and Fenny offered to come. When I heard you were all leaving for Bucifer, I was scared." She stopped a bit and drummed her armrest. "It's almost . . . what Zoho said might actually be true. Maybe I'm nothing without —"

"All right, listen," Ross cut her off and placing an arm on her shoulder, nudged her to face him. "First of all, we're a team. It's perfectly normal if you feel safer with us around. I do too. I feel good when I'm around people I know and trust."

"That's nice of you to say," Ramya replied. "I'm probably making a mountain out of a pinch of dirt. I know . . . I have a sack-load of self-doubt on my shoulders. It's not easy to shake off."

Ross stared at her for a bit, emotions coursing over his face. It seemed he was debating whether or not to say something. In the end, he started abruptly. "When I first saw you, I didn't think you'd amount to anything. But Sosa needed a hand so I thought, all right, we'll keep her around. Then you stayed and worked and . . . earned your keep. You turned into such a presence that . . ." His words trailed off and he looked away for a bit before looking back into her eyes. "That for a while, I was even jealous. I was angry at you when I found out about your family but then, once again, you won. You earned my trust. You earned my respect."

Ramya stared at his intent face, devouring every word he said. Each one of them helped.

"What you did wasn't easy. I'm sure I never made things easy for you. But look at you now. I could trust you with my life."

Ramya couldn't stop the smile from breaking out.

"No, seriously, Rami," Ross said. "You shouldn't, not even for a second, think of yourself as any less than a hero. And right now, you *need* to be thinking like a hero. Can you?"

Ahool crashed into the seat in front of them just as Ramya nodded. "All set?" he asked, and then raised a curious brow at Ramya and Ross. "You excited?"

"Excited?" Ross frowned.

Ahool shrugged. "You have big adventure coming." In the next second, he pouted. "Rida asked me to stay with pilot. I miss all action. Not fair."

While Ross started comforting Ahool, Ramya let out a long deep sigh of relief. Ross had somehow turned her insides back into steel and her heart was light as a feather. Zoho and his presumptions could go to hell. All that mattered was getting this mission completed right.

21

Rida, dressed in tactical combat gear, rounded up her troops at the landing site. She seemed far more at ease leading on the ground than she had been during the air offensive on Bucifer P9.

"All right, people," Rida said in a snappy voice. "We want to wrap this up fast and quiet. Keep the body count low. Clear?" She looked at everyone in turn, then nodded at two men who stood to one side. "Ben and Somi, you go prowl. Stay within three hundred," she barked.

"We'll be around, Lieutenant," one of the men replied and the other simply nodded. Picking up their rifles, they set off along the path into the forest.

Rida turned to a hulking Norgoran next. "Miso, you're on point." As soon as Miso nodded, Rida snapped toward a thin-lipped woman. "Lei, you take the rear. I'll be in the middle with our friends," Rida declared, looking pointedly at Ramya and Ross, her hawkish gaze lingering on Ramya the longest. "Lady Ramya, I know you're driving the mission, but you get to talk only after we've secured the site. Both of you, leave the engagement to us. I don't need any reckless gun waving jeopardize the operation. Got it?"

Ross nodded. Although Ramya wanted to tell Rida that none of them did much in the way of reckless gun waving, she held her tongue. Rida was good at this, and their best option was to trust her.

"Let's go," Rida ordered. Miso and Lei swiftly fell into position and they all started moving into the forest.

Ramya trotted to up Rida as they walked. "You swept Novostra for Locustan presence? Did you find any?"

Rida tilted her head. "We didn't. The GSO did."

Rida's sharp clarification made Ramya smirk a little. Space Fleet and GSO were always clear about the lines that demarcated their territories, as well as their responsibilities. "So they didn't find Locustans here then?"

"I don't know what they found. All I know is Novostra was cleared."

"They couldn't have checked all the islands," Ramya whispered. Novostra had thousands of islands scattered all over. It would take days to scan through each one of them.

"Might've sampled some," Rida said. "Novostra is a low priority planet. No settlements except that awful cult. Who cares if some cultists live or die?"

Ramya bit the inside of her cheek to stop a retort from coming out. What Rida said probably made sense from a tactical point of view, but right now, those cultists mattered. They mattered a whole lot.

"I hope they had this island in their sample," Ramya said. "Wouldn't want to bump into those pests."

"Quiet," Rida hissed and held up her fist. Then she dropped to one knee behind a large boulder. Miso and Lei took cover, as did Ross. Ramya ducked behind the trunk of the tree nearest to Rida's boulder.

"What happened?" Ramya whispered.

"Somi," Rida nodded at the distance. Following her gaze, Ramya spotted Somi's outline, atop a large mound that overlooked the area. He was flashing a bright red light in their direction. "He must've seen something."

Ramya looked around. The forest was quiet, eerily quiet. She saw nothing, no movement at all.

"Hostiles at twelve," Miso shouted at the same instant as Ramya spotted them. She had seen them before, enormous sinewy bodies with powerful shimmery wings. Two Locustans streaked toward them, tearing through the foliage as they careened closer.

"Miso, engage to kill," Rida shouted before raising her own rifle.

Two sharp cracks sounded. There was a thud, then another. Ramya risked a glance around the tree trunk and then slipped out of her hiding place when she saw everyone else coming out.

Ramya held her breath as she took in the sight before her. She had seen them before, but not up close like this. They were enormous, at least ten feet in length, and their limbs were long and muscular. The one closest to them had a bronzed coloring, the other a pale green. Rida and Miso's shots had blown holes through their chests. Their faces—long and wiry like a horse's—twisted grotesquely in the throes of death. They lay sprawled across the forest floor surrounded by a halo of pale-brown blood and a whitish fluid. Even dead or dying, they were scary.

"Fall back," Rida hissed and everyone darted back to their cover. She tapped the communicator on her ear. "Locustans around. Get the WB airborne. Keep it above a thousand."

Rida was instructing the Wentworth-Busa's pilot, Ramya figured. Her heart pounded and her fingers clutched the cannon tighter. There were two issues with Locustans being here. First, they must've harvested any members of the Hand on this island, so the mission was practically useless. The bigger issue was survival. They had not prepared to face Locustans. They had fought off two, and they could probably take on some more, but what if there were a hundred?

"Movement up ahead," Rida said.

Ben's voice crackled over Rida's comm. "One more at three o'clock. I have it in sight."

"Take it down."

Another sharp crack sounded somewhere to their right followed by another thud and crash of branches.

"All clear, let's move," Rida said a second or two later.

"You think it's safe to keep going?" Ramya asked Rida as they marched up. "What if there are more? These pests keep showing up out of nowhere."

Rida's mouth twisted into a smirk. "Scared?"

"Shouldn't I be?" Ramya shot back. "These here are Locustans. And we didn't prep for them. Don't know about you but I'd like to live. So I'm saying, we should probably reassess the situation."

"She has a point, Lieutenant Rida." Ross wasted no time in backing her up.

"You want to abandon your mission, Lady Ramya?" Rida asked and Ramya caught a whiff of scorn in her voice.

"Of course I don't," she replied snappishly. She didn't want to come across as a weakling, but she didn't believe in leading people against insurmountable odds either. It'd be a different thing if she were on her own. "But I'm thinking of our odds. If the Locustans have been here, there might not be any more of the cult left for us to talk to. Is it worth risking all your people's lives for nothing?"

"Tell me, should we fall back then?" Rida asked. It almost felt like Rida was testing her.

Ramya pondered a second, considering deferring the decision to Rida. But that, she figured, would make her look like a pushover. "Not yet," she said in a steady voice. "Let's check out the temple. Then we get the hell out of here."

Rida listened to her with an arched brow. "Sounds good to me," she said when Ramya had finished. "To the temple it is."

They had barely taken twenty steps forward when Ramya caught the flash of red on one of the trees ahead. Rida held up a fist.

"Something's in the undergrowth, Lieutenant," Somi's sharp whisper floated out of Rida's comm. "Movement's slower than the last."

"You have eyes on them?"

"No. I only see a movement in the bushes."

Rida inhaled sharply before giving a reluctant nod. "Take them out," she said.

"No, wait," Ramya blurted to Rida's annoyed glare. "You can't kill them without knowing who they are."

"We do not have the luxury of morality, Lady Ramya," Rida said. "We rarely do in combat situations, even less so when we're on ground fighting Locustans."

"But . . . the movement's different. These may not be Locustans. What if they are locals who've been hiding from the Locustans?"

"You want to take a chance? Risk the lives of all these people?"

Ramya considered Rida's question. This could be a huge mistake. They could very well be a different kind of Locustan, and her judgment could mean death for everyone. But if she wanted to stand up to the likes of Zoho, she had to take chances.

"Yes, I do," Ramya said, vaguely aware that Ross came to stand behind her, clearly indicating his support of her decision.

Rida titled her head a little. "All right. We'll hold fire until we've identified the source of movement."

It happened even before they took another step. A wave rippled through the foliage in a semicircle, swaying the greenery and sweeping toward them in a mad rush. Rifles and cannons swung up just as quickly.

"Hold your fire," Rida shouted. The cannon in Ramya's hand trembled slightly. She kept it pointed at the parting foliage ahead, her finger poised at the trigger. Unless she saw for sure it wasn't a Locustan on the other side, she wasn't taking any chances.

Forms tumbled out from behind the bushes, dark cowls covering their faces, weapons — strange crossbow-mounted units that Ramya had never heard of or seen before — glinted menacingly in their steady arms.

22

A second of silence stretched into two and then more. Ramya held her breath, all her attention on her fingertip resting on the trigger. Her mind raced. Seven of them against the five in cowls . . . if it came to an engagement, they could possibly win. Possibly! She didn't dare take her eyes off her target, not even to look sidelong at Rida or Ross to gauge what they were thinking.

They seemed to stand there forever before a voice, as unfriendly as the weapons pointed at Ramya and the group, hissed, "Who in the name of the sacred Bu'Dai are you?"

Rida replied in a heartbeat. "Lieutenant Rida, Second Fleet. Who are you?"

"We live here," came the reply. Ramya tried to understand which of the five was speaking but couldn't. It was as if the voice was coming through all of them. It had to be some kind of an acoustic effect, she deduced. Or it was simply her nerves. "What business do *you* have here on Novostra?"

Rida gave a slight nod at Ramya.

"We're looking for someone who knows about the Treatise of Ed," Ramya said. She felt a dip around her, as if the air in the area had been sucked up suddenly.

"We're battling murderous aliens, don't have time for fancy books," the voice replied.

"If it helps any, we killed a few of those for you," Rida said.

"How many?"

"Two."

The air around them loosened abruptly. "Are you sure you killed them?"

"You can check out the bodies if you like," Rida said. She tilted her head backward. "They're back there."

One of the cowled figures turned toward the one in the middle. "That leaves three more, Bumassar," he said.

"Bad enough," Bumassar replied. "We have to exterminate them before they take more of us." Ramya had no doubt he was the one who had spoken to them first. She also figured Bumassar was the leader of these locals.

"We'll help you take them down," Rida offered. "If three of them were headed this way, then the others can't be far away."

"We can take care of them ourselves," Bumassar said. "You should leave. We do better without scum from Space Fleet."

Rida's jaw tightened, but she relaxed in the next second. "We'll get out as soon as we've taken the last Locustan out. That's our job. The GSO came through here, but they must've missed a few spots."

Bumassar scoffed. "Few spots? Yes, they sure did. Like I said, we don't depend on useless showboats Space Command sends. We know better than to wait for your kind. Now go back to where you came from, woman, and don't make us fight you."

They raised their weapons a little, and held them tighter still, an act that was not lost on Rida. She tapped her communicator and barked orders. "Ben, Somi! Fall back. We're leaving."

"Got it," Ben replied.

Rida took a step backward, still facing Bumassar and his group, her weapon still steady on them. Miso followed, as did Ross. Other than Lei, who was assigned to guard the rear, Ramya was the last to back away. She didn't want to leave, but Bumassar didn't sound like someone she could reason with. Her steps were sluggish, unwilling. Captain Milos had said they had one shot at this, and that shot was slipping through her fingers. And there was nothing she could do to stop it.

Ramya saw the flash of red just as she was turning her back on Bumassar and his people. It was coming from the right, from among the trees where Ben had been last.

"Rida," she called. At the same instant, Rida's comm blinked and

Somi's voice streamed in. "Hostiles approaching."

"Take cover," Rida barked. "Miso, behind that boulder. Lei, you take those roots. Ross, Ramya, back there."

Rida fell back on one knee behind a broken tree trunk as Ross and Ramya ducked behind a sizeable boulder. Bumassar and his group scattered quickly, reinforcing the semi-circular formation Rida had put in place.

"Contact," Somi whispered. "I see two bugs heading your way."

"All right," Rida whispered back. "Miso, you and I will take the first. Lei, you take the second. Somi and Ben, light them up as you get them."

They waited, seconds ticking past at an agonizingly slow pace. Ramya risked a few glances from behind her boulder, mostly to look at Rida. She spotted two of Bumassar's people to Rida's left, their weapons raised.

Then the world exploded around them. A long, wiry form leaped through the trees and Rida's rifle roared. Ross's cannon thundered next to Ramya and the slug-riddled body of the Locustan flew through the air, landing against the trunk of a tree.

More cracks sounded but before Ramya could see what Rida was firing at, a muffled cry reached her ears. She looked around, realizing immediately that two people who had taken cover to Rida's left were nowhere to be seen.

"Ross, this way," she shouted, darting out from behind the boulder and sprinting past Rida's position.

"What the hell?" Rida shouted, but Ramya didn't stop. Those people were in trouble, she knew it.

Two more steps and she saw it. A Locustan was towering over the duo from Bumassar's group. It held one of them — a young girl who couldn't be older than fourteen or fifteen — on the ground, its clawed feet pressing on her chest. The other, a lanky man, it held in its arms, claws digging into his neck, its mouth open as if to bite the man's head off.

Ramya swung her cannon up, but she was too slow. The Locustan's powerful jaws closed over the man's head, crushing it as if it were made out of clay. Blood flew in all directions, and the girl on the ground screamed. Ross ran up to her, and the Locustan slowly turned its head toward them. For a second, they stood staring at each other. Then it spun around and, baring its blood-drenched fangs at them, it charged. A roar ripped out of Ramya's guts and she pressed the trigger. She didn't budge. She kept screaming and shooting, vaguely aware of Ross firing next to her.

It fell, gaping holes in its chest spewing the brownish blood and white stuff.

"It's dead," Ross whispered.

Ramya lowered her cannon slowly, hesitantly, unable to believe the monstrosity was truly dead.

Rida came up from behind them, cradling her smoking rifle. "You two all right?"

"We're fine," Ross said. He tilted his head at the headless torso behind them. "It got one of Bumassar's, though."

Rida shook her head and sighed. "These things are straight out of hell." She shook her head again. "Anyway, time to leave. Really leave." She turned around and shouted. "Pack up, people. Let's get going. Ben and Somi, back on the ground."

They marched out of the forest in a tight group. Ramya walked in a daze, feeling nothing but the cold, hard cannon in her arms. The scene of the Locustan chomping through that man's head played continuously in her mind. She still wished there was a way to get across to Bumassar, yet she wasn't unhappy to get out of the forest.

"Benj," Rida called the pilot of the WB as they approached the edge of the forest. "You here yet? W-what?" Rida exclaimed suddenly. She held up a fist up and stepped away from the group. The way the woman's face clouded as she spoke with the pilot, Ramya could tell something was terribly wrong even though she couldn't hear the conversation.

Ramya turned toward Ross. He was watching Rida also, his face tight and drawn. Their eyes met and Ramya knew he was thinking the same thing. She was thinking the worst—the Locustans had to have attacked again.

"The iffin Locustans are back," Rida confirmed Ramya's worst fears in the next second with a dour shake of her head. "More of them this time."

"Is Zeta still . . . standing?" Ramya had to struggle hard to get that question out.

Rida nodded, but not with much conviction. "Still is, but at this rate . . ."

The lieutenant didn't finish her sentence but she didn't have to. Ramya understood. If the Locustans kept coming at this rate, Zeta couldn't survive long. Hell, the galaxy couldn't survive long.

"We have to get out of here," Rida said in a rushed voice. "They'll need reinforcements. We simply wasted time here. Let's go."

They set off again, their steps even faster this time. Ramya's heart thudded at a frantic pace. The Locustan threat was getting larger by the moment and she had failed at what was probably the galaxy's only chance of vanquishing the invaders. If the Locustans kept on coming, there was no chance in hell they could defeat them. The last time they had survived simply because the wormhole closed and shut off access to the incoming Locustans, not because the galaxy's forces had overpowered them. That was sheer luck. Now, once again, all they could do was pray for luck. And that was as stupid as praying for a miracle. Yet there wasn't anything else—

"Hey! Wait!" The shout rang out when they had almost reached the landing spot near the shore. Bumassar—his cowl off, revealing a gray-haired, bearded, and scowling man—strode up, behind him a girl. Ramya recognized the girl as the one whom she and Ross had narrowly saved from the last Locustan. "You wanted to find out about the Treatise of Ed?" Bumassar said, panting.

"Yes, we do," Ramya blurted, her mind clearing in an instant.

"Why do you care all of a sudden?" Rida's voice was far more caustic and skeptical. "You didn't want anything to do with the scum Space Command sends, remember?"

Bumassar flipped his palms and shrugged. "That was then. This is now. You still disgust me. However, I shall take you to the keeper of scrolls. You coming?"

Rida let out a wry chuckle and looked at Ramya. "Your call. I don't trust this guy."

Ramya didn't need to think. "We don't have too many choices, do we?"

She studied Bumassar's face. Even though the man was more than offensive, and purposely so, she was going to take his offer. There was no place for pride or fear when life hung in the balance. Ramya stepped forward. "Show us the way," she said without hesitation.

23

A woman, her hair like a halo of cloud around her heavy-featured face, threw a fiery glare at Bumassar. They were in an underground chamber beneath the upturned bowl temple of Bu'Dai, a dark place steeped in the thick smell of incense. Ramya and the group were clustered on one side flanked by Bumassar's deputies while Bumassar spoke with the woman.

"We do not share the scrolls with the uninitiated," the woman hissed at Bumassar. "Certainly not with spies Space Command sends sniffing. You of all persons should know that, Teffera Bumassar."

"But Teffera Aga, they saved Miraya's life," Bumassar said. His voice was low, but Ramya picked most of it up. The woman's name was Aga, she deduced, and the girl she and Ross had got out of the Locustan's claws was Miraya. The way Aga's mouth pursed at the mention of Miraya and the way Bumassar had agreed to help them made Ramya think that the girl, Miraya, was important to these people. Just how, she couldn't figure.

"What does Teffera mean?" she whispered to Ross. He, Ramya knew, was a veritable encyclopedia of contemporary galactic history.

Ross leaned toward her and whispered back. "It's a high position among the Hand of Darkness. I'm not sure how high exactly, but—"

"This is sacrilege," Aga roared, her angry voice echoing through the chamber. "Bu'Dai would never forgive us."

"This is . . . Miraya's . . ." This time Ramya couldn't hear half of what Bumassar said, but his words made Aga's jaw tighten even more.

Ramya shifted her feet, trying desperately to find a comfortable position. They had had to leave their weapons outside in deference to the temple and Ramya felt naked without them. The chamber was cold and damp, and the floor seemed to suck the spirit out of her even through her thick-soled boots. Hope was ebbing quickly. Even though they had come this far, getting to the scrolls didn't seem like a sure shot.

Aga crossed her arms and shook her head. "I cannot commit this sin. Miraya's wish or not, I shall not share our scrolls with infidels. I have sacred oaths to keep, Teffera Bumassar."

Bumassar crossed his arms and bowed. "Teffera Aga, will you let them speak just once?"

"It is a sin that the impure have stepped inside this temple of Bu'Dai, a sin that will take a toll on all of us."

"But this is Miraya's request," Bumassar repeated.

Lips pursed tighter, Aga took a long breath. "I'll let their leader speak. Just once."

"Lieutenant Rida," Bumassar called hastily.

Rida took a step forward. "My respects, Teffera Aga," she started with a quick bow. "We're not here to spy. We're here because of those Locustans that killed your people. More of them are coming. If we can't stop them, they'll take over the galaxy. They'll kill us all." She paused and drew a breath. "There is something in your scrolls, the mention of an ancient weapon I believe, that might help us fight back. That's why we're here. We wouldn't intrude otherwise."

"Weapon?" Aga's eyebrows wrinkled and from under them, her deep-set eyes flashed. Aga stomped to the side of the room and pulled out a large dao from a sideboard. "You think our sacred scrolls discuss weapons? What sort of devious entrapment is this?"

Rida shot a quick glance at Ramya. Before Ramya could open her mouth, Aga raised her arms, the dao flashing menacingly in her hand. "Not one word more. You have desecrated this temple enough. Leave now, or I'll have you dead." Her voice had fallen to quiet depths but the chill in it made Ramya shudder. This woman would no doubt slit their throats without blinking if it came to that.

Rida fell back a step. "Let's get out of here," she whispered. They didn't have to decide for themselves. The guards closed in immediately and the group, herded and rushed, marched out of the temple.

"We came so close," Ramya whispered, mostly to herself. Ross picked up her words and grimaced.

"These people can't be reasoned with," he said. "That woman seems a little off to me. We should be happy just getting out of here alive."

"What's the point, Ross?" Ramya replied morosely. "We're all gonna die in a few months anyway."

Ross didn't say a word but he didn't have to. His downcast, pensive face and the way his gaze fixed on the ground said it all. Ramya's heart sank to the pit of her stomach the moment she stepped out of the temple. A bunch of people, a mob of sorts, stood in an angry huddle. Some of them started shouting as soon as they sighted the group, and fists went up in the air.

"Sacrilege," someone shouted. "Kill them!"

"Burn them all," another voice said.

Ross threw a quick look at Ramya, his face pale and drawn.

"Keep going," said one of the guards. "Keep close."

"Our weapons," Rida hissed. "We need them back."

"You'll get them back when you're away from the temple grounds. Keep walking now," the guard snapped back.

Weaponless and the target of wrathful glares from the crowd whose yells grew steadily louder, Ramya trudged forward with short, bumbling steps. Ross was right in a way, she realized. Even if death from the Locustans was staring everyone in the face, the thought of being lynched by a mob right now was scary as hell. She inched closer to Ross, even though she knew he was just as helpless as she was.

The mob streaked toward them as soon as they stepped out of the temple grounds.

"Keep close," the guards shouted.

"Kill, kill the infidels!"

Ramya held her breath as they swarmed around. Hands flew in.

Someone clawed at her arm. Ramya had barely slapped it away when another hand tried to grab her hair. Ross pushed the hand away and pulled Ramya closer.

"Keep away," another guard shouted, fighting off the crowd.

Ramya couldn't clearly tell what happened in the second that followed. A stick crashed into her back. A sharp pain shot up her arm, making her yelp. Ross grunted and fell to the ground.

As soon as Ross crumpled, a couple of men jumped on him. One grabbed his legs and pulled. Ross tried to fight the men, but they seemed stronger. Fists flew in, pummeling Ross.

It took Ramya a moment to understand what they were trying to do — drag Ross away from the group. She yelled and threw herself on the men. A fist connected with her chin and Ramya toppled. But she got back on her feet in the next instant. She grabbed the nearest assailant by his hair and tugged, screaming her guts out as she did.

Hands clutched her shoulders and dragged her backward. Ramya punched and kicked. She could hardly breathe. The world was a blur. She heard Rida's angry shouts. She saw the guards fight off the attackers. Ross called her name. Ramya punched and kicked and kept on kicking. One moment she tore herself away from the man holding her. In the next, a kick landed on her back and threw her face first on the ground. Ramya rolled, desperate to get away. Fingers digging into the ground, Ramya pulled herself forward. She couldn't go far. Hands grabbed her by the hair, yanked her head up and twisted her around. Pain exploded in Ramya's back and it felt like her neck would snap. She tried to wiggle around but couldn't. Whoever had brought her down was straddling her back. Ramya tried to breathe, her eyes burned. Shouts, screams, cries, filled the air.

A pair of fiery eyes peered into hers. Hate and disgust burned in them. As he brought his face closer to hers, his lips twisted viciously.

"Apologies," he whispered. Ramya blinked, unable to fathom his words. "Had to set this up so I could pass this to you." A hand shoved something roughly into Ramya's pocket before she could understand what was happening.

At the same moment, a brassy voice tore through her senses. "Stop! Let them go!" it said. Ramya recognized the voice—it was Aga's. A hush fell as the woman kept on talking. "They should be punished, I agree. But they also helped save one of our own, so we will forgive their trespass this one time. Today the Hand of Darkness will spare these infidels. We will allow them to live."

A weight rolled off Ramya's back and the man's grip on her hair slackened. She stumbled to her feet, not taking her eyes off the man who had accosted her. He had pulled his cowl low over his face in an instant so she couldn't see his scorching blue eyes anymore. She didn't dare feel her pocket to see what he had pushed into it.

"Rami," Ross called. "Are you all right?"

Blood was trickling from the corner of his mouth, and a large red bruise was growing larger on his cheek, but he looked fine otherwise. Ramya nodded. She turned toward Ross, casting another glance at the cowled man. She stumbled and the man's arm shot out and grabbed her

"Get your filthy hands off her," Ross growled and shoved the man away.

Even though Ramya was surprised by the vehemence with which Ross pushed the man, that didn't hold her attention. She was instead struck by what the man muttered before stepping away. She wasn't sure, but he seemed to say, "Thank you for saving my child."

Ross didn't miss Ramya's stupefied expression as they walked away. He cast questioning looks at her as they hiked back to the shore, this time without incident. It wasn't until they were all secure inside the WB that he finally expressed his concern.

"Are you all right, Rami? What happened back there?"

"I'm fine. Just . . ." Ramya slipped a hand into her pocket, her words fading as her hand touched a sheaf of paper.

Ross scowled and leaned toward her. "What did that scoundrel do to you?"

"He thanked me for saving his child."

"What? What child?"

Ramya pulled the bunch of papers out of her pocket and held them up. "And he gave me this. He said he staged the mob attack so he could pass me this."

"What is that?"

Ramya didn't know for sure. But looking at the yellowed parchment that had been hastily tied into a roll, she had an idea. Her fingers trembled as she tugged at the brown string holding the papers, and it took longer than usual to get them free.

They were pages ripped out of a bound volume and they were old. The handwriting—thin and sinuous, etched in black ink—on yellowed paper was artful and every page had the same inscription along the top—The Treatise of Eternal Darkness.

Ramya looked up at Ross, understanding dawning slowly. "This is . . ." Ramya paused, excitement and surprise choking her throat.

"It's the Treatise of Ed," Ross finished. "I always thought Ed was a person, but it's not."

Ramya gave out a disbelieving chuckle. "No, it's not. It's Eternal Darkness instead." She flipped through the pages, and even though Ramya knew she wouldn't find anything worthwhile just glancing at them, her eyes skimmed them nonetheless. This was a miracle indeed.

"We did it, Ross," she linked her arm through his and shouted in glee. It was finally worth all the pain. If Zoho was correct in his assumptions, there was a chance they could find out how Anomaly Point worked, and there was hope they could close it forever like the ancients did.

Rida walked over, Ahool in tow. Suddenly there was some well-deserved happiness and cheer. Ahool started poring over the contents of the pages right away.

"Could he have been Miraya's father?" Ross said suddenly and it took Ramya a second to realize he was talking about the man who had passed the papers to her.

His deduction made sense. They had saved the girl, and Miraya—what her position was within the cult Ramya had no idea—had wanted them to have the treatise. Perhaps she had realized Aga wouldn't share it, so she found another way to pass it on to them.

"I hope they don't get in trouble," Ramya blurted. The poor girl had just escaped one gruesome death, and Ramya hoped she wouldn't fall into another.

Rida scrunched her brow. "They had to realize the risk of going against that madwoman Aga. Still, they did it. So they must know a way out."

Perhaps they did. Or perhaps they knowingly sacrificed their lives. Looking at the small island below them growing smaller fast, Ramya's eyes clouded. She whispered a prayer for the girl and her family and silently thanked them over and over.

24

El-Iss had been busy when Ramya had left for Novostra but when she returned to the moon, activity was a zillion times more frenzied. It was understandable—troops were being deployed at a frantic pace to Starbase Zeta where the galaxy was fighting a losing battle against the Locustan invaders. People were running around, craft were being loaded in battleships, and the air was tight with anxiety. The worst part was seeing the influx of young people—kids as young as fourteen, Ramya presumed—drafted from every corner of the galaxy in response to the call-to-arms. Faces pale, fear brimming in their eyes as they marched up and down with outsized guns, they were a heart-wrenching sight.

Ross tried to shore up Ramya's spirits. "You aren't that much older than they are." He wasn't far from the truth, but Ramya hardly felt any better.

Rida and her unit rushed away as soon as they touched down on El-Iss. "I have to speak to Admiral Kanaa," she said in a low voice to Ramya and Ross. "And find out where I'm needed. I'll probably head to Zeta." An uneasy silence fell when she paused to take a breath. Ramya didn't quite know what to say—it was possible she wouldn't see Rida ever again, and that was a somber thought. "It was an honor serving with you," Rida added a moment later. With a curt nod, she left.

Ramya, along with Ross and Ahool, headed for Captain Milos's chamber. The doors to his room were closed but they found Fenny pacing the corridor on Vi the Pterostrich. Ramya had seen Fenny riding Vi before, but like always, she stopped and shook her head. Ahool, on the other hand, shrank back a little while Ross scoffed. "The woman's lost her mind," he declared with a shake of his head.

As soon as Fenny saw them, she dismounted and rushed over.

"What the hell happened?" she demanded, looking pointedly at their livid bruises.

"Plenty," Ramya replied. "But we got what we were looking for in the end. So anyway, how did the trip to Bucifer go?"

Fenny shrugged. "Good. The grays had a memorial service. And we came back right after. Dal is here now, with some more of his people."

"And what's going on here?" Ross asked, jerking his thumb at the captain's chamber.

"Some dung from Space Command is here," Fenny said, her lips curling irreverently. "They've been talking for hours now. No one's allowed in."

"What's the update on Zeta?" Ramya asked.

"Barely holding up," Fenny said. "The influx is far larger this time. Anomaly Point closed again but still, doesn't seem like we're gaining the upper hand there."

Ross crossed his arms. "So what do we do now? Just lounge around until the captain is free?"

"No, of course not. Captain posted me here just so I could give you guys instructions. Ross, you and I need to go check on the *Endeavor* and make sure it's flight ready. Rami, you're supposed to keep working on finding the Hinterland with Ahool."

They dispersed quickly, and Ramya headed to her room where Ahool had already started going through the treatise. Together they compared the treatise with the information from Dakrhaeth. A few things were clear right away—the ancients, or the Unosi as the Treatise of Ed called them, had indeed encountered a species they called the Darkness. They broke through space near Anomaly Point. To counter the invaders, the Unosi had constructed means to reach Anomaly Point quickly, which Ramya assumed meant the multiple access points to the SLH in the area.

"They mention Hinterland here"—Ahool pointed at a paragraph—"and it seems like base of operations."

"Unosi HQ?" Ramya muttered to herself. "They had to have something there that even the Locustans know about."

"See, it says here," Ahool said, fingers tracing the handwritten lines on the paper. "The Unosi hurled fury against the Darkness. Fury stitched up the tear in the skies. The Darkness is gone, but only for the moment. It will come back because Darkness is eternal."

"So they knew these Locustans would come back?" Ramya said. Perhaps that's why the Unosi left the galaxy? Because they knew it was only a matter of time before they came back?

A loud, insistent rap at the door made Ramya jump. Her heart was still thudding wildly when she opened the door. She fell back in surprise seeing her father standing outside. He stepped in, his face turning livid as soon as he noted her bruises.

"What have you been up to?" he said through gritted teeth.

Ramya flinched, reddening as she sensed Ahool shift uncomfortably behind her. "We . . . I was at Novostra, looking for the treatise Admiral Zoho told us about. Had a scuffle with the Hand of Darkness."

Her father's face paled in an instant. He seemed to have lost the strength to speak and it was a while before he uttered a sound.

"Y-you had a scuffle with whom?" he said with much effort.

"The Hand of Darkness," Ramya said.

He closed his eyes and rubbed the bridge of his nose. "Can't believe Milos sent you there," he muttered angrily. "I told him not to—"

Was he scared for her? That was new!

"What are you smiling for?" he snapped, and Ramya stiffened. "Do you even realize what those fanatics are capable of? How could you endanger yourself like that?"

There had to be reason for his overreaction, although Ramya had no idea what it could be. He had seen her fight the dreadful Locustans and had barely blinked. "They're just people, Father," Ramya said. "Far less dangerous than Locustans and I've even fought with those."

He crossed his arms and glared. "They are people without souls. They will kill, they will maim for no reason whatsoever. With them, your ability to fight won't matter. You don't stand a chance against madness. Do not underestimate them, ever. Stay away. Do you understand?"

She did understand. Then again, she didn't. Yes, Aga was a madwoman, no doubt. But then there were people like Miraya and her father. Even Bumassar wasn't so bad.

"They aren't all crazy," she argued. "Some are good. A girl risked her life to get the treatise smuggled out."

"The stars help me," her father said, shaking his head with annoyance. "Do you have to be just as stupid as Bryn? Always?"

Ramya hadn't expected him to bring up Uncle Brynden. True, her uncle had left home to join the Hand of Darkness, but that was a long-forgotten saga. Regardless, hearing him call her favorite uncle stupid didn't sit well with Ramya.

"Uncle Bryn isn't stupid," she blurted.

"Of course he was," her father spat out the words. "He paid for his stupidity with his life. At least he wasn't heir to the house. His absence doesn't make much of a difference. Your life, on the other hand, is important. And you don't seem to care."

Ramya blinked. What did he just say? Who paid with his life? Uncle Bryn?

"Uncle Bryn is dead?" Ramya stuttered. It couldn't be. He was in the Fringe somewhere and she was going to find him. He couldn't just be gone.

Her father shifted a little. His gaze dropped and skimmed the floor for a long time. "Yes, they hacked him in pieces and sent him home in a box."

A box? The room closed in on Ramya. Many years ago, she had come across a bloodied box in her father's office. Inside it were severed limbs . . . Ramya could barely feel her legs underneath her. She slumped into a chair, unable to breathe or think.

Ahool scooted over to her side. "Rami, what's wrong?"

"She'll be fine," her father snapped at the young Mwandan. "You go do your job."

She could never be fine. Screams — her own voice from years ago — rang in her ears. The floor was a wave of ivory.

"Why? Why kill him?" she asked finally.

"Not sure," he replied as he lowered himself into a chair across from her. "Had something to do with our family. I think . . ."

"You think what?" Ramya asked when her father's words faded.

"The Moanus had something to do with it," he said in a dark tone. "The stupid boy had this idea of confronting the clan. He wanted to wrest the Kiroff hearth back from them. Always, always stupid and emotional Bryn."

Ramya's fingers dug into the edge of her seat, every word her father uttered cutting like a blade into her heart. She was on a similar path herself, a path not much different from Uncle Bryn's. Her father was right, she was like her favorite uncle in more ways than one. Ramya craved for sunlight, her insides bursting for breath.

"I have to go outside . . . can't breathe in here," she said, her chest heaving. She shot out of her chair and her father followed.

"You have to remember who you are, Lady Ramya," he said when they had walked into the corridor. She turned to face him while his gray eyes bored into her. "You are the future of House Kiroff. You cannot take risks that endanger our family's prospects. There are plenty of expendable people around you. Use them when you can to mitigate threats to yourself."

Ramya barely had the strength to think, let alone speak, but she managed a few words somehow. "So I should just sit here and do nothing."

His mouth curled a little. "Would you do that if I asked you to?"

Ramya crossed her arms and held his gaze, suddenly realizing there was little anger in his eyes. "I can't sit idle and protect my skin while our worlds are getting destroyed out there."

"You think I'm sitting idle, saving my skin?"

"No, you're not," Ramya said. "You're building ships, weapons and everything that's needed to defend the galaxy. But I . . . I don't know how to do that. So I have to find some other way to help."

He let out a sigh. "And that's by inserting yourself into the middle of a war?"

"Yes," Ramya replied without hesitation. "Standing by my friends and comrades."

"Hmm," he said simply. Ramya couldn't fathom what he meant; his face was inscrutable. "Go, have your walk," he added. Then he strode away.

***

Ramya walked about the base in a stupor. Around her, the world moved at a frantic pace. People in uniform rushed about, their faces tight and pale. Equipment of all sizes and shapes was being rolled out of the base and into the sea of spacecraft outside.

Ramya didn't spot anyone she knew and she weaved through the disciplined hubbub aimlessly. Even though she was drenched in sunlight, she was frigid inside. Uncle Bryn's face, every memory of him played in her head in an endless loop. Uncle Bryn was nice and kind; perhaps that's why her father thought of him as stupid. Grappa Abelei called him an idealist, but his face always lit up with a smile when speaking of his youngest son. Gramaman Otis had the sweetest stories of li'l Bryn. Ramya's heart twitched thinking about her grandmother. Did she know her youngest was dead?

"Rami!"

Ramya spun around, trying to figure the direction of the call. She spotted Isbet right away, rushing toward her from the cluster of GSO Astro Scouts. Seeing her best friend dressed in GSO uniform made Ramya smile. This was what Isbet had always wanted and Ramya was happy that her friend's dream had come true. Isbet pulled her into a fierce embrace before she raised her brows at Ramya's bruises.

"You've been busy, haven't you?" she said, smirking.

Ramya nodded. Telling Isbet all about her adventures on Novostra didn't take long at all, just the way it always was with Isbet.

"So, Zoho was right. The ancients . . . the Unosi knew of the Locustans. There could be a weapon out there to get them out of here for good," Isbet said breathlessly.

Ramya shrugged. "Seems like it. The Locustans possibly know of its existence and that's why they were digging around Sector 22."

"Find it, Rami. Find it quick."

She was going to. Even though her heart felt like a mountain was sitting on it, she was going to forge onward. Mourning Uncle Bryn could wait until later.

"Where are you off to?" she asked Isbet.

"Trio," Isbet said.

Trio was a beautiful system with not one, but three homeworlds. Ramya had been there a few times. Tessa, the smallest of the habitable planets, had the most astonishing beaches with bright pink sand, and people from all over the galaxy flocked there. Trio, she realized, was also the closest settlement to Anomaly Point. The thought made her heart drop like a stone to the pit of her stomach.

"Trio? Why? Don't tell me the Locustans reached Trio?" she said, hoping Isbet would reply in the negative.

"Not yet, they haven't," Isbet replied and Ramya let out the breath she was holding. "But Space Command is not taking any chances. If they break through the defenses at Zeta, they'll likely hit Trio first."

"So there's a chance . . ."

Isbet nodded even before Ramya could finish. "There's always a chance," she said. Her voice was thick with worry and her always vibrant face was pallid. Ramya noticed something else — Isbet's eyes were red and slightly puffy.

"What's wrong?" she asked, clutching Isbet's arm as if to stop her from running away. "Have you been crying?"

"It's nothing," Isbet replied, averting Ramya's gaze. It was something, her abrupt tone was proof of that.

"Isbet!"

Isbet stared into the distance for a bit. Then she shrugged listlessly. "Oh well, yes, I've cried some." She stopped and chewed on her lips. "Rownack left."

In addition to being part of the GSO, Isbet's other dream was being with Rownack, a senior from their institute CAWStrat and the scion of House Matteider. She had been ecstatic when the GSO picked both of them as apprentices.

"What happened? Why did he leave? Wasn't he happy being with the GSO?"

Isbet's eyes clouded. "I don't know, Rami. He left last night. Didn't even tell me why he was leaving. He's just gone . . ." Isbet's voice cracked. She forced a wry chuckle in the next instant. "Come to think of it, it's good riddance. Sticking to the GSO's celibacy vows was getting awfully hard with Rownack around. And no one, not even Rownack, is worth getting kicked out of my dream."

Isbet said it bravely enough and forcefully enough, but Ramya could easily see through her façade. Isbet was broken; she was crumbling inside.

"Hey, Isbet! Time to finish up," someone called from the distance.

"I have to go," Isbet said with a quick look at her squad. "Hope I see you soon."

"Fly safe," Ramya said as she released Isbet from an embrace.

"You as well," Isbet replied. A quick fist bump later, she strode away.

Ramya headed back into the base. This was turning into a pretty lousy day with bad news pouring in from everywhere. Isbet's situation worried her the most. Locustans were mighty foes and being heartbroken was certainly the worst condition to be in when fighting them.

25

Ramya had reached her room when she heard the elevator doors open behind her. Not too many people came by the lowermost level of the base that housed only the favored few—Trysten Kiroff and Captain Milos in addition to herself. Curious, Ramya turned to check who was visiting, half hoping it'd be one of *Endeavor's* crew. She stiffened on recognizing the man who strode out.

Lieutenant Gael Arlington of the GSO was heading toward the opposite end of the corridor, the side reserved exclusively for the Lord Paramount. He didn't seem to notice her and for a second, Ramya was relieved that he didn't. She grabbed the handle of her own door and was about to slink inside when a thought hit her.

Isbet was part of Gael's unit and Ramya was sure putting in a word for her friend would help, particularly since Isbet was in a grief-stricken state. Letting go of the handle, she half rushed after Gael.

"Hey, Arlington!"

He turned around and gave a sharp nod when she drew near. "Good to see you again," he said curtly.

Ramya noted how his eyes scanned her face and like everyone else before him, his gaze lingered on the injuries. However, unlike everyone else, he didn't comment.

"Here to see my father?" she asked.

"Yes."

It was a little awkward bringing up Isbet, and Ramya almost thought of dropping the idea. Then she blurted it out. "My friend is in your unit," she said, stringing the words in a hurry. "Her name's Isbet."

"Yes."

Ramya winced inwardly. Did he have to go on with the short replies? They were making an awkward situation even worse.

"Can you keep an eye on her?"

His eyes narrowed. "She's one of my people. Of course I will."

"No, it's —" Ramya was about to tell him how distracted Isbet was but realized it would hardly be proper to discuss Isbet's personal troubles with her superior. She quickly changed her tack. "Yes, of course. Thank you."

Gael's eyes narrowed some more. He seemed to hesitate for a moment or two. "She really needs to get her head back in the game," he said finally. "Boys will come and go, but her life won't."

He knew, of course.

"Isbet is —"

"She's great. She's one of the best pilots I've ever seen. She has the kind of spirit that suits the GSO. But she has to be careful or she'll squander it all. Now isn't the time to mourn someone who was never hers anyway."

Ramya crossed her arms and shifted slightly on her feet. "What do you mean? They liked each other."

"She liked the only son of House Matteider. There was no chance in hell that was going to work out. She may be blind but you understand that, don't you?"

Ramya pulled her arms closer around her torso. She did understand. The fact — Isbet's family was nothing compared to the trading powerhouse that was House Matteider and Isbet was no match for its heir — was cold as could be and just as cruel. Gael was right; love didn't matter as much as money. Isbet should've known better.

"So Rownack was moved away because he was getting too close to Isbet?" she asked, forcing the words through the painful lump in her throat.

Gael pursed his lips and nodded thoughtfully. "Well, that, and his family wanted him out of harm's way."

Of course, they didn't want the future of the house endangered. Her father wanted the same for her. Thank goodness, he didn't enforce it.

"What about you? Doesn't your father —"

"Of course he does. He's never even wanted me to be in the GSO. But that's one thing he can't take away from me. I won't let him."

Once again, Ramya remembered what Gael had said, about losing someone he loved. She yearned to ask him but as much as she wanted to, she couldn't get her words to behave.

"Leaving for Trio soon?" she asked instead.

He nodded distractedly. "Yes, that's the plan so far."

"Be careful out there."

He threw her an amused look. "I'm surprised that you care."

Ramya returned a frown. "Why wouldn't I?" she shot back. "Friends matter to me."

Gael let out a chuckle. "I'm a friend? I'm deeply honored."

Ramya sighed in frustration. Now he was getting under her skin. What was wrong with her? How in the world had she designated him as a friend? It was too late to correct that mistake, so Ramya decided to move past it. "You've gloated enough, don't you think?" she said in the snippiest tone she could muster, nodding at the gaudy door of her father's chambers. "The puppet master will be annoyed if you keep him waiting any longer."

"You're so concerned about my wellbeing. That's . . . I'm truly flattered, Lady Ramya." He put a hand over his heart and bowed, the spectacle making Ramya grit her teeth.

"You're ridiculous, Arlington," she said.

He flashed another aggravating smirk. "See you later, Kiroff," he said before strutting away.

***

All hell broke loose in the next two hours. Ramya and Ahool had been poring over calculations, matching up descriptions from the treatise and Dakrhaeth's memories. The good news was: Both pointed in the same direction. They had made good progress in isolating the location that held the mysterious Hinterland — that was definitely the Kyo-Sedra system. Now, they only had to pinpoint the planet and both Ramya and Ahool were sure another few hours would solve the problem.

However, a frantic pounding on the door disrupted their plans.

"Not a moment of quiet," Ramya grumbled as she opened the door.

A grumpy Fenny stood on the other side. She gestured impatiently at Ramya. "Come on, come on. The captain needs to talk to you."

Ramya found the captain shuffling through a stack of papers. As soon as Fenny ushered Ramya in, he waved Fenny away. "Get set up. We leave in fifteen."

"Where are you going?" Ramya asked, the dreaded emptiness surging inside her once again.

"To Trio," the captain informed her. He fell back on the couch and picked up a half-empty cup of noja. Ramya was sure it wasn't even warm. But Captain Milos gulped down the runny liquid with ease. "Just got news, a squadron of Locustans has broken past Zoho's defenses. And . . ." He paused to take a deep breath and Ramya knew he couldn't have anything good to say. Her heart thumped wildly as she stepped closer to a side table in hopes of support. "And Zoho thinks Anomaly Point will reopen soon."

"Not again," Ramya whispered. The openings were getting closer spaced now, far too close.

"I've been thinking of the last time they came," the captain said, scratching his chin. "It was just like this. The wormhole would open sooner and for longer, until it kept staying open. We're getting close to that point."

"The Unosi called them the Shadowhives," Ramya said distractedly, quoting from the treatise. "The harbingers of the Hive, the core entity bigger than twenty Shadowhives put together. The

Hive is the home of the Locustans' queen, whom they call the Mother. Once the Shadowhives clear the path, the Hive will arrive with her."

The captain chuckled wryly. "We can't let the Hive get here. Hell, I don't think we can survive two more Shadowhive attacks."

"Two?"

Captain Milos raised a pair of bleary eyes. "We're in bad shape. Half of our forces have been wiped out. Zeta is barely there. Look at this." He pressed a switch and a holo image of the starbase flickered into view over the table. Ramya held her breath. What had once been a magnificent horseshoe was now half broken. On one prong was a gaping hole where the tapered end had been. Captain Milos turned off the image quickly, but Ramya continued to stare, held in a trance by the awful visual.

"Rami," the captain's sharp voice made her tear her gaze away from where the image had been. "Any progress on the treatise?"

"Y-yes," she stuttered to life, quickly explaining how their deductions had led them to the Kyo-Sedra system.

"We're hoping for a miracle, Rami," the captain said. "Make it happen."

She was trying. But even if they could find the Hinterland, would they find the miracle weapon hidden there?

"I'm leaving for Trio. As soon as you find something, you report to your father. He'll arrange for a recon mission."

The fear and the emptiness came roaring back. "Everyone's going?" she asked, fighting the tightness in her throat. "Ross, Fenny, all of them?"

"Well, you have Ahool," the captain busily pocketed a few things. "And Chief Dal is staying behind. As well as Lefrasi. You know them well. That ought to be enough."

That *had* to be enough. She had to get to the Hinterland and find the miracle weapon. Fists curling, Ramya nodded. "I'll make it happen, Captain."

She followed the captain out into the corridor. "Godspeed,

Captain."

He stopped and patted her shoulder. "Yes, indeed. Good luck to us all."

26

The Cutlass streaked through the SLH on its way to the Kyo-Sedra system. Inside, Lefrasi checked calculations of trajectories and declinations for the fourth time. Ramya and Ahool sat across from him and Chief Dal and watched.

"It looks clear, Chief," Lefrasi said to Dal after his scan was complete. "Kyo-Sedra-5 is in the direct path from the Akari, the collapsed star in Sector 25."

Ramya leaned forward to tap the coordinates listed in the log. "We figured these coordinates Dakrhaeth gave us are from where the Locustans originate. So we cross-checked with other points in the galaxy and evened out the distribution. That gave us a straight match for KS-5."

Lefrasi nodded thoughtfully. "I see. But you're saying the Hinterland is in KS-5's moon, not KS-5 itself?"

Ramya sat back in her seat. "Well, my father says he did detailed studies of KS-5 when they discovered the crashed Locustan squadron. There was no sign of any underground chamber as large as what is described in the treatise. And he's good at these things. I don't doubt him. Our next, most obvious pick was KS-5's moon."

Chief Dal, who had been excruciatingly quiet since starting on the mission, looked curiously at Ramya. He was probably surprised by her endorsement of Trysten Kiroff, but Ramya hardly flinched. Her father was indeed good at what he did, there was no doubting that.

"Besides, the treatise describes the landscape around the Hinterland and that's almost a perfect match for the moon, 5-1," she continued. "The treatise speaks of three spires and those are near the northern pole. At least that's my guess from what I see of the topographical charts of 5-1."

The entrance of the Hinterland was marked by a triangle of spires, according to the treatise. Ramya assumed that was some sort of landform that pinpointed the site.

"All right, good," Lefrasi said. "I don't know why you're doubting yourself, Rami. Everything fits nicely."

Even though everything fit, Ramya couldn't shake off the dread of failure. It was probably the least dangerous mission she'd been on in a while, yet the responsibility weighed on her shoulders like a behemoth.

"A modest path through the fists of truth reaches the heart of wisdom," Lefrasi read, tracing a line in the treatise. His voice shook Ramya out of her thoughts. "What are the *fists of truth*?"

"We don't know," Ahool replied before Ramya could. "Some protection device maybe."

"Do these symbols mean anything?" Lefrasi asked, pointing at the rows of symbols — there were ten distinct ones repeated in a pattern — that formed a pretty margin on the pages.

Ramya shook her head. That was the problem. They didn't know much. The treatise even had a map — hand drawn and faded — of the Hinterland in it. Spiraling pathways impinged on a central circle; in the middle of that was a star which Ramya thought signified the fabled weapon of the Unosi or a key to it. But she wasn't sure. So much of this was unknown, and that in turn meant all that much more could go wrong. Yet with the Locustans closing in, they didn't have a choice but to check it out even though the information was vague at best.

A dull buzz ran through the craft and Ramya peeked at the window by habit. That buzzing sensation meant they were exiting the SLH, and Ramya could almost pick up the sensation in her sleep now. She was right; the windows cleared a moment or two later and Ramya picked up the hulking form of Starbase Allyses not too far away. Sangfo Milok, the GSO lieutenant in charge of the Cutlass, marched in shortly. Dark haired and tall, Sangfo was a nice, unassuming fellow, courteous and sharp without being glib. Ramya appreciated her father picking Lieutenant Milok for the Kyo-Sedra venture.

"We're about to stop at Allyses," he declared, pointing at the base's silhouette outside.

Ramya nodded, thinking of the plan her father had drawn up. He wanted the GSO to lead the mission since they knew a lot about the Kyo-Sedra system. When Ramya and Ahool had figured out about KS-5-1, all that was available of the GSO on El-Iss was Milok and his unit. The plan, therefore, was to pick up reinforcements on the way. Recon at Allyses—it was a GSO starbase roughly an hour's journey from the Kyo-Sedra system—made perfect sense.

"How many units will join us there?" Ramya asked.

Sangfo's mouth twisted. "There aren't many people around anymore. Everyone is either at Zeta or Trio. I think it'll be a small company, not even a full unit. But we'll definitely have another Cutlass. We'll need space to haul back whatever we discover on that moon."

"How long until we reach KS-5-1?" Chief Dal asked.

"Perhaps an hour at Allyses and then another to Kyo-Sedra," Sangfo said. "Two hours at most."

"An hour at Allyses?" Ramya asked. "Why so long?"

"We're going to switch a few things around," Sangfo replied. "Empty our bay. Move all the craft we have in there to the other Cutlass."

Brows crinkled all around so Sangfo explained some more. "Cutlass 24"—he patted the wall of the ship—"that's this one . . . has a specialized launch bay. In case we find the "fury," we'll bring it back on 24. We want to keep this ship down to the basics, both cargo and crew. In other words, you have to relocate. That's the reason I came by, to give you notice to prep." Explanation complete, Sangfo strode away with a nod.

Ramya had just made a quick trip to the launch bay to check in with Dakrhaeth when the Cutlass docked into the GSO starbase, Allyses. Uniformed technicians streamed in as soon as the gates opened, and most of them headed to the bay. Sangfo came by soon after, along with a man Ramya knew — Amireh, Arlington's second in command. It was funny, no . . . weird, how Ramya's heart did a happy flip on seeing the man with dark, flashing eyes. On a mission like this, it was indeed good to see familiar faces.

"Reinforcements are here," Sangfo announced. "Amireh will move you to *Cutlass 31.*"

As much as Ramya wished she would see Isbet on *Cutlass 31,* there was barely anyone around. She decided to ask Amireh.

"We're running a skeleton crew," Amireh explained as he showed Ramya and the Mwandans to a chamber in the lower deck. "Most of our squad is at Trio."

"How is that effort coming along?" Lefrasi asked. "I don't understand why we don't get regular briefings," he added in a grim tone.

Space Command was letting very little information trickle out of the front lines, if any at all. It was a strategy to keep the general population from panicking, Ramya understood. But like Lefrasi, she wished she knew more. There wasn't too much news floating around and they always had to go sniffing for up-to-date news. Perhaps keeping information from low-level expendables like her was part of the strategy as well, she mused gloomily.

"So far so good," Amireh said with a false smile that made Lefrasi grimace.

"May I have a chamber to myself, please?" Chief Dal said suddenly. "I need some time to meditate."

The request was sudden and strange but Amireh responded with an immediate nod. "Yes, come this way."

Ramya followed Chief Dal and Amireh out, and as soon as Dal had locked himself in the other room, she cornered Amireh.

"Tell me, please, how is the situation at Zeta and Trio?"

"So far so good," Amireh said, his expression calm even as Ramya squinted disbelievingly. He was about to walk away when he hesitated. "Let me check if the lieutenant wants anything from you."

While Amireh stepped away and fiddled with his comm, Ramya assessed what she had just heard. Gael was here, and yet he had sent Amireh in his stead. The Gael she knew would never do that—he always seemed to jump at a chance to speak with her—unless . . . something was amiss. Or maybe he was simply busy and she was overthinking.

"Follow me," Amireh interrupted Ramya's thoughts. "The lieutenant needs you to check on the Stryker."

As Ramya followed Amireh down the corridor, a strange restlessness stirred inside her. It was a jumbled mess of thoughts and feelings, but one thing Ramya was sure of—she was looking forward to meeting Lieutenant Gael Arlington again, perhaps a bit more than she imagined she would. And even though Ramya tried to not think much about it, it somehow made her more nervous than she had ever been before.

27

Ramya had never seen Gael so grim-faced. When she had bumped into him at CAWStrat for the first time, he was not his usual playful self, but he had simply been thoughtful. Even when they had been in the heat of battle, his face had not been as drawn or dark as it was now.

The engineers were performing their final checks in the bay when Amireh led Ramya in and left promptly. Ramya realized when she had last visited this ship's hold, it hadn't been so empty. Now since most of the squad was at Trio, there were only a few craft in it. The emptiness was unnerving.

Gael, who had been conversing with the engineers, flashed a wry smile before nodding at the Stryker. "Make sure everything's all right with the Stryker. It'll be our lead craft into 5-1."

That's what Ramya had suggested to her father also. Even though Dakrhaeth didn't clearly remember the directive he received from the Hive, perhaps a trek into KS-5-1 would trigger a forgotten memory. And even though her father didn't seem to appreciate her leading the way—he was growing increasingly resistant to the idea of her in battle—he had agreed with her line of thought. Clearly, he had instructed Gael likewise. Ramya's steps were lighter, yet firmer, as she walked toward the Stryker.

A thought struck her just as she was about to climb in. The spot across from the Stryker, where Gael's exquisite and rare Mossin—a gift . . . no, a dowry, from her father—had been, was now empty.

"Where's your Mossin?" Ramya asked.

Gael didn't hear. Or pretended not to. Whatever it was, it was weird.

"Don't tell me you lost the most expensive fighter craft in the universe?"

Gael gave a slight shake of his head. "Does it matter where the Mossin is?"

Maybe it didn't matter, but Ramya was curious as heck. She didn't much care what actually happened to the craft, but something about Gael's manner struck her as odd. She tried to forget it, busying herself in checking the Stryker and Dakrhaeth.

"All good?" Gael asked when she got back out. As soon as she nodded, he distractedly beckoned her. "Tell me what you have on KS-5-1. What's the plan so far?"

The more she told him, the cloudier his face grew. He leaned against the wall and ran his hands through his hair when she finished.

"That's all?" he said in a hopeless voice. "That's all we know?"

She had expected support. Not this. Her insides stiffened looking at Gael's gloomy face.

"There isn't exactly a manual out there on how to extract miracle weapons," she said. Ramya had to admit, she sounded ridiculously defensive to her own ears. The thing was, she wasn't half as confident about this as she should have been, and Gael's questioning stance hardly helped.

"Miracle, huh? That's what it is?" he said. "I'll pray for us all then." He turned back to the panel he had been working on.

Ramya frowned at his back. What was wrong with him? She had no trouble admitting the lack of facts, but there was nothing else to pin their hopes on either. Didn't he understand they were grasping at straws? Finding the Unosi weapon could change the odds in a heartbeat. They had to try to do that, didn't they?

Ramya looked at the Mossin's empty spot again and before she could rein in her thoughts, words crashed out of her.

"What really happened to the Mossin? Did you damage it?" she asked, noting the way Gael flinched at the question. Something was definitely not right. "That's it, right?" she asked again when he didn't reply.

Gael had been studying some gauges. Now he exhaled noisily

and looked at her with frosty eyes. "I returned it, all right?"

"Returned it?" Ramya's eyes turned into circles in an instant. "Where?"

"Where it came from, obviously."

"To my father?" Ramya had trouble saying the words. "You returned the Lord Paramount's gift?"

His mouth twisted a little. "Yes, I did."

Ramya scoffed before breaking into disbelieving chuckles. "You must be joking. No one does that. Ever."

"Well, I did."

"All right. Say what you will. I'm not buying it."

He snapped the equipment case shut, with more force than was needed. He started striding away before he stopped suddenly and turned around.

"I don't care if you buy it or not. I didn't think you would anyway. That's why I didn't want to tell you. But you just had to keep asking. So I gave you what I had. The truth. Take it or leave it."

Ramya stared disbelievingly as he stormed out. Then she too walked toward the exit, thoughts ripping through her mind like whirlwind. The fact that he returned the Mossin was one thing, but she was shocked by the way Gael was acting—like something had suddenly come apart inside him. Even though anger left a trail of fire in her head and she wanted to smack that condescending face, she collected herself quickly. This wasn't like Gael at all. Gael was a greedy opportunist, but he was a polite one. And this—

She stopped as soon as she walked out of the entrance of the bay. Gael was outside, rubbing the bridge of his nose as he paced the width of the corridor.

"I'm sorry," he said, looking her squarely in the eye. Before Ramya could reply, he started again. "That was uncalled for and . . . unfair."

He leaned back against the wall and ran his fingers through his hair. "I just . . . This sounds like a wild goose chase. And my squad . . .

I left them at Trio. For what? For something we don't even know exists for sure?"

Ramya didn't know what to say. She was supposed to be outraged when he called the mission a wild goose chase, but instead, her fears clumped around Trio. What exactly was going on there? Amireh had told them all was good but seeing Gael, she was sure it was anything but. She took up hesitant step forward, studying Gael's face as she approached.

"What is the situation at Trio?" Ramya asked. "The Locustans have broken through, haven't they?"

Gael stared at her for a second or two before giving a tired shake of his head. "They're everywhere. Tessa is . . ." He stopped as if he had run out of words. He tapped a button on his wrist-comm and a small holo-image formed instantly above it. "Look at it, look at Tessa."

Ramya shuddered on seeing the image. Tessa was definitely not how she remembered it. Instead of a vibrant green speck against dark space, Tessa was now marred by a swarm of ships. They were ships big and small, and Ramya could easily tell the Confederate ships apart from the tight clusters of black dots that were the Locustans. From time to time, flashes of bright light erupted among the dark swirls. There were too many flashes in too little time. Each flash, Ramya knew, represented death and somehow, it seemed as if death was partial to the Confederate forces. She couldn't see the other two homeworlds from the image Gael's comm showed but she wasn't too hopeful about their situation either.

"Shut it off," Ramya said, falling back against the wall next to Gael. She suddenly realized her fingers were shaking and even if she wanted to stop it, she couldn't. They stood there, in a strange, unnerving, companionable silence until Gael stirred.

"They needed me out there," he said, sighing.

"My father forced you to come here, didn't he?" Ramya asked. She was sure Trysten Kiroff had Gael transferred from Trio just so he could keep an eye on Ramya. The thought didn't make her as angry as it might have. Her father was expected to behave like this, to protect the heir of house Kiroff. There was no making him understand otherwise. Gael, however, was clearly distraught and that, oddly enough, pained her.

"Never mind, I should have expected that," Gael said in an exhausted voice. "I knew what I was getting into. I bought into this. It's no one else's fault but mine. It certainly isn't yours."

Perhaps. But Ramya couldn't shake off the guilt. Besides, she was worried about Isbet. Her best friend had not been in great shape when she left El-Iss and without her commanding officer's guidance, Ramya wondered how Isbet would cope. This was, after all, Isbet's first real war.

"I hope Isbet makes it out of there," Ramya said.

"They'll be all right. If only Anomaly Point doesn't reopen soon," Gael replied.

It would open sooner or later. And what then? The galaxy already had its back against the wall. There was no other way to go from here.

"I know we don't have much information about this mission, but don't you see a miracle is all that can save us?" She looked sidelong at Gael's rock-hard face and saw no sign of it softening. He stared listlessly at the opposite wall. "I wanted to be at Trio also, but Captain Milos believes in this mission. And he has always been right with his instincts. So even if my confidence is nowhere near where it should be, I try to think of the captain and his belief. I have to see this through. I wish you weren't forced into this, but since you're here, maybe we can make it work?"

"You're right," Gael said. "Come to the bridge with everything you've got. Let's go over it together. Have to make some sense out of this."

That sounded better! Even though the odds were stacked hopelessly against them, they couldn't give up before they even tried. The Unosi knew something and Ramya was sure they would find something on KS-5-1.

Gael stopped when they were on the main floor. "By the way, I really did return the Mossin. To the Lord Paramount. He didn't like it but I stuck to my guns."

Ramya chuckled. "You realize that'll lower your standing, right? The Lord Paramount doesn't like such audacity."

"Maybe I'm testing my limits," Gael said with a shrug. "I need to find out how much tolerance he has for me." He paused for a bit, his face breaking into a roguish smile. "Besides, I wanted to see what you would think. Pity the timing turned out to be so awful."

"I think it was pretty stupid of you to give it back. I mean, who in the universe returns a Mossin?"

Gael's brows shot up. "Really? Aren't you impressed even a little by my bravado? What about my selfless sacrifice?"

Ramya shook her head. While having the usual Gael back made for a much cheerful atmosphere, she wasn't sure if her frayed nerves could handle his impish humor for very long either.

28

The galaxy was as good as lost. Even as Ramya forcefully tightened the collar of her parka and prepared for the long trek into the Hinterland, she had little hope in her heart. Or confidence. In barely fifteen days, the galaxy as she had known it was teetering. And that was even before the Hive arrived. Starbase Zeta was partially destroyed, Trio was devastated, and Locustan Shadowhives kept trickling in through Anomaly Point. Half of every available Confederacy squadron was at Anomaly Point, but the allies were taking hits, one after the other, hardly able to contain the Locustan waves. The galaxy's defenses, paltry to begin with when compared to the might of the Locustans, were crumbling fast.

Just before they had left the Cutlass, Gael shared some terrible news. Anomaly Point had opened again and as expected, hordes of Locustans had streamed in. Ramya's thoughts were dark and close to hopeless as she flew Dakrhaeth down to the frozen ground of KS-5-1.

How long would they be able to hold off the invaders? Not very long, Ramya was certain. Unless they found a different way to thwart the pests. In other words, hope rested on finding some information — a clue to a miracle weapon perhaps — the Unosi left behind.

Dakrhaeth, true to her expectations, had remembered a few more things as they flew to the icy surface of Kyo-Sedra-5's moon. The Hinterland was home to the Unosi vaults, Dakrhaeth said. That was what his Locustan squadron had been tasked to destroy, so there would be no known way of stopping them. They would come again. They'd come the first chance they got to slip past the defense the Confederacy had put up. If only Ramya and her team could reach the Unosi vaults before they did.

Reaching the site hadn't been too much trouble. Dakrhaeth had almost fallen into a trance, and even though Ramya was sure where they could find this spire-studded landscape, Dakrhaeth guided them even before she needed to. It was indeed in the far northern reaches of Kyo-Sedra-5-1, and the three spires the treatise mentioned stood out. They formed a rough triangle, the area in between them peculiarly flat in sharp contrast to the spiky surroundings. Most likely, this wasn't a natural landform but expertly built to camouflage as one. A probe revealed a series of spiral tunnels underneath the surface and even though that didn't mean they had found what they came seeking, Ramya's spirits lifted a little. The treatise was not just mumbo-jumbo after all.

That was not the end of surprises. As soon as they reached the area in the middle of the spires, the ground shook and spiraled under their feet. For a second, Ramya thought the moon was crumbling beneath them, that it was a mechanism the Unosi had built to protect the Hinterland. It turned out that the Unosi were showing them the way instead. When the shaking stopped, a hole had formed near the tallest of the spires, and within it, a long flight of stairs that descended into the bowels of the moon. The entire stairwell was lighted with some sort of reflective tape built into the sides.

Needless to say, the unexpected reveal made the party pause. They *had* to go in, Ramya knew that. But fear of the unknown made her hesitate. They barely knew anything about the Unosi, and if they had built the Hinterland here on such an inhospitable moon, it was hard to believe they would welcome just anyone into a place like this. Which, in turn, meant this was a trap. But what choice did they have?

"Ready, Kiroff?" Gael Arlington's voice, sharp and insistent, made her stir. He and his GSO compatriots, as well as Chief Dal and Lefrasi, were dressed like her, covered from head to foot in thick Cavali-thermals to protect themselves in the freezing climate of Kyo-Sedra-5-1. They were all heavily armed as well, just as she was with a Meson Cannon.

"Yes, let's go," she replied in a robust voice. The roof of the stairwell closed above them as soon as the entire party had made it halfway down. One of the GSO tried to sprint up, but he couldn't reach the top in time. Even if he had, Ramya doubted he could've stopped it from closing.

"They trapped us," she whispered.

"Oh well, as long as there is a path forward, I don't mind," Lefrasi said.

They soldiered on, grim-faced and alert. About hundred steps down, the staircase ended. Three doors, each as nondescript as the rocky floor under their feet, stood across from them.

Gael shot a questioning look at Ramya. "Which one do we pick?"

There was no way of telling one door from another, but Ramya remembered the diagram of the spiraling pathways, all of them leading to the central core. It did not matter which door they picked, or so she hoped.

"Let's go with the middle," she said, forcing as much confidence as she could into her voice.

Pitch darkness greeted them on the other side of the door. The Unosi had certainly ceased to be welcoming. Ramya turned the viewer of her HUD on. The cramped tunnel, rocks jutting out in strange and often grotesque shapes, flickered into view. The heart of the Hinterland was about a half hour's walk from the mouth of the underground cave network. The group started off, alert and weapons drawn, along the main vein of the cave with Gael's chief point, Amireh, leading the way. Gael and Ramya walked side-by-side after him, and the rest of the team followed behind in units of two.

For a moment, Ramya missed Fenny and Ross. They were a team; they fit together. She felt safe around them, even in the direst of circumstances. Even though Gael was good and dependable, being with the GSO, and particularly Gael Arlington, was different. But this *had* to be done. The captain couldn't spare his commander or his navigator for the mission, as they were needed to hold off the Locustan onslaught. Then they had to use the Stryker to bring them here, a task only Ramya could carry out. Her father, Trysten Kiroff, had asked for support from the GSO, and Ramya had to agree that strategically they were the best option. Still, it was hard not to miss Ross and Fenny.

Ramya took a long and bracing breath, the cold air chilling the inside of her nose. Well, at least her Mwandan friends were here. No, scratch that. Lefrasi was here but Ahool Petta was up in the Cutlass, and Chief Dal was not himself at all. He was silent for the most part and meditating a whole lot. Although Lefrasi said every Uminato went through such acutely spiritual phases and there was nothing to worry about, Ramya wished the stalwart chief she had known would come back.

They trod as quietly as they could, with only an occasional crunch of their feet. After some time, Gael shot a look at her. "You're awfully quiet," he whispered.

Ramya barely managed to suppress a terrible need to roll her eyes. They were on a critical mission and he expected her to be chatty? She half wished she had left him in the grouchy mood. It was too late now--the old Gael was back with a flourish. "I have nothing to talk about," she said in as quiet a voice as possible.

"Not happy your father put us together on a team?" he asked, clearly unable or unwilling to take the hint to shut up. He wasn't far from the truth. It irked her somewhat that her father had suggested Gael accompany her even though it was likely Trysten Kiroff was not working the matchmaking angle at the moment. But Ramya couldn't shake off the idea or the discomfort entirely.

"Not happy that this may be our only chance of survival," she said, forcing her thoughts in a weightier direction. "I can't believe it came to this so quickly."

"Well, you should be proud that you were on the right side all along," he said with a shake of his head. "As a matter of fact, you sounded the alarm early. And that helped. The shame's not on you."

Wasn't it? They had all gotten too happy with the temporary peace, too busy with frivolous festivities and petty squabbles to remember the immense threat that had never quite gone away. The shame was on all of them. There was no avoiding it.

Gael seemed to sense her thoughts. "All right, maybe we're all to blame for not paying attention. But—"

He stopped abruptly, raising a fisted hand to signal the party behind them to stop. About twenty paces ahead, Amireh had stilled near a bend in the tunnel, his fist raised. Ramya's fingers tightened around her weapon as they stepped closer to Amireh, her heart skipping a beat or two. Her breath hitched in her throat when she looked around the bend and she forgot to blink.

29

Beyond the bend, the ground fell away. They had reached a balcony of sorts and underneath lay a cavern gigantic enough to hold twenty of the ballrooms at CAWStrat. There were no columns holding the roof up so the entire space below was clearly visible. A narrow flight of stairs — fancy with inlaid gold and white mosaic — was carved from the side of the balcony down to a path along the edge. A shiny white balustrade edged this path circling the chamber, opening at regular intervals onto pathways paved in black. These pathways, like the spokes of a wheel, converged from the circumference of the chamber to its center where a large golden dome stood. Innumerable golden protuberances that reminded Ramya of closed fists were scattered around the dome and along the pathways. The chamber was flooded with light and its walls — painted a bright and shiny white with veins of gold crisscrossing it in an eye-pleasing formation — shone almost blindingly. There was a gossamer feel to the walls, as if a curtain was hanging over them. Overall, the scene before them was right out of a lavish dream.

However, it wasn't the unexpected opulence that made Ramya hold her breath, but the prostrate forms that lay scattered around the central dome. They were unmistakably dead Locustans. And these weren't old skeletons but newly killed bodies.

"The Locustans are here already?" Ramya whispered. "But how?"

Gael shrugged. "I'm guessing a few squads gave us the slip and ended up here."

"But the Unosi got them in the end, huh?"

"Hmm. And they'll get us too. No wonder they opened up the stairwell for us. They knew we couldn't get too far along anyway."

That made sense. Probably the opening of the outer gates was nothing but bait to lure them in.

"But how did the Locustans get in?" Ramya asked again. "We didn't see any craft outside when we landed."

"Maybe there's another entrance," Gael said.

That had to be it. Perhaps the Locustans had found another path to the Hinterland. Although she could not think how. The Unosi had not advertised the location of the Hinterland and the treatise was vague at best. How did the Locustans even know about the Hinterland, and then find the secret path into it?

"There is a doorway down there right across from us," Amireh said. "That must be where they got in."

"We need to make sure no more of them are coming," Gael said. He tilted his head at Amireh. "See the path along the edge? That leads straight to the other entrance. You and Boone cover that." He turned toward Ramya next. "Guessing we have to get to the dome in the middle?"

Ramya nodded. Nothing else in the room stood out and the way the Locustans were scattered around the bulge, it was the obvious point of interest. Still, she decided to check with Ahool.

"Ahool, can you hear me? Do you see this?" Ramya said tapping the small communicator button built into the side of her HUD. Gael's engineer had set up a channel from their HUDs to the communication system on the Cutlass. Ahool had been tasked with monitoring their movements along with Sangfo's unit. While the Mwandan boy was upset when he heard he had to stay behind yet again, Ramya liked the arrangement of having a pair of eyes monitoring them and helping them in case they missed anything. Ramya heard Ahool's excited chirp almost instantly.

"I hear you, Rami," he said. "I see too."

"We are heading to the big mound in the middle," Ramya said. "What do you think?"

"Yes, there has to be something there," Ahool replied.

Seeing Gael frown worriedly Ramya stepped closer. "Do you think there are more Locustans out there?"

Gael shook his head slowly. "Well, there are thirteen bodies I can see from here, and the Locustans usually work in units of five. So we have three units that arrived here. That's a reasonable number."

"Fifteen? Two are still missing then?"

"Maybe," Gael said. "Maybe they're on the other side of the dome. Anyway, two missing Locustans don't worry me."

"What is it, then?"

"What could've killed them? All of them were killed the same way. They all have a hole in their chest. Something killed them in an extremely precise and most effective way."

"The fists of truth?" Ramya asked no one in particular.

Ahool's voice buzzed in her ear right away. "What you say, Rami?"

"Those little bumps all over the floor are the fists of truth, Ahool," Ramya said. "Don't you see their shapes?"

"So fists are killing machines?" Ahool asked. His voice had a hint of a tremor in it.

"They might be," Gael replied. "But the thing is, those bumps . . . fists are everywhere. I don't see how we can avoid them."

"Lieutenant," Amireh called. "Seeing where the Locustan bodies are, they were killed only when they came close to the central dome. Nothing seems to have happened to them when they were at the edge of the chamber, right?" He paused a second and when no one replied he started again. "My point is, we should probably go on and secure the other entrance while you figure out a path to the dome."

Gael nodded, although Ramya sensed some hesitation. Amireh and the other man, Boone—a fair-haired, dimply-faced man who Ramya guessed was no more than a couple of years older than her— had started down the stairs when Gael beckoned one more GSO from the rear of the party. "Tamara," he called the wide-shouldered woman with vivid blue eyes. "You go with them."

As Amireh proceeded down the stairs, Gael called the rest of the team together. He looked at each of them in turn before starting with his instructions. "Chief Dal and Lefrasi, you go with Nohr," he said nodding at the heavyset man who was bringing up the rear along with Tamara. "Kiroff, you'll come with me."

They started off when Amireh was halfway down the stairs, treading warily, weapons raised, eyes scanning the chamber constantly. Ramya's heart pounded. A dull fear numbed her mind and made her ears buzz. The more they descended, the smaller she felt, until at the base of the stairs she was thoroughly overwhelmed by the immensity of the room. But however much her limbs grew numb, Ramya had to admit the mission was going well. Amireh and his team had reached the other entrance without incident, and he signaled an all-clear after checking the area.

Gael pointed at the nearest golden protuberances. "We have to avoid them. Although they might not be what we are thinking. Something else could get us." He pointed at the closest path to the dome. "We'll take this one. You take the next," he whispered to Nohr.

As soon as Gael and Nohr took their first steps, all sorts of hell broke loose. The golden fist nearest to Gael rattled a little and then shot up from the ground, elongating into a column. It swiveled around as if looking for the source of the disturbance. Then the fingers unfurled revealing a gaping hole in its palm.

Ramya screamed, "Get down." Gael threw himself down on the ground and rolled back to the edge, but Nohr wasn't as fast. A blast of fire ripped through the air and caught the man in the shoulder. He flew backward, one side erupting in a shower of blood. Before his body fell to the ground, another fist behind him shot up and fired. Nohr's head vaporized in an instant. As Ramya stood with her mouth wide open, her icy fingers shaking on the cannon she cradled, she realized the impossibility of the task ahead of them. The Locustans had at least made it across half of the chamber; they had not even started and had already lost one.

Gael fell back against the wall noisily. He stared, stiff-jawed and chest heaving, at Nohr's mutilated torso and finally gave a shake of his head. "Iffin hell!" he said through gritted teeth.

For a long time, they stayed quiet, everyone looking back and forth across the chamber checking the numerous fists that dotted the floor.

"This is impossible," Gael said after a while. "There is no clear pathway to the center. The Locustans almost made it because they're faster. I don't see a way of getting through, unless . . ."

The way Gael's words trailed off made Ramya take notice. His jaw had hardened and his eyes turned steely as he kept scanning the layout of the chamber. Ramya looked also, and she could see no clear way. All the paths looked exactly alike, except for a couple to the sides that seemed to be at a level lower than the ones just ahead of them. But even around those, there was no dearth of the bumps. There was simply no way in unless they drove an armored vehicle.

Lefrasi leaned in. "Do you have any shields that could hold up to these things?"

"Counteract these things?" Gael shot a disbelieving look at Lefrasi. "Did you see the color of the bolt? I believe these are plasma weapons. No, I don't have anything strong enough to withstand that."

"How about we try to blast them?" Lefrasi said.

Gael closed his eyes and shook his head vigorously. "No, I don't think that's a good idea. First of all, I'd rather not use a weapon in this chamber at all. We do not know what the ancients were up to and what they put in to protect this chamber. Besides, I don't think any weapons we have will be enough to bring down all of these buggers. And then, these might not be the only weapons built to secure this place. There might be worse things. I'd rather not awaken every hidden demon the ancients have planted in here."

"What do we do then?" Ramya asked. "Leave now?"

They had spent so much time and effort and pinned all their hopes on finding something here. Going back now, and empty-handed, would be the worst possible outcome. But then, after seeing Nohr being shredded to bits within seconds, she had no conviction left in her, nor the strength to imagine sacrificing the rest of the people.

"Absolutely not," Gael said. "We can't retreat now. Nohr can't die for nothing."

Ramya took a long, deep breath. "I think we will all die. They'll slaughter us just like Nohr. You ready to take that chance?"

"I thought you believed in this mission," Gael said, raising a questioning brow at her. "Now you don't?"

"Well, I thought I could do this. But I'm not so sure anymore. We're no match for these things. And I don't think sacrificing ourselves here would do much good. I'd rather live and go fight at Anomaly Point. Maybe that way I can buy the galaxy some time."

Gael scoffed. "I remember you saying something different just a few hours ago and I agreed with your point. I still do. I think our only hope rests on a miracle. There is no chance we can win this war with what we have. Two things can save us from the Locustans. The first thing is Anomaly Point closing, and the second is us finding this miracle weapon of the ancients. We have no way to influence the first, but we can try doing the second. Perhaps we'll die trying but we'll have tried."

Gael was right. That was exactly what she had thought. But that was before she had seen Nohr blow up in a shower of burnt flesh and blood within seconds of stepping into the chamber.

The idea of coming here had spread from her—she had noted something Dakrhaeth had mentioned, added Zoho's theories on top, and run with it. What if there was no miracle weapon? The deaths of all these people would be on her. She had no trouble risking her own life, but leading everyone to death? She couldn't imagine that.

Lefrasi stepped near. "What are you thinking, Rami?"

Ramya's eyes burned as fear churned her guts. "What if there's nothing here?"

"There *has* to be something here," Lefrasi said. "Why else would the Locustans come here? Why else would the Unosi fortify this place?

There is something here that can change our fates."

"Now is not the time for a debate," Gael said in a scathing tone, frowning at Ramya. "You've rallied people and now you're having doubts? Well, it's too late for second thoughts. You can't turn back now."

Anger coiled in the pit of Ramya's stomach. "I don't want to turn back. But at the same time, I don't want to send you to your deaths."

"We are not risking our lives for you," Gael snapped. "We're doing this to save the galaxy. Your job is to guide us, so do that. Please don't get in the way of my plan."

Ramya crossed her arms. "And what is your plan exactly?"

Gael threw a quick look around. "We'll run for it. In a group, shielding each other. That's what the Locustans did too. Not all of us will make it to the end but I'm hoping at least one of us, the one person we keep at the center, will."

"All right, maybe one of us will get to the dome. And how will they get back out?" Ramya asked. Gael didn't answer. He couldn't. There was no answer. This was an unsolvable problem. "We can't do this, Arlington," Ramya said. "We will come back when we find a way to shield ourselves."

Chief Dal had been sitting on the floor with his back against the wall, eyes closed. He suddenly tottered to his feet and spoke in a strange, high-pitched voice. "It's here, it's here. It's calling us." His eyes fluttered open and he looked at each of them in turn. Then he walked to the balustrade, his gaze fixed on the golden dome as if hypnotized by it. "We have to get to the dome. It holds the key to the fury. I've seen the memories of our ancestors. The fury saved them, and it'll save us now."

Gael gave her telling look, and Ramya let out a sigh. She didn't know what Chief Dal had seen in his meditation, but the fact remained that the fists of truth wouldn't let them pass. Unless they found a way to make themselves impervious to their fire, the problem remained the same.

"But how do we get there?" she said.

"Take the modest path," Dal replied in a distracted voice and sat down on the ground again.

Ramya jolted upright. She had read of the modest path in the treatise. She had agonized over its meaning. Now she was sure it was an important clue. But what could it mean? She scanned the chamber again. She saw nothing. Only the paths converging like spokes of a wheel at the center near the golden dome. Every path was guarded by the fire-shooting protuberances, none of them seemed safe.

"Hey," Ramya shouted as something caught her eye. She had noticed it before but it only clicked now. Two of the paths were sunken below the others. What if the lower paths signified modesty?

As soon as Ramya finished explaining, Gael rushed toward the closest sunken path, Lefrasi in tow. Ramya followed with the chief, her heartbeat rising to a crescendo.

30

Gael stopped for a minute at the head of the path and studied the area. Then he looked at the others, more pointedly at Ramya. "I'll head in first, all right? No one follows until I give you the all-clear. Not even to help me."

"Rami," Ahool's agitated whisper streamed through the comm just as Gael took his first step forward. "I am reading treatise again. Listen what all of it says! A modest path through the fists of truth reaches the heart of wisdom. Stray from the core, unsettle the bounds, and you shall burn."

The gears in Ramya's head spun furiously. The first line they understood but what did the other mean? It *had* to mean something.

Core . . . center . . . middle.

Bounds . . . limits . . . edges?

Core . . . center —

"Gael, stop," Ramya shouted as an idea bubbled up. "Stay in the center of the path. Don't touch the walls."

He nodded and crept forward slowly while Ramya held her breath. Her heart jumped into her parched throat. She scanned the nearest fists constantly. Even though there was not much she could do other than scream and warn Gael, she was not taking her eyes off the killing machines. Gael made it past the first step and then more. After he had taken about twenty steps, Gael gestured them to follow.

Ramya darted in, keeping her head as low as she could, her finger alert on the trigger. Lefrasi followed with Chief Dal bringing up the rear. They continued in a tight line and nothing but the dead Locustans' bodies came in their way.

"What now?" Gael said. They had reached the end of the path. The enormous golden bulge stood a few steps away, a heap of dead Locustans littering the space in front of it.

"Ahool," Ramya called. "Does the treatise say anything about the golden dome?" Ramya didn't remember reading anything about it, but still, she needed to be sure before she walked up to the dome.

"Nothing," Ahool replied.

Ramya turned toward Gael. "Guess we just walk up then."

Five more heart-numbing steps and they were up on the platform with the dome. They kept checking but nothing moved. No one was coming to kill them.

"Looks fine from here, Lieutenant," Amireh's voice drifted over the comm.

Ramya started inspecting the dome more closely. Lefrasi followed her around. It seemed like a solid mound. She saw no openings, none at all. Strange, otherworldly symbols etched its golden surface from top to bottom. Ramya kept looking, scanning the surface for a telltale crack or opening. But even after circling it a couple of times, she found no mechanism to get it open.

Ramya stopped near Gael after finishing her third fruitless circle around the dome. "It's like a solid block. There's nothing to open or enter it," she said to Gael who had been monitoring the periphery.

Gael's worried face darkened a bit more. "And worse yet, I don't see the two missing bodies," he said.

For a second Ramya didn't understand what he was talking about. Then she realized — they had found thirteen dead Locustans. But Locustans supposedly moved about in units of five. So two of them were missing.

"You think they could be still alive and lurking?" she asked, her voice a tight whisper.

Gael shrugged. "Don't know. Amireh, stay sharp. We have two hostiles unaccounted for."

Two hostiles they could probably deal with, but Ramya was worried about worse. What if more Locustan squadrons had slipped past the defenses at Anomaly Point? What if they arrived here now? They couldn't linger here too long, that was for sure.

Ramya hastened back to the dome, running her fingers over the designs, her eyes blurring from the golden glare. She didn't know what to do next and time was running out fast. She kept touching the symbols, feeling the cold notches and grooves under her fingers as she traced their outlines.

They had to call this off sometime, sooner than they wanted, and she would have to return with the weight of failure on her heart. Gael would probably mock her again but they couldn't stay here forever hoping for a miracle to happen.

"Anything?" Gael asked when she circled back to him. Ramya shook her head. Gael tilted his chin toward Chief Dal who stood with his back against the dome. The chief's eyes were closed once again. "He says this is indeed the receptacle of wisdom. It was sealed by the Unosi to protect it from invaders. His ancestors said the path to wisdom is painted."

The painted path? Ramya had seen the Uminato in action before and she wasn't skeptical of their powers, but she wished Dal's ancestors had given them some better clues. Distractedly, she poked at the designs, almost falling back in fright when one of them emitted a sharp sound.

Heart pounding, Ramya stared at the surface of the dome. She had touched and poked many symbols, but only one of them — the last one she had pressed — glowed a vivid red.

Gael flashed an anxious look at her. "Is it supposed to do that? Please tell me you haven't armed a detonator."

Ramya didn't know. She sure hoped she hadn't started a countdown to their annihilation. Something bubbled at the back of her mind. But hard as she tried to pin the thought down, it spun in a crazy spiral in her head. There was something she was missing, something very obvious.

"Rami! The symbols!" Ahool's screech tore through her ears and in that instant she knew. It wasn't a detonator she had fired up, she had stumbled on a key.

"Yes, I know," Ramya shouted back, barely stopping from breaking into a dance.

Some of the symbols on the surface of the dome matched the ones depicted on the pages of the treatise. The one she had just touched was one of those.

"They make a key," Ramya muttered. "The symbols are a key to the dome."

But there was more than one symbol in the treatise. Ramya was sure they had to find them all and press them in a certain sequence. She was also certain the pattern of ten symbols that formed the edges of the Treatise of Ed was the pattern of the key.

"Ahool, tell me the pattern," she shouted into her comm. Ahool was ready. In the blink of an eye, he was reciting the pattern, describing each symbol to Ramya while she scanned the surface of the dome. It was a task easier said than done and it took Ramya and the rest of the squad quite a while to locate all the symbols. Then, one by one, Ramya pressed them in sequence. Every symbol sounded a different note, each of them lit up a different color.

"The path is painted," Chief Dal muttered behind her.

It was indeed painted in rainbow hues. But that was it. Nothing else happened. The symbols stayed lit while Ramya and the others stared, their hopes dwindling as swiftly as they had built up. Then the entire dome erupted in a rainbow of colors and sounds. The notes emitted by each of the keys played over and over, like music.

Gael leaned closer to whisper in her ear. "What do you think? Is it going to explode on us?"

Ramya sure hoped it wouldn't. The music sounded friendly enough, at least not ominous. Or perhaps the Unosi had a dark sense of humor and were just toying with them. She didn't have to wonder long. The vivid show of lights on the dome faded a bit and then went out completely. A tremor started under her feet.

"Something's happening," Lefrasi shouted.

Something was surely happening. The tremor grew stronger by

the second and the light in the chamber dimmed. Suddenly, a wail, an ear-piercing screech rather, shattered the atmosphere.

"Fall back, fall back," Gael ordered. Even before Ramya could take a step, the dome transformed. It opened up like a blooming bud, its surface split into eight equal-sized sections. Ramya held her breath, watching as the inside—lit a vivid but soothing red—came into view. Except for a column at the center, the inside of the dome was empty. On top of the column was a small black cube that looked very similar to the memory cubes widely used in the galaxy.

"That's the receptacle of wisdom!" Chief Dal's loud voice shook Ramya out of the trance. The chief—his eyes wide and unblinking—pointed at the black cube at the center. "I have seen that in my dreams. That is the path to our victory. The ancients left it there for anyone who would come after them."

Ramya exchanged a quick look with Gael. Were they supposed to pluck the black cube out and walk away with it?

They didn't have a chance to ponder. Two voices—it was Amireh at the door and Sangfo from the Cutlass—both alarmed, blasted through the comm. For a bit, Ramya could barely make out what they were saying but one thing quickly became clear. They were both shouting, "Get out of there. Right now!"

They had to get out. The floors were crumbling under their feet. Around them, the golden fists crumpled. A chunk of masonry from the roof crashed to the ground close to them, shattering to bits. Part of the staircase they had used to climb down to the chamber collapsed with a gut-wrenching thud. Ramya stood, her feet rooted, her thoughts scattered. A piece of the roof crashed dangerously close to the column holding the black box. Flying debris—sharp and painful—clawed at her face and Ramya stumbled back.

"Lefrasi, we can't get out the way we came. Get to Amireh," Gael shouted.

"The receptacle," Chief Dal cried. Ramya had torn her eyes off the box for a second and now that she looked back at it, her heart sank like a boulder to the pit of her stomach. The unfurled petals of the golden chamber had begun to close.

Dal tried to rush forward but slipped over a pile of debris.

"Lefrasi, get the chief out," Gael shouted again. "Go, go, go!"

They *had* to get the receptacle. Ramya cast a quick look at the roof above. Then she jumped over the unfurled surface of the dome and lunged at the column with the black box. She grabbed the box and pulled it with all her might. It didn't budge.

"Come on, come on," Ramya pleaded. "Get out of there. I know you were meant to come with us."

The tremors grew and grew. It was hard to keep her balance. The golden petals kept on closing.

"Come on, Kiroff," Gael yelled from outside the dome.

"I can't get it out," Ramya yelled back. They couldn't leave empty-handed now, not when they had come so close. But she didn't have too long to try. The petals were half-closed already.

Gael rushed in and grabbed the box. Together they pulled. It was stubborn but at the third tug, it came free. The petals stopped closing and fell open with a loud clang.

"Yes!" Ramya shouted. For a second she forgot the rapidly disintegrating chamber around them and simply laughed.

Flashing an indulgent smile, Gael patted her shoulder. "Well done. Let's get out of here now."

They skidded out of the dome. It was hard to recognize the chamber from when they had first seen it. And it was changing even more. Gaping holes covered the once mosaic-paved floor. Ramya and Gael jumped, hopped, and skipped across the broken surface, barely able to stay on their feet as the ground swayed under them. Lefrasi and Chief Dal were already outside and only Amireh stood at the door, beckoning them wildly.

Debris came from everywhere. It rained on them, it flew from the sides, and it even ricocheted from the bottom. Plumes of smoke rose from the ground, filling the chamber with silvery-gray mist. Ramya had to keep blinking hard to clear her vision as she careened after Gael. They rushed, breathless, weaving, ducking, and dodging through tumbling masonry.

Ramya had only a few paces to go when a large section of the wall came crashing down behind her and a part of it slammed into her shoulder. A scream left Ramya's throat as she flew sideways. Something thick and hard hit the side of her head. A hand clamped onto hers. Grainy blackness spread across her eyes.

31

The blur lifted from Ramya's eyes after a moment. Her senses, however, took a while to stabilize. People dragged her out of the underground chamber. Someone pulled her HUD visor off, patted her cheeks, and set her down on the ground. A bit later, the sound of chaos streamed in. She was sitting on the ground, her back against a rough pillar. They were in a clearing of sorts, surrounded by an army of rocky spires. Chief Dal and Lefrasi were huddled to one side. Boone and the woman Tamara circled the clearing, weapons raised and eyes scanning the periphery. A few steps away from her, Amireh and Gael were talking, their brows knit and faces drawn.

The tremors under her feet had subsided considerably, Ramya realized. The only thing that bothered her now was the dull ache in her head and the stickiness on one side of her face. She lifted a shaky finger to touch her forehead and realized she was bleeding. Gael and Amireh noticed the movement and Amireh walked over and kneeled by her side.

"You all right?" he said, his voice tight with anxiety.

Ramya managed a weak nod. "What's going on?"

"Lieutenant Sangfo is coming to get us. We came out from the backside of the Hinterland."

"But the Stryker . . ." Ramya's words trailed off as a blinding pain shot through her head. "The Stryker is at the front. I have to go get it." She tried to get up on her feet but her legs were like jelly underneath her. She slumped back, hitting the hard surface of the pillar.

"We'll get it," Amireh said. "You rest a little."

Ramya closed her eyes and slipped a hand into her pocket. A smile curled her lips as she felt the black box they had extracted from the golden dome. She didn't know how they would get information out of it, but at least they had something. Nohr's death would amount to something.

"Hey!" Ramya forced her eyes open. Gael kneeled in front of her, his intense gaze burning into her face. "Some scare you gave me. Try not to do that ever again, all right?"

A wry chuckle rose up Ramya's throat. "Lord Paramount Trysten Kiroff would be mighty displeased if his heir died on your watch, wouldn't he?"

Gael's face tightened some more. "Yes, that too," he replied gruffly.

"Hey, I didn't get hit on purpose, you know," Ramya said. "Besides, I wanted to give up on this a while ago. You wouldn't let me."

Gael had barely opened his mouth to retort but he didn't have a chance to get his words out. Another rumble, one that rose from deeper within the bowels of the moon, shook them. Ramya jolted upright, forgetting the pain in her head. Not again!

"Move away from the rocks," Gael shouted, as he tapped furiously at his comm. "Sangfo, how far out are you?" he shouted. "The whole damn moon is breaking up."

Ramya scrambled to her feet. "The Stryker," she said frantically. "We can't lose it."

Gael shot her a look and Ramya knew—saving the Stryker was way low on the list. With the Astro Scouts still some distance away, their own survival was not guaranteed. Ramya's eyes burned and a lump of pain grew bigger and thicker in her throat but she knew there was nothing she could do to help the Stryker now.

She didn't have the time to mourn her loss. A wave, the likes of which she had never seen in her life, rose in front of her. It was a wave of rock and dirt, the ground swaying and crumbling, rising and falling in a constant ebb and flow. Ramya's heart pounded at the base of her throat and she instinctively inched nearer to Gael.

"Do you guys see that?" Sangfo's incredulous voice drifted through the comm. "I don't believe it."

Ramya couldn't believe it either. The waves of crumbling ground had created a crater of sorts behind the back entrance. Something rose from it. Something shiny and white and immense. It looked like a spacecraft, but it was different from any other spacecraft she had ever seen. The metal had a strange shimmer to it, and its surface was inlaid with the same symbols that had covered the golden dome inside. Could this be the miracle weapon? Was this the *Fury*? Whatever it was, there was no question about its origins. It was clearly something the Unosi built. They had kept it hidden, perhaps to reveal it when the time was right. Or perhaps they thought they would never need it again. Now it stood in front of them, glittering in the bright light, and Ramya felt more hopeful than she had felt in a very long time.

"You have to be joking," Gael muttered. "All these years this thing has been sitting here and no one had an inkling. No one but a bunch of lunatics."

"And crazy Zoho was right after all," Ramya said. Even though she herself had difficulty keeping faith, now that they had discovered so much, she had no doubt all of Zoho's theories were true. This had to be the *Fury*, the weapon to drive the Locustans away. But they still had to find a way to use this thing.

"And you were right as well," Gael said. He reached to thump her shoulder. "Your crazy antics might have just saved the galaxy, you realize?" He flashed a lopsided smile and placed a hand over his heart. "Respects, Kiroff!"

Ramya flushed a little. This was just the beginning of hope, nothing more. They had a long, long way to go from here. Yet Gael's earnest gesture warmed her insides. Above them, three Astro Scouts zoomed into view.

"Finally!" Gael exclaimed on seeing the trio. He turned toward Ramya and explained quickly. "I'll have you and Chief Dal out of here first. You need medical attention." He paused to wave away Ramya's protest. "Get Chief Dal to the medics. He's been in a daze for a while. Lefrasi thinks it's fine but I'm not so sure."

Ramya had barely finished explaining about the psychic powers of the Mwandan Uminato when the Scouts landed. Gael didn't waste a second getting Ramya and Chief Dal into the nearest one.

"Don't forget my Stryker," Ramya said as she settled down.

"Get your head fixed, Kiroff," Gael said. "I'll see you later."

The Scout took off and they had barely flown for a minute when the pilot yelled. "Two hostiles on the ridge," he said into a crackling comm. "I see spacecraft, three spacecraft, all Locustan."

A chill sped up Ramya's spine. She leaned over to look at what the pilot was seeing, her heart pounding at a frantic pace. Had more Locustans arrived? They didn't have enough people on the ground to fight off a horde.

Her panic subsided the moment she saw the scene below. Two Locustans stood staring at the enormous crater with the Unosi craft inside. These two, Ramya reasoned, had to be the ones that were missing. They were possibly the pilots.

"We have eyes on them, but they are out of our firing range," Gael replied.

"Should we engage?" the pilot asked.

"No, we got this," Gael replied in a heartbeat. "You need to get your cargo to safety."

The Locustans didn't seem interested in engaging, either with the team on the ground or with the Astro Scout as it pulled away from KS-5-1. Their behavior was strange and worrisome. Even after she was back in the safety of *Cutlass 31*, Ramya couldn't shake off the feeling of dread about the two watchers.

32

The extraction went faster than Ramya had expected. One by one people and craft were hauled back to the two Cutlasses. After the dutiful medic aboard *Cutlass 31* released her, Ramya waited eagerly near the hold for Lefrasi, Amireh, and Gael to return. The Unosi craft, the one Ramya and the others had dubbed the *Fury*, had been docked in the other Cutlass.

Gael's face was pensive when he walked out of the hold. He walked past hurriedly with barely a nod. He clearly didn't want to strike up a conversation and that was weird. Lefrasi and Amireh came right after. While Lefrasi rushed away with Gael to check on Chief Dal who had been confined to med bay by the medic, a glum-faced Amireh lingered.

Ramya asked Amireh the question at the forefront of her mind. "What happened to those Locustan stragglers?"

"We killed them both," Amireh said casually. "It was weird. They hardly put up a fight, almost as if they wanted us to kill them."

That was weird indeed. Why didn't they fly away? They had three Locustan craft with them, and they could've taken off if they wanted. Yet they didn't. Ramya stole a look at Amireh's drawn face. Was that what was worrying the man?

Ramya decided to tackle the issue directly. "What's the matter? Something troubling you?" she asked Amireh.

Amireh gave a shrug. "Anomaly Point just opened again. Zeta is in bad shape."

Ramya inhaled sharply. This was what they were all dreading. Ramya recalled what Captain Milos had said: They couldn't hold up against too many more openings.

"What about Trio?" she asked, her voice trembling a little. Captain Milos and his crew were out there, as was Gael's unit and

Amireh's mates.

Amireh's face darkened a notch. "Admiral Kanaa is dead," he said. "Her entire fleet was wiped out."

"Rida! Was she—"

Amireh shook his head mournfully even before she could finish.

"Where?"

"Palisades."

Palisades was another homeworld at Trio, a bigger planet with close to fifty million inhabitants. On top of that, Palisades had one of Confederate Space Fleet's training stations or FTS as they were commonly called. Losing that would be a major blow and Ramya almost didn't dare ask Amireh the outcome of the battle.

Amireh said it anyway. "Ninety percent of Palisades is destroyed. The FTS is decimated."

Ramya turned away; rage, frustration, and grief jumbled into a heavy, painful ball in her throat. Did the Locustans know of the FTS? Had that been the real reason they attacked Trio?

"What about Nakee?"

Nakee, the third and the smallest of the homeworlds at Trio, had nothing but some mining settlements on it, and Ramya didn't have high hopes for it surviving. Palisades and Tessa had advanced shielding tech and even they had not stood up long against the Locustans.

"We were able to drive the Locustans away from Trio before they got to Nakee. But the damage was done at Palisades."

Ramya released the breath she had been holding. At least some lives were saved and that was good news, but . . . the situation was grim as heck. There were other questions—difficult and fearsome ones—that needed to be asked, so Ramya voiced the first one.

"Have you heard from Captain Milos?"

Amireh nodded. "Captain Milos has been promoted to fill Kanaa's place. He's off to Zeta now."

"And . . . is your unit all right?"

Amireh shook his head. "We lost two of ours."

"Isbet?" Ramya blurted, nails digging painfully into her palms as she awaited an answer.

"No, Isbet's fine. It's Conley and Ree. I don't think you've met them."

She hadn't even heard those names before. But she was sure they were gallant young soldiers. No wonder Gael and Amireh looked so excessively glum. On top of the ravaging of Trio, this loss was personal to them. Seeing Amireh's dejected face, Ramya almost felt guilty of being relieved about Isbet. "I'm sorry," she added hurriedly.

"Yes, it's sad," Amireh said. In the next second, he pursed his lips and squared his shoulders. "Well, this is war. There won't be a happily ever after for everyone." He scoffed loudly. "Well, with the way things are going, there won't be a happily ever after for anyone."

Even though it sounded brutal and made Ramya's gut churn with anxiety, she knew Amireh was right. As a member of the GSO, he was trained to accept the inevitable outcome of war — death. That was how Gael could handle Nohr's gruesome death so easily. Ramya checked her thoughts — it couldn't have been easy, but Gael had taken it stoically.

Now he seemed far more affected and Ramya couldn't stop wondering why. She hesitated to pry further, but curiosity got the better of her in the end. "Any of them related to the lieutenant?"

Amireh shot her a funny look. "Ree is . . . was Sela's kid brother, of course."

It was Ramya's turn to be surprised. "Sela? Who's that?"

Amireh's lips moved, but no sound came out. "I-I thought you knew," he stuttered a few seconds later.

Ramya shrugged. "I don't."

Amireh was behaving oddly and she didn't understand why.

"I shouldn't be speaking about this," Amireh said. He picked up his weapon and turned to leave but Ramya's hand shot out faster to block his way.

"Wait! Why can't you?"

"It's a personal matter, of course," he said.

Personal? Pieces flew in — thoughts, conversations, ideas — to form an ill-fitted puzzle. Sela had to be the one Gael had lost, the love of his life. A sudden and unexpected emptiness made Ramya's stomach turn. "Come on, Amireh," she pleaded without even realizing what she was saying. "It doesn't seem like much of a secret anyway."

Amireh gave out a resigned sigh and cast a quick look around. "She was the lieutenant's sweetheart. They had known each other all their lives — grew up together, went to CAWStrat together, joined the GSO together. I knew them for a while. They made a perfect pair, pretty, funny, and sharp. But . . ."

"What happened? Did she die?"

Amireh broke into a chuckle. "No, no. She's fine. Just got married off in a hurry about a year ago." He paused and took a long breath. "He's never been the same since."

"So she liked someone else?" Ramya asked, knowing well the answer would be something different.

"Of course not," Amireh said. "She loved him just as much he loved her. But . . . Tucker Arlington wasn't having any of that. She was of low standing and she stood in the way of his son's future. So Tucker Arlington had her removed."

Ramya gasped for air as if she hadn't breathed in years. It wasn't Tuck alone. Her own father had orchestrated this . . . ruined two people's lives and their chance at happiness.

"I should be going now," Amireh said. Ramya nodded vaguely, lost in her thoughts as she watched the man walk away. She had always blamed Gael for her situation, not realizing how much he too had suffered. Perhaps she was just as selfish as her father, only in a different way.

She walked back to the room they had been assigned and sank into a seat. Kyo-Sedra-5-1 had already grown distant and soon the Cutlass entered the SLH. Ramya's thoughts drifted and she didn't know when she fell asleep. When she awoke, Ahool was sleeping, curled into a bundle in the seat across from her. Lefrasi, however, was furiously pacing the room. He walked up to her as soon as she stirred.

"Rami, you have to stop this. They've kept the chief under observation," he said. "I keep telling them to let the chief be, but they won't listen."

"They're just worried about his health," Ramya said groggily, hoping to calm Lefrasi down. "He's been a little strange lately and the medic just wants to —"

Lefrasi sank back into his seat noisily. "Our ancestors were there when the Unosi fought the invaders hundreds of years ago. They know how to use the weapon. And the chief is trying to speak to our ancestors."

"Oh!"

"Yes, and that's why he's sinking deeper into what you call a trance. We have to let him go. He has to reach the voices of our ancestors."

"No one's stopping him."

Lefrasi rolled his eyes. "Yes, but probing and poking isn't helping him meditate, Rami. You have to make the medic understand . . . the Uminato are born different. They're not regular people like me or you. Please, make him understand."

Lefrasi had a good point. They knew precious little about Mwandan physiology anyway, let alone the mystic sensibilities of an Uminato. The best way was to let the Mwandans handle themselves. But she also knew that Mett, the medic of *Cutlass 31*, was almost as stubborn as Sosa. Still, she had to make sure the medic's intervention was not hurting the chief.

"All right, I'll talk to him," Ramya said, forcing her tired legs to stand. Lefrasi followed her out of the room. They had not made twenty paces along when a bone-numbing tremor rippled through the Cutlass. The lights dimmed and even before a gasp of surprise could escape Ramya's throat, the entire corridor plunged into darkness.

33

Ramya stood in the pitch darkness, bewildered. Her heart drummed in her ears, her breath was a nervous wheeze. She sensed Lefrasi's presence behind her.

"What's happening?" Ramya asked, regaining composure swiftly. She hardly expected Lefrasi to answer. How would he know? This was as unexpected a situation to him as it was to her.

The one time Ramya had seen a ship's lights nearly blacked out was when the pirates had taken over the *Endeavor*. That couldn't be happening now. Space pirates wouldn't mess with a Cutlass belonging to the GSO. So if this ship could not have been similarly compromised, and since Ramya could still sense the movement of the ship in space, it had to be a failure of some kind in the ship's systems. Given that the ship was still in motion, it couldn't be a total failure of every system. So, she deduced quickly, perhaps the secondary power supply had some problems. "Let's get to the bridge and find out," she suggested.

They stumbled forward, bumping into walls every now and then — less as their eyes adjusted to the darkness — as they made their way. Had this been the *Endeavor*, Ramya would have had a good idea of the layout of the corridor. But this ship was unknown and she had to feel her way along the corridor like a blind person. They had not taken more than fifty steps when the lights came back on.

Ramya breathed a sigh of relief but then, instantly, she froze. There was light indeed, but this was not the ship's normal light. This was different, almost a glow that seeped from the walls around them and bathed them in a golden hue.

Ramya's heart picked up the pace when her eyes adjusted and she took in the scene. This was not the Cutlass. Somehow, they had been transported to a different place in a different time. She snapped around to look for Lefrasi, relaxing a little when she saw the Mwandan next to her. He looked just as bewildered, and even in the dim light, Ramya could tell his face was ashen.

"W-where are we?" Lefrasi stuttered.

Ramya wished she could answer. But she did not know. They were in a gigantic chamber with a sunken pit at the center of it. In that pit, a series of buttresses held up a large metallic object. People walked around the edge of the pit, studying the object. Ramya squinted but it didn't help her see better. She was too far away to see clearly, almost like a bird hovering far up in the sky.

"Can't see," she whispered. Lefrasi responded immediately with a nod. "Wish we could get closer."

Ramya regretted her words as soon as they left her mouth but it was already too late for regrets. It was as if someone was waiting to grant her wish. In the next instant, the chamber grew bigger around them, almost as if a magnifier had been inserted in between. For a moment, Ramya wanted to whack herself. How stupid could she have been? She did not know where she was and who those people were. They could be Locustans for all she knew. And now she had just wished herself closer to a dangerous enemy.

There was no room for regrets anymore. The chamber was big now, dwarfing her. Ramya hung awkwardly over rows of equipment scattered along its periphery. She tried to straighten herself, to get herself to stand and move, but couldn't. Realization dawned. She was not in the chamber physically—nothing and no one had transported them there. She was seeing, only seeing. This was a vision, a grand, unimaginable hologram of sorts.

"Rami, I know," Lefrasi's excited whisper floated to Ramya's ears. "It's . . . it's the chief. He's projecting his visions to us."

Incredible as the idea was, that was the only thing that made sense. But where were they? Who were those people? And what were they up to?

Wait! Ramya squinted again. She knew that enormous shape that lay at the center. It was the weapon they had just retrieved from Kyo-Sedra-5-1 — the *Fury*.

Heart pounding, Ramya looked again at the people around the pit. They were humanoids, but they were a species Ramya had not seen before. They were all very tall, with a shiny golden skin tone, and skinny . . . almost skeletal. She couldn't tell if the golden folk were male or female. They were all dressed alike, draped in floor-skimming white cloth with a golden belt at the waist.

Only a few among them were shorter and Ramya recognized that species as she scrutinized their forms. She was looking at Mwandans and . . .

"The Unosi?" the word came out of her with a disbelieving gasp. Could these golden-skinned people really be the legendary ancients? Were they seeing a vision of the past?

Lefrasi pointed at a person standing next to a gigantic array of portals, levers, and switches. "Look, they're using the black box."

It sure looked like the black box they had retrieved from the dome, or something identical. It was hooked to the side of the array and as the person fiddled with the controls, the *Fury's* door opened. Everyone around the podium turned to look at the open door. A few moments passed by, and Ramya could tell the assembly was waiting with bated breath for something to happen. It happened soon after. Two people — both golden-skinned but wearing pilot's attire in white — walked out of the *Fury*.

People rushed forward to greet them, some even embracing them. It seemed to Ramya the duo had just returned from a mission. But it couldn't have been a wildly successful mission because gloom hung in the atmosphere. There were bowed heads and woeful shakes that clearly indicated failure.

One of the Mwandans pointed at the equipment array with the black box and Ramya looked also. Holo images had formed over the array now and Ramya could easily identify a couple of them. The biggest one was of a wormhole, surrounded by a gigantic fleet of golden ships. Ramya was sure the ships were Unosi and the wormhole was none other than Anomaly Point. It seemed to shake and dim from time to time, as if it were about to vanish any moment.

Ramya turned her attention to the next image — a galactic map. It showed star systems and it only took a quick scan to be sure it wasn't their galaxy. Ramya moved on to the third and the strangest image. It was a dimly lit planet, its surface dark. Ramya could've sworn she was looking at Morris II from a distance. It could've been any of the Mwandan sanctuaries, for that matter, since they all looked the same, covered with the Manoko — the dark-leaved, sentient vegetation revered by the Mwandans.

She couldn't see the planet for long because it disappeared when the technician brought the image of the wormhole forward and it hid the others from view. The wormhole had clearly shrunk in the last few seconds. Not just shrunk, it was closing. Ramya looked at the crowd of Unosi. The wormhole was closing — yet they didn't seem happy. Why? Because they knew it would open again?

She turned to ask Lefrasi what he thought about it, but before she could, the ground shook underneath her feet. The scene around them contracted as rapidly as a pierced balloon. It was gone, just as suddenly as it had appeared. Ramya found herself back in the corridor of the Cutlass, blinking at the brightness. The lights had probably never dimmed at all. Only her mind had played a trick.

"Let's go check on Chief Dal," she said and Lefrasi agreed heartily. The medic, Mett, gave them a concerned look as soon as they stepped into med bay. He had been adjusting some monitors around Chief Dal who slept soundly on one of the beds.

"Good that you're here," the medic said to Lefrasi. "Your chief isn't well at all. His vitals sank and —"

"He's fine," Lefrasi snapped.

The medic crossed his arms. "Well, per my knowledge he's not. He's close to slipping into a coma."

The duo glared angrily at each other and Ramya was almost

about to throw herself in the middle when Gael and Amireh rushed through the door.

"Mett, don't disturb the chief," Gael said right away. "Just let him be."

"Why would I disturb him? I'm just monitoring him," Mett said, throwing an accusing look at Lefrasi. "Take him out of here if you like," he added gruffly. "See if I care. All this for —"

"No one's taking him anywhere, Mett," Gael interrupted. "Just don't move him or —"

Mett rolled his eyes and threw his arms up, before stomping away. Gael and Amireh exchanged a look. It seemed like Mett's temper was something they were used to around here.

"You saw it too," Ramya said as comprehension trickled in. Gael and Amireh had to have seen Chief Dal's vision also. That's why they had rushed here. "You saw the scene Chief Dal projected."

"Yes," Gael said. "We saw it. The ancients used the *Fury* to shut the wormhole down. The Mwandans were there also." He tilted his chin at the sleeping form of Dal. "I'm sure he's trying to find out more."

"I still don't understand," Amireh said. "If they had closed the blasted wormhole already, why in iffin hell did it open up again?"

Gael shrugged. "Wish I knew, Amireh."

It would have been a sure win if they understood how Anomaly Point worked. But they didn't. Ramya suppressed a sigh as she stared at Chief Dal's prostrate form. Whatever the secret of that wormhole was, they had to find out fast.

34

Ramya forced her tired legs to walk faster as she sped toward her father's chambers. She was running late. The request for her presence to discuss how to proceed with the discoveries at the Unosi Hinterland had come two minutes earlier. The guards parted the doors and Ramya slunk in. When her father didn't shoot a disapproving glare at her, she cast a quick look around to assess the situation.

Four of the five screens in Trysten Kiroff's underground meeting chamber — now dubbed the Combat Room or CR — were ablaze when Ramya entered the room. It was funny that the room itself was relatively empty and quiet but the giant screens buzzed nonstop.

The screen in the middle was devoid of a central figure. Ramya knew that was the feed from Zeta and the screen was reserved for either Admiral Zoho or Captain Milos . . . no, make that Admiral Milos. At the moment a managed hubbub of officers and soldiers at the starbase ebbed and flowed across the screen. The main person was missing. Ramya presumed that was the reason conversation was held up here.

Marson Hale, the Chief of Fleets, filled the screen to the right. Although he was the one in focus, a room full of grim-faced officers hovered in the background.

On the screen to Marson's left was a view of an opulent pool with clear blue water. At the edge of it, seated on a throne of sorts, was Molen Danukis, the Chief of Chairs at the Galactic Senate.

Ramya's lips curled in disgust. Could Molen be any more flagrantly irresponsible, showing up like this when the galaxy was at the edge of annihilation? If there was a way to reach across the screens, she'd have landed a punch on his flaccid belly or at least chucked him off that ridiculous throne into the water.

Trysten Kiroff sat at the head of the table, his fingers tapping the dark-grained wood relentlessly. Lord Wultoph Aristide, her father's right-hand man, sat to his left. The chairs around the table were all taken—mostly by officers of the Space Fleet and quite a few house leaders, mostly allies of House Kiroff—except for one to his right. Her father looked up at her and gestured at the empty seat. Ramya gave him a nod and slid into the chair, smiling inwardly.

It was funny to think this was what she had craved all her life, a position of importance, respect from her illustrious father. Now that she was seated to Trysten Kiroff's right, she wasn't half as elated as she had hoped to be. That was plain weird and unexpected. Did she want more? Or did she want something else altogether?

"How is everything?" Lefrasi, who sat two chairs down, leaned forward to speak to Ramya. He was asking about her trip down to Chief Dal's room, specifically about the chief's condition.

"The same," she said, without going into too much detail in front of the whole council. Chief Dal's condition was a topic her father was intentionally keeping under wraps.

Lefrasi's face grew glum. Ramya understood his worries. The chief was still in a deep trance that all the doctors classified as a Level-5 coma, which meant a severe lack of consciousness. They wanted to support his life functions, but Lefrasi objected. Lefrasi was sure the chief was trying to read the memories of their ancestors and find a way to use the Unosi weapon they had discovered. So, per his request, the chief had been put in a quiet room surrounded by Manoko plants and praying Mwandans. Yet so far the chief had not projected any more visions. Although Ramya had not told Lefrasi, that fact worried her.

Trysten Kiroff's guttural growl made Ramya stir and look up at him. "Where the hell is that man?" he muttered angrily. His brows had furrowed. Clearly, his anger had something to do with Milos's absence.

Although Trysten Kiroff wasn't exactly looking for Admiral Milos for his personal gain, his manner irritated Ramya. If Milos was late, he had to have a good reason. The man was busy defending Zeta and trying to shore up a collapsing defense against another wave of Locustans, and that wasn't a particularly easy task. As much as she wanted to defend the new admiral's absence, Ramya was determined not to get into an argument with her father about it. She had gotten better at putting some emotional distance between herself and her father and she found that space served her well.

Ramya tore her eyes away from his clouded face to the fourth screen on the wall. It showed a view of the main lab. Engineers scuttled around and clustered everywhere. Some were around a workstation. They were investigating the Unosi black box, with little luck so far. The *Fury* was on the far side of the labs and more engineers surrounded that.

"What the hell is taking him so long?" he father snapped, this time loudly enough for everyone present to take notice.

Marson Hale shifted uncomfortably in his seat. "We haven't had news of another incursion. Have you?" he said in a nervous, raspy voice. "What if the sorties brought on a new wave?"

Ramya squinted at Hale, unable to follow what he meant.

Molen scoffed. "I think his grandiose mission into Anomaly Point has fallen flat. So now he is too embarrassed to show his face. And here I was preparing to celebrate our grand success."

A mission into Anomaly Point? What in the stars was Molen talking about?

"Milos is sending in fighters to assess the wormhole. He wants to bombard the structure, hopes to destabilize it," Lefrasi explained as soon as she asked.

"When did this come about?" Ramya asked. Even when she'd stopped by the CR an hour ago, she hadn't heard of such plans.

"We heard of it a few minutes ago," Lefrasi replied, nodding surreptitiously at Molen on the screen. "Obviously, people are displeased at the sudden change in strategy."

Obviously.

"Success or failure, we need to know," her father grumbled.

Molen Danukis chuckled lightly. "Those men are undependable. Always have been. I don't know what better you expect of them."

The fire in her head that Ramya had been desperately trying to keep down, lit up in an instant. The Danukis family had been all talk in these days of terror. None of them — not even the CAWStrat trained Armand who was Ramya's ex-classmate — showed up at the battlefront. What right did the likes of Molen have to criticize Zoho or Milos?

Molen grumbled on. "Here we are, struggling with food rations and mandatory drafts, and look at the people who are leading the fight."

Struggling? Food rations? Ramya blinked at the enormous plate next to Molen's chair. It was piled high with what could only be roasted legs of Canila fowl.

"They're at the forefront of the greatest crisis we have seen in the galaxy," Marson said. "If they need more time, then — "

Molen sat up in his monstrously gaudy chair. "They are undependable. Undependable, you understand? You had to be incredibly foolish to entrust the protection of Zeta to those fools."

Ramya looked at her father. His finger tapping had sped up but his lips were pursed. She drew a breath and turned her burning eyes toward Molen's screen. She was not going to take his insulting Milos lying down.

"Perhaps you should get to Zeta then, Molen?" she started in a scathing voice. That was not the way someone like her with no official title should address the Chief of Chairs, but Ramya didn't care about the consequences. This had gone on far too long and Molen didn't deserve the respect. She sensed eyes widening around her, but she didn't stop even to breathe. "Oh wait, I forgot. You and your family are cowards. All you can do is lounge around and impugn the brave men who are risking their lives to protect yours."

Molen's face had flushed when Ramya started and now it was a flaming red. The colorful drink he held in his hand visibly shook, the sight making Ramya's mouth curl in satisfaction.

"How dare you?" Molen whispered. "You--"Molen tore his glare off her face and threw it at her father. "This is what a Kiroff heir looks like, eh, Trysten? An uncultured mutt with no control over her tongue? You're lucky I excused her behavior at the hearing but there's a limit to misconduct. You better rein your pup in, Trysten, or you'll regret having known me."

Before Ramya could reply, her father broke into chuckles. "Is that a threat, Molen?" he said. He was still chuckling but there was no mirth in it. "My daughter might be young enough not to know how to speak, but you should know better than to threaten me."

Ramya squared her shoulders and drew in a long breath, her father's words cutting at her heart. She knew well enough how to speak, she just wanted to put Molen in his place.

"Besides, Molen" — Trysten had not finished yet — "given what my daughter has done for the galaxy, she has earned the right to speak whatever way she likes. You want to make her stop? Go ahead, try. I dare you. Trying to incite me won't help you at all because I support every word she just said."

Molen squirmed out of his garish throne, trembling on his stubby legs. He wanted to say something — many things, Ramya presumed — but he couldn't. His mouth simply opened and closed, and opened and closed again. Five times, Ramya counted. She put in everything she had to make sure she didn't burst out laughing.

Thankfully, right then, the taut face of Terenze Milos filled the central screen. "Apologies for keeping you waiting," he said gruffly. Ramya noted his tired eyes, the sallowness of his skin. The stubble on his chin had now grown into a scruffy clump. "I have dispatched my envoys and they should arrive soon with my message. I wish us all luck."

Ramya sat up at his strange words. Where was the update on the planned sorties? Besides, they needed Milos and his counsel to strategize about the Unosi artifacts. He said nothing about that. Instead . . . envoys? And why did his message sound like a final farewell?

Ramya—or anyone else for that matter—couldn't get as far as asking the question. The screen flickered and a heartbeat later, it went dark.

35

Zeta—the entirety of the starbase—had gone dark. There was no live communication channel from Zeta whatsoever after Terenze Milos transmitted the message. Engineers, on El-Iss and at every other station Space Command had, scanned and probed but no one could find a way to communicate with Zeta. Probes around the starbase worked fine and Zeta still existed, but that was all the information anyone outside of Zeta had. An hour later, other than sending a recon mission to check on Zeta, no one knew what to do.

Except for Molen Danukis, who wasted no time scoffing at Marson Hale. "This is what happens when you put the gateway to our galaxy in the hands of a pair of mavericks. Once this is over," —Molen wagged a threatening finger at Hale— "I will make you stand trial for incompetence and reckless endangerment of our galaxy."

Ramya didn't have to air her choicest words for Molen because Marson Hale raised a hand to silence him immediately. "Do that. But first, let us survive this." He addressed Trysten Kiroff next. "I will meet with you soon, Lord Paramount. After I've dispatched the recon mission to Zeta."

As soon as the screens shut down, Trysten Kiroff stood up. "I'm going to check with engineering," he announced. Ramya jumped to her feet. She was not about to miss a chance to tour the labs with her father. People were always much more willing to share when the big boss came by.

Her gambit didn't go unrewarded. The always uncommunicative and unapproachable Norgoran chief scientist, Eiger, and his assistant rushed up to them as soon as they approached the *Fury*. A hopeful smile tugged at the corners of Ramya's mouth when the chief scientist started to speak, her heart thumping eagerly for news that they had decoded the *Fury's* secrets.

"We haven't been able to get inside, Lord Paramount," Eiger said apologetically, and Ramya's hopes sank like a lead weight. Eiger, probably sensing the hopelessness, quickly pointed a finger up. "But . . . we know a lot about this craft. It is made of a metallic compound that's far more resilient than the strongest materials we know. It has a tiny cockpit, probably can seat up to two people. But it has a weapons bay that fills more than half of the craft. The rest is the propulsion system. The layout and the emphasis on the weapon carrying capability make me think this was used primarily for weapons delivery.

"They are studying the controller back there," — Eiger jerked a thumb at the sprawling workstation where engineers were crowded around the black box — "and I believe that's the key to opening this craft up."

Ramya recalled the scene Chief Dal had projected to them. The Unosi had been tinkering with the box . . . controller when the door opened.

"We need more people on this," Trysten Kiroff said in a grim voice. "We don't have the luxury of time."

The coldness of his voice made Ramya's spine tingle with fear. He was right, time wasn't on their side. Getting the Unosi weapons meant nothing if they didn't know how to use them. Right now, they had no clue how to even get the craft to open.

Her father tapped his chin thoughtfully. "The propulsion system," he said, pointing at the *Fury*, "we need to find out more about what fuel it uses. We need to get this thing spaceworthy as quickly as we can."

Eiger nodded. "Yes, Lord Paramount. Once we can get inside the craft—"

His sentence remained unfinished. Trysten Kiroff's aide, Casten — he was like a shadow to her father — had been hovering a few steps behind them. He shot forward.

"Lord Paramount, an unscheduled flight from Zeta just arrived," he said in a rush, checking his communicator frequently. "Commander Ross Pornell is here in a WB from Admiral Kanaa's fleet. Says he has an urgent message from Terenze Milos."

"Ross?" a gleeful shout escaped Ramya's mouth.

Casten nodded, casting a bewildered look at Trysten Kiroff who started walking to the exit. "Bring them to the Combat Room immediately," Trysten ordered.

The tour of the lab postponed, Ramya and her father hastened back to the CR. Ross was already in the room when they reached it, along with Fenny and a few officers of the Space Fleet. As soon as Ramya and her father entered, Ross nodded curtly.

"So happy to see you," Ramya cried, rushing to bridge the distance between them.

Both Ross and Fenny broke into smiles but Ramya didn't miss the tiredness in both of their eyes, and the gashes scattered over their faces. They seemed to have aged years in just a few days. Obviously! They had been through hell and it showed.

Ramya knew it was a grim moment that asked for seriousness, but she couldn't stop the all-encompassing relief taking over her senses. Rather, she didn't want to. She didn't know who would survive this war and moments like these were precious. She threw her arms around Fenny and Ross and held them for a second. Her family, that's what they were, and Ramya whispered thanks to the stars for keeping them safe so far.

Fenny patted Ramya's shoulder and chuckled. "Hey! Come on, kid. We're all right. We'll make it."

Ramya wasn't so sure. She tried to suppress the huge sigh that flooded her insides but it slipped out regardless.

Ross held her hand and gave it a squeeze. "Have faith. We couldn't have come so far without it."

He had a point. Faith was all they had and they couldn't lose that now. Still, fear of inevitable doom kept Ramya's insides cold. Even after discovering the weapon of the Unosi, they hadn't made much progress. And time was running out. Fast.

Ramya sensed her father's presence behind her and moved a step away. She wasn't ashamed of how she felt. She didn't worry about her father's disapproval. Emotions had always meant a lot to her, and with the galaxy's clock ticking down, she didn't want to shy away from showing people she cared. But at the moment she had to focus and hear what message Terenze Milos had sent them.

"Commander Ross, good to see you. You have a message from Admiral Milos?" her father asked, his voice cold and his eyes like stone.

Ross bowed a little before replying. "Yes, we do," he said curtly. He was trying to match Trysten Kiroff's coldness, Ramya understood, but he was no match for her father.

"And what is it?"

"He wants us to take the Unosi weapon to Zeta as soon as we find out how to use it."

"They're still investigating it," Ramya said. "No breakthrough yet."

"What was the status of Anomaly Point when you left Zeta?"

Ramya didn't miss the pall of darkness that fell across both Ross and Fenny's faces at her father's question. "It is open but there's no activity. Sometimes, if we're lucky, it takes a day or two before the first of a new wave comes out after the wormhole opens, so . . ." Ross left the sentence unfinished.

Her father crossed his arms and took a long bracing breath. "Can Zeta hold up against another wave?"

"Depends on how big it is," Ross said. Ramya fought back the chill in her bones and digested the information. Ross didn't say it, but she knew Zeta couldn't fare well for too long. And if Zeta fell, that would be the end of the galaxy.

"Tell me the man has a plan in place," Trysten Kiroff said, his jaw as hard as a rock.

Fenny pursed her lips and looked away. Ross shifted on his feet uncomfortably under Trysten Kiroff's glacial stare. "He plans to send sorties into Anomaly Point," he said. "Shelling the wormhole might make it collapse."

Trysten Kiroff looked up at the roof and let out a long breath. "I heard about that. But what will he send in? WBs? Does he even know if they can withstand the conditions within Anomaly Point?"

"There was a recon mission earlier today. Some WBs went in."

Trysten Kiroff crossed his arms. "And?"

"And . . . the good news is . . . they flew in and out of there fine. But, they could only go so far."

"What do you mean?"

"A few seconds in, they were blocked."

"How?"

Ross shook his head. "We don't know. But it doesn't matter right now. We can still go that far in and bomb the heck out of the wormhole. It may not destabilize Anomaly Point completely but perhaps—"

Ramya didn't hear Ross anymore. Her mind had hit a worrisome snag—if the Locustans were blocking entry, the *Fury* was useless. They'd been hoping in vain. But her father found a completely different interpretation.

"Perhaps that's why they needed the *Fury*," he said. "Maybe it can get past this blockage."

Fenny chuckled. "That's funny. Zoho thinks the same. He thinks the Unosi encountered this exact problem. And that's why they built *Fury*."

Her father closed his eyes and shook his head. "Still, these sorties are a bad idea. We hardly know anything about Anomaly Point."

"We know enough," Ross countered vehemently. "We have determined preliminary strike points. If we can hit those, we will cause enough damage." The more her father frowned, the more adamantly Ross continued. "Besides, do you see much of a choice, Lord Paramount Kiroff? We either try something new or just wait like cattle to be slaughtered. Would you rather die a coward?"

For a moment it seemed to Ramya her father would slap the living daylights out of Ross. She was ready to jump between them and given how Fenny's eyes darted back and forth between Ross and her father, Fenny had to be thinking the same.

Thankfully, the taut atmosphere dissipated quickly. "Why couldn't Milos talk to us directly?" her father asked. "Why did he cut the channels off?"

Ross cast a quick look over his shoulder and leaned forward a little. "He believes they're spying on us," Ross said, his voice barely a whisper.

"What?" Her father sounded incredulous and Ramya felt the same disbelief herself.

Who would be spying on them? The Locustans? How?

Ross cast another quick look around. "He believes the Locustans chose to attack Trio for a reason. No, not because it was the system closest to Anomaly Point, but because of the FTS. And they will be taking out all of our defense installations one by one." Ramya drew a sharp breath. She had had the same thought not too long ago. The precise way the Locustans had spread into the galaxy was strange. It was almost as if they had a map laid out in front of them. Ross continued, "They know everything about us and they're probably listening to every strategic conversation we're having out here."

"You mean they have spies among us?" her father voiced the darkest question that had long stirred in Ramya's head.

Ross and Fenny exchanged a look before Ross shrugged. "We're not sure. All we know is they seem to have very precise information about us and that's plain—"

"Unexplainable," her father completed. He shook his head and rubbed the bridge of his nose for a second or two. "That's why Milos cut off communication?"

"Yes."

A frown that had been rippling on her father's forehead

deepened. "Well, we can't just fly in the dark. I could use my private network internally but—"

"I wouldn't do that," Ross interrupted. "The scientists at Zeta believe they're preying on certain predictable wavelengths. Your network could be compromised as well. Then they'd take out all your factories and—"

"So what then? Work in disconnected, guerrilla groups? That's a recipe for disaster."

"Well, we don't have to," Ross said. "We have the Mwandans. The Uminato among them can set up communication channels. All we need to do is place the Uminato at strategic points."

Trysten Kiroff stared disbelievingly at Ross for a few seconds. Then he chuckled. "That's a good idea. Good old Milos."

"Um . . . actually," Fenny interrupted. "You should thank Ross for that idea. It was all his."

"I see," her father said. He nodded appreciatively at Ross. "That was unconventional thinking, Commander. I wouldn't have thought of Mwandans."

"Ross knows everything there is to know about Mwandans," Ramya added. "Or any of the races, really. He's a history buff."

Her father's brow crinkled. "What's a history buff doing on a freighter?"

"Trying to get food on my plate," Ross replied in a heartbeat.

An uneasy silence hung in the air for a second. Ramya knew the reason Ross was working on a freighter was because he had no other choice. Had his family's livelihood not been upended by the Kiroff family's greed, he'd probably be a teacher at a university. Ramya made a mental note—after the war was over, if they ever made it out alive, she had to speak to her father about Halperion. She had to fix everything the Kiroffs had broken on the planet.

"Well, get some rest," her father told Ross. "The Chief of Fleets should be here shortly. We'll discuss our next steps then. We'll need you there."

Ramya studied her father's face, the emotions coursing surreptitiously across his eyes that no one but Ramya could read. She knew it was hard for him to speak with as much respect as he did to Ross — anyone without noble blood was automatically at a lower standing with Trysten Kiroff and he also suspected his daughter and heir had a thing for this nobody — but he did it nonetheless. Ramya was thankful for his grace, almost proud of it.

"Well, look at that" — Fenny crossed her arms and raised a brow at Trysten Kiroff as he walked away — "Nasty Kiroff actually praised you, Ross. That's something I never thought I'd see. I think he likes you."

Ramya lingered in the CR, unexpectedly catching her father throw a worried look at Ross as he walked out. She scoffed inwardly thinking how far off Fenny was from the truth. She knew her father didn't like Ross. He was only trying to keep the peace.

36

A day later Ramya stood in the CR along with every leading member of the galaxy that was currently present at El-Iss and watched the first confederate sorties take off toward Anomaly Point. The screen didn't receive its feed from the regular communication channels anymore. Instead, it was now enabled by a Mwandan Uminato who sat cross-legged below the assembly of projection screens. In a flurry of activity, Uminatos had been placed at certain strategic points across the galaxy and more were on the way to cover all the bases.

Ross stood next to Ramya and wrung his hands endlessly. Everyone else was just as nervous or worried as they watched the shiny specks that were the Wentworth-Busas streak out of the battered starbase. Every eye in the room followed their trajectory until they vanished into the darkness—the Uminato's vision was not nearly as sharp as the probes that aided the regular feeds—and then stared hopefully at the giant ring of light that signified the mouth of the enormous wormhole that was Anomaly Point.

Over the past day, a zillion iterations of trajectories and payloads and every other thing that was needed in a shelling operation had been run and the precise calculations made. The ten WBs—most likely on a suicide mission into Anomaly Point—were to drop the shells starting from inside out in the periphery of the mouth. Ramya didn't have much hope for this first mission but she prayed for a miracle nonetheless.

Her father had been skeptical of the plan at first but then, after he had run a few simulations, he had nodded thoughtfully. "The Locustans have found a way to stabilize the wormhole. That has to be achieved by a careful balance of matter within the structure. So if we can destabilize it just a bit, then perhaps . . ."

He hadn't said much more after that--he was a pragmatic man

who believed more in facts than in conjecture--but Ramya knew he had some hope simmering inside him. That was enough for her to believe.

"There they are," someone shouted on the other side of the assembly. Ramya had to squint hard to see them, but she located them in the end — tiny dots that stood out against the vivid rim of the wormhole. It was a brief view; soon the WBs blended once more into the gaping blackness near the mouth.

With a loud beep, a timer next to the screens started its countdown from twenty. This was another device her father had fashioned, a simple means to predict the moment to expect results from the attack. Ramya turned around to check on Trysten Kiroff. While everyone in the room had gathered around the screens, her father was at his seat at the head of the long table, his sharp eyes fixed on the screen, fingers tapping his cheek as he waited.

Lieutenant Gael Arlington — he had just returned from Trio with his unit, many of whom needed medical attention before they shipped out to Zeta — sat like a statue carved of stone to her father's left. Ramya grimaced a little, albeit much less than she used to when she first knew of her father's plans for Gael. She had gotten used to seeing him around and hardly disliked his company anymore, but a speck of resentment still lingered deep inside.

Another beep signaling the end of the countdown made her turn back to the screen.

"Any moment now," Ross whispered. Ramya shot a quick look at him. The muscles of his face were rippling with excitement, and his eyes gleaming.

Nothing happened. No telltale sign of destabilization, not even a flicker near Anomaly Point. The clock completed another countdown from twenty. The wormhole loomed, just as menacingly glorious as it had always been.

With a soft sigh, Ramya turned away and made her way out of the crowd. Pondering a second, she walked to the end of the table where her father and Gael sat. Trysten Kiroff threw a quick, appraising look at her.

"What do you think?" he asked as soon as she lowered herself into the chair to his right.

"About what?"

"That, of course," he flicked a brow at the screen lit up by the wormhole. "Think this will work?"

Ramya stiffened. How was she supposed to know? The calculations were vague at best since they had no facts to go by, no previous experience at having done such a thing as bombing a wormhole. She fixed her eyes on the screen, trying to ignore her father's impatient frown on her face. She sensed Gael shift uncomfortably in his seat. Was this a test of some kind?

"You don't have an opinion?" her father asked again. "Or are you too scared to voice it?"

Did he have to keep poking at her fragile ego like that? Of course he did. He was good at it. He enjoyed riling people, pushing their buttons, particularly hers. Perhaps what he was doing now was entertainment to contain his own fears.

For a second Ramya thought she'd let it pass. Then she gave in to the temptation.

"Don't you know by now that I'm not afraid to voice my opinions?" she asked, holding her father's steely gaze with equal poise. Well, almost equal. And even though her voice never quivered, her heart thumped wildly. This was not how one spoke to Lord Paramount Kiroff. But his question had been a tease, and she had to show him her strength. It was right now, or never.

Her father's lips thinned. "Then what do you think of that?" he asked again, his voice glacial.

Gael, Ramya noted, had conveniently fixed his gaze on the screen, refusing to look at the quiet duel between father and daughter.

"I don't know —"

Ramya realized her mistake right away. However, before she

could veer herself away from the hesitant beginning, her father hissed at her. "Never, never, ever start with an 'I don't know.' It makes you look weak, and makes you look like a fool." He paused to draw a sharp breath through gritted teeth. "Do you realize your odds of succeeding in this world, Lady Ramya? You're a girl in a galaxy run by men who are neither trained nor willing to give you respect. You have to wrest it from them. You can only do that when they perceive you as strong . . . their equal or better yet, their superior. All these years, I've tried to make you tough and sharp. I thought you were getting better. But here you are again, unprepared . . . shaky."

A flush surged up Ramya's face. Even though no one except Gael was within earshot, her father's harsh words—although even in the haze of ear-burning humiliation, Ramya had to admit this was indeed the bitter truth about the world she lived in—made her want to flee the room. She didn't, though. She barely even flinched.

"All right, let's try it again," her father said.

This time around, Ramya was ready. "I think there's a chance they'll do some damage to the wormhole, but . . ." she paused to take a breath before continuing, "but I doubt it'll do significant damage. We hardly understand how they built this thing. How can we break it? I mean, we could get lucky. But that's all we can hope for."

"The *Fury*. We have to get through to it," her father muttered. He looked up at Ramya's drawn face and frowned again. "You're not excited about that either. Why not?"

"Because we're nowhere near the tech level of the Unosi. And even they failed to shut that monster wormhole, even with the *Fury*. Not to mention that we're running out of time."

He stayed silent for a while. Then suddenly he leaned over and placed a hand on her shoulder. "Hope is a slippery thing, Bella. Grab it with everything you've got. The true end comes only when you give up on hope."

She must've looked like an idiot, her mouth shutting and opening like a fish out of water, unable to blink, let alone speak. She didn't care how she looked. For Ramya, cuddles and hugs from her parents were things dreams were made of. She could hardly even recall the last time her father had patted her shoulder. Then, to call her Bella? She hadn't even expected him to know the name Grappa Abelei, Trysten's father, always lovingly called her. Yet he did. The back of her eyes stung and a dull ache came to life at the base of her throat. Why now? Couldn't he have called her that all these years?

A loud cheer behind Ramya stopped the tears from trickling past her defenses. Barely. She hastily dabbed her eyes, acutely conscious of Gael's curious stare, before she looked at the spectators near the screens. They were cheering. Loudly. Ross turned around and flashed a mighty grin at her before she could fathom the cause for celebration.

On the screen above them, Anomaly Point had started to flicker. And it had already shrunk a bit.

"I'll be damned," her father said. "We've destabilized that monster."

It was a miracle indeed. Although Ramya worried it wouldn't last very long—the wormhole showed no apparent sign of collapsing totally—but at least this bought them some time. Perhaps they could get the *Fury* up and running by the time it stabilized again.

At that precise moment, the doors swung open and a man—his ample girth barely made it through the door—with bright red hair swaggered in.

Oh no! Ramya shrank back in her chair as she recognized Tucker Arlington, Gael's loud-mouthed father. This was unexpected. The decision to shut down most of the communication channels was partly to blame for the lack of announcements that usually preceded anyone's entry into the CR. They needed to get the damn comms on again, Ramya thought, wincing as she braced herself for the storm that was Tucker Arlington.

"So, this is our command center," Tucker said to the man accompanying him. Ramya recognized the Chief of Fleets, Marson Hale, right away. He looked like a midget next to Tucker, and his face was drawn into a look of extreme annoyance. Ramya was sure, if Marson Hale could, he would slap Tucker Arlington into silence. Tucker, however, paid no heed to the Chief of Fleets' displeasure. "Lord Kiroff, always a pleasure," he added, beaming.

Trysten Kiroff rose to greet the two men, and Ramya was just about to slink away from her chair and mingle with the crowd near the screens when a short figure shot past the open doors and careened inside.

"Rami," he shrieked as he made a beeline for her.

"Ahool?"

"They open the *Fury*," Ahool shouted, heaving. "Fenny and Merin, they did it."

"Really?" A grin spread over Ramya's face even before Ahool nodded to confirm it. Heart thrashing against her chest, she followed Ahool out of the CR. It was probably the best day the galaxy had had since the war began.

37

The laboratory was in a state of heightened activity when Ramya entered with Ahool. She had not waited for anyone else, not even her father. Trysten Kiroff didn't want the entire troupe of people in the CR to descend on his labs and when Ramya left the CR, he was reminding everyone of the strict protocols and procedures for visiting.

Down in the lab, people were running around and more people — Ramya spotted Eiger and his two assistants near the craft's entryway — had crowded around the *Fury*. Instead of heading toward the golden craft, whose surface now had a reddish glow, Ramya looked for Merin — a Mwandan engineer who was also an Uminato — and Fenny. She located them not near the craft but instead near the workstation that held the black box.

The last time Ramya had been here, the scientists and engineers of Kiroff Industries had been all around the box, with Merin and Fenny trying to peek in from the sidelines. Now the scene had changed drastically. The two outsiders sat like a pair of queens at the center of the workstation, while the staff stood behind them, as if waiting on them, assisting from time to time but for the most part watching curiously.

As soon as Ramya reached the workstation, Fenny flashed a wide grin. "Guess what? Dal finally came through. He took us through a scene where they handle the iffin box and after that, it didn't take too long to hook this baby up the right way and crack it open. The ancients used five-point electrical sources, did you know that?"

She didn't, but Ramya knew they used a three-point, far different from a five.

"As soon as we set up the right voltage differentials, the controls came alive," Merin said. "Look!"

Indeed, the surface of the black box had lit up, revealing rows of symbols that glowed red like the *Fury*. At first glance, the symbols looked familiar to Ramya.

"These look like Mwandan script," she said, recalling seeing them once, long ago on Morris II. "Are they?"

Merin smiled. "You're right. And wrong. They definitely are similar to the letters we use presently but they are an ancient form. I believe this was what we used back when the Unosi were present in the galaxy."

Ramya chuckled as a random thought streamed through her mind. "It's funny that the Unosi would leave us a box coded with Mwandan script, isn't it? As if —"

"As if they knew we would come looking." Ramya almost jumped at her father's voice. She had been so engrossed in her conversation that she had not noticed when he and his entourage — a tiny selection of the crowd that was present in the CR — had come in. Most of the officers and the house leaders had gone to look at the obvious attraction, the *Fury*, and only a handful came to the workstation.

"They *had* to know," Merin said confidently. "Mwandan customs and culture haven't changed much over the years. Our government wouldn't let us change, they wouldn't let us adopt a single new concept from any of the other races. That has been the reason we have been revolting against our government for years. But now I believe our people's self-imposed seclusion was for a reason. They didn't want us to change. If we had let outside influences in, our language would have evolved more. It couldn't have been as easy giving this box commands as it is now.

"Look, I say 'close.' And watch there." Merin entered the word on to a console and pointed at the *Fury* in the distance. Just like magic, the doors of the craft shut.

"It's all basic commands," Fenny explained. "This is a remote controller for that honking big ship. We think the thing could be flown both ways — with personnel inside or via this."

"We have to find out the maximum distance the controller works," Trysten Kiroff said.

"We have to find out a hell lot of things, Lord Paramount," Fenny said thoughtfully. "We've just uncovered the tip of an iffin iceberg. We know next to nothing about it. It'll take time to — "

"We don't have time, Fenny," snapped Ross, who'd been standing behind Trysten Kiroff, tapping his feet non-stop. "You better get the basics figured out fast so we can hurl this thing into Anomaly Point."

Fenny had been hunched over a console. Now she slowly uncurled herself like a spring. Crossing her arms, she frowned at Ross.

"What do you mean, hurl?"

"Well, not exactly hurl," Ross said, waving impatiently at her. "But quickly get the controls figured out and then send it into the wormhole to shell it."

Ramya had a whole lot of things to say against that reasoning, but Fenny beat her to it. "This is our biggest hope, Ross. The one weapon that might make a real difference. We have to understand it better before we even take it out of here."

"Well, I have news for you. We don't have the time to lounge around and research away."

"No one is lounging, Ross," Trysten Kiroff said. "But we have to give it the time that is needed."

"Says the man who has never been to the front lines."

"Calm down," the Chief of Fleets, who had been quietly standing next to Trysten, said snappishly. "I know you're not officially part of the Space Fleet, but still you're operating under its protocols. Insubordination is always an offense and it applies to you as well."

"Throw me out, then," Ross roared back. "You shouldn't blink. I'm sure you have a galaxy of people willing to lay their lives down. One of them can replace me right away."

Marson Hale's lips thinned to lines but he didn't reply. Ross scoffed and cast a mocking look back at Fenny. "You should know better than them, Fenny."

Fenny had just opened her mouth when Trysten Kiroff raised his arms. "That's enough. Let's spend what little time we have in a constructive manner, yes?" The way he said it—like the flustered adult trying to break up a fight in a playground full of toddlers—made Ramya chuckle.

Ross, however, went red in the face and huffed. "People are dying out there, do you understand?" he said, glaring at Trysten. "It's easy for you to spit out fancy words but every second counts out there in Zeta."

Ramya bit her lip. She understood the frustration Ross was feeling. Besides, even though what he was saying was illogical and unsound, he was her compatriot. She couldn't fall out with him when the whole world was watching. She owed him loyalty.

But then, wasn't Ross being unfair to her father? Trysten Kiroff had dedicated every factory the Kiroffs owned to supporting this war and he certainly did not deserve this disrespect. Didn't she owe some loyalty to her father and her house?

"I think I've found something new!" Merin's excited shout broke the taut atmosphere in the blink of an eye. Forgetting disputes and dropping debates, everyone turned toward the engineer. "Wait, let's try this."

Merin's long knobby fingers danced over the console, and a second or two later, a ball of intense, blinding light erupted from the top of the black box. Someone shrieked, a few fell back in surprise, and for a second, Ramya clamped her hands over her eyes. In the next moment, a sharp, shrill sound, like the screech of a dying bird, rose from the box and reverberated across the room. Ramya plugged her ears with her fingers, but the mind-numbing screech still kept coming. Fenny was doubled over on the floor. More people fell to their knees around her, grasping their heads, writhing in agony.

This is the end.

She was wrong, they were all wrong. The Unosi weapon was

probably not meant to save the galaxy, it was probably meant to kill them all.

She craved a sip of water. The drinking station was near the wall and she had to get to it. If only getting there was as easy as wishing. One step and then another, Ramya stumbled forward, her gaze blurry, her head throbbing. She had barely taken ten steps when the screech rose to an unbearable pitch. Ramya's guts churned before she careened into a sightless and thoughtless fog.

38

Ramya had no idea how much time had passed when her senses cleared again. She felt exhausted, her body sore, her mind sluggish, her throat parched. She realized the terrifying noise was gone, as was the light. She turned around slowly, almost afraid that turning around too quickly would make her crumble.

Everyone else in the lab was recovering also. Most were still hunched over, or curled on the floor, but many were slowly getting to their feet. Ramya looked for her father—he was slumped in a chair, massaging his temples as he stared fixedly at the workstation with the black box. Merin and Fenny were both sitting up, as straight as they could be. Just like her father, their eyes were fixed on the black box, or rather—Ramya realized it wasn't actually the box that had their attention as soon as she looked up—on the image that was hovering above the box.

The unmistakable form of a Unosi—golden-skinned and tall, resplendent in their customary white outfit—floated in a golden, grainy haze. The figure's lips were moving . . . he . . . or she ... was saying something. Ramya could hear his voice but it was barely a mumble in a strange tongue.

"Eiger," her father's voice cut through what was left of her stupor. The chief scientist ran to his side and rushed away as soon as Trysten Kiroff had given him orders. It only took a few moments to understand what those orders were. Eiger and his assistants brought over equipment and set it up around the black box, and not too long after, the clear, almost musical voice of the Unosi rippled across the room.

"What in the iffin hell is he saying?" Fenny's loud voice hurtled across the room seconds later. "Someone tell me you understand that shit."

Not one head nodded. It was indeed a strange tongue, perhaps Unosi. The hope that had made Ramya's heart soar for a moment deflated once more. There wasn't exactly a handy translator lying around that spoke Unosi.

A babble of murmurs rose around the room. People clustered together and the hum rose to a fever pitch until Merin raised her arms. "Wait, I think I know this," she said in a rush. "I recognized one of the words. This might be an ancient Mwandan tongue or simply Mwandan spoken in a very different accent than we are used to hearing now."

This time Eiger scooted away before Trysten Kiroff uttered a word. He soon placed another piece of equipment, a sleek cylinder, next to the voice amplifier they had set up earlier.

Marson Hale looked curiously from Eiger's team to Trysten Kiroff. "What's that? What are they doing?"

"It's a translator," her father explained. "It simply translates from Mwandan as we know it now. Of course, we have no knowledge of what it could've sounded like thousands of years ago. But it's an excellent machine. It should do better than us in understanding what he's saying."

Soon a stream of letters lit up the space next to the image of the Unosi. It didn't take long to realize that while there was some garbled text, there were plenty of complete sentences. The atmosphere in the room turned buoyant and chirpy once more.

"Restart the recording," Marson Hale ordered.

As Merin's fingers flew in an intricate pattern over the console, Ramya looked around at the huddle that surrounded her. She was separated from most people she knew and in her immediate proximity there was only the staff of the laboratory. She needed someone she could speak to and Ahool was nearest to her, only two women standing between them. Ramya sidestepped toward him, as surreptitiously as she could. Ahool flashed a brilliant smile at her and she had just nodded back when the Unosi started speaking. The translator scrolled on.

"*Greetings, people of the future. My name is Sombata Melis Un. I am the principal science officer of the Unosian Domain of the D'arol Sector. If you have found this message and understood it, I hope you have come in peace and the darkness has ebbed. If not, I wish you the blessings of every star. May their lights be with you as you fight the dark universe.*

"*Ten thousand eons ago, we, the Unosi, settled this galaxy. For ten thousand eons we have lived peacefully here. Now that darkness is seeping in, we have to leave our beloved home forever. But we couldn't leave without a message for our friends, the Mwondahn stalwarts who want to keep guarding our lost world, who refuse to leave their homes to the darkness that is coming to devour it.*"

"Mwondahn?" Ramya muttered to herself.

"Must mean Mwandan," Ahool whispered.

"*The darkness is the shame of the Unosi. Without us, they would not be here. We did not create the soulless, lightness beings that make up the darkness--Unosi did not stoop to that, thank the stars--but we did show them the way to our home.*

"*All we wanted was to chart a path to the legendary Hapotah. Calculations showed it was . . . could be in the Lantis sector. It was too far away, so brilliant Unosi minds came up with the idea of digging a shorter path through the space that separated us. There was much research done, much time spent in debate. The Selan group said we should go from the galactic north, while the Boyson group wanted to start from the west. In the end, we did both. We built two gigantic pathways – marvels of Unosi technology – out from our galaxy.*"

"Two pathways? So they built two wormholes?"

Ahool looked up at Ramya with wide, beacon-like eyes. "Anomaly Point is one. Where the other, Rami?"

Ramya wished she knew.

"*Little did we know one of the paths, the one in the north, would lead us into a universe so foul that it would make nightmares for us for ages to come. The darkness, we call them. They are strong creatures, soulless but sentient,* with nothing but the endless need to consume any organic material that comes their way. As soon as we stumbled on their hive, we realized the threat these creatures posed to our existence. There was no reasoning with these creatures, no placating them. They were driven only by an insatiable thirst to consume. We turned back, but it was already too late. We tried to close the gates to the pathway between the dark universe and ours, but the darkness had already molded the gates to their liking and had altered the structure at the heart of the pathway.

"We tried to stop them, but years of war later we realized they were relentless and we could not keep up with the volume of them. So we decided to evacuate. It was the only way to save our race. Luckily for us, the western pathway had led to Hapotah, and we knew that returning to our ancient roots was the only way to save ourselves. We would hold off the darkness at the gates as long as we could, while we emptied the galaxy from another end. Once we had all left, we would shut the western gates forever. Yes, the darkness would claim this beautiful galaxy, but they would stop there.

"The plan would have worked flawlessly had it not been for our faithful friends, the Mwondahns. They refused to leave with us. This is where they were born and this is where they wanted to die. The Unosi could not leave them behind to die alone and defenseless. Since our regular warcraft were being blocked easily by the darkness, we had to create something special. So we created a mighty weapon. We named it the Fury. That is what you behold today, beings of the future.

"Fitted with ten immensely powerful proneiux bombs, the fury is a bomber that could flatten a mountain range in a blink. It was to be flown by two of our most skilled flyers and the charges dropped along the length of the northern pathway. If we could execute the mission in the correct fashion, we hoped to destabilize the structure of the pathway enough to make it collapse on itself. If successful, it would close forever."

Ramya knew that didn't happen. The two flyers had returned with grim faces—she had seen the moment, courtesy of Chief Dal.

"The mission was completed, but it wasn't as successful as we hoped it would be. Perhaps the bombs weren't as powerful as we thought they would be, so they didn't damage the structure of the pathway as rapidly or as deeply *as we expected. Even so, the pathway was unstable enough to close. But we knew it was only a matter of time before the darkness forced it open again. The readings were clear – the damage wasn't extensive enough to close it forever.*

"Our time in the galaxy had run out. With our best wishes for our Mwondahn compatriots, we left. And we left the fury for you. Should the future bring the darkness back, you could use the fury once more. We wish you better luck than we had. We hope you can close that dark pathway forever. Good luck, beings of the future."

The Unosi paused for a second and then started reciting a series of codes. *"These codes will open the information archives within the data store. I have placed within it all the schematics – of the pathway, the Fury and the bombs within it. I hope they come to good use."*

Merin busily pressed the keys and fed the codes and soon next to the image of the Unosi, a series of schematics lit up the air. This was indeed a treasure. Her eyes fixed on the diagrams, Ramya made her way to her father's side.

"This is it, Lord Paramount," Marson Hale said. "I suggest we drop everything else and focus on this."

Her father nodded. "Yes, I agree. Now we have everything we need to get it functional. Let's have everyone working on this, Eiger."

Almost immediately, the humming crowd around the workstation fell away. Smaller huddles formed, all busy and purposeful, as they discussed.

"I think we should ship the *Fury* to Zeta right away," Ross said suddenly. "We know it comes loaded with bombs. We can figure out the details on our way."

Marson Hale glared mercilessly at Ross. "Know your place, Ross Pornell," he said in a caustic voice. "You have not been thrown out of this room only because you're a trusted assistant of Terenze Milos, and we all respect him. But I won't tolerate rampant disregard of protocol for very long, no matter who vouches for you."

Ramya held her breath. She had expected this scathing rebuke to come from her father, and a long time ago. Curiously enough, Trysten Kiroff stayed quiet, even as Ross and the Chief of Fleets stared murderously at each other.

Ross finally broke the silence with an indignant huff. "All right then, since I don't have a place here, I'll leave. But I'll also have a chat with Milos and see what he has to say about this," he declared. Then he spun around and walked off.

"Oh, come on, Ross," Ramya called after him. He stomped away regardless, without another look behind.

"Let him be," Fenny said. "He can be so pigheaded at times."

Part of Ramya wanted to listen to Fenny and let Ross go and cool down a bit, but somewhere deep inside she felt sorry for him. Ross wasn't doing this for his personal gain. He was fighting to save the galaxy, just like the rest of them. It was just unfortunate that he was thinking along a different tangent. Ross was a good soul and in this hour of darkness, they couldn't afford to lose good people.

"I'll go talk to him," she said distractedly to Fenny before rushing to the door after Ross.

39

Ramya caught up with Ross right outside the main laboratory entrance. "Ross," she called again before grabbing him by the arm. "Ross, stop."

"And do what?" he snapped back. "Wait around forever while Zeta is wiped out?"

Ramya took a bracing breath. She knew his temper well, and she knew it would take a long time before Ross saw clearly again. He was a passionate man, whose faith in certain things and distrust in others often turned him blind. Everyone behaved like that once in a while--she did too--but with Ross the peaks of angst were extreme.

"We're on the same team, Ross. None of us here wants Zeta to fall. Why are you fighting us?"

"You haven't seen it, Rami," he said. "You haven't seen the abomination that is Anomaly Point. It's one thing to look at the wormhole on the screen, but when you see it in front of your eyes, it will chill your bones and turn you into mush. It needs to be closed. Right now!"

He spat the words out with such vehemence that Ramya fell back a little. Staff who were walking along up and down the corridor threw curious glances at them. Ramya clutched Ross by the elbow and opened the nearest door. If they were going to have a fight, she'd rather have it in private. Thankfully, Ross followed her inside. Better yet, the room—a smaller laboratory from the looks of it—was empty. Ramya didn't have time or interest to study her surroundings. She had a job on her hands.

Crossing her arms, Ramya locked stares with Ross. "So you think we should take the *Fury* out even before we understand how it works?"

"We know enough. We can figure out the rest while we transport it to Zeta."

"Enough? We only know they used it against the Locustans once. And it worked, somewhat. You saw the Unosi guy wasn't happy about how it worked. They knew they had not damaged the wormhole enough to close it forever. That's why they didn't take a chance and left the galaxy before it opened again."

Ross looked away in a huff, but Ramya continued. "The Unosi had the tech to relocate themselves, Ross. We don't. This galaxy is our home, our only home. We can't carry out a rash mission and fail. There is no room for failure here. Don't you see?"

He spun around, lips curled in rage, and glared at Ramya. "Why don't *you* see? That a rash mission is better than no mission at all? The shelling has bought us a little time, maybe a day or two. That's all we have. The next time a big Locustan wave comes through that blasted wormhole, we won't have enough forces left to stop them from getting to the inner galaxy." He paused and placing his hands on his hips, he took in a sharp breath. "Even if we simply guided this thing via its controller into Anomaly Point and detonated it, the wormhole would collapse. I agree it wouldn't be completely destroyed, but it would give us a few hundred years, even a thousand if we're lucky, before they regenerate this thing again."

Although Ross had a good point, it was almost entirely based on hope. And it counted solely on luck. Even though Ramya knew nothing good could come from showing Ross the gaps in his logic, she had to.

"What if the controller fails? Do you know from how far away it can guide the *Fury*? Do you know whether the weapons, the thousand-year-old proneiux bombs that have been sitting in an underground chamber, will detonate like we hope they will? I sure don't. None of the scientists in there know. How can you?"

A soft breeze tickled the back of Ramya's head and she realized someone else had entered the room. But she had to finish this conversation, so she continued without looking back.

"The *Fury* is a gift, Ross. Our only hope. We can't squander it on a whim. We have to be sure, 110% if not more, that when we send that damn thing in, it'll shut down that iffin wormhole forever."

"Squander it on a whim? My idea sounds like a whim to you?" Ross whispered, the words barely trickling out past his gritted teeth. "Only you'd know the best way, right? You're so much better than anyone else, aren't you? You're a Kiroff after all, and your father's daughter. You're god, deciding the lives and deaths of mere mortals like us."

"Ross—"

"Don't Ross me," he shouted. "You go cozy up with your all-powerful father and his cronies. I'll run my whim by Milos and see what he has to say. I think he'll appreciate it more than you privileged people around here do."

His words stung like hell, but Ramya swallowed the insults, one word at a time. "Please, Ross, now isn't the time to fight among ourselves," Ramya tried one last time. But he brushed past and didn't even as much as cast a half-glance at her.

Ramya rested against the nearest table, her fingers curling around its sleek, cold edge. She had to be calm, they all had to. They were staring at total and complete annihilation—Ross was right about that—but that didn't mean they would run in firing blindly. Now was the time for level-headed thinking no matter how impossible it seemed as an idea.

"Sorry about that." Ramya jumped, Gael's voice catching her completely by surprise. In the heat of the fight with Ross, she had forgotten all about the person who had entered the room.

"What are you doing here?" she demanded, not trying to hide her annoyance. "What do you need?"

"Your father was looking for you and I said I'd find you."

"Congratulations, you've found me," she said bitterly. She reined in her anger in the next moment. "I'm sorry, I'm just—"

"No offense taken," he said. "We're all . . . pushed to the edge and it's not a good place to be." He paused and ran a finger over the arched back of a chair. "Even if the controller can fly the *Fury*, I don't think those old bombs will work. We have to replace them with something we know will cause enough damage. This is our one shot, and you're correct, we have to be damn sure we're doing everything right."

Ramya scoffed at the thought of Ross's fuming face. "Why doesn't he get that? He called me my father's daughter."

"And what's wrong with being Trysten Kiroff's daughter?" Gael asked, his gaze steady on her face. "Your father has one of the steadiest and sharpest minds I've come across. It's a pity he isn't the Chief of Fleets."

There wasn't anything wrong with it at all. But Ross hadn't used the moniker to praise her father, he had wanted to remind her of all the vile things Trysten Kiroff had done over the years to benefit his family.

Ramya didn't get a chance to explain her thoughts because Eiger barged in, an assistant in tow. He bowed hastily, before rushing to Ramya's side.

"My lady, you shouldn't be in this room," he said. "This is a hazardous area. We're testing a new weapon here and it's not very stable—"

Ramya cast a look around. She hadn't paid any attention to the room at all, but even now, she couldn't see anything extraordinary about it. Or perhaps her thoughts were too muddied to see anything clearly. She was angry at Ross, and angrier at herself for failing to get across to him.

She scanned the room once more anyway. There was equipment scattered around on the benches, but nothing that announced the presence of a weapon. If there was indeed a weapon in here, it had to be a minuscule one.

As Eiger ushered them out of the room, Ramya's gaze lighted on a glass-enclosed area at the farthest end of the room. It looked small from the door, but she thought she saw a row of black pebbles on pedestals. Even though something looked eerily familiar, she couldn't quite remember what it was.

40

Lit up by the fading sunlight of El-Iss, the *Fury* was a sight to behold. Ramya sat on an escarpment that overlooked the training grounds to the rear of the base, watching the members of the Space Fleet maneuver the behemoth around.

"You sure you don't want to come, Rami?" Isbet, who'd been sitting with her, watching the maneuvers, asked for the third time that evening. Ramya replied with a firm shake of her head, for the third time in a row.

Isbet, along with her GSO unit, was scheduled for their session with the *Fury* next. They — along with the Space Fleet corps — had been at it for a day now. For a craft that was thousands of years old, the *Fury* was handling extremely well. They had not taken to the skies yet, but the ground maneuvers to test out the controls went without major setbacks.

"You know you're welcome to check out the *Fury*, right?" Isbet asked, slipping her hands into a pair of mocha gloves.

"I do, Isbet," Ramya said. "I don't see any reason to distract you while you're working. Flying the *Fury* isn't my job, and if we're going to get this done right, we have to stick to our specific assignments. Otherwise, if we all start to poke our heads in everything, it quickly becomes a mess. We need discipline, even when we're panicking."

Isbet let out a sigh. "The Chief of Fleets sure gave a speech, didn't he?"

Ramya couldn't help but chuckle. Isbet didn't miss that Ramya had just quoted bits and pieces of Marson Hale's speech from the previous day. Marson Hale had gathered all personnel and lectured them on the need for discipline even in the face of complete disaster, probably spurred on by Ross's outburst.

"Well, I agree with things he said," Ramya declared.

"All right, then. I'll be off. Don't want to miss my chance at it," Isbet declared, jumping off the rock they'd been resting on. "See you at dinner."

Ramya watched her friend striding away, her steps buoyant and forceful. She smiled a little. Isbet looked happy once again. Ramya was sure she wasn't totally over the Rownack fiasco, but she was getting there. The *Fury* had helped. Learning to tame it was a challenge Isbet had taken very seriously, and having a lofty goal in front of her had taken her attention away from pining over useless matters.

"You show them, Isbet," Ramya whispered as she watched her friend's form grow smaller until it disappeared behind a bluff. Isbet had been doing extremely well at the trials, not surprising given her skill at flying. She had always been the top flyer at CAWStrat, and Ramya was sure they'd pick her as one of the prime contenders to fly the *Fury*.

Hearing a steady thumping approach from behind her, Ramya turned around. Fenny and Vi, both breathing heavily as they careened toward the escarpment, were quite a sight. Ramya didn't jump away as they hurtled close, the way she used to. She hardly even winced anymore. She knew they'd stop right on time. And they did. Fenny grinned and slipping off Vittoria, she patted the Pterostrich's neck appreciatively.

"Good girl," she said. "You're the best girl ever, aren't you?"

It was funny to see Fenny croon, and even funnier seeing the huge bird that towered over her—it was the twice the height of an average human already—nuzzle its fearsome beak against Fenny's chest. Fenny had taken good care of the bird, who didn't seem to have a disloyal bone in her. Vi was almost like a dog now, following Fenny around, hissing at people who would dare—mostly stupidly—to cross Fenny in the slightest possible way. Now that it was huge and growing bigger still, Trysten Kiroff wouldn't allow the Pterostrich to walk around inside the base, but he had built her a sturdy coop near the rear entrance. Twice a day, Fenny took Vi out to breathe the fresh air. Ramya didn't miss a chance to accompany them. It was her chance to breathe freely also, and for an hour or so, forget the doom hanging over them.

"So, the GSO's up trying the *Fury* now?" Fenny sat down noisily next to Ramya after she had tied Vi up to her post. "We better get it flying quickly," she said when Ramya nodded. "I doubt they can hold the pests much longer at Zeta."

Two days had passed since the first shelling of Anomaly Point. No Locustan fleet had come out of it since. Then this morning, the mouth stabilized once more. Milos did not dither for a second. He sent in the bomber ships. Five of them, each carrying a hundred mag-prot warheads, released their payloads inside the wormhole. This time, aided by the new schematics of the Unosi, the delivery was more precise, at the points deemed most vulnerable. This time, the mouth shrank further. But it still didn't close completely, only buying them some time.

"I think we have a few more days," Ramya said. "Should be enough to get the *Fury* airborne."

Fenny scoffed and shook her head. "It's not just the delivery system, Rami, it's also the payload. The Unosi proneiux didn't test out positive. We have nothing."

That was the bigger problem. The Unosi bombs were duds, all of them. Eiger and his team had industriously studied the details the Unosi had left on the bombs, but while they easily understood the structure of the weapon, its constituents were far more advanced than what was commonly known in the galaxy at present. So even if they could get the *Fury* flying, without the original payload their chance of succeeding was as good as none.

"My father is getting some new warheads assembled to fit the *Fury's* weapon delivery mechanism," Ramya said. The Kiroffs didn't build weapons, but some of the allied Houses—the Arlingtons prime among them—had munitions factories. They were working round the clock to build the warheads to peripheral specs. "I'm hoping they'll work."

"I'm sure they will. But only outwardly, Rami. There's no fundamental change. He's assembling the same mag-prots that we used today, nothing special."

Ramya didn't reply. There was nothing left to say. Fenny wasn't wrong, she was dead right. The *Fury* couldn't do magic. Simply delivering the same mag-prots wrapped in a shiny new cover wouldn't make any difference. Ramya cupped her face in her palms and rubbed her eyes. It was tiring, the never-ending ebb and flow of hope and despair. She was trying hard to stay positive, but it was hard as hell to keep thinking straight.

A sharp nudge on her arm made Ramya look up. Fenny flashed a smile. "There's no point stewing about this," she said. "My fault. I shouldn't have brought it up. All the big shots are on it, they should be able to find a solution. We should stop thinking too much. Discipline, Fenny," she ended with a stern word to herself.

Ramya had to laugh. Marson Hale's speech had made quite an impact, and not in a bad way.

"Rami, want to ride Vi?" Fenny asked. "That'd take your mind off this shit."

Ramya stole a look at the Pterostrich. She had mounted the bird twice, once even rode a few steps. But that had been it. While she had ridden horses often, riding a Pterostrich was a much different thing. It was faster, stronger and its two-footed gait felt strangely unbalanced. It was scary as hell.

"Yes, I want to," Ramya said eagerly. "If we're all dying in a week or so, I'd rather die knowing how to ride a Pterostrich."

Fenny thumped her back. "That's more like the Rami I know," she said.

If riding Vi was scary, it was also fun. Heart thudding and mind numbed except for the one thought of holding on to Vi, Ramya savored the rush. Cool evening air brushed her cheeks, the dusty ground rose and fell around her. Heels dug into Vi's sides, Ramya fought to keep her balance. By the time night skies rose around them, Ramya was drenched in sweat. As they walked back into the base that evening, her body was sore, but her heart was free from fear.

41

As much as her spirits had lifted that evening, by the time she retired that night, Ramya was back in her foulest mood. She paced her chamber endlessly, cracking her knuckles, thumping her fists, tugging her hair. There had to be something they could do to close Anomaly Point. If the Unosi had found a weapon that could damage the wormhole enough to close it for thousands of years, why couldn't they?

"Because their tech is a zillion times more advanced than yours, stupid," she shouted at herself. That was the sad truth. As advanced as they thought they were, the galaxy of the present wasn't even halfway to where the Unosi had been.

Ramya flopped onto her bed and stared at the ceiling, rage and frustration coiling in her guts relentlessly. She *had* to do something. The Chief of Fleets had asked for discipline, and she wasn't planning to poke her nose into everything, but she couldn't stop worrying and trying to think up a plan. Unfortunately, groundbreaking plans didn't come by often. And right now, her mind was like a pot of mud, a lump of nothing. It was driving her crazy.

"All right, that's enough. Let's take a walk," Ramya muttered to herself and rolled out of bed. Wrapping a coat around herself and tucking the blaster into it, she walked out the door.

The corridors on this level were deserted, which was expected at this time of night. Deciding to check up on Dakrhaeth, Ramya took the elevators up to the entrance level. This part of the base was always active, although much less now than it was during daylight hours. Grim-faced soldiers walked about, technicians rolled parts and pieces of aircraft down to the underground hangars.

Ramya started off in the direction of the hangars on the north side. Dakrhaeth was docked there along with many other craft of the

Space Fleet that didn't need to be taken out as often. She stopped for a moment on reaching the cavernous hangar. It was buzzing like a hive at the peak of summer. People loaded, fitted, and inspected crafts. More ran around with parts and pieces and equipment. The air was taut and the lights, as bright as they were, failed to lift the gloom from the enormous cavern-like chamber.

"Rami," a familiar voice called when she had walked halfway to the Stryker.

"Lefrasi?" Surprising as it was to find the Mwandan there, he was not alone. He, along with another Mwandan from Chief Dal's group, sat on a bench to one side. Between them, huddled under a blanket, was Chief Dal himself. Even though the chief smiled at her, he looked tired. He looked much better than when she had last visited him at the infirmary but he still had a long way to go. His coloring was faded to a pasty beige, a far cry from his usual deep, eye-catching brown skin tone. Ramya knew the doctors had released him from the constant monitoring. It was obvious Dal was far from his usual strength.

"We're taking the chief to Bucifer P9," Lefrasi explained. "He's still too weak and the medicine here isn't helping much. We think the Manoko groves will help him heal, and even faster if we could get Temihula to bless him."

The Manoko was the vegetation that grew on every Mwandan sanctuary — the miraculous sentient vegetation that Mwandans venerated. Ramya had seen firsthand how the Mwandans — particularly the Uminatos like Chief Dal — communicated with the flora, and she was quite sure being among the Manoko would help him heal. Temihula was the resident spirit of the groves, a deity the Mwandans believed was the forefather of all Mwandans.

Ramya kneeled in front of Chief Dal and grasped his hands. They were icy in hers. "You have shown us so much, Chief. Without your help, we'd be nowhere. We're close to flying the *Fury* now. Perhaps by the time you return to the base, we'll have figured a way to block off that wormhole."

His lips moved, but no sound came out.

"You shouldn't exert yourself by talking, Chief," Lefrasi cautioned.

"Yes, please rest," Ramya said, jumping to her feet. "I should be going. Just wanted to thank you." She bowed to the group hastily. "Godspeed."

His raspy whisper stopped her in her tracks. "Rami," Chief Dal said, the effort of speaking making his eyes roll backward. "You know everything. Everything there is."

"All right," Ramya nodded. "All right."

The chief, utterly exhausted now, slumped back into the bench. Right about then, a uniformed soldier of the Space Fleet walked up behind the group. "The transport's prepped," he announced. "We'll board when you're ready."

They gathered up their belongings and left with the soldier. Ramya hoped and prayed with all her heart that the chief would feel all right soon. Her thoughts flew to the time she had met him for the first time on Morris II. It was a terrible time. Stranded when the Mwandan government shot down the Stryker, with the *Endeavor* trapped in the reliquary grove, and the Confederacy hot on their heels, they had nowhere to run and no one to ask for help. The Chief had led them inside the grove and they had found and freed the *Endeavor*. Of course, she had had to fight the grove's resident spirit, the Mwandan god, Temihula, on the way in.

Ross! Her thoughts soured the moment she thought of him. He had risked his life trying to save her when Temihula went on a murderous rampage. He deserved more loyalty from her, more patience. He was struggling to fit in and she had hardly helped. She had to try harder to support him, to back him up.

Fists curled into balls, Ramya turned. She didn't need to speak to Dakrhaeth now, she needed to talk to Ross instead. Help him find his footing. She was marching out of the hangar when it hit her like a sack-load of stones.

The Drigganstone! Temihula's gift to her . . . the Mwandan government used it to build weapons. What if . . .

She had to talk to her father.

Ramya broke into a wild sprint along the corridors as a barrage of ideas surged like an avalanche through her brain.

42

Ramya almost collided with Ross coming out of her father's private meeting room. Eyes popping out, he seemed just as stunned seeing her as she was to see him.

He quickly composed himself. "Hello, Rami," he said curtly. Then, even before she could utter a word, he rushed away. It was almost as if he wanted to run away from her as fast as he could.

Ramya hesitated at the threshold. As much as Ramya wanted to ask Ross what he was doing in Trysten Kiroff's chamber, she had other urgent matters on her mind. So instead of trying to catch him, she walked into her father's chambers.

Another surprise awaited her inside—her father wasn't alone. Gael and his father Tucker, as well as Marson Hale, were in there also, a pile of blueprints scattered on the long table between them. The other people's presence didn't surprise Ramya much, but the mirthful look on their faces did. And the fact that they all looked a bit surprised at seeing her enter. Her father raised a questioning brow.

"What was Ross doing here?" Ramya demanded.

"I thought you'd know already," he father replied, his mouth twisting a little amusedly.

Ramya crossed her arms. "Well, I don't. Is it something you can share with me?"

"That boy is a friend of yours, Lady Ramya?" Tucker Arlington asked, swaggering by her.

"Yes, he is," she replied. She didn't like the tone of his question at all, as if he was putting her through an inquisition. She swallowed her indignation and turned to her father again.

"He came here to offer his apologies to the Chief of Fleets," he said as soon as their eyes met. "He was quite sincere in his efforts. All of us appreciated that."

Ramya had to scrunch up everything she had to suppress a frown. Ross apologized? Why? That was utterly unlike him. Did Milos make him do it? She didn't have to stay bewildered for too long.

"He wants a chance to try flying the *Fury*," he father explained seconds later. "What is your opinion of him?"

She didn't get a chance to reply. Tucker jumped in. "He's her friend. Of course she'd approve."

Ramya gritted her teeth and stopped a retort from slipping out. She wouldn't approve of just anyone — not even herself if it came to that — flying the *Fury* unless they were really capable. Tucker obviously failed to understand fairness and objectivity. She decided to ignore the loudmouth and addressed her father and the Chief of Fleets instead.

"He's co-piloted with me on the Stryker many times. I've found him quite capable."

"Trustworthy?" Marson Hale asked.

"Loyal to a fault," Ramya replied in a heartbeat. "Once he identifies with the cause."

Marson Hale exchanged a quick glance with Trysten.

"Milos wouldn't have kept him around if he didn't have his heart in the right place," Gael said suddenly, breaking the stifling silence. "Besides, what is he going to do anyway? Crash the *Fury*? I'll have my top pilot with him if that makes a difference."

Gael's support was unexpected. But Ramya was grateful that he spoke out in support of Ross. Ross could be stubborn at times but he would lay down his life for the cause without hesitation.

"All right, Lieutenant. Let's let him try tomorrow."

"Yes, sir."

Another bout of silence followed. Ramya, unsure if it was appropriate to share her wild idea in the presence of such a large audience, lingered.

"I need to speak with you," she blurted when Trysten looked curiously at her.

"So speak."

So much for hoping for some privacy. The Arlington spawn she had learned to handle, but the loudmouthed Tuck was annoying as heck. And judging by the way he was studying her, Ramya was sure he would make an idiotic comment or two at least. Besides, she didn't want the whole world in on her finding. She wanted to talk only with her father — Kiroff to Kiroff. But her father refused to take the hint.

To hell with it.

"When we were on Morris II, the Stryker was hit by projectiles fired by the Mwandan government. They almost brought the Stryker down, ripped one of its wings apart."

Tucker Arlington guffawed. If Ramya could've thrown a fist against that big, round nose of his and get away with it, she happily would.

"You forgot to get your craft's shields up, dear girl?" Tucker didn't seem to appreciate her rake-you-over-the-coals-if-I-could look. "It's all right. We all make mistakes. You're just a little girl."

"The shields were up, Lord Arlington. The projectiles still got through," Ramya said, coldly, as pointedly as she could. If not Tucker, her father — the designer of the Stryker — would understand what she was implying.

Trysten Kiroff crossed his arms. "It went through the Stryker's shields?"

"Yes."

"So . . . so what?" Tucker asked.

"So . . . just hours before, the same shields took fire from a Drednot and cruised through just fine. And yet that powerful shield came apart at the first shot from the Mwandans," Ramya replied. She looked at the faces surrounding her. There was no doubt she had them all engaged.

"That's impossible," her father muttered.

"It happened, Father. I know it's possible," Ramya replied. "And I keep wondering what would happen if we somehow infused our most powerful mag-prot warheads with whatever the Mwandans are using. Would that be the superweapon that could close Anomaly Point once and for all?"

Tucker Arlington tilted his head at Trysten. "What do you think? Sound reasonable to you?"

Marson Hale was on his feet, pacing around with his hands behind his back. "Even if this were true, the Mwandan government is a bunch of stubborn asses. They'd die before they tell us their secrets." Marson Hale walked to the door. "But I'm going to speak with the Mwandans anyway."

As soon as he left, Trysten Kiroff's eyes narrowed, his gaze boring into Ramya's face. "You know what the Mwandans use in their weapons, don't you?"

She didn't know for sure, but she had heard enough from her Mwandan friends to venture a guess. She hadn't said it in front of everyone just because she wanted to share it with her father first.

Ramya nodded. Gael and his father were still in the room and she wasn't sure—

"Drigganstones, isn't it?" her father said.

Of course, he had enough clues to conclude that already. Ramya realized he had been testing them. The room she had accidentally stumbled into with Ross, the one with a row of pebbles in the far end, was, in fact, the lab testing the Drigganstone she'd given her father. He suspected their potential use in weaponry as well. They were volatile, Eiger had told them before he whisked them out of that room. It all made perfect sense now.

"I think so," she replied.

The confused look on Tucker Arlington's face was a sight to behold. His gaze darted between Trysten Kiroff to hers for a few times before he blurted, "What's this Drigganstone?"

By the time Ramya had explained what a Drigganstone was, his eyes were bulging like a toad's.

"You know about this stone, Trysten?" he stammered.

"I have one sample in the lab here," Trysten Kiroff said. "We tested it a little bit. It is indeed stronger than any weapon we've seen so far. But with everything else going on, we—"

Tucker Arlington wrung his meaty hands together. "I'll get some of my people here right away. They know all there is to know about weapons. We will sort this out together."

Ramya noticed her father was hardly as excited. Could it be because he didn't believe Drigganstones would be as miraculous as Ramya hoped? Or did he dislike sharing this information with Tucker?

Tucker Arlington, however, went on and on. "We'll have to get more stones, of course. One sample won't be enough."

"Tucker, these stones are extremely rare," Trysten Kiroff said after they had watched Tucker pace around the room in a daze. "You don't come across them just anywhere."

Tucker stared at him disbelievingly for a while. "Well, there must be a way." He snapped toward Ramya and plodded up to her. "You know a way to get these things, don't you?"

Ramya wanted to glare at him until he caught fire. Wasn't she just a little girl a minute ago? Now *she* had to know a way?

"You think a little girl like me would know?"

Tucker's face turned a flaming shade of red that almost matched his fiery hair and beard. He stayed quiet for a bit before his brows danced. "Well, you're not just any little girl. You're Trysten's heir, after all."

Ramya sucked in a long, deep breath, willing herself to stay calm. There was no winning with some people. No matter what you did, they'd paint you in the small, petty way they had always known. Just like Tucker was doing right now—he *had* to bring her down to being someone's heir.

Her father swiftly stepped between them and placed a hand on Tucker's shoulder. "Ramya's much more than just my heir, Tucker. She knows these things because she went beyond being my child, so I think we owe her experience that respect."

Tucker was about to say something—retort, most likely—but Trysten Kiroff's hint was not lost on him. He quickly clamped his mouth shut and gave Ramya a short bow.

"My mistake," he said in a grave voice. "Please forgive my rudeness, Lady Ramya. I'm a foolish man from a bygone era, my lady. I do not much understand the ambitions of the young. My sincere apologies."

There was very little that was sincere about his speech. Ramya could tell that easily from the gleam of mockery in his eyes. He was simply playing with her. She'd have to let this pass, though. This wasn't the time to throw tantrums, but Ramya made a mental note of it. Someday, she'd put Tucker Arlington in his place.

"Is there a way to get more Drigganstones, Bella?" her father asked.

"I'm not sure. I could try asking Temihula," she said.

Her father's eyes widened. "You'd have to go to Morris II?"

"No, I don't. Temihula resides in every Mwandan sanctuary, among the Manoko groves. I could find him on Bucifer P9."

"That's excellent," Tucker Arlington exclaimed. "How many of these stones do we need, Trysten?"

"We'll have to figure that out."

"All right, I'll get my people started on this," Tucker declared before leaving.

Her father watched him leave. He didn't speak until the door closed behind Tucker. "I don't want you to go to Bucifer," he said finally, his eyes dark with worry.

"Well, I don't want to go either. But unless the Mwandan government has a hidden stash of Drigganstones and decides to share them with us, there's no other way, Father," she said. "What do you think of this? Is there a chance we could use it to make our warheads stronger?"

"Maybe," he replied slowly. "But there are too many unknowns here. It's a leap in the dark."

"Remember the vision Chief Dal projected to us when we were getting back from KS-5-1? Remember the three images the Unosi displayed?" Gael's voice almost made Ramya jump. He had been so quiet that she'd almost forgotten his presence in the room. She tried to recall the vision they'd seen.

"There was a view of a wormhole. There was a map of a galaxy," she said. "The last one was a dark planet. I only understood the meaning of the wormhole. It had to be the one the Locustans came through."

Gael left his chair and walked over. "The wormhole part was fairly obvious. The meaning of the other two images wasn't clear to me. The galaxy they showed had to be either where the Locustans came from, or where the Unosi were building their future home. But what about that planet? You know, it reminds me of a typical Mwandan sanctuary, lit by a dim star, with dark foliage covering its surface."

Ramya's heart thudded with excitement. She remembered it clearly now. She also recalled thinking of a Mwandan sanctuary at the time she'd seen it. "You think there was a connection?"

"I'm quite sure there was a connection," Gael said. "Perhaps their proneiux bombs were made with Drigganstones?"

"Or maybe they were simply worried about leaving their Mwandan friends behind," her father said.

"That's a possibility," Ramya said. "But you know that's not the likely reason. You already knew Drigganstones could be used as weapons. The Mwandan government already does that."

"We need to run more tests to be sure," her father countered. It seemed as if he was desperate to find an excuse. "Eiger can get some results in a day and maybe then—"

"Every day we spend waiting is a day wasted. It's not like my going to Bucifer to get some Drigganstones will jeopardize our main plan. So why not keep a backup plan running?"

Her father held up his hands. "All right, all right. Go to Bucifer P9 and get some stones," he said, his worried gaze moved from Ramya to Gael. "You will be with her the entire time, Gael. I want my daughter back here safe and sound."

Ramya studied her father's grim face. She had walked into far messier situations before this. He had not sounded half as paranoid as now. What happened all of a sudden?

"Yes, Lord Paramount. Of course. I won't let her out of my sight," Gael replied, far too chivalrously for Ramya's liking. What was she? An iffin newborn?

"Thank you," her father said to Gael, before turning toward her. "And Bella, please do me a favor. Please ask Gael to use the Mossin. It's far safer than the Scouts. I understand he cares about your approval, but it's ridiculous to put one's safety at stake to score good opinion."

"That's not—" Gael, red-faced and stuttering, had just started when her father cut him off.

"I have to go speak with Eiger about the Drigganstones now," he said. "You two sort out the details of your mission."

As soon as he left, Ramya turned toward Gael and fixed a stare on his still flushed face. "You told him you gave up the Mossin because of me? That's sweet," she said. "But my father's right. You should take it back."

"What's done is done."

"I thought you cared about how I felt."

They stared at each other for what felt like an eternity, a battle of wills raging in the silence. Finally, Gael broke the quiet.

"So we're off to Bucifer again? I wasn't looking forward to visiting that planet anytime soon."

Ramya shot him a telling look. "That's what happens when the boss favors you. You get handed the most difficult jobs."

His eyes crinkled. "In this case, it translates to babysitting his impetuous daughter."

Ramya held back the retort bubbling inside her. "Why did you back Ross?" she asked instead, watching intently as the question made his eyes widen briefly.

"Didn't you want me to?" he said.

"You didn't answer my question."

Gael shrugged. "Sure I did," he said. "I assumed you wanted your beau to get his wish. So I helped."

"He's not," Ramya shot back. "But thank you."

"Anytime," he said before leaving. "I'll see you in the morning, Kiroff."

"Make sure the Mossin comes along too," Ramya shouted as the doors closed behind him.

43

The blustery morning the next day drained hope out of Ramya's heart the moment she peeked out of the base looking for Gael and his team. The wind cut into what little of her face was exposed and she almost teetered at its raw force when it hit. She didn't have to go far to find what she was looking for. Amireh, Gael's right-hand man, came out of the first Cutlass near the hangar.

"Lady Ramya," he greeted. "We're off on another adventure then?"

"Is Isbet coming?" Ramya asked, ducking into the hold of the craft as quickly as she could. Getting the wind off her face felt good.

"No," Amireh's reply dashed her hopes. "She's working the *Fury*. Turned out she's very good at it. So we've been getting her do some more training."

No wonder she hadn't seen Isbet since her trials. Ramya swelled a little with pride for her friend. Isbet had always been an excellent flyer and Ramya knew getting a chance to fly the *Fury* would be a dream come true for her.

"She might even be the one who takes the *Fury* in on its final run," Amireh said. "

His words sank in slowly, and as they did, Ramya's joy at Isbet's success drained out like water through a sieve. Whoever flew the *Fury* into the wormhole didn't have a huge chance of surviving the flight, which meant—

Her thoughts drifted with the winds, courtesy of Gael who arrived with a handful of people. He gave Ramya a quick nod and started barking orders. Minutes later, they were airborne. Ramya lingered on the Cutlass's sprawling bridge as they drew farther away from El-Iss. This would be a quick mission, Ramya was sure. She would ask Temihula for Drigganstones, and he would either bless them or not. It would likely not be a long-drawn-out process. Ahool, their guide to the Manoko groves, sat to one side, studying a holo-map of the planet. Ramya joined him, her eyes skimming the various groves the Mwandans had pointed out. Those were the spots where the spirits would be the strongest, and they had to pick one of those to land. She hoped Ahool would easily locate the best of them.

Gael strolled over when the Cutlass was passing the next planet—El-Domme was a coral-hued gas-giant—on the way to the AP. "What do you think?" he asked Ahool right away. "Can you find the right site?"

Ahool looked at him, his eyes pensive. "I think so. I try."

Ramya wished Gael wouldn't scare the boy. This was new to all of them and all they could do was try. "You know, even if he finds the grove, there's no guarantee Temihula will hand us the stones just because we ask."

"I know," Gael said with an understanding nod. "Well, Hale had a good talk with the Mwandan government last night. There's a chance they might share their stock of Drigganstones with us."

"Really?" Ramya's heart skipped a beat. If that were true, it'd take a lot of weight off her shoulders.

Gael shrugged. "They were still talking when I last saw them, so nothing's done yet."

Even so, the fact the Mwandan government was willing to talk about sharing Drigganstones was a huge step forward.

"Any update from the labs?" Gael asked.

"Eiger's team has been working all night," Ramya said. She had spent a good deal of time in the labs herself, watching the work. "Eiger said they now know a good deal about how the proneiux were built. They were a hybrid radioactive and electromagnetic weapon, fortified with a layer of an unknown substance. He thinks that layer is a mesh made of Drigganstone."

"So all we really have so far is conjecture. And talks of hope."

Ramya winced at the abrupt statement. The truth always hurt. It was indeed all just inferences at this point, nothing set in stone.

"Eiger is trying to replicate the layer with the Drigganstone sample he has," she said, noting that her statement hardly made Gael's face any brighter. He tapped the table for a bit before chuckling loudly.

"Well, there's one piece of good news," he announced. "Your friend Isbet is the top pick to fly the *Fury*. At least one person's happy on that base."

Ramya grimaced. Strange how things were—being the top pick on the suicide squad made an eighteen-year-old's day.

"Hey, at least she's not moping over that deadbeat Matteider spawn," Gael said, noticing her gloomy face. As soon as a smile trickled across her lips, he smirked. "And your beau, Ross, did quite well at the pre-evals also. Nifty for a guy who doesn't have formal training."

Even though Ramya was happy for Ross, Gael's words made her frown. Her frown quickly built up into a glare. "For the second time, Arlington, he's *not* my beau."

He chuckled and took a step back. "Don't blame me. Your father said he was, and I just—"

Ramya was just about to share a piece of her mind but Amireh's call interrupted their conversation.

"Lieutenant, I see a ship. It's en route to El-Iss," he said. There was an edge to his voice that not only made Gael rush to his side, it also made Ramya follow.

"What do you mean, ship?"

"On screen, Rooh," Amireh ordered and the giant viewing screen filled up with a grainy picture of a dark shape steadily moving forward. Darkened by the shadow of El-Domme, it was not clearly visible, and Ramya couldn't tell what sort of craft it was. But it was indeed headed toward El-Iss. Only instead of taking the direct path from the AP to the moon like most regular ships, it was on a circular path skirting the next planet.

Gael squinted at the screen. "It doesn't look Locustan. They could be the people my father is shuttling in to work on the warheads. But why would they take a roundabout path to El-Iss?"

"Your father wouldn't have the shuttle waste time going around El-Domme. That'd easily add ten hours to the flight time. Besides, that doesn't look like a standard shuttle to me," Amireh said. He gave them another shake of his head. "The only reason anyone would do that would be to evade detection," he added grimly.

There was a moment of perfect silence as everyone stared wordlessly at the craft stealthily creeping forward on the screen. Then Gael clapped his hands.

"Sound an alarm, call El-Iss," he shouted. "And turn around. We're going after them."

"They're too far out, Lieutenant," Amireh said. "They'll reach El-Iss before we catch up."

"Well then, we'll meet them there."

In a heartbeat, the bridge erupted in a frenzy of activity. Ramya saw everything unfolding slowly. Her heart was frozen with an unexplainable terror and her eyes feverishly scanned the grainy shape on the screen. There was something ominous about how the craft moved and she doubted they had friendly intentions in mind. However, who they were and what they wanted was anyone's guess. All she knew for sure was — there was too much at stake at El-Iss.

44

The stealth craft had reached El-Iss by the time Cutlass 31 caught up with it. It was a ship carrier, a stripped-down version of an Eradicator model of the past decade. These were discarded after the Locusta-Vanga war and you could only come across their crumbling skeletons in the ship graveyards. Whoever owned this one obviously had one salvaged and retrofitted to make it marginally faster than a Cutlass. To Ramya, it looked like the handiwork of space pirates.

"Hail them again," Gael ordered for the sixth time. But just like the previous times, no response came from the hulking carrier.

"Come on, come on," Gael kept muttering as the distance between the ships closed. He was waiting to get into striking distance. His plan was simple, use the traction beams to hold the carrier and find out what they wanted. Ramya, however, doubted that the crew of the Eradicator had any wish to cooperate with them. What they wanted was unclear, but their actions so far didn't seem friendly.

"We're within striking distance, Lieutenant," an officer announced.

"Train the traction beams," Gael said.

Fighters streaked out of the Eradicator at the precise moment the traction beams switched on. They were all old model Gullwings but clearly retrofitted to rival the speed and agility of current confederate fighter craft. Most of the fighters whizzed toward El-Iss while about five came directly at the Cutlass.

"What the hell?" Gael shouted. "Blast them out."

"That's going to be hard, Lieutenant," Amireh said. "Keeping our traction beams on the Eradicator steady is seriously compromising our agility. All we can use are the surface cannons."

"Well, use those then."

Ramya wished for a different course of action. The Stryker was in the Cutlass's hold and it would be far easier to attack the fighters with it. However, Gael had vehemently rejected the idea of taking the Stryker out when she suggested it minutes ago. Remembering the last time they had fought over disregarding protocol, Ramya waited. As two of the fighters fired potent salvos at the Cutlass's bulkhead, creating a tremor under their feet, Ramya decided to break her silence.

"Let me take the Stryker out," she said. "Please. Before it's too late."

Another barrage of fire shook the Cutlass. Gael nodded. "Go, go, go."

Ramya dashed. Gael and four more of his unit—Tanaka, Munro, Alys, and Kata—came right behind her. It only took them minutes to get into their respective craft, but to Ramya, every second seemed to crawl by.

"Depressurizing now," Amireh's voice came on.

Ramya took a long, deep breath. She had to get out there, as fast as possible. The base's hangar—that's where she had to go first. They had to save the *Fury* at any cost.

The side panels of the Cutlass parted noiselessly. Ramya released the docking clamps and eased the Stryker over the deck toward the edge. The reddish-orange surface of El-Iss peeked through the opening. Ramya gripped the flight stick tight.

"Here we go again, Dakrhaeth," she whispered. She pressed on the throttle and shot out of the bay like a torpedo.

She turned when there was some space between the Cutlass and the Stryker, tugging the flight stick to point the craft toward the backside of the base.

"Let's shake these pests off the Cutlass first, guys," Gael's voice came over the Stryker's comm. As logical as the order was, it made Ramya wince. About ten Gullwings had flown off to the base and every second they spent here was time the base was left unassisted.

"Not interested in sticking around, are we?" Dakrhaeth commented, sensing Ramya's reluctance to turn the Stryker around.

"Of course I am," she shot back. "Just worried about the base, that's all."

She pulled the flight stick with more force than necessary, channeling her annoyance at both Gael and Dakrhaeth.

"Well, the sooner we wrap things up here, the faster we get to assist the base."

Didn't she know that?

"Plasma gun, Mihaal?"

The cheeky bastard. He knew her well.

"Why not? Prep it up."

"All right."

Ramya's eyes skimmed the Eradicator, locating the position of key components and weak parts. She did not know how these were built but the curve near the fuselage looked vulnerable. She was busily calculating the angle of attack when Dakrhaeth blurted, "No."

"What?"

"Mihaal, I feel her," Dakrhaeth said, his unexpected and weird comments scattering Ramya's thoughts in an instant.

"What do you mean?" she asked. "Who?"

"Our mother," Dakrhaeth said in a distant, morose tone. "The Hive. She's on the move. I can hear her call, stronger than ever."

"What is he talking about?" Gael's voice came over the comm. "What about the Hive?"

Ramya was about to ask the same. Before she could, Dakrhaeth yelled. "A bug on your tail, Mihaal."

Ramya glanced at the rear displays. "I see it."

Damn it, Rami! This was the price to pay for her distraction. She should've focused on the immediate instead of mulling over things to come.

She dove, twisting the Stryker sideways as the Gullwing fired. Ramya zigged and zagged, swooped up and down, carving a path over and around the Eradicator, trying to shake the pest off. It turned out to be a tenacious thing. The shield took most of the hit, and even though the Gullwing wasn't firing torpedoes, the systems on the Stryker moaned and screeched with complaints.

"Damn that—"

Ramya couldn't complete the sentence. A bright white light flashed behind her, dazzling her for a second. The Stryker shuddered from the shockwave of the blast. Ramya steadied her grip on the flight stick, but her eyes darted to the rear display. A fireball had erupted behind them and the familiar shape of the Mossin streaked over it.

"You're welcome, Kiroff," Gael's voice said.

"He's good and timely," Dakrhaeth commented in a wise manner. "I'd give him—"

"Good to know, Dakrhaeth," Ramya cut off his monologue. "What's the status of the Plasma gun?"

"Ready to fire, Mihaal."

Ramya looked around and took stock of the situation. Gael and his people had destroyed all five of the Gullwings that had come for them. The Eradicator was held helplessly in place by the Cutlass and its traction beam. There was no point blasting the ship carrier. Instead, the crew could provide information on who had dispatched them and why.

She hit the comm switch regardless. "Lieutenant Arlington," she called, remembering Gael's lecture on protocol. "What do we do with the Eradicator? Gut it?"

"No. We'll take prisoners. They're low-level ops very likely, but still . . ."

Just like she had thought. "Permission to head to the base?" she asked next.

"Yes, disengage."

Ramya banked hard and turned the Stryker around. She pressed on the throttle and shot away. The view of the base became clear in a few minutes and the scene brought both fear and relief.

Clearly, there was significant damage to the entrance and evidence of a fight. Smoking rubble—remnants of Gullwings and a few WBs also — was scattered around the area. While Ramya couldn't tell how bad a beating the base had taken, seeing the way a dozen WBs circled overhead, she was sure their side had won against the pirates.

"Looks like we won, Lieutenant." Ramya recognized Munro's voice. He was the youngest of Gael's lot, a junior at CAWStrat recently recruited as an intern. His excitement was infectious and Ramya's heart did a flip.

"But who the hell are these people?" Tanaka, an older hand brought up the gloomier question.

"That's the zillion-liere question, Tanaka," Gael said. "Hoping our prisoners will provide some answers."

In any case, they had won this battle. Ramya eased her finger off the throttle and was about to tell Dakrhaeth to disarm the plasma guns. Before she could, an ear-splitting explosion made her jump. For a second, Ramya thought the Stryker had exploded. Then she realized the source — the Eradicator. Instead of a view of the dated ship carrier, the Stryker's rear display was now filled with flaming skies and a shower of debris, the Cutlass flung aside by the aftershock of the explosion.

"What just happened?" Munro said, clearly shaken.

"The ship carrier just blew itself up," Tanaka replied, his voice as disbelieving as could be. "That's . . . unbelievable."

"Amireh," Gael yelled. "Amireh, respond for star's sake."

Silent moments trickled by. Ramya held her breath. She could still see the Cutlass, and it was still in one piece. They could be injured, but they had to be alive.

"Amireh!"

The comm crackled, faintly at first, then in a normal way. Amireh's voice — shaken but coherent — drifted out.

"All good, Lieutenant," he said. "The shields took a beating and the secondary systems dropped dead for a second or two, but — "

Ramya could hear Gael's relieved sigh. "Get out of there. Get back to the base," he said.

"Why the hell would they do that?" Tanaka's incredulous voice drifted through the comm.

Indeed. Space pirates were a greedy and seedy bunch. They'd do anything to survive, anything at all. Blowing themselves up in the name of honor—Ramya doubted there was any such thing in a pirate's dictionary as honor—wasn't a pirate's way of doing things.

Unless . . . they weren't pirates at all. Only staged to look like them.

"I'm landing," Ramya announced. She didn't care about permissions or protocols anymore. These were no ordinary space pirates. Someone had sent them here with a very specific agenda. And even though Ramya didn't know what it could be, dread made her spine tingle at just the thought of it.

"Right behind you," Gael said.

"There's a perfect spot to the right of the entrance, Mihaal," Dakrhaeth said helpfully.

Ramya eased the Stryker down on the training ground near the front of the base, heart pounding furiously as she jumped out of the craft. Gael had landed his Mossin nearby and he caught up as she neared the battered front gates.

45

Ramya could hardly recognize the base she had left behind merely hours ago. Plumes of smoke and dust rose up in thick coils, making breathing and seeing difficult. The main entrance had a gaping hole carved out on one side. People were running, while many lay on the ground, bloodied and battered. Ramya streaked in — Gael was at her heels — her eyes skimming over the remnants of mayhem, her mind focused on locating just a couple of things — her father and the *Fury*.

Her steps slowed to a halt as she neared the private elevators that'd take her down to the lower levels. Casten, disheveled, blood trickling down his cheek, trudged out of the elevator. His eyes brightened as soon as he saw her and he stumbled forward.

"I didn't see them coming, my lady," he wailed. "I just didn't. We were walking from the hangar to the CR when . . . I — I . . ."

Ramya did not have the strength or will to think. Something bad had happened, something that was beyond the mess she had seen at the entrance, something far more personal and scary.

"Casten, look at me," she forced the words out with everything she had. "Where's my father?"

Casten kept mumbling, fat tears rolling out his bloodshot eyes. "The Octus came out of nowhere, and they started firing. I tried to get the emergency protocol engaged, but by the time the steel ingresses closed, he was shot."

"Shot?" Gael asked. "Who was shot?"

The air was full of dust and the smell of blood. Every breath she took seemed to scratch Ramya's nostrils raw. She could barely sense her legs beneath her. The entire world was collapsing furiously into a blur and a dull drone.

"Is he dead?" she asked even before Casten replied to Gael. She braced for the worst, but she knew she wasn't ready for the answer.

She'd never be.

"No," Casten almost screamed. "Lord Paramount is in the surgical unit. He will recover."

For a long, thick moment, Ramya's mind was like a pane of glass, blank and cold. Then thoughts bubbled up and streaked across her mind at lightning speed. She didn't know what she was thinking, thoughts came and went so quickly. A nudge on her arm made Ramya stir.

"He is alive," Gael was saying. "He will be all right."

She wasn't supposed to feel this empty. She wasn't supposed to care about him that much. Yet the numbness in her limbs refused to go away.

"Anyone else hurt?" she asked, barely squeaking the words.

"The Chief of Fleets," Casten whispered. "He's dead. What do we do now, Lady Ramya?"

Ramya closed her eyes and leaned against the nearest wall. How could this be happening? Why? Why now? This was the direst, darkest moment the galaxy would ever see. Now was the time to come together. Yet the Octus chose to attack.

All right, Rami. Calm down. Focus. Think of right now. People need you to lead them. They need your strength, your resolve, not shaky ineffectiveness.

"I need to speak with the doctors. Can you take me there?" Ramya asked as soon as she calmed her thoughts a bit.

Casten hastily showed them the way. As Ramya walked immersed in her thoughts, she heard Gael question Casten. "And my father?"

"He had some injuries. None too severe."

Ramya looked back at Casten. "Did you take any prisoners?"

"One or two, I believe," Casten replied between sighs.

"And the *Fury*? Any damage to it?"

"We got lucky there," Casten forced a sliver of a smile. "They were able to secure it in the hangar. The thugs didn't get that far."

The sharp, clean smell of the medical unit hit Ramya's nostrils even before the elevator doors opened, and grew stronger when they walked through the bright orange door of the surgical section. The smell stoked the fear that had settled down a bit in her stomach and churned it relentlessly. Ramya walked in breathing deep and fast, struggling to rein in her urge to throw up.

A medic rushed up in an instant. "Lady Ramya, please come here." He ushered them into a smaller room to the left. The place was designed for waiting, a bare, square room ringed with stiff-backed, metal chairs. "Please take a seat," the medic gestured at the nearest chair. Ramya happily lowered herself into it. The chair was hard and cold under her and it was just what she needed. Firmness, a touch of steel, and stability. Strength surged back up her spine, at least for a moment.

"We will have Lord Paramount Kiroff out of surgery soon," the medic informed. "The doctors will be able to brief you then."

There was no mention of his wounds being minor or words of hope, Ramya noted. Only a precise and dispassionate evaluation of the situation. Not a good sign.

Ramya pushed her hands as deep as she could into her pockets, hardly finding the warmth she was desperately seeking. As much as she wanted to curl up in a corner, her situation didn't allow such luxury. She couldn't mope over this for too long. The galaxy's clock was ticking down fast. She had to get things under control quickly.

"Casten," Ramya called. "The prisoners. We need to interrogate them. Find out what they wanted, what their plans are. We need information. Now." Casten had stepped away when Ramya called him back. "Whatever it takes, Casten. Beat them to a pulp if that's what it takes."

Gael, who had briefly disappeared into a side room where his father was being treated for wounds on his head and arm and fractured legs, walked over to her side as she spoke to Casten. He fixed a worried stare on her face.

"Is now a good time to get back at them?" he said in a low voice. "I'd like to get even too but now —"

"This has nothing to do with getting even," Ramya replied. She looked him squarely in the eye. Revenge was not why she was doing it, and that needed to be clear right away. "I need to find out if there are more threats out there. We can't have any more disruptions if we are to make good on our promise to Milos."

He held her gaze for a moment, his stare intent, before he nodded. "Got it. Anything I can do?"

"Yes. Check the hangar. We need to take stock of our losses." Before Gael could leave, the orange doors swiveled open and Eiger rushed in. He was in front of her in the next instant.

"I'm so sorry, Lady Ramya," Eiger gushed. "My sincere thoughts —"

"He'll be fine," Ramya said through gritted teeth, ignoring how Eiger blinked fearfully when she snapped. He meant well, but she had to get past the fear of her father dying. Trysten Kiroff was going to pull through, he just needed some time to get better. She had to hold it together until then. "Any update from the lab?"

Eiger gulped and nodded. "The Mwandan government sent us some of their studies. And now we have a better understanding of the molecular structure of the stone. I have some ideas. We could create something similar to the covering the proneiux has . . . a Drigganstone mesh you could call it . . . that'd give the warheads extra power to rip into the core of the wormhole. Lord Arlington's engineers are on their way from LBX-02, and we'll put it together, I'm sure. But we need some more of the Drigganstones."

The Drigganstones!

Had this ambush not happened, they'd have a good chance of getting the elusive stones. Now all their well-laid plans had gone awry. Anger bubbled in Ramya's veins and left a scorching trail along the rim of her head. Everything was a hundred times worse now. Now, with her father wounded and fighting for his life, she couldn't leave El-Iss until things were secure.

"What happened with the Mwandan government?" she asked. "Aren't they going to share some of their stockpile of stones?"

Eiger shrugged but Gael volunteered eagerly. "I can find out," he said.

"No, I will," Ramya declared. "I need you to check on the status of our fleet here. I'll go to the CR." She shot a look at the medic's station. "I'm not much help here anyway."

They walked out of the surgical unit soon after. Gael pulled her aside for a moment before heading for the hangar at the back of the base. "Are you all right, Kiroff?"

Concern shone in his eyes and Ramya was thankful for it. But on the other hand, she didn't want her misery to become the subject of conversation around the base. They couldn't afford that. Not at the moment.

"I'm fine," she said, staring distractedly at the floor as a new thought barged in. Her hand flew up to clutch Gael's arm. "Do something, Arlington. Secure the *Fury*. And Ishet and whoever her backup pilot is. Secure it, do you understand? Come see me in the CR when you're done. And bring Ahool with you, please."

He looked confused for a second, but it passed quickly. "Yes, of course," he said.

With a short bow, Gael left. Ramya took a long breath and started along the corridor that led up to the Combat Room, Eiger in tow.

46

The Combat Room was in disarray when she entered. People clustered around, and a dull drone filled the air. Ramya looked around for a familiar face, her eyes quickly settling on her father's right-hand-man, Wultoph Aristide, who stood with a few officers, talking animatedly. He spotted her almost as quickly and hastily walked over.

"So relieved to see you here, Lady Ramya," he said with a quick bow. "We need someone to keep things moving while the Lord Paramount recovers."

Ramya let out a small sigh of relief as she nodded to acknowledge Wultoph. At least Wultoph didn't start with sympathies.

She decided to cut to the chase. "What's the status of talks with the Mwandans?" she asked.

"The Chief of Fleets was negotiating with them this morning. They shared their findings on Drigganstone, but they seem unwilling to give us their stockpile."

"We don't need their entire stockpile, do we?" Ramya asked Eiger.

"Well, depends on how much they have," Eiger responded. "But yes, I don't need too much. The protective material can be constructed from a medium-sized sample. With what we have left from the one sample Lord Kiroff gave me, I can arm at least two of our mag-prot warheads. But I don't think two warheads will be enough to destabilize that wormhole. The Unosi had ten of them loaded in the *Fury,* and even that didn't shut the monster down completely. We need to do better."

"So how much do you need?"

"Five stones the size of the one I had. They should be at least ten drams each."

She had to find him five. She couldn't leave the base at the moment so she'd have to haggle with the Mwandans. Make them give her what she wanted. Somehow.

"You can go back to your work if you want," she said to Eiger who flashed a grateful smile immediately. "I'll see you soon, hopefully with good news. Get started on getting the two warheads prepped with Drigganstone mesh."

As soon as Eiger left, Wultoph leaned closer and whispered in her ear. "Follow me, Lady Ramya." It was weird but Ramya followed him to a corner without questioning. She could feel eyes on her back as they walked, some curious, some hostile, and the remaining, contemptuous. "Space Command is trying to wrest the controls from our hands, now that the Chief of Fleets is dead and the Lord Paramount is unwell. They want to call the shots." He paused, his light-brown watery eyes boring into Ramya's. "Now if you so wish, I will grant them a transfer of word from the Lord Paramount. But . . ."

"But?" Ramya had to prod when he refused to finish the sentence.

"But the Lord Paramount would've liked us to be in charge. House Kiroff and its allies have spent an enormous amount . . . both effort and money . . . in this war and it'd be a loss to give up the reins now."

Ramya crossed her arms. She wasn't planning on giving up anything. But she also knew the wizened creatures that made up Space Command wouldn't easily bow to her authority. She'd have to make them. And it wouldn't be easy. Or pretty.

She saw a coterie of people, all suited in Space Command uniform, approach their corner. *Here they come!*

"Back me up, Lord Aristide," she whispered. "They're coming."

"Always in your corner, my lady," Wultoph whispered back and turned to face the officers.

Ramya shot a sidelong glance at Wultoph's determined face and smiled. "Now'd be a good time to stack up on security at the doors, Lord Aristide."

Wultoph's watery eyes barely had a chance to rest on hers when the Space Command officers walked up to them. A Norgoran at the head of the group placed a hand over his heart—fingers outstretched—and bowed his head. "Lady Ramya, I'm Vice Chief of Fleets, Romolo Mara. My sincere sympathies for your circumstances, my lady. I admire your strength. So much courage at such a tender age. I weep at the unfairness of fate. This is cruel. You should not need to worry about this war when your father needs you so badly by his side. Leave this to us. We will take care of this for you."

As if she didn't understand what he really wanted. All he wanted was to be in control, and that, she wasn't giving him. Ramya didn't let her derision show. She simply bowed, lower than he had, with all the grace that had been instilled in her over the years.

"Your words are very kind, Vice Chief Mara," she said. "But all my father needs right now is attention from the doctors. And they're all right by his bed. So please don't worry about me. Allow me to see this through."

Ramya watched as his eyes changed, feigned kindness draining out of them slowly until all that remained was a stone-cold gleam.

"You're just a child and this war is no place for a fatherless little girl to be in. We will take the Unosi craft and the new warheads from here and head to Zeta. We appreciate the hospitality House Kiroff has shown us thus far, but we couldn't impose on you anymore."

Ramya didn't know how Wultoph did it so quietly and so fast, but she smiled at seeing armed guards file into the room and take position around the doors and the corners. No wonder her father depended on the man. He was good.

She smiled at Romolo as sweetly as she could. "You're correct. I won't officially be an adult for a few more days. But I'm not poor, neither am I a little girl, and certainly not fatherless. Also, let me tell you, this war is the perfect place for me to be. And like it or not, you're going to have to live with the hospitality my father and the late Chief of Fleets agreed to. Let's make this clear, you aren't getting your hands on the smallest scrap from this base, let alone the *Fury* or the warheads. Not on my watch. Unless of course, you don't care about your well-being. You seem the sensible kind, but then, with the Locustans about to destroy us all, we've all become a little foolhardy these days, right?"

"Did you just threaten us, Lady Ramya?" Romolo said through gritted teeth. "Have you forgotten we're officers of the Space Command? That you're merely an underage civilian? Even your father had more respect for protocol."

"Well, I'm not my father." She had started away from the group, Wultoph following, when she stopped. She couldn't leave without a parting shot. "If I were you, Vice Chief Romolo, I'd pray for my father's quick recovery because I don't think you're going to like me at all. You see, I have no patience for decorum."

Their glares burned into her back, but Wultoph had a wicked grin plastered on his face that said it all—she had done well against the sniveling worms of Space Command. But there was more to be done, worse things to handle. She walked up to Merin, the Uminato, seated at a platform under the screens. The Mwandans took turns setting up the communication channels and today must be Merin's rotation.

"Can you set up a channel to your government, Merin? We need to pick up from where the Chief of Fleets left off this morning."

Merin gave her a telling look before assuming her meditative posture. Wultoph leaned closer to whisper. "Just so you know, my lady, the Vice Chief just spoke with them," he informed with a quick glance at Romolo and his associates. "It didn't go very well."

Ramya took a long breath and thought it through as Merin set up the channel. All she needed was five Drigganstones, whatever it took. Five stones. A movement to her left distracted her for a second. Gael, along with Ahool, was back.

"All properties are secure like you wanted," he whispered. "No one will even see them if I don't want them to." He paused and smirked at Ramya. "Not even you. So treat me well, my lady."

Ramya chuckled, thankful for the momentary levity.

"You called on the Mwandans?" he asked next. "You know what you're doing, right?"

"Hardly," Ramya confessed. "But I do have a gamble in mind."

Soon the view of a room flashed across the central screen. A bunch of people — male and female — sat in a row of chairs facing them. More sniveling worms, Ramya thought to herself, before smiling warmly at the screen.

"Greetings, Councilors," she said.

"What is the meaning of this?" asked an imposing female — a tag on her lapel announced her name, Nessa — in the middle of the row. "We just told you, we've given you everything we can. There's no more we can share, so please don't call on us every few minutes."

Someone chuckled behind her and Ramya was sure it was Romolo. So much for presenting a united front.

"My apologies," she continued calmly, even though all she wanted was to shake some sense into the Mwandans. "I'm Ramya Kiroff, Lord Paramount Trysten Kiroff's daughter. My father is unwell, so I'm speaking in his stead. I'm often told I'm too young and inexperienced and that's probably true. But I simply thought . . . no, I hoped, you'd reconsider. I made some friends on Morris II," — she took a moment to pat Ahool's shoulder — "and they've put their lives at risk for this cause. I just hoped you too would —"

"Whoever said you're inexperienced said the right thing," the Mwandan female spat the words out so venomously that it almost seemed to sear the screen. "You think you're impressing us with your friendships. You're actually insulting our pride. Those you call your friends are blemishes on Mwandan history, traitors, rebel filth. You're harboring our most-wanted fugitives. That makes you our enemies by extension, and that's what you are."

Ramya let the silence sink in and the anger settle down. The bait was cast and the Mwandan Council had taken the first nibble. She just had to play it up some more and make them swallow it all. Ramya took a step closer to the screen.

"I don't want to be your enemy, Councilor Nessa," she said as calmly as she could. "Is there anything I can do to win your alliance? Anything at all?"

Nessa gave her a blank stare, then she looked back and forth at her associates on either side. They whispered amongst themselves for a while before Nessa fixed a beady stare on Ramya's face. "Give us our traitors and we'll send you the Drigganstones," she said in a voice raspy with greed.

Ramya sensed Ahool move behind her but she didn't look back. She couldn't. There would be time for that, later.

Ramya placed a hand over her heart and spread out her fingers. "You have my word," she said. "Give me a hundred drams of Drigganstone and I'll send all your rebel filth back to you."

"Rami!"

She willed her eyes to stay on the screen and not look back at Ahool. Nessa's mouth twisted into a triumphant smile. "You will get what you want. When are you sending them?"

"I can't right now. I don't have enough ships left--the pirates destroyed whatever was left of the fleet here. But I have a transport heading this way that will pass by Morris II, and if you want, you can send your envoys in it. They can bring us the Drigganstones and secure your fugitives once they get here."

Lips pursed, Nessa took a long breath. "All right. Remember, Ramya Kiroff, you just took an oath. I hope you know the punishment for breaking one."

Ramya held her gaze steadily. "I would never," she said.

"All right then," Nessa replied. "We shall expect your transport at Morris II."

As soon as the screen turned off, Ramya found herself surrounded. Ahool was at the fore, his eyes brimming with unshed tears. "Rami, you traded us off? How could you?"

She wanted to console him, tell him what she truly wanted, but it was too risky. Romolo's suspicious gaze was stuck on her and the best thing to do at the moment was to up the ante. She tore her eyes away from Ahool and Merin's accusing eyes and faced Wultoph. "Please secure all the Mwandans on the base, Lord Aristide. Right away."

She turned toward Gael as Wultoph scuttled away. Her breath caught in her throat seeing his blazing eyes and furrowed brows. His anger didn't bother Ramya as much as the disappointment written on his face.

"Your father's shuttle is on the way from LBX-02, isn't it?" she asked. He barely nodded but that was enough. "Have it stop by Morris II, please," she added curtly.

"That's not right, Kiroff," he said when she started to walk away. "What you just did was not right."

She had to cut his dissent off right away or earn the reputation of being soft forever. She turned slowly and locked stares with him.

"Yours is not to question if I'm right or wrong, Lieutenant Arlington," she said in the iciest voice she could deliver. "Yours is to carry out my orders. Is that clear?"

Ramya saw the light ebb in his eyes. She saw Ahool's wilted face and Merin's look of disgust. Ramya didn't flinch. She turned away from them slowly and walked out of the CR. She had put a few props in place. Now she had to go wait for her father to wake up.

47

The walk out of the Combat Room was lonely, but Ramya had never stood taller. Things had gone exactly as she had planned, and given that she was hardly in a state to plan something meticulously, the ease with which things had fallen into place gave her a much-needed boost of confidence. The guards at the door made way for her as she left the room, and it seemed to Ramya they were lighter and faster on their feet than they had ever been.

They'd found more to respect, perhaps? No, more to fear most likely.

She inhaled sharply at the thought. It didn't matter why. The result was all she cared about.

"Lady Ramya." Wultoph's call made Ramya stop. She waited for the man to lumber up to her. "You were serious about holding the Mwandans?"

"Yes," she replied. "Why would you doubt anything I said?"

He opened his mouth, but then it shut just as quickly. "I shouldn't," he said finally. His eyes, hesitant and curious, said a different story. "I'll carry out your order, my lady."

"And don't let the Space Command folks out of your sight," she reminded him before walking away.

The medic greeted her when she entered the surgical unit. Much to Ramya's disappointment, he had no new updates to share. She slid into the chair farthest from the door and rested her head against the wall behind. Her shoulders throbbed and shook, as if a sack-load of bricks hung on them. She craved a soft, warm bed and . . . darkness.

Ramya didn't remember when she had dozed off, but she sat up with a start at the sound of a door opening. Gael strode up to her, his face just as gloomy and inhospitable as it had been in the CR.

"I made contact with our transport. They'll stop by Morris II and pick up the cargo you asked for." He paused for a bit, probably waited for Ramya to answer. "Is there anything else you need me to do?"

"No. I think that's—"

The door flew open before she could finish and Fenny marched in. Ramya barely needed a glance to tell the woman was furious. It only took her a second or two to locate Ramya, and then she stomped over. Nostrils flaring, she crossed her arms and glared.

"Iffin hell, Rami," she started. "Is it true that you traded away the grays?"

Gael looked from Fenny's flaming face to Ramya's exhausted one, lips pursed in disdain. Ramya had no doubt he was on Fenny's side.

"You lost your tongue, Rami?" Fenny snapped when she didn't reply. She hadn't lost much, only the strength to fight her friends. Fenny was having none of her silence. She grabbed Ramya's shoulder and shook it. "What is wrong with you? How could you?"

"How else were we going to get the Drigganstone, Fenny?" Ramya asked. "Everything's falling apart, don't you see? I can't leave the base and go looking for Drigganstones now. That was the only way. Our captain is counting on us."

"Don't you dare!" Fenny raised a shaking finger and hissed at Ramya. "Don't you dare bring Captain Milos into this. He would die a thousand times to protect innocents. And you . . . you just gave away your friends. That little boy saved your behind how many times now? And you . . ."

Fenny turned away and started pacing the room. Ramya stole a look at the medic's station. The man was still there but seemed oblivious to the commotion in the waiting room.

"Who's next on your list, Lady Ramya?" Fenny stopped and turned an indignant chin at her. "Me, Ross?" She paused and waved at Gael. "This GSO guy?"

"No one," Ramya replied. "But once you calm down I need a favor from you."

Fenny, who had started pacing back and forth once again, stopped abruptly. Turning her saucer-like eyes on Ramya, she shook her head for a while. Then she thumped Gael's shoulder.

"Can you believe this girl?" she asked. "She thinks I'll help her. After she's handed off her friends . . . our friends to be executed."

"Will you please calm down?" Ramya whispered.

"Calm down? Hell no, I won't," Fenny said. She spun away toward Gael. "Please make her shut up before I smack her face."

"I haven't handed off anyone, Fenny," Ramya said, but Fenny didn't even look at her, simply shook her head. "The Mwandans are still here, aren't they?"

"Right now they are, but you'll eventually hand them off. You have to. You've taken an oath, Lady Ramya," Gael said coldly. "It's done."

"Nothing's done until it's done," Ramya said.

For a whole minute or so, Gael stared wordlessly. It took Fenny just as long to turn around and look at her.

"You don't mean to back out on your word, do you?" Gael found his voice first.

Ramya shrugged. "What's stopping me?"

Fenny closed her eyes and shook her head, as if she were trying to wake herself up from a bad dream.

"They'll come after you with everything they've got," Gael said. "You don't—"

"Only if we survive the Locustans, Gael," Ramya said. "Right now, all that matters is getting Anomaly Point closed. Whatever it takes. If we live through this, I'll find a way out." She looked up at Fenny's large and sad eyes. "No one lays a finger on my friends, Fenny. Not on my watch."

Fenny sank into the chair next to her and sighed. "You could've told us."

"No, I couldn't. There wasn't time and I needed the reactions to look real," Ramya said. "I still don't want anyone knowing."

"I still don't think taking an oath with intent to break it is a good idea, but you have some guts, Kiroff." Gael paused and rubbed the bridge of his nose. "And I iffin hate it sometimes."

Fenny scoffed. "Yes, I second the lieutenant here."

For a minute or two, they all stayed silent. Then Fenny nudged Ramya. "What favor did you need?"

"The Octus prisoners. I need them to talk, to tell us who sent them and why. I'm not sure if Casten is having any luck interrogating them, so I need you to use Vi."

Fenny sat up straight. "You must be joking. Use Vi?"

"Yes."

"But Vi doesn't do violence."

"Maybe. But those mercenaries don't know that."

Fenny ran a hand through her hair and sighed. "I don't know, Rami."

"Don't sweat it, Fenny. I don't want to force you. Wanted to ask just in case."

Fenny was about to reply when the medic at the entrance rushed over. "Lady Ramya, your father wants to see you." Ramya jumped to her feet, her heart thudding like a drum gone berserk. Her father had made it after all. She noticed the anxiety clouding the medic's eyes a few seconds later. "Please hurry," he said, wringing his hands nervously.

Hurry? That only meant they were running out of time.

Ramya's heart dropped like a lead ball to the pit of her stomach. Cold tingled at the base of her spine and spread up her limbs. She followed the medic like a puppet on a string, unthinking, unfeeling.

Halfway, she stopped. She needed to do something else.

"Gael," she called. Her voice seemed to come from a world away.

"What is it?"

"You should come too."

His eyes were wide, uncomprehending. "Why me? This is your time with your father."

Her mouth was parched. "He likes you. It'd make him happy to see you."

"No. You should go alone."

A chuckle, lifeless and dry, slipped out of her. "That's the other thing. I need you there."

***

The room was cold as hell, colder than the frozen moon of Kyo-Sedra-5-1, and far more vicious. It bored into her heart and her soul, ate through her bones and left them hollow with barely any strength to keep standing.

Her father lay on a bed, his entire upper body wrapped in white. Things coiled in and out and around him — tubes, probes, and a zillion other wires that fed into an uncountable number of machines that blinked and beeped nonstop. It was cruel that a man whose presence dominated an entire galaxy could be made so small by a bunch of lifeless machines. Ramya could hardly keep her eyes on him when they ushered her in, or off the monitor at the foot of his bed that announced his plummeting CHS score. No wonder the medic had asked her to hurry.

His wheezing breath echoed in the room, and for what felt like an eternity, Ramya simply stood at the door listening to the brutal sound, her vision getting blurrier by the second. Until Gael nudged her forward. She found herself right next to her father, peering into his faded eyes, her heart agonizing over his drained face and purplish lips. The shaking palm he opened for her was icy. And his fingers desperate to hold on to hers.

"Bella . . ." He stopped and wheezed.

"You shouldn't talk," Ramya said, sobs spilling over her words.

"You have an instinct, Bella," her father said, ignoring her plea to stop. "Don't ever doubt it. Follow it. Always."

His eyes strayed over to Gael for a second before coming back to her again. "Find . . . good people and keep them close."

His eyelids drooped. Did his fingers loosen a little? Ramya tightened her grip on his cold hand.

She leaned closer. "Father?"

"Family comes first," he said, his voice fading into a whisper. "Take care of House Kiroff."

"I will, I promise," Ramya said.

His eyes stayed closed. The wheezing that had filled the room moments ago was quieter now. Ramya held his hand against her cheek. Her tears coursed over them like a river spilling over a ruptured dam.

"Bella . . ." His broken whisper floated like a specter across the room. "You make me proud . . . every day," he said, gasping for a breath, his face contorting with the effort and pain. "I'm . . . lucky to be your father."

His eyes closed once more. Ramya waited, his limp hand held tightly in hers, her heart open, eager to hear his voice again. She only realized a few moments later, other than the sound of her sobs and the steady beeps of the machines around them, the room had turned deathly quiet.

48

Trysten Kiroff left behind a million myths that grew stronger every second after his passing. Overnight, Ramya found herself enveloped in a strange halo. The way people looked at her changed; it was as if she had walked out of a fable. But if there were gazes of admiration, there were plenty more skeptical and even dismissive looks thrown her way. Ramya didn't care. She didn't have the time to care.

She only wished she could grieve away from thousand pairs of eyes watching her every move, but that was not to be. She wished she could speak with Gramaman Otis, but that couldn't happen because of the communication blackout. She could only send the word out to Somenvaar the old-fashioned way via an envoy. Ramya wished she could take her father's remains back home and perform his last rites, but that wasn't about to happen anytime soon either. So she held on to her father's last words and kept her interactions limited to close friends over the next day and a half. The rest of the world could stay away for a little while.

There was plenty to cheer for, though. The Drigganstones had arrived and Eiger and his team were busy prepping the warheads. The plan was to get the *Fury* transported to Zeta as soon as the warheads were ready. Isbet was doing great with the *Fury* and Ross — he had briefly stopped by to offer his condolences to Ramya — seemed to fit in well with Isbet. Pieces of the grand plan were finally falling into place. At least it felt that way.

Ramya was studying the blueprints scattered on her father's desk when Gael and Wultoph arrived.

"The Mwandan envoys are demanding we give them their prisoners, Lord Paramount," Wultoph announced worriedly.

Ramya's brows crinkled at the name he used to address her. "Why are you calling me that?"

"Because it's your title now, my lady," Wultoph explained. "No woman has inherited this title before you, so there is no notion of a Lady Paramount. Hence . . ."

Ramya let out a resigned sigh. "All right. Please tell the Mwandans that we can't spare them any transport back to Morris II. They are welcome to enjoy our hospitality until we get the fleets back from Zeta. Then they can take their prisoners to wherever they want."

Wultoph's face darkened. "You do not intend to give them what they want, do you?"

Ramya studied Wultoph's face for a second. The man — cunning and unscrupulous for as long as Ramya had known him — had been her father's trusted ally since . . . forever. She could trust him, she had to. But then, Wultoph was an old-timer and to him, the idea of breaking an oath could be the line that could never be crossed. What if he defected?

"These are my friends, Lord Aristide," she said, praying that her faith in the man would see her through. "The Mwandan government will probably execute them at first sight. So no, I don't intend to send my friends to the gallows."

Wultoph's face puckered. "I'll hold them off. We'll have to find a way around the oath you took. But please, Lord Paramount, let's strategize a bit next time?"

Ramya felt a flush creeping up her cheeks. "I didn't have the time."

"I understand," Wultoph said. "Besides, had I known, I couldn't have put on the shocked expression I had when you announced your deal. It was a good gambit but oaths tend to be sticky."

"Well, if anyone can unstick it, it'll be you, Lord Aristide," Gael said. "Deflecting them for a few days should be easy." He hunched over the table and looked at Ramya. "Milos is sending out another sortie into Anomaly Point now. That's it. The next one in has to be *Fury*."

"We're ready," Ramya said. "The warheads are prepped. Eiger is happy with them. We have fifteen of them in all. So in case we fail once, we can —"

"There can't be any failures," Gael interrupted. "We get one shot, that's it."

The way he said it made Ramya frown. There was a strange edge to his voice, an anger that he was struggling to keep down. Gael ran his hands through his hair when her gaze narrowed on his face.

"For all we know, the *Fury* isn't coming back from there, Kiroff," he said with a stoic sigh. "I got the stats from Milos today. During the last mission, of all the twenty-one ships that went in, only two made it back out."

Ramya slid into the nearest chair and dropped her head on her palms. This was bad, this was almost a certain death.

"We have to tell Isbet and Ross," she blurted. She had always known this was a risky mission but the odds were so much worse than she had imagined.

"They know," Gael said. "We've been working . . . strategizing with Milos."

Of course they knew. And they still wanted to do it.

"We need an engineer on board also," Gael announced.

"Don't tell me Fenny volunteered."

"No, she didn't get the chance. But Merin did."

They had all lined up, all her friends, to sacrifice their young lives. There was nothing she could do to change their minds. She wouldn't even try; that'd be insulting their valor. But she couldn't stop fearing for herself. She'd have to live on, mourning them as long as she lived. Ramya inhaled, long and deep, to fill that cavernous emptiness inside her. But she knew already that all the air in the room couldn't fill her lungs, no matter how many times she tried.

She pushed the chair back and forced herself up. "So, we're all set to leave for Zeta then?" she asked Gael.

"We can leave in six hours."

"Let's do that." Ramya stopped briefly at the door to speak with

Wultoph. "Lord Aristide, I want you to stay here at the base, keep the peace. I'll get back in touch when all's done."

Wultoph nodded and walked away but Gael lingered. As soon as Wultoph was out of earshot, he strode up to her. "Where are you off to?"

Ramya wished he hadn't asked. "I want to check up on Fenny. See how the interrogation is going."

His face hardened. She had known this already—he wouldn't like her pursuing the Octus right now. It probably wasn't the most sensible thing to do, either. But she *had* to find out. Whoever had taken her father's life had to pay.

"This is not the time," Gael whispered. "You know that. There will be a time and place for payback. But not now."

She bridged the distance between them with a quick step and reached for his hand. She returned his intense gaze with earnestness. "Trust me, I won't lose it. I know what the priorities are. But I need some sort of closure before I leave for Zeta."

He looked at her for a long time, as if trying to gauge her thoughts. Finally, he tore his eyes off her face and sighed. "All right. I'll see you later at the hangar."

Ramya watched Gael walk away. Then she headed to the holding cells in the northwest corner of the base. Fenny was inside the mercenary's cell, and a white-faced Casten was in the observation chamber watching Fenny and Vi prowl around the hulking Octus. The mercenary was bleeding in places, but his demeanor was far from broken.

Fenny left the cell as soon as Ramya called, looking almost relieved as she trudged out. The woman was disheveled, as if she had just come back from breaking up a scuffle. She wiped her brow with her arm as she walked up to the table.

"Got bad news for you, kid," she announced. Pulling a chair out noisily, she slid into it. "This bastard is as hard as they come. The other one is useless cannon fodder, but this one . . . he knows things.

I'm sure of that."

Ramya sat up and held her breath.

"Looks like the Octus weren't the ones driving this. Someone else hired them from Octus Laurden to get in here and eliminate some specific targets. He tried to spin it as a simple piracy-gone-wrong, but when Vi nibbled on his ear, he was more than happy to give us part of the truth. Isn't that right, Casten?"

Casten, who had been sipping from a glass of water, nodded hastily.

"So who did he say sent him?"

"That he wouldn't say. He's sticking with the 'I have no idea' defense." Fenny rubbed her temples and shrugged. "That's what he said. Over and over. I don't know what to do. I said I'd set Vi on his other ear and he still wouldn't budge."

Ramya tapped the table as she studied the battle-hardened face of the Octus mercenary. "Maybe it's time to bring out the carrots."

"Huh?"

"The stick didn't work as well as I expected. And I can't think of a bigger stick than a Pterostrich gnawing on your ear. So . . ."

"Bribe him?"

Ramya got off the chair and walked to the door. "Try to."

Fenny jumped off her chair and rushed up behind her. "Don't tell me you're going in. That thing's dangerous. And I think it was sent to kill Kiroffs. If it—"

Ramya parted the right side of her jacket to show Fenny the mini-stunblaster she had tucked in there. "That's a special make from Eiger's lab. All I need is one shot and he'll . . . crack his shell and die."

Fenny didn't say much after that. A minute later, Ramya was seated across from the Octus. The Octus, with their thick layer of natural armor and plentiful limbs, were always fearsome to look at, but this one was built more heavily than most. Even though a large open space separated them, his towering presence was unnerving.

"What's your name?" Ramya started, drawing an immediate glare of his near-luminescent green eyes.

"I told the bitch with the bird I don't know who bought this mission," he growled. "Can you just kill me already?"

Ramya smiled, taking her time to shake her head at the Octus. She could see how it was irritating him already. "What's your name?" she asked again.

His thick lips ground against each other. "Macuso," he spat it out with a grunt.

"You have a family, Macuso? Wives? Children? Parents?"

"What's that got to do with anything?"

Ramya leaned forward, holding his repulsive green gaze as best as she could. "I bet you haven't seen them in a while, have you?" she said slowly, waiting for telltale signs of his rage to show. "Macuso is a common name from the Lexi settlement and I think like most Octus from that area, your family is in containment."

He let out a long, torturous breath. She had come close. Lexi was a mess of a gangland that the Galactic Confederacy had tried to clean up for a long time. Their latest—and stupidest, in Ramya's opinion— move had been to round up the families from Lexi and send them to prisons across the galaxy.

"They're in some Confederate prison camp, aren't they?"

"So?"

"So, if you want to see them, I can help arrange that. I don't think your mercenary boss, whoever it is, has the power to do that."

His fat lips bent at the corners, his eyes crinkled at the apparent hilarity of her words. "And you, a pathetic little woman . . . child has some magical power to make the impossible happen? How? Does your mother sleep around with prison wardens?"

Ramya wanted to whip out the stunblaster and fire him into oblivion. Yet she simply folded her hands in her lap and pushed the next words out of her mouth. "Well, yes I do have the power," she replied calmly. "You see, my name is Ramya Kiroff. Lord Paramount Ramya Kiroff now, thanks to your murderous rampage. I can make the impossible happen."

It was satisfying to see the laughter die on his blubbery face. Ramya got to her feet slowly and fixed a cold stare on the Octus. "I'm making you an offer, Macuso. Tell me what you know and I'll get you your family. Maybe even buy you a plot of land somewhere in the Fringe. Don't tell me and you'll spend the rest of your life here, in this room.

"Give it some thought. If you have something worthwhile to say, just shout. The bitch with the bird will be right outside."

The air in the room was unsettled when Ramya walked out. She couldn't tell if Macuso was about to cave, or when, but one thing was clear—Macuso was seriously pondering the bait. It was only a matter of time before he bit.

49

It was ironic that the galaxy's last hope, the *Fury*, would be transported with such little fanfare. However, with the depleted resources of the Confederacy and the recent ambush by the pirates, a Drednot and two GSO Cutlasses were all the base had in working condition. Daybreak was still a few hours away when the trio of ships took off from El-Iss.

Ramya had pondered traveling in her father's state-of-the-art personal craft, the *Kinvari*, but she dropped the idea over security concerns. Even though the Octus prisoners hadn't spoken of more attacks being planned, who knew? The Kiroff family's enemies were numerous and strong and it wouldn't do to underestimate them. Someone could be out there waiting to get her. Since the *Kinvari* was known across the galaxy as Trysten Kiroff's personal ship, it would be an obvious target. So Ramya chose the familiarity of *Cutlass 31* instead.

She was one of the first ones to board, under the cover of darkness and secrecy. Amireh had escorted her down to a private chamber that Ramya had been to many times now. Alone in her chamber, she had watched people board the ships. She kept twirling a small data cube Fenny had passed her before she herself headed to the Drednot with Ross. The cube contained a statement from Macuso, one Ramya had gone over a hundred times already.

The name Macuso had given hadn't surprised Ramya much, but the fact that her hands were tied at the moment and that she couldn't do anything with the rage that swirled incessantly within her, didn't give her a moment's peace. Besides, she couldn't talk about it with anyone.

Well, except maybe Gael. However, he too wasn't around, likely busy at the bridge. It was funny how she had grown to trust him, confide in him, and long for his company. It was all because of the strain and rush of war, Ramya was sure. She wouldn't find him half as much a kindred spirit in everyday life. Or would she?

Ramya shoved the question away with a firm hand. *Useless thoughts!* Everyday life was a far cry from now, almost an improbability from here. And there was no point in focusing too much on the impossible. She shifted deeper into her seat and tried to clear her mind as she watched El-Iss grow smaller.

Someone knocked on her door after the tiny fleet had entered the SLH. Ramya opened the door, hoping it'd be Gael, and it was.

He took a long, hard look at her face before coming in. "What's wrong?"

Ramya shrugged. "Just worried about what's coming, that's all."

On the one hand, she wanted to share with him what Fenny had discovered, but on the other, she didn't want to be sucked back into thoughts of vengeance that would amount to nothing.

"Oh," he said simply. As he slid into a couch across the table from her, his gaze skimmed over the data cube sitting in the middle, eyes narrowing briefly as he looked, yet his face hardly even twitched. If he realized a connection between the cube and her current state of unrest, he didn't seem to want to show it. "We'll reach Zeta in five hours or less. Outlook is good. The last sortie went well, so Milos projects we'll have half a day to prepare for the final attack with the *Fury*."

"Is Romolo happy now?"

Gael chuckled. "Nah. He didn't like that I loaded the *Fury* in this ship and the warheads in the other Cutlass. Tried to twist my arm into putting it all in the Drednot. In the end, I offered him an audience with you, and then he backed off. He's scared of you, Kiroff."

"Of course he is."

From what Ramya had researched in the last two days, Romolo Mara had graduated from CAWStrat with the Danukis patriarch, Raan. Their connection over the years had stayed strong. Perhaps she was being overly suspicious, but Romolo had probably known that

House Danukis had ordered a hit on Trysten Kiroff. Maybe he was worried about being found now.

"What do you mean?" Gael asked.

To hell with pretenses! If she wanted to share this with him, she was going to. Ramya pushed the data cube toward Gael.

His face hardened, eyes narrowing to slits as he went over the contents of the cube. His fists had tightened into balls when he finally spat out, "Molen ordered the hit? Molen Danukis?"

"That's what the hired hand says. I'm not sure. But it's a start. If we make it through the fight tomorrow, I'm going to start digging for proof. It has to be out there somewhere."

Gael fell back in his seat and sighed. "What the hell was Molen thinking? That he'd get away with this? That no one would ever find out?"

"That's what all criminals think before committing a crime, don't they? That no one will ever find out. If they were smart enough to realize that's never the case, there'd be no crime at all."

"Molen! I always thought he was the sanest in the family."

Molen Danukis! Ramya recalled his pudgy face, his shiny button-like eyes, and a voice that oozed a sickening cadence of entitlement. But it couldn't just be Molen. The whole family was involved. Upstaged and beaten by Trysten Kiroff every step of the way, House Danukis had finally found a way to retaliate. They were going to pay, all of them.

Gael rubbed the bridge of his nose. "I know it's not easy but please try to keep your mind off it for a few more hours. I hope the *Fury* works a miracle and you won't have to go into the combat zone, but you never know. Have to keep your head straight."

She knew that. She wasn't going to do anything right now. But she was going to wipe them all out when the time was right. They sat for a while in uncomfortable, awkward silence. Then Ramya swung her legs off her couch.

"I'm going to walk around a bit. Isbet's on board, right?"

Gael nodded. "Yes, she is. She's a bit . . . jittery."

She had to be. After all, she was staring death in the face.

"Well, we'll cheer each other up. We have a few hours to kill anyway."

This turned out to be the best decision Ramya could have made. As soon as she located Isbet—she was alone in the fitness center, working with a set of weights—time flew, and in a very pleasant way. They hadn't spent much time together in a while and now was the perfect chance.

They sparred—Ramya found the exercise extremely helpful in lifting her spirits—and chatted about everything from CAWStrat to the present.

"You should make up with Ross," Isbet said as she took a jab at Ramya's shoulder with her training saber.

Ramya jumped away, caught by surprise at Isbet's comment. "Make up? I didn't fight with him, Isbet. Is that what he told you?"

"No, he didn't tell me anything. But he gets jumpy whenever I mention you so I deduced as much."

Ramya propped her saber on its stand and took her helmet off. "It's not like I started it. He—"

"Who cares, Rami?" Isbet said. The melancholy in her voice hit Ramya like a sudden punch in her guts. "In a few hours from now, things will change forever. Will it matter anymore who was right and who was wrong?"

No, it wouldn't. Ross would probably never return from his mission. All that would stay with her were the memories. And the guilt of not having done the simplest of things, not having said she cared.

"You're right, Isbet," she said. "I'll talk to him."

Isbet flashed a smile and Ramya suddenly realized how much they had all changed in just a few weeks. The carefree Isbet she knew had long vanished, and in her place was this thoughtful woman with the depth of the oceans in her eyes.

"Why are you looking at me like that?" Isbet flopped onto a sofa and fixed a frown on her. "It's like you're staring at an animal in a zoo."

Ramya chuckled. "It's nothing. You sound very wise, that's all."

"Hey, watch it, girl!" Isbet puckered her face in mock anger. "When have I not been wise?"

They broke into loud giggles and would've laughed for a long time but a loud beep interrupted. Isbet flipped her wrist to look at her watch.

"Aah," she said. Then slipping her arm around Ramya's shoulder, she touched her head with hers. "It's your birthday, Rami. Don't tell me you forgot again."

Ramya sighed. She didn't like birthdays. Ever. Growing up in Somenvaar, it meant lifeless parties, being paraded in front of strangers, being appraised by a zillion eyes. Then, when the guests left, her father would hand her a list of deficiencies she had displayed through the day. Getting into CAWStrat had meant escape from that routine of humiliation, and Ramya, desperate to get rid of painful memories, tried her best to forget the day. Isbet, however, never did. Not even now.

"Don't make that face, Rami," Isbet chided. "This is a special one for you. You are officially an adult now."

Yes, it was supposed to be special indeed. She was officially free in every way. She was finally her own person. It was something else altogether that just like every other year before this, Ramya didn't feel the slightest happiness. It was just another day, nothing else.

Isbet jumped to her feet. "Let's go, Rami. We have things to do."

"No, Isbet," Ramya warned. "You're not telling anyone about this."

Her caution was lost in the wind. Isbet flashed an impish grin. "You know how it's going to work, Rami," she said before bounding out of the room. "We're going to have a party."

Ramya followed, knowing she could do little to stop Isbet

completely. But maybe, she hoped as she picked up the pace, at least she could do some damage control and keep it low key.

50

Ramya had seen the image of Anomaly Point many times. However, nothing had prepared her for the sight when the Cutlass slipped out of the Drednot-flanked mouth of the SLH on its approach to Zeta. She stood at the bridge with Isbet and no matter how abysmal the chilly pit in their hearts grew, neither she nor anyone else present there could take their eyes off the view of the wormhole. It was enormous and . . . beautiful in a menacing, haunting sort of way.

"That's something," Isbet whispered.

It was indeed something. It looked like a gigantic window into the heavens, but it had been more appropriately described by the Unosi as a gilded pit leading into a soulless, dark universe filled with merciless beings only capable of endless aggression.

Ramya tore her eyes off the beautiful circle and scanned the space around it. She spotted the dark spot that was Zeta, its size in stark contrast to the gaping mouth of the wormhole. A shudder, sharp and strong, sped up her spine and shook her violently.

"I don't want to look at it," she said, turning away from the view. Just a few minutes ago, she'd been happy—as much as the circumstances would allow anyway—and distracted from the looming troubles by Isbet's impromptu birthday celebrations. One look at the monstrous wormhole and the warmth inside her had ebbed. Now she was back in a dark hole of fear and hopelessness, the insignificance of her existence made utterly clear by the monstrous wormhole.

She burrowed back into her chamber along with Isbet and they spent the rest of the journey to Zeta barely speaking to each other. Thankfully, the rest of the trip was short. Ramya had hoped her dwindling spirits would get a reprieve once they reached Zeta, but she quickly found out how wrong she was.

Zeta looked and felt like hell. It was one thing hearing about war — glorified, sepia-hued scenes of valiant soldiers marching off to the front lines — from a distance, and something else altogether being in the middle of it. Ramya had seen carnage before, but it was nothing compared to this. This was as near complete chaos as could be. Everything around seemed broken and dilapidated — the base as well as the people milling around with no apparent order. Children, no more than ten or eleven, were hauling parts and assisting the technicians. While all that was bad enough, the worst part was the look on people's deathly pale faces, the complete and utter absence of hope on them. These people had already lost the war.

Next to her, Isbet trembled a little. And as much as Ramya wanted and tried to say something . . . anything to cheer her up, she couldn't find the strength. They simply stood, stunned and devastated by the near-destitute conditions around them.

"Rami!" The voice came like a shaft of sunlight through the darkest clouds and pulled her out of the misery. Ramya's heart hung on to the sound as if it were a lifeline, her dazed eyes scanning for the source. They finally came to rest on a tall Norgoran woman dressed in a medic's white coveralls heading toward her from the far side of the docking port.

"Sosa," Ramya could barely stifle the sobs as Sosa's arms wrapped around her and held her close. Fear, hurt, and every doubt that had made home in her heart in the last few days ebbed in an instant. She was home, she was finally with family again. "Sosa, my father's dead," she whispered.

"I know, child. We all know. We've been waiting for you. Come, let's get you someplace quieter."

She wanted to. But she couldn't just take off because she wanted to. There was work to be done.

"I wish I could, Sosa, but I can't," she said, pointing at the workers streaming into the hold of the Cutlass. "I have to see this through. I promised —"

"Go, Kiroff." She hadn't noticed when Gael had walked up

behind them, Amireh in tow. "We've got this. You go, take a break. It won't be a long one anyway."

Isbet nodded vigorously and Sosa pulled Ramya away. "Like the lieutenant said, it won't be a vacation. But you need to unwind a bit while you have a chance," she said as they walked away.

Sosa's room on Zeta was tiny, but what it lacked in size, it more than made up for in character. Familiar fairytale creatures romped about on all of the walls except the one with a sturdy set of shelves. The shelves were stacked from floor to ceiling with Sosa's favorite concoctions and a smile flooded Ramya's face as soon as she saw a large beaker filled with the familiar blue-green Pax.

Sipping on goblets full of the warm Pax, they caught up on everything that had happened since the *Endeavor* had left El-Iss. Sosa told her about the dire situation on Zeta and the hopeless outlook on the galaxy's future.

"Zoho's a wreck," she said. "He's tired of seeing his people getting wiped out by the Locustans and Space Command's carelessness. When Terenze came here from Trio, Zoho was on the edge of a breakdown. This place was a worse mess than it is now. Marson called and offered Terenze Admiral Kanaa's seat." Sosa scoffed and took a long sip of Pax. "As if Terenze cared about positions. But seeing how Zoho was acting, he had to stay. It was a good thing too since Zoho has given up on everything since then. All he does now is sulk and mope." Sosa stopped and scrunched her nose. "Zoho's a fool if you ask me, a fool wrecking the name of Norgorans in the galaxy. Making a display of weakness goes against our grain. Besides, he's an admiral for stars' sake. He's supposed to lead the people on Zeta no matter what. But not Zoho."

Ramya sort of understood both sides of the argument. True leaders would lead stoically despite the circumstances, but then, Zoho had been through hell and back.

A loud rap sounded and in the next instant, the door swung open. Admiral Terenze Milos, his beard much more than stubble now on his drawn face, sauntered in. His rock-hard eyes softened as soon as they fell on Ramya and an adoring smile lighted up his face.

"There's my girl," he said, pulling Ramya into an embrace. "We have to end your Pax session now, I'm afraid," he announced. "I want to speak with you before the final scramble."

He waited patiently until Ramya had taken leave of Sosa. "Gael mentioned something Dakrhaeth had told you about the Hive. What was that about?"

It had almost been a momentary flash. They were in the middle of fighting the Octus ship when Dakrhaeth had blurted something about it. She hadn't spoken to Gael about it later, but he had remembered.

"Sorry, I didn't pay much attention to it then. I was — "

"You went through immense trauma, Rami," he cut her off forcefully. "From what I'm hearing, I'd say you did better than I could've pulled off myself, given the circumstance. So, don't beat yourself up over a tiny slip or two."

"Well, Dakrhaeth said the Hive was on the move and the call was stronger than ever."

His face darkened. "No wonder our attacks are getting less effective every time. I think the Hive is messing with the ships or the pilots somehow." He scratched his chin as they walked. "I wish Trysten was here. He'd think of something to counter."

"Well, I'm not Trysten Kiroff, but . . . I brought Eiger along. He's our chief scientist and I thought he might help."

"Of course that'll help," Milos said. "Good thinking."

He didn't notice her downcast face until a few paces later. He stopped and turning toward her, he placed a hand on her shoulder. "I'm sorry about Trysten, Rami. I wish it hadn't happened. I truly do."

Ramya stifled a sigh, blinking to relieve the sting in her eyes. "Molen was behind it," she said.

His eyes stilled for a second. He walked a few paces backward. Then forward a few times before he stopped. "Despicable scum. They knew everyone would be distracted."

Ramya crossed her arms, debating inwardly if would be wise to share her doubts about Romolo. In the end, she decided to go for it. "I think Romolo knew."

"That doesn't surprise me," Milos said right away. "Romolo has always been their dog. He and Raan Danukis were the best of chums since they were kids. After the Locusta-Vanga war, they went at it like a bunch of pigs. Raan was put in charge of funding Zeta and other defenses around Anomaly Point. Some defense system he built. All they cared about was pocketing the benefits. When people protested they were cornered and exiled." Milos paused and sighed. "Good people like Zoho got pushed away to the fringes."

"People like you?"

His jaw hardened for a moment but Ramya knew that was the truth. Milos, the hero of the first Locustan invasion, had been turned into a nobody for a reason. The reason was scheming dogs like Raan and his cronies. Her father had not done much better, but at least he tried to help in the end.

Milos shifted his feet and fixed a worried gaze on her face. "Well, never mind me. I've seen these games for a long time. I'm no friend of Space Command."

"Was Marson Hale the same way?"

"No. Marson was weak but he wasn't rotten."

Then perhaps removing him was part of the Danukis agenda also. Marson Hale had become friendly with her father, and that couldn't have made Romolo and Raan happy.

"What is it?" Ramya asked, seeing how vigorously Milos tapped his chin. Something new was bothering him for sure.

"I'm worried about you. Molen will be joining us."

For a second or two, Ramya could hardly believe her ears. Then she found her voice. "Here? Molen Danukis is risking his life coming to the front lines?" Ramya broke into disbelieving chuckles as she understood suddenly. "Of course he's coming. He wants to swipe the credit if the *Fury* works."

Milos nodded, his brows dancing. "You got it. There's a void in the galaxy's power structure and House Danukis and its allies are planning a coup. They're hoping to be masters of the galaxy when this crap settles."

"Only *if* the crap settles, right?"

Milos laughed. "They think we'll win. They have immense faith in our abilities. You have to give them credit for that."

"What if I survive along with the galaxy? You think they'll come after me?"

His head snapped upward, eyes flashing. "They wouldn't dare. Not while I'm standing. And it's not just me, Rami. You have friends. Your father, your family, has always had allies. You are not alone. You'll never be alone."

At least the thought that she had potential backers was comforting. It didn't stop the dread from tap dancing on her spine. Her enemies were many, and tenacious.

"Ah well, let's just get through tomorrow," she said, pushing away the cumbersome thoughts. She'd deal with them later, after they'd finished with the Locustans.

51

The crap showed no sign of settling down. In fact, it was piling up higher and higher. Five hours had passed since Ramya reached Zeta and while the Fury was prepped and ready for its flight into Anomaly Point, Milos had thrown a spanner into the plans. Now, they—everyone conversant with the upcoming offensive with the *Fury*—were crammed inside the Command Center on Zeta, staring at the huge display screen that showed two Wentworth-Busas approach Anomaly Point.

"What the hell are you trying to prove, Milos?" Molen Danukis roared after they had watched for a bit.

Milos shot him an icy look. "That would be Admiral Milos."

Molen turned a shade of red. When he spoke again, his voice was as close to courteous as could be. "Apologies, Admiral," he said, forcing a simpering smile. "Could you explain to a simpleton like me the meaning of this exercise?"

Ramya shifted her feet. The exercise was simple enough, only Molen was not willing to accept the implications of it.

"Yes, I'll explain," Milos replied patiently. "When we sent the first sortie into Anomaly Point, we could only go a third of its length. However, all ten of the WBs that went into it returned after discharging their payloads. That was a perfect mission—zero loss of life, Anomaly Point dimmed and turned unstable for two whole days."

Molen nodded and flashed a grating smile. "With someone as capable as you at the helm, what less could we expect?"

Ramya let out a breath remembering how barely a week ago, the same Molen had been quick to paint Milos as just the opposite of capable. She wished she could smack all the teeth out of his chunky jaw. Thankfully, for Molen anyway, the whole breadth of the room separated them. Ramya felt Gael's sidelong glance on her face. It was no accident that he had found a spot next to her. He was there to make sure she didn't hurl herself on Molen, and Ramya believed Milos had something to do with the arrangement as well.

Milos continued with his explanation. "But that changed rapidly after. The next sortie, we were blocked earlier. And we lost all our WBs. The wormhole was affected by the shelling, no doubt, but not as badly. Things have been getting worse since. In our last mission, two pilots made it back home. They complained of a blackout, they had no idea how and when they discharged their payloads, no memory of how far they had traveled within the wormhole. Nothing!"

Molen grunted. "These people you're sending in . . . are they good enough?"

A silence — so thick and heavy that you could smother someone to death with it — fell in the room. Ramya felt Gael stiffen next to her.

"I-I mean . . ." Molen stammered to life, realizing his mistake. "I mean they are all tired and exhausted and —"

"They are all as fit as can be," Milos cut him off coldly. "It's not them. It's the wormhole. We believe the Locustans are doing something, messing with our pilots and our craft somehow. The Unosi said the same. The *Fury* was built specifically to counter the Locustan blocking."

"I don't understand," Romolo said. "If the *Fury* is immune to the block, send it in. It releases the warheads and we're done. End of story."

Milos grunted. It was a while before he replied. "We didn't want to send the *Fury* in unescorted. What if the Locustans happen to swarm out at the same instant the *Fury's* going in? It will be a sitting duck."

"Why's that?" Molen asked.

"Other than a basic shield, the *Fury* hardly has any built-in defense mechanisms. It is simply a carrier of weapons," Milos explained. "So, we want to have our fighters clear a path, at least to a strategic point."

Once again, a deathly quiet enveloped the room when Milos stopped speaking. But the silence was not for long. An unfamiliar, gruff voice broke the quiet. "What if we can't? What if none of our fighters can get inside? We don't send the *Fury* in at all?"

It was Melroon, Molen's uncle. Ramya remembered him from the close encounter at Nebeca 21; he had the hard, cruel eyes and the typical square jawline of the Danukis family. He was clearly a quiet, shadowy presence who spoke very little, at least compared to his nephew.

"Of course not," Milos replied, his voice steady and cold. "If all else fails, we send it in unescorted. But I'd like to know outright what we're up against. And plan likewise."

Melroon raised an eyebrow. "So, what's the grand plan?"

"The plan is to see if we can find out how they're affecting us. It's useless otherwise to send in people, knowing they'll be rendered ineffective once they get inside Anomaly Point."

"I thought we didn't have time?" The sarcastic comment came from Romolo Mara, who had, tellingly enough, seated himself between Molen and Melroon. "Now, all of a sudden, we're back to doing a basic investigation?"

"Yes, we are," Milos replied. "Before we fire our most valuable weapon, we need to be sure we're firing it right. I thought someone from Space Command would understand the need for the pause."

The scathing rebuttal shut Romolo up. Pursing his lips, he turned his attention back to the display. Molen, however, waved at the screen.

"So . . . how long will this take?"

"The pilots are sending us their feedback now. As soon as we analyze the data—"

Molen shook his head vigorously. "Can't we do it faster? That blasted wormhole is stable now, isn't it? What if more Locustans are on the way?"

"You're right. It's been almost a day since we last shelled it. So the destabilization is about to wear off completely." Milos paused to look at his watch. "I'd say in an hour or so. Once that happens, there's a chance Locustans will come through."

Romolo sat up and turned around. "Damn it, Terenze. Send another sortie, get this thing destabilized. Then we can do the damned analysis."

"Scared, are you?" Milos let out a dry chuckle. "Well, I wish we had enough expendable people and craft to send in, but we don't."

Molen shook his head again. "You can't find ten people to carry out a mission? And you call yourself an admiral?" He leaned over the table and shot a mocking look at Romolo. "This is who you picked? He's just as useless as Zoho."

That was the last straw. Ramya just couldn't take it anymore.

"Perhaps you should find your brother, Armand. He liked to flaunt that he was the top cadet at CAWStrat, so he could've pulled off a miracle here. Oh wait, I forgot, he's hiding to save his skin."

Molen glared across the table at her. "You again. The illustrious Kiroff brat. Always speaking out of turn and without permission."

"I speak when I want to," Ramya returned icily. "I don't care about your permission."

Molen kept glaring but Ramya didn't relent. She held his hostile gaze until he looked away angrily toward Milos. "All right, so you're running analysis. Who's doing that? Why can't they hurry up?"

"My scientists are running the analysis. And they'll be done when they're done," Ramya replied.

Molen's face puffed, as if it would come apart in pieces. "All right then. Let us know when you're done twiddling your thumbs, Admiral," he said, almost spitting the words out at Milos. Pushing his chair back noisily, Molen stomped out of the room. Melroon, Romolo, and the rest of the coterie followed.

As soon as the room cleared a bit, Eiger spoke. "They're seeing a massive surge of Therym-Bay particles near Anomaly Point,

Admiral," he said to Milos. "This is unusual, so focused and . . . I think it's some sort of a scattering weapon."

Milos rubbed his forehead. "So our fighters won't be able to get far, will they?"

"I'm afraid not. They can sustain the interference for a maximum of ten seconds, maybe. Any longer and the pilots will be disoriented and their equipment will probably fail," Eiger replied. "Even if we were to build a shield of sorts against these particles, that wouldn't counteract everything. There's an organic lattice that forms a base of this blocking mechanism they're using. It's most unusual."

A gloom fell in the room until Milos spoke. "Well, the *Fury* goes in alone then. That's the only way."

A moment of silence and then a group of Space Fleet officers clustered around Milos.

Ramya walked over to Eiger. "There's really nothing we can do?"

Eiger pressed his temples and shook his head morosely. "Apologies, but I haven't seen such a mix of — " He stopped abruptly, his rapidly-widening eyes fixed on Ramya. "No, wait, I've seen this before. In the Strykers. The homing calls. The muffler we made to counteract the homing calls were sort of . . ."

Ramya wanted to break into a dance right there but she had to adhere to some form of decorum. So she simply broke into giddy laughter. "That would work against this blocking?"

"Well, not exactly. The Stryker couldn't automatically counter these beams. Yet. But . . . I can tweak the mechanism we have in the Stryker. And maybe . . . I think it might work."

Ramya wanted to wrap Eiger in a tight hug. But then again . . . it wouldn't be proper. "Good," she said simply before whirling around to find Milos. He was still surrounded by the bevy of Space Fleet officers when she walked up. "I'd like to propose something, Admiral."

His eyes narrowed immediately, as if he knew what she was about to tell him. He didn't say a word, simply looked around the room to check who was still present. Zoho hadn't left, he still sat with a vacant look on his face. Eiger's assistants were still hunched over a portal. Gael and Amireh had hung back as well.

"Yes, Rami," Milos said in a resigned voice.

"The Stryker, if you remember, has a mechanism that keeps it from latching on to homing calls from other Locustans," she said. "Eiger can try to tweak it so it can counter the blocking mechanism of the Locustans."

Ramya had expected Milos to look hopeful, if not happy, but instead, his face clouded. However, Eiger, who had followed Ramya, beamed.

"There's a possibility, Admiral."

"Can you build similar mechanisms into the other craft?" Milos asked.

Eiger's eyes dimmed. "No, Admiral, there just isn't enough time."

"But I could lead the *Fury* into Anomaly Point," Ramya said. "I know one Stryker doesn't make a squadron, but it's better than sending the *Fury* in on its own, isn't it?" Milos gave her a vacant stare so Ramya continued. "And who knows . . . maybe the Stryker's presence will confuse the Locustans. They won't know what to do with one of their own and maybe that'll give the *Fury* a chance to get even deeper inside."

Milos seemed intent on counting joists so Ramya turned toward Eiger. "Can you please start looking into this right away?" she asked.

The officers around Milos snapped their heads toward her, their faces hard, and Ramya realized she had breached protocol yet again. She could feel Gael's frown on her back. She recalled his words from way back when — all she was allowed to do was propose a plan. The final decision had to be the Admiral's, not hers.

Swallowing the lump of trepidation choking her throat, she turned toward Milos. "Apologies, Admiral. I jumped too fast. Do I have your permission to get Eiger started?"

"There is no guarantee it'll work," Milos said slowly. "Besides, you'd be risking your life for . . . what might amount to nothing."

"Maybe. But maybe it'll work like a charm."

"I couldn't ask you."

"You aren't asking me. I'm volunteering."

His nod was barely there. It was enough for Ramya. She gestured Eiger to follow and bounded out of the room. She had to speak to Dakrhaeth first and foremost.

Before she could reach the Stryker, Isbet and Fenny accosted her. She had just finished explaining the plan to them when Gael appeared in the docking bay. He was sporting an impressive scowl and Ramya guessed he was mad at her for volunteering. It didn't take long to find out she was right.

"You just *had* to throw yourself at their feet," he said, arms crossed as he stomped up to her. Isbet muttered something and backed away immediately. Fenny, however, stayed put and watched Gael soak Ramya in a glare.

"So you're going to sacrifice yourself? Give the Danukis weasels what they want?" he hissed at her when she didn't reply to his earlier question. "I'd hate to see them win so easily."

As much as Ramya wanted to keep calm, frustration raised its head within her. Why didn't he understand? She didn't want to hand the Danukis a win either, but there was no other way.

"I told you already. You know what it means if the *Fury* flies inside unescorted. The Locustans might rip it apart even before it's able to reach the strategic spots. Someone has to clear the path, and I can with the Stryker. If we're lucky, they will even be confused by the Stryker, thinking it's one of their own. That'll buy us time." She paused to take a deep breath. This fight was tiring and she wished Gael would relent. "If the *Fury* fails, we're done anyway. All of us. Me included."

"You don't see the Danukis risking their necks, do you?" he said stubbornly. "Is Armand Danukis here? No!"

"Armand doesn't have the Stryker, does he?"

Gael's lips thinned. He didn't like that answer. Ramya continued regardless.

"Besides, I have greater ambitions than Armand. I'd like to be the one who beat the shit out of the Locustans."

"So Stryker or no Stryker, you'd never listen."

"And you would?" Ramya shot back.

For a few moments, they simply stared at each other. Then Gael shook his head. "Your father wanted you to take care of your family. Don't you remember?"

She did remember. "I *am* taking care of my family, Gael. If I don't do this, they'll die."

He ran his hands through his hair and sighed. "All right, I get it, Kiroff. I get it."

"I'll come back, Arlington. I'll find a way."

"I wish it were that easy," he said before marching away.

Fenny rolled her eyes as they watched him leave. "You two match each other perfectly, you know that? Loud, stubborn and . . ."

Fenny stopped when Ramya cast an annoyed look at her. Then she shrugged and left. Ramya walked toward the Stryker. It was going to be one long chat with Dakrhaeth.

52

Time couldn't have trickled by any slower. Eiger was busy. His entire team descended on the Stryker and for hours, they probed, poked, and ran tests. The longer Eiger took to finish, the greater the anxiety grew around the base. It meant Anomaly Point was stable and open for the Locustans to pass through, and knowing that wasn't a happy thing. Molen kept breathing down Milos's neck, and even Ramya made frequent and quite a few unnecessary trips down to the docks to check on Eiger's progress.

Milos had picked a squadron of fifteen, codenamed the Fenix Force, to fly into Anomaly Point with the *Fury*. All of the fighters except the Stryker and the *Fury* would turn around at five seconds in. Ramya would continue further, hopefully long enough for the *Fury* to reach strike point.

While Ramya didn't like the plan much—the other fighters were on a suicide mission against the Locustan blockage—she did like the name a lot. The Fenix was a mythical bird, one who rose from the ashes. The story of its rebirth was a favorite of hers. She still remembered how Gramaman Otis always ended the story. House Kiroff is like the Fenix, she'd say, and she'd go on to tell how the family had risen from being destitute to kings. Ramya would fade into dreams of the bird with plumes of gold.

There was no room for dreams at the moment. The Fenix Force had started its day with a sharp and precise address by Milos early in the morning. It was not a real morning—there were no mornings near Zeta since there were no stars nearby, or it could be thought that right now, it was always morning since the wormhole continuously cast a glow—only a standardized time relative to Xandria.

Milos went over the details. A Drednot would carry the Fenix Force—the *Fury* and the rest of squadron—close to Anomaly Point. He explained the formations, the precise locations where the *Fury* would drop its payload, and when the fleet would have to turn around and get out of Anomaly Point. Ramya listened, her senses strangely sharp and dull at the same time. Numbers, instructions, orders penetrated her mind, while everything else floated past like a hazy mist.

Milos walked up to her after the assembly was dismissed. Zoho, his face as deathly pale and shrunken as a desiccated mushroom, was with him. "Rami, you will turn around precisely at twenty seconds in, all right? You will leave Anomaly Point then no matter what. Do you understand?"

"Yes, of course."

She couldn't fathom why Milos shot a worried look at Zoho whose face darkened another notch.

"You're leading this squad, so I expect you to follow orders," Milos said. "Can I have your word?"

Did he question her commitment? Or was he simply reining in her adventurous side? *It had better be the latter*, Ramya thought to herself.

"I don't understand," she said aloud.

"I don't want you to spend one second more inside the wormhole than is necessary. I need you back here, understood?"

Ramya's brows crinkled. Lieutenant Arlington surely had something to do with this.

"Yes, Admiral." She hesitated a second before pulling out the data cube with Macuso's statement from her pocket. "I want you to keep this safe for me. It has a message for you and my family just in case."

A deep frown furrowed his forehead. "Make sure I do not need to use it," he said stiffly as he accepted the cube. "Remember my directive. Twenty seconds and no more. Good luck."

After Milos and Zoho left, Ramya stood there nursing a prickly annoyance. She wasn't a child anymore; she didn't need the constant shepherding. Gael, and now Milos, seemed to think otherwise and that was—

She discarded her thoughts on spotting Ross around the corner. Talking to him before they headed out into the unknown was top on Ramya's agenda, so she bounded up to him. Ross, however, hardly looked thrilled at seeing her approach. Heck, the way he glanced over his shoulder, it almost seemed like he was looking for a place to run.

Ramya placed herself squarely in front of him. "We haven't talked in a while, so . . ."

She had banked on Ross picking up the thread, but he didn't. So they stood in awkward silence for a while.

Until Ramya forced herself to speak. "I'm sorry if I offended you the other day. I didn't mean to—"

"You meant what you meant, Lord Paramount Kiroff," he said in a voice so abrupt and sharp that it made Ramya catch her breath. The way he lingered and stressed her title was particularly irksome. Ross continued, the acid in his words hardly diminished. "I forgot my place, I said too much. Well, I've learned to make peace since then."

Ramya crossed her arms and then uncrossed them again. She was sure she'd get her thoughts out all wrong. She tried nonetheless. "It had nothing to do with your place, Ross. I just thought . . . I thought we needed to think it through some more."

Ross smiled, but there was no peace in it, just ridicule. "So what's the problem? You were right, I was wrong. We're all square."

The problem was simple—Ross was not willing to see her side of the argument, at all. Everyone did it at one time or another, but in the end, when things cooled down, they understood the opponent's point of view. Or they at least tried. Not Ross. Not now.

"Well, good luck on the mission," she said, not finding anything else to talk about.

Ross scoffed. "Oh no, not me. You need all the luck," he said. "See how Milos is more worried about you than the mission? You know why? You see, the galaxy's future depends on you. You're important, Lord Paramount Ramya Kiroff. I'm expendable. So, take my luck. I'll be fine without."

What the hell was wrong with him? Anger and frustration coiled and melted in Ramya's guts, and she could barely hold it in. She didn't reply to his scorching monologue and simply stood and watched him walk away.

Her heart was leaden as she headed to the Drednot's docking bay, her mind lingering over the frustrating conversation she'd just had. Ross had snubbed her cruelly. Did he have to? They were headed into an impossible mission; couldn't he pretend to be civil for a few minutes?

Forget him, Rami! Focus on the mission, she kept telling herself. Ross was tired and worried. One didn't just glide into Anomaly Point every day. Even the thought of doing it was enough to make people snappish.

Looking at the positives, at least she had tried.

Fenny was working at the docking bay along with Gael and six technicians when Ramya walked in. They were setting up the craft, arranging them in order of launch. While it wasn't critical, a good sequence could save precious minutes on a mission. Ramya decided to join them, hoping it would clear her thoughts. She could do without brooding over Ross's sullen face and stinging words.

Ramya noticed an apparent inconsistency right away. Instead of the *Fury,* Gael's Mossin was placed next to her Stryker. She walked up to Fenny and jerked her thumb at the lineup.

"Hey, are those in the right sequence?"

Fenny took a look at the Mossin and then gave Gael a curious look. "I think so," she said.

Ramya looked one more time. "I don't. I'm going first, then the *Fury.* The rest come behind. Unless you don't care how they launch."

Once again, Fenny shot her a furtive glance. Then she cleared her throat in a weird way. "Umm . . . Lieutenant," she called Gael.

Gael wasn't half as flustered as Fenny when he heard Ramya's question. In fact he wasn't flustered at all. He simply shrugged. "Nothing's wrong. I'm flying right behind you."

"What? No, you're supposed to bring up the rear. You're turning around at five, don't you remember?"

"That was before. Things have changed, and so have my plans."

"Milos didn't say that. He—"

"You always follow orders, do you?"

Things were going wrong. Very, very wrong.

"It's not the same. I'm a civilian with nothing to lose. You on the other hand—"

"That's my problem. Now, if you'll excuse me, I have other matters to attend to," he said and turned away.

Ramya shook her head at his back for a long moment before she turned toward Fenny. If she had hoped for support from the woman, she was mistaken. Fenny flashed a look and shrugged. "That's his choice, kid. If you get to choose your way, he does too."

So much for a peaceful start to the mission of their lifetimes.

53

The Drednot, a dot in the darkness beyond the far rim of the wormhole, hung still. All was quiet, nothing stirred, except for the light and colors around the wormhole. In reality, there was no peace in the situation. Inside the Drednot, a group of seventeen people, young and old, male and female, resolutely marched into their craft. Their faces were grim and their jaws clenched, not out of fear but conviction.

On nearing the Stryker, Ramya pulled Isbet aside. "Be safe, all right?" she said, releasing her best friend from a desperate embrace. They all knew the odds. Ramya knew chances were she'd never see Isbet again and the thought made her heart weigh like a rock in her chest.

Isbet however, flashed a bright smile. "Come on, Rami. Stop making that face," she chided. "I'm the best flyer there is, you know that. There hasn't been anyone in the history of CAWStrat with stats like mine. And yet you think one stupid wormhole is going to get the better of me?" She paused and patted Ramya's shoulder. "I'll be out of there in no time. You'll see. I'll destroy that iffin wormhole and come out laughing."

There was no fighting the sunshine that was Isbet. Ramya nodded and forced a lifeless grin. "Yes, you will," she said.

"There you go. Now let's get out there and give those bugs hell."
Now that, Ramya had no trouble getting behind. A fist bump later, Ramya strode up to the Stryker. She took a long breath as she slid into her seat and fastened her harness, her hand instinctively slipping over the flight stick. It had been a long journey in a rather short time. From the moment she slipped out of CAWStrat until now — it had been the ride of a lifetime.

"Ready for the final reckoning, Mihaal?" Dakrhaeth said. Ramya thought his tone was rather forbidding, yet it brought a smile to her lips.

"I am," she replied, chuckling as she thought how far Dakrhaeth had come as well. "Are you, Dakrhaeth?"

"Always."

Ramya wondered how he felt about heading toward the world he came from. Before she could ask, the comm crackled and Lohau, the captain of the Drednot they were in, spoke.

"Fenix Force, Admiral Milos would like to have a word."

"A wise man, my superior and friend, once told me, a person shows his true colors not when there is nothing to lose, but when there is everything to lose." Ramya shuddered a little. She knew those words well; Grappa Abelei said them often. On the comm, Milos continued. "Today, we have everything to lose. Our lives, our homes, our families. Today we need to show that mighty enemy who we really are. We have one goal, get the *Fury* to its target." He paused and Ramya realized her nails had dug deep into her palms, enough to draw blood. "Let the Fenix rise."

A wave of cheering rolled out of the comm and filled the Stryker.

"Fine words," Dakrhaeth said. "Your kind sure has a knack for them."

Ramya hit the mute button and shook her head at the AI. If Dakrhaeth had been a real person, the galaxy's penchant for protocol would have had him exiled by now.

"Let's keep our thoughts to ourselves, all right? Particularly non-flattering thoughts about our superiors," she chided.

"Non-flattering? Really, Mihaal? I thought I said the —"

He stopped. The comm still roared with the sounds of cheering, but Dakrhaeth's sudden pause unleashed a dread that instantly drowned the noise.

"Dakrhaeth?" Ramya called. She couldn't stop her voice from trembling.

"They're coming, Mihaal," he whispered.

Ramya hit the mute button off and shouted. "Locustans approaching. Cut us loose."

In the blink of an eye, all chatter stopped.

"Rami?" Milos called, his voice steady as a rock. "Dakrhaeth tell you that?"

"Yes."

"Captain Lohau, set the Fenix free," Milos ordered. "Fenix Force, unless they come for you, do not engage with the Locustan fleet. I repeat, do not engage. You have one task only, taking the *Fury* inside Anomaly Point safely."

"Depressurizing," the captain said as soon as Milos stopped.

A babble came out of the comm, and even though Ramya focused her senses on the darkness outside the parting doors of the bay, she caught bits of the chatter. It was a conversation on Zeta, and Molen was yelling.

"Let's go. Let's get out of here before they come."

"You really shouldn't," Milos said. "The safest place is here, inside Zeta."

"You think I'm a fool? I'm not sitting in this ratty starbase and waiting for those pests to eat me alive. I should've never come here. I'm leaving now."

The last sounds Ramya heard from Zeta before the channel cut off with a click were of footsteps, loud and stubborn, fading away. She couldn't help chuckling to herself and hoping that Molen would be stupid enough to venture out of Zeta. The incoming Locustan swarm would take care of him and his cronies. Getting the biggest name off her kill list this easily? That'd be good.

"Time to go, Mihaal," Dakrhaeth said. Ramya eased the Stryker over the lip of the bay and pressed on the throttle. The Stryker zoomed out into the darkness.

A string of craft trickled out behind her. Ramya checked their progress on the rear display, lips curling in annoyance when the Mossin fell into place right behind her.

"I don't need you protecting me," she hissed into the darkness. Once this mission was over, she was going to give Gael a piece of her mind. That'd teach him to stay within bounds.

Now though . . . she needed to focus.

They couldn't go too far out and dash headlong into a Locustan swarm, so they had to wait it out on the sidelines until they came. Hopefully, they'd take their attack straight to Zeta and not notice the Fenix Force at all. But where the hell were those Locustans? Had Dakrhaeth felt it right?

Captain Lohau's breathless voice answered all of Ramya's questions. "There they come."

They streamed out, perhaps a hundred in total, in a thick, twisted wave of darkness. Ramya held her breath, thrusters down to a minimum as they waited and watched. The swarm veered right and away from them, making a beeline for Zeta.

"We just let them pass," Lohau said in a low voice. "Let them go."

Ramya said a prayer for Zeta. Admiral Milos would have a tough fight on his hands, but there was no way out of it. They had to let the Locustans go so the *Fury* could get a clear path in.

"All right, Fenix, let's get moving now," Lohau said after a few minutes.

Ramya pressed on the throttle again, and the Stryker shot forward. The rest of the fleet followed. For minutes that seemed to creep forward, they made their way with ease, their formation perfect, their speed optimum. The gaping mouth of Anomaly Point loomed just a minute's distance away when Ramya, desperate to keep her jitters in control, broke the tight silence on the comm.

"That was smooth sailing, wasn't it?" she said, chuckling. "Looks like we'll be in and out in seconds, Fenix."

"Here's hoping, Rami," Isbet replied.

They had hoped too soon. As if on cue, a bunch of Locustan craft careened out of Anomaly Point just as the Fenix Force approached the entrance.

"Stragglers," Tanaka shouted.

There was no turning back now. No avoiding them. No hiding from them either. Ramya eased on the throttle, mind racing. She counted them. Eight in all. They had to take them on.

"Fenix, Engage," Lohau said. "Protect the *Fury*."

Fighters from the back — Tanaka's Astro in the lead — broke out of formation, as the Locustans shot forward. Tanaka's cannons lit up the first two on the left instantly. "Two down," he shouted. Two WBs swooped on the next couple. "Three!"

"And four."

Ramya picked a Locustan to the right. She lunged at the craft, arming her rail guns as they bridged the distance between them. Its guns erupted, Ramya swerved. The shield monitor complained — 95%.

She banked the Stryker hard, and as soon as she was level with the Locustan craft, she fired. It flew at her through the fire, it kept on coming even when it had broken into pieces.

"Make that five," she shouted.

"Three more to go," Tanaka said. "Munro, there's one on your tail."

"Move, Munro. Shake it off." Gael shouted. Ramya tugged the flight stick as hard as she could, spinning the Stryker around. She saw a Locustan rip into Munro's Astro, turning it into a fireball.

"Damn it, Munro," Gael's frustrated whisper hung in the air. But grief got only a moment's attention.

"There's one going for the *Fury*," one of the WB's pilots yelled. Ramya threw her weight on the flight stick, pushing it with all her might to turn the Stryker around again.

"We're under fire," Isbet's scream shattered Ramya's focus. She spotted another straggler on the far side of the *Fury*, front guns blazing. "Shields are holding up, but . . ."

They couldn't hold up forever.

"I got my eyes on one," Ramya declared.

She dove, aiming for the Locustan craft. It saw her coming and bolted. Ramya pressed on the throttle, nose glued on the Locustan's tail. She didn't want to waste a torpedo on the puny craft but the rail guns weren't an option anymore.

"Dakrhaeth!"

"Torpedoes armed and ready, Mihaal."

Ramya's hand caressed the flight stick. She lined up the Stryker and steadied her finger over the firing controls. The targeting scope blinked green and beeped. Ramya hit the launch button.

"Don't miss. Don't iffin miss," she muttered. The Stryker shuddered under her as the torpedo streaked out.

Ramya held her breath as the torpedo bore down on the Locustan. The Locustan banked to the left. The torpedo grazed its wing and exploded. The Locustan swung away from the ball of fire, intact.

"Damn!"

Ramya's hand flew to work up the throttle. This Locustan was tricky, hard to follow. Its craft was small and far more agile than the Stryker. Thankfully, it wasn't as cunning as it could be. It flew away from the *Fury* and the rest, and at least Ramya didn't have to worry about endangering her comrades during the chase.

"Dakrhaeth, engage the turbo," she ordered. She was close. Her hand hovered over the firing controls.

The Stryker picked up speed. Ramya's fingers danced over the targeting controls until the scope blinked green again. The Locustan swung in the direction of the *Fury*. Ramya pressed on the throttle. She had to take the Locustan out before it got too close to the Fenix.

In a sudden burst of power, the Locustan craft shot forward like a missile.

"What was that?" None of the other Locustan craft had been so fast.

"Must be a better version than the rest, Mihaal," Dakrhaeth concluded calmly.

Perhaps it was. But the Stryker was no dated toy either. Ramya cursed and pressed harder on the throttle. She cursed again as the targeting scope beeped and flashed red, signifying lost aim or out of range. Possibly both. She couldn't catch up with it. It shimmered and melted against the lights of Anomaly Point, and vanished.

"Dakrhaeth, do you see it?"

"It seems to have gone into stealth mode, Mihaal. But I feel it, coming closer."

Ramya looked — left, right, up, and down.

Nothing!

"Rami!" Isbet shouted. "Look up."

The Locustan had come back out of nowhere. It swooped straight at her from the top. Ramya froze. She had to pull up the nose of the Stryker. But the Locustan was too close. She wouldn't have time. She tugged at the flight stick anyway, even as she braced for impact. And death.

"This is it, Dakrhaeth," she whispered.

Something flew over her. The Mossin! It glided over the Stryker and fired its front cannons, and the lone Locustan craft disintegrated. The Mossin careened forward through the debris, until it didn't. Something, an invisible barrier stopped the craft and flung it backward. The Mossin went into a tailspin and plummeted into the darkness.

"Gael," Ramya screamed.

No one replied. Ramya dove, the Stryker's nose pointed at the shape of the Mossin below her. Two other craft dove along with her.

"Lieutenant Arlington," Ramya shouted again.

Was he dead? A cold wave of panic swept up her spine and numbed Ramya's fingers. "Come on, Arlington," she muttered. "You can't die on me. Not now."

"Lieutenant," Tanaka, piloting the Astro next to her, called on the comm.

The Mossin kept spinning away, out of control and directionless. As Ramya circled around it, a series of realizations, sharp and relentless, riddled her mind like gunfire. That out here in the endless void of space where the circumstances were unforgiving, unless Gael came to quickly, his chance of survival was minuscule. That there was nothing she could do, nothing at all to help Gael. And that she'd give anything to get him back.

"Please, respond," she muttered over and over.

A faint crackle came at the end of an endless, heart-numbing silence. Then a raspy breath. "I'm here," Gael whispered. His craft steadied.

Ramya fell back against her seat and let out the breath she'd been holding. She slowed the Stryker and brought it level with the Mossin. She couldn't see Gael clearly but her eyes took in what little that was visible.

Gael chuckled as he veered the Mossin back toward Anomaly Point. "Quit worrying, Kiroff," he said. "I'm fine, still alive and just as annoying."

Ramya smiled to herself. Thank goodness for that. Not that she was ever going to tell him how relieved she was to hear him talk, annoyance and all. She eased the Stryker back toward the entrance of the wormhole, frowning as she approached. All the craft hovered in an odd, almost-straight line, as if stuck on an invisible paper. Something wasn't right.

Ramya groaned. What now?

54

Ramya waited until she was level with the rest of the fleet. She knew something was wrong, and she dreaded asking what.

"Did you catch the last two?" she forced her question out.

"Got one. But then, some weird shit stopped us right here," a nasal voice on the comm replied. Ramya recognized the voice as Wez Lander's, a Norgoran piloting a Wentworth-Busa. "We can't seem to go any further," he said. "They're blocking us right here. That last straggler went past it and back into the iffin wormhole."

Ramya slowed, her eyes sweeping over the sensors. Nothing seemed out of place.

"What do you see, Dakrhaeth?" she asked, just to be sure she hadn't missed anything. Although there was nothing out of place at a glance, Ramya knew Wez wasn't wrong. She had seen the Mossin hit a barrier just seconds ago.

Some of the new gadgets Eiger and his team had installed bleeped and blooped merrily until Dakrhaeth spoke. "I see a wall of Therym-Bay particles, Mihaal. An immense, dense wall."

A wry chuckle bubbled up Ramya's throat. The Locustans were primal in their instincts and it was almost surprising seeing them use such advanced tech. In a matter of just days, they had moved the blockage this far out to counter the galaxy's offensive. They had built an invisible wall dense enough to fling the Mossin off like a twig. Had the Locustans not been creatures bent on the annihilation of her galaxy, Ramya would've openly voiced her admiration for their intelligence.

Now was no time to admire the enemy. That could wait until they had won this war and shut the bastards out of the galaxy.

Steeling herself, Ramya pressed gently on the throttle. "Let's see if Eiger's magic works. On we go, Dakrhaeth."

Ramya braced herself for impact as she eased the Stryker forward. Eiger's counters beeped louder. She held her breath as the nose slipped past the invisible line. The beeps rose to a frantic peak before ceasing abruptly. "I got through," Ramya exclaimed.

"Let me try," Isbet said.

Ramya watched the *Fury* inch past the sticking point, and slowly, without incident, its entire body coasted in as well.

"I didn't feel any resistance at all," Isbet declared.

Thank the stars for that. The Locustans had put in place a barricade that kept the galaxy's regular craft at bay. That was a smart move. It'd have been the end of the galaxy if they blocked the *Fury*. They couldn't. Not yet anyway. But they had better hurry before the Locustans came up with something new.

Gael's faded voice came over the comm. "We can barely hear you, Kiroff. I sure as hell can't get anywhere nearer. They have blocked us for good."

"We'll carry on then," Ramya said. "I'm heading inside, Isbet. Follow me."

The two craft moved in a straight and steady line, the Stryker leading the way. They had barely come halfway from the barrier to the entrance when a Locustan craft—the lone straggler that had escaped beyond the wall, Ramya deduced—shot out of Anomaly Point. It streaked toward the Stryker with the speed of a lightning bolt, rushing in a mad fury. Ramya banked hard, barely in time to avoid being rammed by the Locustan. The craft zoomed past, almost grazing the top of the Stryker. There was no avoiding its gunfire though, and the Stryker's shields went into complaining mode immediately.

Ramya tugged on the flight stick and swung the Stryker around, her eyes following the swiftly-moving shape of the Locustan craft.

"Isbet," she yelled as soon as her sight had steadied. "I'll take care of this pest. You—"

"We're already on the move," Isbet replied, her voice rock steady.

The hulking shape of the Fury shot past the Stryker in a sudden burst of speed.

"Godspeed," Ramya whispered. She muted the comm and called Dakrhaeth. "Looks like we'll get to use the plasma guns again after all, Dakrhaeth."

"They're ready, Mihaal."

Ramya shot a quick glance at Anomaly Point to check on the *Fury*. The Unosi craft was barely visible anymore, a speck against the wormhole's gaping mouth. Smiling, Ramya turned her attention back to the Locustan—it was coming back toward her.

"All right. Now we hold steady."

She pressed on the throttle, her eyes glued on the Locustan zooming at her, her finger steady on the firing controls. It was coming straight at the Stryker, and she was going to take it head-on.

"You're going to let it ram us on the head?" Dakrhaeth asked. "Have you considered the possibility of our plasma guns failing? Or our adversary possessing a shield that can withstand our fire?"

Ramya chuckled. Dakrhaeth, cheeky to the end.

"I have faith in the Stryker, Dakrhaeth," she said. "And in you."

A moment of silence hovered in the chamber.

"And we couldn't have been in better hands, Mihaal."

Ramya was still smiling at Dakrhaeth's words when the Locustan whizzed within range. It was like a sliver of darkness, its contours undulant like ripples in a murky, bottomless ocean. It came at her with the bull-headed confidence of one who was sure of their win.

Ramya fired.

Warmth flowed out of the Stryker in a pulsating wave. A blast of plasma shot out and hit the Locustan craft on its nose. Metal warped and melted in an instant into a ball of fire that swept over the Stryker in a blinding flood of heat and light.

Alarms screeched and parts of the instrument panel lit up like Somenvaar on her birthdays. The aftershock slammed Ramya back into her seat, knocking the air out of her guts. Ramya kept smiling through it all.

As soon as she had caught her breath, Ramya swiveled around to face Anomaly Point. She dashed toward the wormhole, hitting the communicator button as she careened in. "Isbet! Isbet, do you hear?"

No one replied. A barrage of fear descended on Ramya's heart and turned it numb. Had the *Fury* even survived in here? What if it didn't?

"Rami!" Isbet's voice was distant but steady. It was the sweetest sound Ramya had heard in a while.

"What's the status, Isbet?"

"All good. We're almost near the final strike point."

"I'm behind you."

"You should leave, Rami. You don't need to be here anymore." Isbet's voice was sharp and as if to keep her company, a loud beep sounded from the instrument cluster. Ramya frowned. The temperature gauge was throwing a fit and Ramya's frown grew deeper as she squinted at it.

"Dakrhaeth, what's wrong with the temp gauge?"

"Nothing's wrong with the gauge, Mihaal. For some reason, the temperature is spiking. I have never experienced such a rapid increase before. Unless we are aiming to be roasted alive, we have to turn back."

Ramya had suspected as much. "How far can we go?"

"Ten more seconds, maybe."

"All right." Ramya placed her thumb on the throttle and pushed. The Stryker hurtled forward, but not as much as it usually did. The thrusters were weak and growing weaker. The Stryker teetered.

"Dakrhaeth," Ramya shouted. "What's going on?"

"All my systems are complaining a whole lot. They're starting to malfunction."

"Why?"

"This wormhole is built differently, Mihaal. I don't believe my new body was engineered to withstand the radiation patterns inside this."

Indeed! The instrument panel was a sea of red and yellow lights, while random beeps and wails filled the inside of the Stryker. It was warm in the cockpit, and getting hotter by the second.

"Isbet," Ramya called. "I'm burning up here," she said. "How are you doing?"

"Cruising," Isbet replied. "The Fury was built for this, Rami. Guidance systems have come alive, shields that never showed up before are up and running now. Merin is all over it. We will finish this. You don't need to be in here anymore. Go. Get out of here before the Stryker breaks down."

There was no doubt she had to leave. And soon. The instrument cluster — that annoying temp gauge in particular — was flashing, not in a friendly way. But how could she leave the *Fury* behind and run?

"What if you need help — "

"Stop, Rami!" Ross didn't yell, but his voice leaped out of the comm and almost grabbed Ramya by the throat. "For once, can you just listen? We'll do this, have some faith."

"See you later, Rami," Isbet said. "We're approaching strike position. It feels beautiful in here. I almost — "

Her voice died abruptly.

"Isbet! Isbet!" Ramya screamed, pressing the comm button like a mad woman. She found nothing but silence.

"Dakrhaeth," she called. "Anything?"

"I don't hear them, Mihaal," his prompt but deliberate reply came in a heartbeat. "I suggest we turn around. My shields are wearing off fast and surface temperature is . . . well, it's almost beyond warning levels now."

What about the mission? How could she know if they had pulled it off? And how could she return empty handed without the *Fury* and its crew? Without her friends?

"Mihaal! Shields down to twenty percent."

Ramya grabbed the flight stick and twisted it to the side. Ross was right, she *had* to learn to trust others. This world was not hers alone to save. Others needed and wanted to do their part also. She had to let them. By the time the Stryker's nose swung around, the temp gauge was flashing red.

"We're getting out of here, Dakrhaeth. Engage the turbo," she ordered. Aligning the Stryker straight to the mouth of Anomaly Point, Ramya pressed on the throttle. Fifteen seconds and she would be outside. She started counting down.

Ramya was down to ten when she first felt the tremor.

Nine . . . eight . . .

The heat was seeping inside the walls. Beads of sweat trickled down Ramya's forehead.

Seven . . . six . . .

Just a few more seconds.

The air felt hot in her nostrils, and her throat parched.

Wait! Did the walls just dim a little?

"Dakrhaeth?"

"The structure around us is morphing, Mihaal."

"R-a-mi!" Isbet's scream made Ramya jump. "Rami, it's here. It's huge. W-warn them."

Ramya stared at the comm, unable to follow. What did Isbet mean?

"Isbet?"

Isbet didn't reply but Ross's faded voice drifted out of the comm, "Locked into strike mode. Hold position—"

The comm died abruptly but Ramya's attention was taken by Dakrhaeth's terrified whisper. "Mihaal, it's the Hive. It's behind us."

Ramya pressed harder on the throttle as she leaned forward and squinted at the rear display. She had never felt so cold. Even as the temp gauge in the Stryker screamed and sweat poured over her face, a terrifying chill engulfed her core.

Then she saw it. It was a brief flash of darkness behind her, but she saw enough of its sprawling structure, the size of fifty Drednots put together. Long, thick protrusions from its sides writhed like tentacles as it lumbered toward her. It was slow, probably because of its massive size. Its body seemed to morph and melt as it approached, and Ramya realized she wasn't looking at one massive ship. This thing—ship or creature, whatever it was—was made of a million smaller entities that clung together to form this immense arrangement. As nightmarish a sight as it was, Ramya couldn't take her eyes off it. Not until it vanished from the viewer just as suddenly as it had appeared.

Ramya fell back in her seat. "The stars help us all." The words, a prayer almost, slipped out of Ramya's mouth as the Stryker shot into the darkness, spiraling out from the light-swept mouth of Anomaly Point. There were no other craft at the mouth; likely everyone had fallen back to the Drednot. Ramya's thumb ached from pressing down the throttle for so long, but Ramya kept it pressed still. As she shot toward the safe zone, to the waiting Drednot in the distance, Ramya hit the comm.

A voice crackled on the comm before she could speak. "The Stryker has returned, Admiral." Captain Lohau of the Drednot, Ramya recognized. A cheer broke out and Ramya had to yell to be heard.

"Captain Lohau! Admiral Milos. The Hive is coming."

The shouts of joy died even before she could finish, as abruptly as a candle snuffed out by a gust.

"How far, Rami?" Milos asked, his voice a whisper.

"It should be here anytime now, Admiral," Ramya replied. "I saw it right behind me for a second."

Lohau's resolute declaration took only a moment to come. "We will engage, Admiral. Until you can send reinforcements we'll hold the Hive with whatever we have."

They had nothing. Thirteen puny fighters and a Drednot was nothing compared to the monstrosity that was the Hive. However, there was no other option but to engage. Besides, there were hardly any reinforcements to spare at Zeta. What was left had to be still fighting the last swarm.

Ramya slowed, her hand was sluggish when she turned the Stryker around to face Anomaly Point. This was it. This was how it would end — with a pathetic, insurmountable battle against a merciless colossus.

"All right, Lohau. Prepare to engage." Milos ordered. "Rami, what's the status on the *Fury*?" he asked next.

"I left them inside," she said. Guilt made her voice dip. "Last I heard, they had reached strike position."

"They'd better have reached strike position or we're all dead," Lohau said breathlessly. "Admiral, we have just sighted the Hive."

It was here. The thing she had briefly seen on the Stryker's display was not a distant image anymore. It was real, and it was hovering at the mouth of Anomaly Point.

"What in the name of the unholy is that?" Tanaka's incredulous voice came over the comm. "How the hell are we going to fight that monster bug?"

Indeed, it looked like a bloodsucking mite supersized a trillion times, a creature right out of hell. Its huge, dark body crept toward the mouth of Anomaly Point like a living nightmare, its appendages reaching out of the lighted mouth of the wormhole.

"Fenix Force, engage," Lohau ordered.

The Mossin shot forward and Tanaka's Astro followed. Ramya placed her thumb on the throttle and pressed. They streaked through the darkness, tiny specks in the endless void of space, toward a nameless death.

Ramya hardly felt any fear. The chill was gone from inside of her. An intense pride, for everything they had achieved together, for every person that had selflessly sacrificed for the galaxy's cause, made her heart swell. She hit the comm. "It has been an honor flying with you all."

"Same here," Tanaka replied. A wave of cheering rose, the sounds making Ramya sit up taller, straighter, and steadier. She was ready to take the beast head on, whatever the consequence.

Gael was the last one to speak. "Been an honor knowing you, Kiroff."

Ramya wanted to tell him how she felt the same way, but an unexpected and sharp pang of regret twisted her heart and turned her mute for a moment.

Wish I could get to know you better, Arlington.

"Abort." Lohau's frantic shout tore through Ramya's thoughts. She lifted her finger off the throttle and the Stryker slowed immediately. The crafts around her slowed as well. "Fenix Force, abort mission. Fall back," Lohau yelled again.

Ramya tugged at the flight stick and turned the Stryker around. Lohau's voice came over the comm again, and it almost sounded cheerful. "Seems like the *Fury* hit it dead on target, Admiral."

Ramya looked back, her disbelieving eyes glued to the wildly flickering view of Anomaly Point. The wormhole was unstable, more than it had been during any of the other strikes. At its mouth, the Hive lurched. It was trying to crawl out but a stronger force was pulling it back in. The enormous appendages clawed at the mouth of Anomaly Point as if desperate to cling to life. Ramya could tell it wasn't about to give up trying.

"Close up already, you iffin wormhole," Tanaka shouted.

Anomaly Point started growing. Its mouth flared suddenly and for a breathless moment, Ramya almost thought it would swallow them all. Then, like an enormous balloon that had been pricked, it shrank. Until it was no more.

Ramya blinked furiously to make sure she was seeing it right.

There was nothing but empty space where Anomaly Point had been.

"Isbet—"

A sob shook Ramya and stole the rest of her words. She didn't know how long she stared at the darkness. Or how long her shallow breathing was all she heard. The disbelieving silence hung in the air for what seemed like an eternity. Then, like a volcano erupting in the dead of night, wild cheering ripped through the quiet. Shouts of joy, sobs of relief, and laughter poured out of the comm and filled the Stryker's cold interior. People yelled and shrieked. They congratulated each other. Ramya wanted to share their glee, but couldn't. All she could think of was her friends who were lost forever in that darkness. The sounds kept washing over Ramya's senses like relentless waves in a stormy sea, bringing little happiness. Until she reached for the button and turned the comm off with shaky fingers. Stillness rushed back in, embracing Ramya in its desolate arms.

"Dakrhaeth?" she whispered after an eternity of waiting in the dark. "The *Fury* . . . do you see them?"

He didn't reply right away. When he did, Ramya was sure there was a hint of a tremor in his voice. "No, Mihaal. Looks like we've won the war but lost the *Fury*."

WAR'S END

Ramya stood alone in Admiral Zoho's observation room, staring in the direction of Anomaly Point. The heavens had gone dark again. It was strange not seeing the brilliant wormhole in the distance and what was stranger still, Ramya missed seeing it.

Two days had passed since it closed and now, the idea that it'd likely never open again was slowly sinking into even the most skeptical minds. As much as that was a relief, to Ramya it meant something more – Isbet, Ross, and Merin were lost forever. Even if they had somehow survived the collapse of the wormhole, they wouldn't have a road back home. They were trapped in a distant, dark universe, sealed in a tomb until death.

Ramya shuddered violently as a chill sped up her spine. She had always known loss was inevitable, but she hadn't known how difficult each loss would be to bear. Regrets, scores of them, welled up in her heart ceaselessly.

Why didn't she spend more time with Isbet at El-Iss? Did she have to fight Ross until the end? Couldn't she have been more giving with him?

There was no respite from the thoughts, yet barely time to mourn. There was so much to do – homeworlds to resurrect, fleets to regrow, people to find and train to replace the lost.

She had to find in herself the strength to lead House Kiroff. A sob formed a painful lump in her throat as she thought of the road ahead. Her father's absence was the worst to deal with. Now that the Locustan threat was gone, it hit her full force and knocked the air out of her guts every time she thought of it. She realized that his presence had shielded her from the responsibility of wearing a thorny crown. Now the weight of the world was on her. She had to carry on, keep the Kiroff flag flying high. She'd have help, but she'd be the one alone at the top. That thought was far from comforting.

She knew little about the intricate politics of the galaxy. She knew very few people she could trust. Her thoughts flew to Milos, the one she could depend on the most. He would always be around. He had promised her. But pulled into the immense task of rebuilding the galaxy's defenses, he couldn't be right next to her even if he wanted to. And if rumors had any truth in them, Admiral Milos was set to become the Chief of Fleets soon. He was already at Xandria, far away from here. Fenny had gone with him, but Sosa, Wiz, and Flux had stayed on Zeta to help Zoho rebuild the starbase.

Ramya's eyes studied the massive outline of Zeta that stretched into the darkness ahead. Zeta was a far cry from what it had been originally. The prongs of the horseshoe were heavily damaged, the left one broken near the midway point. It was all lit up, right up to the ripped end, and Ramya knew people were working non-stop on the repairs. Still, it would be a long time before Zeta was fully restored.

A patch of light fell across the darkened room as the door slid open behind her. Footsteps, light and hesitant, approached. Even without turning her head, Ramya knew who it was—Casten, a faithful inheritance she was happy to have around.

"What is it, Casten?" she asked after she'd sensed him bow.

"Should I make arrangements to travel back to Somenvaar, Lord Paramount?"

Lord Paramount . . . the words weighed her down like a mountain. But there was no escaping them. She wasn't ready for that title yet, but she didn't have the luxury of time either. She had to respond, she had to fill up the enormous void her father had left behind before her ambivalence made it even bigger.

"Yes, please do," Ramya replied forcefully. Casten had tiptoed away to the door when she turned around and called him back. "We shall stop at El-Iss on the way to Somenvaar. Please tell Lord Wultoph Aristide that I want to be briefed on the status of . . . everything."

Another bow later, Casten left the room. Dark descended once more along with quiet. Ramya lowered herself into the plush chair that faced the largest of the windows in the room. This was supposedly Zoho's favorite place on Zeta. Sitting here, he watched the battles unfold around the gigantic starbase. Zoho had left his office to her when she had asked for some privacy. Deference, that's what it was. Was it because of her newly inherited position as head of House Kiroff or was it because of how she had led the Fenix Force to victory?

It doesn't matter why, Rami, she told herself. *You're here, and you earned it.* She had done well, losses notwithstanding, and she deserved every bit of the respect. She had to remember that. Yet, faced with responsibilities that loomed like a never-ending nightmare, Ramya always shook a little.

Summoning up all the willpower she had left, Ramya focused her thoughts. Or tried. In her mind, she went over Kiroff Industries' various holdings, the factories, the mines, and most importantly, the list of allies. There was a chance they could dither, now that Trysten Kiroff and his larger-than-life presence was no more. She had to find a way to keep their old friends together, and she hoped Wultoph and Uncle Lynden would help her with it.

She didn't know how much time had passed while she had been alone in that dark room, but she sat up straight when the telltale patch of light fell across the room again. Someone had entered, but Ramya could barely hear footsteps.

A dim light came to life near the workstations that ringed the walls — this being Zoho's observation room, it was heavily equipped with various control and communication units — and even the distant and faded light made Ramya shield her eyes. She swiveled around in annoyance, making out the blurred form of a man in a blue uniform approaching.

"Didn't know you liked to bask in the dark, Kiroff," Gael Arlington said. The mirth in his voice was a welcome and much-needed change that Ramya hadn't even known she was craving. In an instant, she forgot to be angry at the intrusion.

"I don't," she said. "I just . . ." She let her words trail, hesitating to voice her fears and . . . weakness.

"Hiding from the world?" he asked, teasing words poking too close to the uncomfortable truth.

"Something like that," she confessed. "I don't know what I'll do. I'm nothing like my father."

Gael shrugged and slipped into a chair next to her. "Of course you're not Trysten Kiroff." He watched her, brows crinkling as her face tightened. "That doesn't mean you're any less capable than he was. It only means you'll do things differently."

She only hoped she could keep things together. "What brings you here?" she asked, jumping topics.

He held her gaze for a second before replying. "You know, we need to start rebuilding our defenses from the ground up. There are relief operations we have to support on Trio and some of the inner worlds that were touched. There's a whole lot of work and it needs to start right away. So, I'm heading out."

"Right now?"

"Yes, right now," Gael replied. "I came to say farewell to you."

Her insides weren't supposed to crumble to pieces like that but they did. Ramya chided herself swiftly. What was she expecting? That he'd wait around and serve her? How did she come to this? Wanting to keep Gael Arlington around? He stood for everything she'd tried to escape—the stifling patriarchy that refused to give her a chance to prove herself and a life that'd keep her locked away in a gilded cage.

Ramya's gaze roamed over Gael's battle-exhausted face and came to rest on his sharp but earnest eyes. Well, Gael was none of what she feared. Quite the opposite, actually. She felt free around him, stronger, braver, surer of herself.

She had to tell him that. Hesitation raised its head swiftly. Ramya shoved it away. Hell, she had seen up close how fragile life was, and she wasn't about to use false pretenses to look invincible like her father.

"I thought you'd stay," she said, eyes still locked on Gael's.

His face broke into a craggy smile. "I wish I could. But I'm honor-bound to my duties as a GSO." He paused a second before smirking. "You have to get to work as well, Kiroff. We all have to. Can't sit here forever and stare at the dark."

If he had said that a month or so ago, Ramya would have exploded in a fit of rage. But she knew better now; she knew he meant well.

"Have to let the past go," Gael continued, his voice soft and kind. "The future needs you."

"I know."

Gael tapped the armrest of his chair and tilted his head. "Well, this is it then. I should be going now."

He rose to his feet and Ramya followed. "Wish you the best, Lord Paramount," he said, bowing.

Ramya winced. "Can you not call me that, please?"

Gael frowned a little. "You have to get used to that quickly, Kiroff. Don't underestimate the power of that title. Use it. Use it for good."

Ramya nodded. He had a point. She couldn't let her vexation show. She tried to recall the forever-unperturbed face of her father — that was something she had to emulate quickly.

With another bow, Gael took a step back, leaving a gulf of cold around her. She wanted to make him stay, she craved his warm presence. Yet she couldn't just reach out and embrace him. As close as they had come since that first meeting at CAWStrat, a wall still remained. She wanted to throw her arms around him before he left, but . . .

"I'll see you again soon?" she asked. She was certain Tucker Arlington, Gael's father, would pay her a visit soon to remind her of the promises made by her father. To collect his debts, so to speak.

Gael smiled and shook his head. "Unless everything falls apart again, I'd say you're rid of me for good. Or unless you need my services of course, in which case I'm happy to be of any use, Lord Paramount." He paused and shot her a quizzical look. "Which reminds me . . . when are you planning to make war?"

He meant payback against House Danukis, of course. As much as she wanted to raze the Danukis scum to the ground, Ramya knew she needed time to plan it right. She needed to build up her strength before she started wiping out her enemies.

"Not right away," she said. "I need some time to think it through."

He flashed a relieved grin. "I like that thought. I had hoped the Locustans would take care of Molen."

She had wished the same—that Molen would head out of Zeta around the time the last Locustan swarm hit the base. They would've destroyed his ship in an instant. Molen, however, had stayed back in the base.

"Too bad for him," Ramya said grimly. "That would've been a less painful end. Now he has to face me. Eventually."

Gael crossed his arms, his gaze growing sharper on her face. "Now you're scaring me, Kiroff."

Ramya broke into a grudging chuckle. "Don't worry. I won't go about cutting off people's heads. And I won't go after them right away, anyway."

He studied her a while before speaking. "In that case, we won't be seeing each other anytime soon."

That didn't make any sense. Trysten Kiroff had promised Gael her hand in marriage. Now, with her father gone, the word was on her. Vows like those weren't reneged upon, particularly not in times like these when she needed to rebuild and bolster House Kiroff's alliances without her father. She couldn't get rid of Gael and House Arlington, not even if she had wanted to.

Ramya crossed her arms and frowned. "You're forgetting my father's promise to yours."

"No, I'm not," he replied in a heartbeat. It seemed as if he had thought this through a zillion times over. "That was Trysten Kiroff's word, and his word doesn't transfer to you."

"Of course it does. I'm his heir. All his debts and dues transferred to me on his passing."

"This wasn't a debt or a due, Kiroff," he explained. "It was a simple agreement that would've translated to a binding one only after you had reached adulthood. But you were a quasi-adult when your father passed, so his non-binding agreements didn't transfer to you. I'm sure my father will try to convince you otherwise, but the fact is, Trysten Kiroff's word on this matter died with him. You're free."

Ramya took a long breath and let the cold air settle at the pit of the stomach. Free? Yes, indeed. That was what she'd wanted all along. Funny though, as much as she reveled in the idea that no one could force her into doing anything, freedom didn't seem a perfect situation either. True, she was free to walk away from her father's wishes. But she didn't want to.

The deal with freedom was, it went both ways. Gael was just as free to walk away from the agreement as she was. Surely, the idea of having Gael in her life made her smile. But that didn't mean he wanted her. Gael always said he was dragged into this agreement, and he didn't seem unhappy to announce that the terms had expired with Trysten Kiroff's death.

"What if I don't want to break his promise?" It took all the strength she had in her to utter those words. Heck, baring her heart was a zillion times harder than flying into that iffin wormhole had been. But once it was said, Ramya stood taller.

Gael's eyes narrowed, his curious gaze burning into her face. "You left home because this agreement was forced upon you. And now you want it back?" A teasing smile curled his lips as they studied each other. "Am I that irresistible, Kiroff?"

Ramya let out a surreptitious sigh. He was always going to hold this over her head, but she didn't give a damn as long as she got what she wanted. However, he didn't need to know that, did he?

"It's strategy, Arlington. Can't have Tucker baring his claws at me," she said, cramming as much ice into her voice as she could find. "The stars know I'll have to face enough flack in the senate thanks to House Danukis and its underlings."

Gael's brows shot up before he scoffed. "That is cold, Kiroff," he said. "Who says you don't take after your father? I'd say you surpassed him right there."

His words, casually flung at her, plunged ferociously into her core. That wasn't what she wanted. Her father's biggest flaw—he would never show how much he cared—couldn't be hers as well. She wouldn't let it take her the way it had taken him.

She stepped closer to Gael and looked him in the eye. "That was wrong of me to say. And offensive. I didn't mean to—"

"I won't hold it against you."

"That's very kind of you," she said, bowing her head just a little. A smile slipped out as she framed her thoughts. "I wouldn't go as far as irresistible, but I do like you. Quite a lot." Gael didn't say a word, his features frozen into an inscrutable expression. Ramya tore her eyes from his face, seeking the comfort of a distant corner as a dark thought muddied her spirits. She found the strength to look back at him shortly. "Even though I can't deny the strategic advantage of the agreement, I wouldn't . . . couldn't force it on you. Ever. It doesn't matter if a hundred Tucker Arlingtons shred me into bits in the senate because of that."

She had never seen Gael's eyes any wider. She had never known silence so deep. For what seemed like an eternity, they stared at each other. Until Gael spoke. "I don't know what to say," he said finally. "That's the most earnest speech I've heard in a while and I totally respect your offer. But I have no idea how to respond."

Ramya's gaze scoured his face; his solemn eyes, to his proud nose, down to his lips . . . and away. "You could kiss me," she whispered, barely able to believe she had said that aloud. "That'd seal the deal," she added hastily, forgetting to breathe as she studied his reaction.

He froze for a second. Then, looking in the direction of the windows, he shook his head. "You're always unexpected, Kiroff. But . . . no, I couldn't."

The smile died on her face in an instant. There it was—the outcome she was dreading. She had known there was a good chance he'd spurn her offer, but she didn't expect her insides to shrivel in mortification the way they did.

You knew it was a gamble. You took a risk. You lost. So what?

It was humiliation like she'd never known before. The room receded until the only thing Ramya could feel was an intense cold. Shame—fearsome, frosty—slashed her insides. Her mind fought back.

Snap out of it, Rami, she yelled inwardly. *Get a grip on your senses. It's not like he's the last man in the universe.*

The room came back in focus, albeit slowly. She could see Gael's lips move, his voice came from a distance, like a dull hum.

"As much as I want to oblige," Gael was saying, "and believe me I do, I have to uphold my GSO vows."

The cold around her ebbed as swiftly as it had arrived.

GSO vows? Of course. Every new initiate took a ten-year-long vow of celibacy and Gael was still somewhere within his term.

Gael kept speaking. "It'll be a couple of years before we can get any closer than this. That too long for you?"

Ramya stepped nearer until all that separated them was a paper-thin wall of air. "What if you break your vows? Who would know?"

She had half-expected Gael to jump away. He didn't. He simply smiled, his smoldering gaze flitting over her face. His hand snaked around her waist and pressed against the small of her back. He pulled her just a bit closer, enough to make their foreheads touch when he leaned forward. He was so close, his breath tingled her face, her lips yearned to melt into his.

"We don't want to start our life together with a deception, do we?" he asked, his voice thick and soft in her ears.

No, she wanted to do it just right. No falsehoods. No pretenses.

He pulled away and she let him.

"Be good, Kiroff," he said from the door. "See you soon."

Ramya watched him until the doors closed on him. Then she walked back to the curved windows.

She took one last look at the distance where the gaping wormhole of Anomaly Point had been and inhaled deeply, letting the slightly-metallic air settle inside her. This would stay with her forever, the view of Anomaly Point, the smell of Starbase Zeta, the memories of the wins and the losses. They would spur her on; give her strength to carry on.

Ramya tore her eyes from the darkness. She couldn't afford to look at the past anymore. The future needed her attention. This war had drained the galaxy and House Kiroff. She had to rebuild it and take it beyond the heights her father had dreamed. She had to rebuild her life as well. Right now, she decided, was the best time to begin.

Ramya turned around and walked out of the empty observation chamber with resolute steps.

–   The End   –

GLOSSARY

From the Previous Books

The Characters:

Ramya Kiroff – Protagonist of the Dark Universe. Seventeen-year-old Ramya has a life anyone in the galaxy would give anything to have. But only Ramya knows that it's far from perfect. Her father, Trysten Kiroff, is the richest man in the galaxy and he has impossible expectations of her. All her life she tries to prove her worth to him but fails. When she's taken to task for dishonorable conduct at CAWStrat, her father terminates her education. Furthermore, he threatens her with a marriage to benefit his business and the family. With no way to avoid her father's punishment, Ramya sneaks out of CAWStrat and hitches a ride on the *Endeavor*.

Captain Terenze Milos — Veteran of the Confederate Space Fleet, Captain Milos is the legendary hero of the Locusta-Vanga War. His stand against the Locustans during the first Locustan invasion brought the galaxy back from the brink of extinction. He offers Ramya the job of the medic's assistant when she rescues the Stryker's pilot on Nikoor. She doesn't reveal her true identity but it is revealed later that he knew she was Trysten Kiroff's daughter. Captain Milos also served with Abelei Kiroff, Ramya's grandfather and Trysten's father, while in the Space Fleet.

The *Endeavor* – Battlecruiser-turned-freighter commanded by Captain Terenze Milos. Home to our protagonists, the ship is a Class II battleship, from before the Locusta-Vanga War. One of many battered battleships discarded by the Space Fleet after the Locusta-

Vanga War, it was salvaged from a junkyard by Captain Milos and repaired. The *Endeavor* is antiquated but has a sound frame and is well maintained. The crew of the *Endeavor* is fiercely loyal to the ship.

Commander Ross Pornell — Second-in-command of the *Endeavor*. He is at the helm when the *Endeavor* comes across the debris field of destroyed GSO spaceships. He changes course and orders the investigation of the beacon for help. Quiet but contentious at times, Ross wants to impress Captain Milos with his competence, more so because of Milos's legendary stature and Ross's newly hired status. Ross is snappish to Ramya and suspicious about her. However, he saves Ramya when a deadly Pterostrich chick attacks. He also accompanies her in the Stryker during the final showdown with Admiral Kanaa at Totori.

Fenny – Navigator of the *Endeavor*. Foul-mouthed and opinionated, Ramya often describes Fenny as a pocket-sized powerhouse. She can navigate a spaceship, wield a cannon, or nurse a Pterostrich chick with equal ease. She befriends Ramya from the moment they meet, becoming more of a confidante to her as time passes.

Wiz -- Pilot of the *Endeavor*. He is a nervous sort of person, easily worried over small matters.

Flux – Engineer of the *Endeavor*. He is seldom seen outside his cave, the *Endeavor's* engineering bay. Although extremely skillful and smart, Flux is often overextended and has trouble keeping the old ship in top shape.

Sosa – Norgoran medic of the *Endeavor*. Sosa is anything but ordinary. Eclectic to stir-crazy, she is fiercely loyal to Captain Milos, whom she has known for decades. She is also the only person on the ship who calls Captain Milos by his first name. Ramya addresses Sosa as Domina, which is a respectful title for a Norgoran of high birth, and what comes naturally to Ramya on seeing Sosa's regal bearing and age. Sosa is also the masterful maker and mixer of potent concoctions, particularly her signature "Pax."

Habardein – Original pilot of the last Stryker. He is rescued when the *Endeavor's* crew salvages the Stryker from the debris field in Sector 22. He wants to report the incident at Sector 22 to his employer Trysten Kiroff, which goes against the directive of the Space Command. When stopped, he sneaks out of the *Endeavor* and is beaten up by a pair of thugs until Ramya rescues him. His injuries are grievous and he soon slips into a coma. He regains consciousness for a bit and recognizes Ramya as Trysten Kiroff's daughter. He tells Ramya about the Stryker before his condition worsens again.

The *Stryker* – A space fighter designed by Kiroff Industries in Sector 22. It has embedded Locustan technology, with a Locustan Viriskshi (AI) controlling the major components of the craft. The Stryker is paired with a pilot who is the only person allowed to control the AI. Directives from the Kiroff family can override all other directives in a properly functional Stryker.

Dakrhaeth – An AI aboard the last Stryker, or as Dakrhaeth likes to call himself, the soul of the ship. Dakrhaeth is smart as he is snarky. A Locustan Viriskshi whose craft crashed into Kyo-Sedra-5 along with its squadron, and lay buried for years in the frozen planet until Kiroff Industries discovered and resuscitated them. He considers Trysten Kiroff his creator and mistakes Ramya for her father during the initial genetic scan. He addresses Ramya as "Mihaal" which means creator in the Locustan tongue. He allows Ramya access into the Stryker and bonds with her.

Trysten Kiroff – Ramya's father and the leader of House Kiroff is an enigma. During his time, House Kiroff has grown into a galactic powerhouse. He's shrewd, ruthless, and indomitable. Even though the Confederate Senate is the seat of power in the galaxy, it is said that real power is in Trysten Kiroff's hands. To Ramya he's always dismissive and cold. He holds her to impossibly high standards. Ramya believes that being a female firstborn, she has let her father down since the moment she was born.

Lynden Kiroff – Lynden is the younger brother of Trysten and Ramya's uncle. He is currently serving in the Senate where Trysten Kiroff is said to have placed him.

Brynden Kiroff – Brynden is the youngest brother of Trysten and Ramya's other uncle. He's the black sheep of the Kiroff family who left CAWStrat before graduating and vanished. He's supposed to have left for the Fringe to wrest the Kiroff family hearth from the usurper, Callen Moanu, and bring honor back to the family. However, he's not been heard of since. Ramya has fond memories of Uncle Bryn and when she leaves CAWStrat, she wants to follow Brynden's footsteps to the Fringe and complete his quest to regain the Kiroff hearth.

Abelei Kiroff – Ramya's grandfather and Trysten's father. Abelei was a member of the Confederate Space Fleet and one of the first to face the Locustans during the first invasion and perish. Ramya's memory of her grandfather is faded, but she remembers him as courageous and upright. Captain Milos served with Abelei Kiroff during his time in the Space Fleet.

Sonya Kiroff – Ramya's mother and Trysten's socialite wife. She likes spending time with her galaxy-trotting friends more than with her family. To Ramya, Sonya's presence is like a specter; she's never really there, even when she's physically next to her.

Armand Danukis – Scion of House Danukis and a staunch enemy of House Kiroff and Ramya. He insults Ramya's mother after he's lost a duel to Ramya. This causes Ramya to lose her temper and she punches Armand in the face and draws blood. This is considered dishonorable conduct at CAWStrat and Ramya is threatened with expulsion from the institute.

Istapol Maroni – Trainer at CAWStrat who is present at the duel between Armand and Ramya. He is also a veteran of the Confederate Space Fleet.

Callen Moanu – Usurper of the original Kiroff hearth. After losing the hearth to the Moanus, the Kiroffs were branded hearthless vagrants as was the custom during the time when the galaxy was settled. The mark has stayed on the family since, even though they are currently the richest and most powerful house in the galaxy. Over the centuries, many a Kiroff has tried to wrest the family hearth back from the Moanus but none have succeeded.

Leona Calibe – Administrator at the CAWStrat. She's fond of taking Ramya to task for the smallest of issues. Ramya suspects she likes to show her power over Ramya to take shots at Trysten Kiroff, who is otherwise insurmountable. Leona's threat to send Ramya packing for punching an offensive classmate makes Trysten pull Ramya out of CAWStrat instead.

Isbet – Ramya's best friend at CAWStrat. She is one of the younger daughters of a lesser noble family with insignificant standing in the galaxy. Isbet's network of spies at CAWStrat ensures she's on top of every bit of breaking news in the galaxy. She also holds her year's flying record, much to the annoyance of her male counterparts. Isbet has two dreams: join the GSO and marry Rownack, a handsome senior at CAWStrat.

CSA Stevan Helves/Lieutenant Gael Arlington - Ramya bumps into a mysterious stranger in a blue GSO uniform during her last gala at CAWStrat and dances the last Decosset with him. She lies about her identity and unknown to Ramya at the time, he does the same. Later, she finds out his real name, Gael Arlington. He belongs to one of House Kiroff's major competitors, House Arlington. Gael serves as a Lieutenant of the GSO and commands a state-of-the-art Cutlass but is allied with Trysten Kiroff. He tries to secure the last Stryker but Captain Milos outmaneuvers him and the *Endeavor* escapes.

Wultoph Aristide - A lesser lord and ally of Trysten Kiroff. Wultoph is a known spokesperson for Trysten.

Admiral Kanaa - Admiral of the Confederate Space Fleet. She wants to destroy the last Stryker and the *Endeavor* along with it. She knows Captain Milos from his days in the Space Fleet.

Ahool Petta - Mwandan boy, training to become a doctor, and member of the Mwandan rebel faction, the Berkari. Rescued by Ramya and Ross on Morris II, Ahool becomes part of the *Endeavor's* crew and Ramya's staunchest admirer. Being very young, he speaks the galactic tongue in a stilted way.

Chief Dal Uminato - Chief of the Berkari faction on Morris II. He helps Ramya and Ross reunite with the *Endeavor*. He and a retinue of his people later join Captain Milos on the *Endeavor*. He is also a Uminato—a Mwandan with extrasensory powers.

Lefrasi—Another Mwandan from Morris II, he is Chief Dal's second-in-command. He is a fierce and loyal presence, and often joins Ramya on her quests.

Temihula—Resident spirit of the sacred reliquary grove. The Mwandans believe Temihula is the father of their race and worship him. Offended by *Endeavor's* intrusion into the sacred grove on Morris II, he almost kills Ramya and her cohorts as punishment. However, in the end, he relents and gifts Ramya the rare Drigganstone.

Amireh—Second-in-command to Lieutenant Gael Arlington, Amireh has known the lieutenant for a long time and he is loyal to Gael and GSO. Not a skilled pilot, Amireh is often in charge of *Cutlass 31* when Gael is out on a sortie.

Octus Laurden—Owner of Nebeca 21, a space station on the outskirts of the galaxy. He also commands the loyalty of a sizeable pirate squad, one of which he sends after the *Endeavor* to secure the Stryker.

Chief Mifek—Leader of the Berkari faction on the Mwandan sanctuary of Bucifer P9, Chief Mifek first notifies Captain Milos of strange activities in the Fringe. Later, his own colony is attacked by the Locustans and assimilated. Ramya arrives at Bucifer P9 to evacuate the survivors but she is unable to get to them in time.

The Places

Sector 22 – A largely uninhabited sector where Kiroff Industries has a secret research center and factory for conducting experiments with Locustan technology. A large GSO fleet stationed in this sector is eviscerated by unknown forces with a lone survivor—the Stryker, a space fighter embedded with Locustan tech. This precipitates the event of the Dark Universe.

Kyo-Sedra-5 – The fifth planet of the Kyo-Sedra star system where the secret Kiroff factory is located. This is where a squadron of Locustan spacecraft crashed during the first invasion.

Nikoor – Home planet of the Kiroffs and the location of CAWStrat. It is classified as a prime planet because CAWStrat is situated on it.

Somenvaar – Home estate of House Kiroff.

The Fringe – A group of quasi-autonomous star systems at the northern outskirts of Confederacy space.

Totori – Star system neighboring the system of Alameda, known for its mineral-rich asteroid belt.

Alameda – A prime planet and the seat of the GSO. It is also home to the Kiroffs' staunchest rivals, the Arlingtons.

NAB – Noxillian Asteroid Belt. It is a mineral-rich belt off the AP at Totori. Captain Milos plans to drop off the Stryker on one of the asteroids during the handover with Admiral Kanaa.

Kashiyap – Star system near Totori with one habitable planet, the Mwandan sanctuary Morris II.

Morris II – A planet in the Kashiyap system, a Mwandan sanctuary.

Anomaly Point – Anomaly Point is the gateway to the Locustan world. It is a wormhole that closed at the end of the Locusta-Vanga war. It has stayed closed since, but the worry remained that it could open again someday. Not knowing why it had opened and how to stop it in case it did again, the Confederacy has since erected stationary defenses in the area and positioned several Confederacy fleets around it.

Bucifer P9—The ninth planet in the Bucifer system, a Mwandan sanctuary. It is located in the Fringe. Chief Mifek, who heads the rebel Berkari faction on the planet, notifies Captain Milos of unusual activity in the area. By the time the *Endeavor* reaches the planet, Locustans take over and assimilate all the inhabitants.

Nebeca 21—A space station near the Fringe, owned by Octus Laurden. It is the last fueling station in the galaxy before the Fringe and being lawless, also a favorite place for outlaws and miscreants.

Starbase Zeta—The galaxy's only base near Anomaly Point, built after the first Locustan invasion to watch over the area. A third of the galaxy's forces are stationed at Zeta. It is headed by Admiral Zoho.

The Terms

COM – Core Operations Module. It is the command center of the *Endeavor*, a scaled-down version of a ship's bridge.

SLH – Super Luminal Highway. These are a network of wormholes discovered when the galaxy was settled that interconnects the various colonized systems. Spacecraft can move through it at faster-than-light speeds. It is not yet known who built them and when, but without the SLH, the Galactic Confederacy could not exist.

SL mode – Super Luminal mode, also known as Faster Than Light or FTL mode. This is the mode spacecraft switch to when entering the SLH. Outside the SLH network, spacecraft can use the ordinary mode.

AP – Access Point. A gate that allows entry into the SLH. There is usually one AP per star system.

Galactic Confederacy – An alliance of four races—human, Norgoran, Mwandan, and the Octus. They are bound by laws that are passed by the Galactic Senate.

Confederate Space Command – The top leadership of the Confederate Space Fleet.

GSO – Galactic Special Ops. It is the premier defense agency of the Galactic Confederacy, where most students of CAWStrat hope to score an internship. GSO recruits take a ten-year vow of celibacy when they "don the blue."

CAWStrat – Commerce, Administration, and Warcraft Strategy Institute, or CAWStrat. A premier institute in the galaxy where the scions of every notable family train before taking up their vocation of choice.

Norgoran – One of the allied races that form the Galactic Confederacy. They are green-skinned humanoids with long life spans.

Mwandan – One of the aboriginal races of the galaxy, and currently allied with the Confederacy.

Octus—Another race of the Galactic Confederacy. The Octus are Crustoids, with shells of various colors and eight limbs. The Octus do not actively participate in the Galactic Senate on a regular basis. However, they own and operate most of the space stations in the galaxy. The Octus are also said to wield the allegiance of space pirates and other outlaws.

WB—Wentworth-Busa, favored fighter craft of the Space fleet, built by Kiroff Industries.

AS—Astro Scout, the GSO's standard issue fighter craft, built by Kiroff Industries. Although smaller than the WBs, the Astros or AS are more agile and pack far greater firepower.

CHS—Comprehensive Health Score, a measure of a person's health used widely in the galaxy by medical practitioners.

The Events

Locusta-Vanga War – The Locusta-Vanga War began a decade before the events of Dark Universe. It started with the opening of a wormhole at Anomaly Point through which Locustan swarms arrived in the galaxy. The war almost pushed the galaxy to the brink of extinction and only ended when the wormhole closed. There have been no signs of the wormhole reopening. Regardless, the Confederacy has since erected stationary defenses in the area and positioned several Confederacy fleets around it.

About the Author

Alex Sheppard has always wanted to be an author. And even though that dream eluded Alex for a long time, now, finally, the ducks seem to have lined up. This is the third book in Alex's space opera series.

When not obsessively guzzling books (mostly scifi), tinkering with gadgets and gizmos, and wrangling rambunctious little ones, Alex likes to write.

Want to follow Alex's adventures in the writing world? Check out https://thefarworlds.com.

www.ingramcontent.com/pod-product-compliance
Lightning Source LLC
Chambersburg PA
CBHW020238200626
46816CB00001BA/21